SICKS

Image © 2018 by d. bRENT iSBELL

d. bRENT iSBELL
SICKS

Cover art and illustration by D. Brent Isbell; text and graphic arrangement provided by Naomi Corrie https://beholdentolove.deviantart.com

Printed in the United States of America
First printing: December 2018

ISBN
978-0-692-12109-2

Sincere appreciation:
Tarah, David A., Sandy, and Caroline

Many thanks to active supporters:
Karla, Erika, Chrissy, Lee Ann, Patrekr, and Tina I.

Additional thanks to:
Tommy, Dave P., Kelly, Tina S., and all others who have encouraged me in this endeavor

d. bRENT iSBELL
SICKS

For Jimmy (1972-1976)

The untimely loss of innocence at the hands of those with diseased minds produces a lingering rottenness that shatters the soul and divides the spirit. We who have died before our time, yet breathe, and think, and trod this earth, scant function among the sane apart from the unyielding aid of a deliverer, a love who adores us more than we ourselves. We need something, *someone*, more effective than mere random chance; we require an intelligent and purpose-driven force upon which we may depend.

"I got your *six*..."

d. bRENT iSBELL
SICKS

d. bRENT iSBELL

SICKS

JULy 29: LATe AFTERNOOn

A deep bronze hellion with hair as black as pitch, and dark smoldering eyes, tantalized her quarry with a rhythmic, vibrating shudder of her hips and buttocks. The salacious *twerking* nymph backed against the object of her seduction, dressed in a G-string thong and a thick, form-fitted sweater. She squirmed free of the upper garment. Her plump, bare breasts bounced from their textile cocoon. The dusky brunette flashed a shy, puppy dog glance with wide doe eyes and pouty lips in an attempt to feign girlish naïveté. Her partner knew she was anything but naïve. The woman grinned and purred as she walked her fingers up one of his exposed thighs. Anticipation boiled. Her eager subject's anatomy throbbed. She faced her quivering observer, then straddled him and scooted backward on her knees. The woman licked her lips then went down with her mouth opened wide. The pressure was firm, wet, and amazing! She groaned and massaged the man's *boys* while she worked her magic. He erupted.

The woman sat up and glared at the man with blazing, purple eyes. Her facial features were gone. She screamed in a booming male voice from a cavernous black mouth emptied of teeth. The emanation penetrated her partner's bones as it shook the bed and rattled the window glass. A nondescript bird descended toward the man from behind the faceless woman. A tiny white rabbit scurried away, making no sound at all, with arrows in its back. The bird's foot was chained to the rabbit. It was snatched away into darkness.

The man jolted into consciousness. He thought his heart had leaped from his chest. The intense, yellowish-white afternoon haze burned his retinas with a granular itch reminiscent of fiberglass dust. His eyelids fluttered as he tried to adjust to the light. He sat up and rubbed them with the heels of his palms. He trembled.

The waking reality of the man's environment took shape as he lowered his hands and shifted his eyes toward the grass to diffuse the sunlight. He became aware of the sticky warm splatters on his bare abdomen as he realized he had fallen asleep sunbathing. The splatters cooled as they thinned and oozed. Within seconds, they felt no different than the sweat that dripped from his naked torso except in spots where the tacky liquid had dried.

The man's mind and heart rhythm settled. He had never experienced a wet dream that had ended in horror. He wondered whether he had yelped aloud. A ten-foot wooden privacy fence lined the perimeter of his backyard. The closest neighbor's house was at least a hundred feet away. The man questioned whether the barriers had been adequate if he had issued an audible alarm. He hoped he had not drawn any unwanted attention. As he pondered, his vision focused on a new horror that stood before him.

The apparition watched with dark cocoa eyes leveled at the man's pelvis. Though saturated in striking, deep brown pigment, the vision's eyes reflected no spark, like a fish's dull stare. She licked the backs of her hands and sucked her fingers. Her face was void of expression; no emotion radiated.

The man's brain was in a vice as he tried to process what stood before him. The platinum blonde creature remained in an almost catatonic trance. Her thick, wintry wardrobe defied the stuffy, volcanic southern heat. The man's blood turned to ice when he recognized the strange creature standing before him was shy of four feet tall, and she was not an adult.

The child turned. Her long, high-riding platinum ponytail swayed as she walked toward the back door of the man's house then scaled the steps as if she lived there. Panic-stricken, the man stood from his flat beach lounger. He frantically inspected his manhood and his drying mess.

"Damn it!" he barked as he pawed himself. He shivered from mild emotional shock in the muggy afternoon furnace. "Shit!" the man whispered when he remembered he had left his clothes in the house.

Vivid dreams were nothing new. The man's senses had been fooled by plenty of them in times past, but this was too real. He hoped he was locked inside another bizarre imagination from which he would soon awake.

This can't be happening! The man's ears burned in frustration. *Damn it! I am awake! It's not a dream!*

He scanned the backyard. Standing naked in broad daylight was no longer a concern even if his neighbor had heard. He needed answers, and there was no time to *pussyfoot* around.

How did she get in here? What the hell's going on?

The man strutted the perimeter of the fence, looking for a breach. He found an opening beneath the house where the privacy wall abutted a vinyl skirt. It was at the corner of the house's raised foundation near a pillar of concrete blocks that supported the floor joists. The opening was large enough for a medium-sized dog to slip through, but a dog had not slipped past, a child had, and she may well have performed the unthinkable. Adrenaline invaded the man's veins. He wished he had known for certain.

The man hurried up the cement steps and pulled on a rickety spring-bound screen door. Behind it stood another door that accessed the kitchen. It had been left open. The pint-sized little girl was scrounging the refrigerator.

The man covered himself with his hands, then asked the girl if she wanted a sandwich. She stared at his covered groin from behind the appliance door. Her dark brown eyes were still dim and listless, and her face void of emotion. The man had experienced many scares throughout his life, but none like this. The girl's blank stare was unnatural, almost hideous. The man was tempted to doubt his senses, to convince himself he was still dreaming.

The girl's reluctant host asked a second time whether she wanted a sandwich. She said nothing and remained fixed on his nether-region, registering no surprise and no discernable curiosity, nothing resembling what the man could consider normal. The man's ears and forehead burned while nervous embarrassment washed through him. His covered turtle withdrew into its shell.

"Wait here a minute," the man told the girl. "I need to get dressed, and then I'll fix you something to eat. How does that sound?"

The little girl closed the refrigerator door and remained in place. She continued staring without a sound. The man walked out of the kitchen and returned a few seconds later wearing a pair of sweatpants and a T-shirt. He was barefoot. The girl had not moved. The man struggled to ignore her intense gaze.

"Can you talk?"

The child did not respond. She did not blink. *Damn, this is creepy*, the man thought. The girl appeared less like a fish and more like a possessed doll.

Speaking in a gentle tone to avoid spooking the child with his mounting frustration, the man asked, "Do you understand me?"

She remained still and fixated.

"Damn it!" the man huffed loud enough that the girl heard. Something changed in her eyes. Her breathing grew rapid and shallow. Her nostrils flared. The man thought he heard a whimper.

"Sweetheart," the man lowered himself and duck-walked toward the child, "I am not angry with you." He took her hands and tried to look into her eyes. She bowed her head toward the faded linoleum floor.

"I do not understand," the man said. He turned his head aside for a few seconds as he tried to figure out the best approach. A chill and a sense of darkness washed over him. Goose bumps arose. He looked around. *Where did that icy draft come from?* The man pushed on the refrigerator door. It was closed. It did not budge.

The nervous adult faced the child again and asked, "You were not trying to earn some food out there, were you? Did you do something while I was asleep, thinking I would not give you any food unless you did?"

The child angled her head toward the ceiling. Her breathing calmed. The gloss in her eyes faded as a single tear eased down her cheek. The man's stomach felt sour. His heart began to break. Though he had no answer to the gnawing question, it was becoming clear that attempts at verbal communication were a waste of time. Giving in, he pulled the child close and hugged her. He stroked the girl's dirty, tangled ponytail, and swept her long bangs to each side to give her a clearer view.

The man arose and ushered the girl toward an old metal-framed vinyl kitchen chair. "Sit here, sweetheart."

The child climbed onto the chair then watched the man remove a loaf of bread and a jar of crunchy peanut butter from a cupboard. He took a jar of strawberry preserves from the refrigerator. The man paused and looked out the window above the sink to observe the road for a few seconds. He set down the spreading knife he had retrieved from a drawer then turned to face the window on the opposite wall. The road was empty on that end, too. He wondered whether anyone was looking for the girl. Something in his gut told him no. He prepared a fold-over peanut butter and jelly sandwich on a single slice of white bread, then trimmed the crust and left it on the countertop. He poured some milk into a ceramic coffee mug. Having not been in the company of small children for years, he was not sure whether a regular glass would be too awkward for the child to manage. She seemed old enough to handle one, but he was not willing to take the chance.

The man glanced over his shoulder. The girl's eyes were glued to him. *Strange, strange kid*, he thought. *Cute, but I don't know? Something's way off.*

He estimated her age at five or six, too young to be prowling alone outside. Years ago, it would not have been a problem. He remembered waddling his old neighborhood, unaccompanied as a pre-kindergartener, in old-fashioned cloth diapers. The community had been full of wandering, exploring children and watchful neighbors, but the times have changed. *It's a risk for full-grown adults in broad daylight in some places,* he thought. *At least she has some advantage out here in the woods, I suppose?*

The man leaned against the counter and looked at the stone-faced little girl a short while longer. She watched him like a hawk. He took closer note of her appearance. *Why not? I mean, if this is what it's all about, then why shouldn't I also stare at you? Try to figure you out?*

The girl's ponytail was soiled and tangled but not matted. A single patch of dirt extended from one cheek to her forehead. Her lips were supple with remnants of fire engine red lipstick in the corners of her mouth. Her fair skin was lightly tanned, and her nose and cheeks were sun-ripened with a garnish of light freckles. The child's left ear was outlined from lobe to peak with stud earrings. There were a few thin scrapes on her neck that appeared to have dried blood on them, the result of a close brush with woodland vegetation the man figured. He recalled from the hug that the girl smelled sour as if she had not bathed in weeks and had stewed in sweat in the same clothes for days at a time. He considered the significance of that thick winter jacket in the summer's afternoon heat contrasted by thin denim jeans tucked into weathered, scuffed, pink slip-on cowgirl boots.

The man set aside the crust from the bread and presented the sandwich on a dish, with a soft homemade oatmeal cookie, and a powdered mini donut from a bag. He set the mug beside the plate. The child licked her hands and sucked her fingers again.

"You're washing them, aren't you? That's what you were doing outside? You were washing your hands, hoping to get some food?"

The man examined the girl's hands. Her nails were painted pink. The ends were jagged and torn, and they extended a little past her fingertips. The undersides were black with earth. Dirt lined her cuticles. Polish was caked and chipped. A few of the child's knuckles were banged up, and the back of one hand was scraped, with a light tan bruise. There were a few insect bites. The man sniffed the child's hands. All he could smell was the musk of her saliva.

"You have a hard life, don't you beautiful?"

The man picked up the child and carried her toward the kitchen sink, then sat her on the counter and swung her feet into the basin. She was tall enough to reach the faucet, had she stood tiptoed with her hands outstretched, but it was easier this way. He turned on the water.

Well, this is awkward. The girl had to bend at the waist a little lower than the man had anticipated so that she could reach the sink. Standing or sitting, she was just the wrong size. A light, golden-tan *plumber's crack* beamed from the scrunched, elastic waistband of the girl's trousers. The sight of her shiny little bum made the man grin. He almost chuckled.

Cute little squirt. Interesting: no panties. "Huh," the man grunted and tilted his head. *No tan line, either. Her little boo-hoo is the same shade as the rest of her.*

The man lathered the girl's hands with dish soap and scrubbed them, paying close attention to her nails. *Can't afford to get worms sucking on those things. Too late, I'm sure?* He dried her with a towel.

"Let me see your teeth, puddin."

Without hesitation, the girl opened her mouth wide and rolled her tongue but kept her eyes averted. The ragged little child's teeth were pearl white and perfect. It appeared a few molars had fallen out, and their adult replacements were just breaking through the gums. Her upper and lower central and lateral incisors were intact. They were larger than the rest of her teeth. They reminded him of a squirrel. He fought a grin as he leaned in close. Impressive as the little girl's choppers were, the overall picture was bleak.

"Breathe on me."

The girl kept her mouth locked open with her tongue withdrawn as she pushed out a breath as best she could. It smelled like a bag of plain potato chips mixed with creamed corn, but it was a world better than the vile dog breath he had remembered from other children. The man grunted.

"I can't really tell," the man whispered. He sniffed again then realized his pulse was increasing. "Might as well leave it at that."

The man carried the little girl to the table. Her boots dripped water onto the old linoleum tiles. Small white puffs of soapsuds rolled off her jacket and soaked into her jeans. Once seated, the tiny platinum blonde girl picked up the sandwich and started nibbling. Her eyes brightened a little, though her face still lacked expression. She rocked her head from side to side. Her ponytail swung and brushed her collapsed jacket hood.

The man pulled up a chair and sat beside her. He attempted to communicate again. "What is your name, angel?"

The child met his query with silence.

"How old are you, princess? Four? Five?" The man spread the fingers on one hand and held them in front of the girl. She paid no heed. "Are you this many?" He extended a finger from his other hand. "What about this many? Are you six?" More silence.

"Are your folks close by? Your mommy and daddy?"

The child laid her sandwich down and presented a balled-up fist in the man's direction with an extended middle finger. A burning scowl entered her eyes as she flipped him off and glared hard at her plate. She held the *bird* in place for about eight seconds, then sighed and resumed eating. A girl this young, throwing a vulgar hand gesture would ordinarily be a bit comical to the man but not in this context. Though seemingly mute, the child's reaction confirmed she could hear, and comprehend, and communicate.

"Aren't you hot with that jacket on?"

The girl continued to nibble. She turned her head to look the man over, still avoiding eye contact.

The youngster's behavior did not add up. As her adult host tried to weave this strange patchwork into a coherent tapestry, he remained focused on the most obvious concern: the fluffy pink elephant in the room.

"Does your jacket make you feel safe? Is that why you wear it in this heat?"

Still no response.

"Do you have anything in your pockets? Anything that might tell me where you live? A telephone or maybe a piece of paper with a number for a babysitter, perhaps?"

The girl picked up the mug with both hands and drank. She gulped air as the milk went down. A light trail trickled from one side of her mouth. She set the mug down, then wiped the milk with one hand and licked it. She used the side of a straightened finger to squeegee her liquid mustache then licked her finger. The man had never seen a child do that.

The girl belched.

The man snickered. "I'm glad you liked it. May I look through your pockets?"

The girl kept eating and eyeballing the man. He fondled the pocket over the right side of the girl's abdomen. She did not react to the invasion. The pocket was empty. The man stood and moved toward the girl's left pocket. A zipper sealed it. She watched without resistance as he opened it.

I really wish you wouldn't stare at me like that, he thought. *Of course, I could ask you to stop.* He held his peace.

The pocket contained two folded envelopes. They were not sealed. The man opened them. Each contained one thousand dollars in cash in different denominations. The man's blood gelled while his heart sank. His skin crawled, and his ears burned. There was no writing on the envelopes and no notes inside. There was nothing else in the girl's pocket.

"Stand up a minute, sweetie."

The girl slid down and stood beside the chair. Her rear trouser pockets looked flat. The man patted them. *Solid little tushy,* he thought. "You must spend a lot of time out there in the woods?"

The child did not bat an eye. Feeling nothing in her rear pockets, the man reached around and fished inside the baggy front pockets. He felt flesh.

"Nope, definitely nothing in there, except you!" The man kissed the child's forehead, hoping the light-hearted attempt at humor might loosen her up. It did not. He guided her back into the chair. The girl resumed eating.

The man stepped away, then retrieved his phone from his bedroom. He stared at it and debated whether he should call the sheriff's department. He considered the money in the child's possession, the heavy coat in stifling heat and humidity, and her apparent lack of distress. He reflected upon the condition of the girl's teeth. They triggered a thought: *Never look a gift horse in the mouth.* The old saying did not fit the circumstance, but the underlying wisdom did. Intuition urged him to tread lightly. *Don't get too carried away with your sense of compassion. Don't be hasty. Think!* As compelled as he was to seek help for the child, the man chose instead to err on the side of caution.

The man set his phone down and returned to the kitchen. The girl was still there, eating the soft oatmeal cookie. She had already devoured the sandwich and the powdered donut. The man walked to the refrigerator and poured himself a glass of tea. As he poured, the girl licked the crumbs from her plate then walked to the kitchen counter. She retrieved the discarded bread crusts.

"I don't put sugar in my tea like other folks around here," the man informed the child.

The girl expressed no interest in his statement. She crammed down the bread crusts.

"I used to when I was younger, but I started getting fat."

The child walked to the man as he drank then groped the crotch of his sweatpants with a disengaged look. He sprayed tea and tussled with the glass as he fought to maintain control. Most of the tea splashed into the girl's hair and across her back and spilled onto the floor. She strolled through the screen door and down the stairs. The man hesitated for a few seconds, still shocked by the physical contact. He realized the child had passed from sight during the distraction. He debated whether he should follow her or wipe the floor. Feeling he could waste no more time, the man set the glass on the counter then rushed outside.

The child stooped beneath the house.

The man hurried down the steps and crouched to watch her slip away. "If you ever need something to eat, it's here for you."

The child's pace did not falter. She did not look back to acknowledge the man as she shimmied through the opening between the vinyl skirt and the privacy fence.

What have I done? What am I getting myself into? Why is it that every time life seems to finally start going pretty decent, something comes completely out of left field and slaps me upside the head?

The man realized he had not seen in which direction the girl had departed. He rushed back into the kitchen to watch her through the opposing windows, but she had already evaded the property with the stealth of a feral cat. He hurried through the house and out the front door to survey the narrow, sun-bleached and weather-beaten, rural asphalt road. The pavement ended about fifty yards to his left. A powdered, red clay dirt road continued past there. In the opposite direction, he saw his closest neighbor's house and the next two houses about fifty yards beyond that. Thick, evergreen woods stood everywhere else, except for a large, clear patch of undeveloped land, perhaps four squared acres total, on the opposite side of the road. The girl could have disappeared into one of several tree lines or navigated the overgrown kudzu thickets that preceded them.

There's a whole lot of country out here, the man thought. *No telling who all's up in these woods?* His ears tuned-in to the distant buzz of cicadas. They, along with the sweltering, muggy heat, intense sunlight, and overall rustic setting, conspired to leave the man with an eerie sense of isolation he had not experienced since his youth.

A fORMEr AUTUMn

A young boy sat at a school desk. His head was bowed, and his were eyes lowered. The rest of the class dipped into their boxes of eight, sixteen, and sixty-four crayons. They colored in the books they had brought from home or purchased from the visiting bookmobile earlier that week. Some of the children ate nontoxic paste from their glue jars, and a few giggled and whispered. Except for occasional chatter, the environment was comfortable and quiet, almost as if in a vacuum. The boy did not move. He had not raised his hinged wooden desktop to withdraw the cardboard cigar box that contained his art supplies so that he may indulge in his favorite school period.

A large woman approached the somber-looking boy. She noticed he had been inattentive during the first two class sessions. She was accustomed to the youngster being distracted. He had always been a well-behaved child, though unlike his peers, he never could seem to focus for more than a few minutes at a time. She knew his dyslexia had a lot to do with it. She also recognized the boy's intelligence was a few notches above the other students. The woman figured his elevated IQ was affecting his unusual mood in some way. He had always been quirky and strange. He was imaginative and artistic, and less predictable than his classmates. He paid more attention to seemingly insignificant details and less to important subjects than any second-grade student she could remember. She had often referred to the child as "touched in the head."

Today was different. The boy was a lot more *off* than his teacher had ever observed. It seemed his mind had not entered the classroom at all. Less predictable than his peers or not, he had recognizable patterns; this behavior was not among them. The usual energetic mannerisms of this student appeared to have been replaced by depression. Two hours of minimal, lethargic participation in silence was cause for alarm, especially during art period.

"Are you okay, honey-child?"

The boy did not answer.

The teacher placed her hand on the boy's back. He recoiled as if she had touched a sunburn. "Baby, are you okay?" she asked.

The boy burst' into tears and lowered his head further.

"I'll get you to the office to see the nurse." The teacher walked to an intercom that hung on the wall behind her desk. She pressed a button. The intercom buzzed.

"Ms. Nathan, speaking," a female voice answered.

"Ms. Nathan, this is Ms. Bettis." She pronounced Ms. as Mizz. "I'm gonna take one of my pupils to see the nurse. I'll need a student volunteer from Ms. Hollins' class to keep an eye on mine while I'm out. I'm in unit two. They're in art period right now, so they shouldn't be any trouble."

"Yes, ma'am, I'll send one over."

"Thank you, ma'am."

The large, dark-skinned teacher adjusted her gold-toned, metal-rimmed prescription glasses. A small chain dangled from one side. She walked back to the little boy who was sobbing.

"Come on, baby, let's get you to the nurse." The teacher ushered the boy away from his desk and led him by the hand out the door of the portable classroom.

The school nurse was unable to figure anything out. The boy was not talking. His back was indeed not injured as she had thought based upon Ms. Bettis' description of how he had reacted when she had touched him. She brought the results of her examination to the attention of the principal and recommended the child see a counselor. The school had none on staff. The principal speculated the boy might be getting bullied by other children. He also considered the child's home life might have taken an ugly turn. Whatever the case, he recognized it was psychological, as he had seen many students from dysfunctional and broken homes come through the school.

"Hello? I'm trying to reach Mr. Moffat," a voice said over the phone.

"Mr. Moffat is at work. This is his wife, Nelda. How may I help you?"

"Mrs. Moffat, this is Principal Zeigler over at Pierpont Elementary School. I'm calling about your son."

"Is he okay? Did he get into some kind of trouble?"

"No, ma'am, he's not in any trouble, but I can't say for sure whether he's okay. He was taken to the nurse's office. His teacher said he's been unusually quiet and distracted. He flinched rather harshly when she went to his desk. The nurse couldn't find anything wrong with him, but he's not talking. Mrs. Moffat, has your son said anything at all about being bullied by other children?"

"No, sir. He's been a little under the weather since Friday afternoon. The poor dear was playing in the woods after school, and he got bit by an insect. He had a mild allergic reaction, but he's fine other than being a little tired. He spent most of the weekend in bed."

"An insect bite, you say?"

"Yes, sir."

"Begging your pardon, Mrs. Moffat, but his behavior is not indicative of a bug bite. Forgive my forwardness, but are things good between you and Mr. Moffat?"

"I don't see what business that is of yours, Mr. Zeigler, but if you must know, things are fine between me and my husband."

"I'm terribly sorry, madame. I did not mean to insinuate anything, but I had to ask. Your son is way out of sorts, and we're just trying to look out for him, is all. I'll have the nurse ask what kind of a bug bit him. Meanwhile, I'll have his teacher keep an eye out on the playground and in the lunchroom for a few days to see if any other children are harassing him. Thank you for your time, ma'am."

"You're welcome, Mr. Zeigler. I'm sorry if I sounded a little snippety? I know you meant well. Things are fine here, sir. We'll check to see if he got into a tizzy with one of his little neighborhood friends. Thank you for the call, sir."

"Good day, Mrs. Moffat."

WINTEr: YEARs LONg GONe

Her ears rang, and her vision mocked her wide-open eyes as the images fled. Throbbing pressure hammered the female's forehead, ears, and sinuses. The woman's brain felt too large for her skull. She could not process what had happened and wondered whether she had died. She wished she had when her teeth rattled almost immediately afterward. Pain enveloped the lady's left jaw. Her ear was muffled; the ringing intensified. She thought the entire side of her head had caved in.

The woman's vision returned as her head snapped the other way, rocked again by blunt force. The right side of her face felt as if it, too, had collapsed. She screamed. A crushing blow smashed the base of her nose and upper lip. A searing hot and icy sensation radiated from the roots of her teeth throughout her face. She caught a glimpse of a fist as it recoiled, prepared for another strike.

The woman tried to scream again but was hindered by the coppery flow of blood that ran onto her teeth and into her mouth. It dripped from the back of her nasal passage and down her throat. She gagged and coughed as she tried to expel the blood. The pain mounted, and the pressure increased. Her head was an overinflated balloon that would not stop expanding while she asphyxiated.

The woman clawed at the motel bedding with one hand and fumbled around the floor with the other. She hoped to lay hold of any object she could use to fight her attacker. He pinned her left leg against the bed and her right to the floor. She kicked against the frame as she tried to gain leverage against her assailant, who sat atop her twisted body.

The woman's attacker wrapped his hands around her throat. "You fuckin' whore!" he spat. "All the ways I've loved you and taken care of your sorry ass, and this is how you repay me? Huh? Who the hell do you think you are?"

A booming knock shook the motel room's front door. It startled the occupants. "Hey!" a male voice called from the other side. What's going on in there?"

The woman's assailant yelled back, "Mind your own damn business!"

"*Police!*" the other voice replied, filled with intensity. "Open this door now!"

Muffled words followed, "You said you have the master key? Open it!"

"Holy shit!" the man mumbled. He looked around in panic. "Where the fuck did they come from?"

The attacker leaped up. The woman heard him scuffle about as the main room's doorknob violently rattled. The cooing of an infant arose amid the din, seconds before the man scurried into the bathroom and locked the door behind him. The outside door burst open. Two bearded men rushed inside with firearms drawn.

The woman remained on the motel room floor, topless and bloody in a pair of black lace panties. Her belly piercing had been ripped out. Blood still oozed down her throat. She managed to choke the words, "Help me!"

The two men glanced around the room, then rushed past the woman. She frantically drew a deep breath then screamed, "My Baby! Oh, God, my baby!"

An infant's tote carrier sat atop the motel room's bed. The woman could not hear her child. She struggled to her knees and reached across the mattress toward the portable seat. The two rough-looking men kicked the bathroom door open. It was empty. An open window stood above the toilet.

TIMEs PASt

The boy did not know any better. He was too young and was void of understanding.

A man groaned and whispered, "Ah... Yes! Perfect!"

A small girl sat on a tattered, soiled sofa a few feet away from them. Her eyes looked as black as a bottomless pit.

The man added, "Straight from the bottle and the pacifier. An easy transition with this one. The way it should be!"

The girl grinned and said with a southern twang, "He looks funny doing that, don't he?"

"Funny ain't exactly the word I had in mind, but yeah, sure, I guess? If that's the way, you want to look at it?"

"He's not better than me. He'll never be as good as me."

"First of all, it's not a 'he,' it's an *it*, just like those others. Secondly, we don't need another one like you runnin' its damn mouth all the time. We have too many like you already."

The child stuck out her tongue. "I speak my mind. So, what makes him and the others an *it*?"

"We ain't gonna raise it like one of us. Think of it the same as those damn dogs out there: just a little mutt on the end of a chain, until we're ready to put it to work."

The girl laughed, "We're gonna keep him chained up with the dogs?"

"It... *it!*" the man corrected the child. "No. That was just a figure of speech. I'm moving it out of the van. It will live in here with us from now on. It just won't be allowed to sleep with us or eat with us or anything else. And you ain't gonna go talking to it and trying to make friends. You understand me?"

The little girl kicked her head back and sneered, "Why the hell would I want to? I mean, look at it!"

The man groaned and closed his eyes. "Yeah," he sighed. He grunted and moaned. "This one's gonna bring some decent cash. It helps when they don't have a fuckin' thought in their head."

The girl giggled. "It looks stupid! I'm much better!"

"Only if you learn to quit gagging and spitting! This one don't."

The girl scowled then stormed away.

JULy 29: LATe AFTERNOOn

"Hey there, cutie pie! How are you doin'?" A slim woman with sun-bleached dishwater blonde hair flagged down the man as he returned from the store. He pulled up beside her and rolled down his window. The woman's eyes were amber. Her skin was deep reddish tan and coated with light freckles, with a few mild sun wrinkles. She was aged with character: a little hard looking but attractive. She wore a pair of loose-fitting shorts with cuffed legs and a high waist, and a button-up long-sleeved shirt embroidered with a single rose. The sleeves were rolled up, and the tails hanged out behind. The front was tucked. The top three metal snaps were not fastened. She was barefoot.

The woman spoke in a thick southern accent that many would consider mush-mouth hillbilly. "I'm your neighbor. I live in this house right here." She pointed behind, toward the house closest to the man's. Her voice was raspy like a persistent smoker's. Aside from the accent, it was obvious to the man that she was tipsy from drinking. He could smell the beer on her breath.

The woman went on, "I ain't never seen you before today, but when I seen you walk out of your house in them jogging pants and that tight-ass T-shirt a little while ago, I said to myself, 'Mmm-m! That's one mighty fine-lookin' hunk o' man right there! Fine-as-wine!'"

The woman placed her longneck beer bottle into her left hand then reached her right into the car window. "My name is Charlene."

The man loved the twangy upswing she used to pronounce the last half of her name. He shook her hand and nodded with a grin.

Before the man could respond, Charlene added, "I hope you don't mind me being so forward and all, but why don't you park this thing," she pronounced thing as *thang*, "and come on over so we can get acquainted? I promise I won't bite...unless you want me to?"

Charlene's voice cracked with a single laugh. She leaned her forearms on the windowsill to prop herself and dangled her beer inside the car. She wagged her butt back and forth. "Nah, I'm just funnin' with ya. Come on down and let's hang out for a spell. And don't worry, I got no man, and I ain't lookin', neither!" She paused.

The man wondered whether she was awaiting a reaction.

Charlene was still wagging her backside. "I just want to say hey for a little bit, that's all. I got plenty of cold beer or some other stuff if you'd like? Come on over. We can start a fire in the backyard. I have a pit."

The man thought for a second. "Let me get myself situated, and I'll be right over."

"Situated? What does that mean? You gotta use the commode or somethin'? I got one! I don't mind if you use it, as long as you promise you ain't gonna try no funny stuff once you're inside the house! Pull your car on over here, and let's go out back and get us a fire goin'!"

"Well, okay, then. I reckon I'll do that? Watch yourself." The man glanced at Charlene's arms. She giggled and withdrew them. He parked beside her car and got out, holding a paper sack that contained a bottle of liquor and a box of cigars.

The woman beckoned in a protracted manner, "Hey!" and pointed at the bag. "I see you're bringin' something, too! I reckon we're gonna have us a bonafide party tonight?"

Charlene strutted toward the backyard. "Come on now! Let's get this party started! I'll cook us up some food first. I got steaks in the house. We'll grill 'em outside, then start a bonfire after we eat!"

The man chuckled and followed her, shaking his head. "Alright, let's do this," he mumbled with a big, goofy grin. "A party it shall be!"

d. bRENT iSBELL
SICKS

JULY 29: LATe AFTERNOOn: ELSEWHERe

"**Y**ou want to be clean, you little faggot?"

A gruff male interrogated a child. The boy screamed, but duct tape muted his agony. He choked, as a mix of water and mucus sprayed from his nostrils. His eyes burned from being dunked into the foul water in an old tin washtub. The water engulfed the child's head. A tall, slim man with long, black-and-gray hair, suspended the boy upside-down by his ankles. The man's thin arms trembled from the weight of the child. A cigarette adhered to his lower lip. It bounced as he spoke.

"You like gettin' all freshened up?" the long-haired man asked, with an air of relaxed smugness. He dunked the child again and held him under for a few seconds. The boy thrashed his head back and forth and rocked his torso. Duct tape bound his hands at his waist. The man lifted him. The child's eyes were bloodshot and his face red. His muffled screams did not escape the cleared perimeter of the immediate grounds.

"You will never be clean," the man taunted. "You were not even supposed to be born. God hates your sorry little ass, and I ain't too damn fond of you, neither!"

The longhaired man lowered the boy again. He dunked and raised the child until a light, strawberry-red trail of thinned blood ran from his nose toward his brow. The child's eyelids fluttered.

A girl asked, "Now, can we bury it in the woods?"

The man scowled at her. "Get your ass inside!" he barked.

The girl huffed then walked away. "I swear, I don't know why we keep that damn thing!"

The man dropped the boy, face-down onto the sand. The boy's mouth and hands remained bound.

"I gotta take a shit," the man said as he walked toward the trailer.

The boy lay upon the ground, crying, while the sun beat upon the side of his wet face. His vocabulary was limited, but his mind asked in its unique language, *Who is God? Why does he hate me? What did I do? Why was I not supposed to be born? I promise I won't be bad again! I don't understand!*

~ 21 ~

The child's soul sank as the questions crowded his brain. A shadow crept over him. He turned his head to see what cast it. The little one's eyelids flickered from the intensity of the sun. A person moved beside him, blocking some of the light. The boy could not see any details in the darkened silhouette.

"You filthy, demon-possessed little fag," a female voice sneered. An obese, pale, redheaded woman with freckles loomed over him. She wore a bright patterned sundress with no bra and flip-flop sandals. The woman stared at the boy while she drank 150-proof alcohol straight from a bottle. The boy turned his head away. His rib cage heaved, and rapid breaths from his nostrils pushed up small puffs of dust.

"You're crying again, ain't you?" The woman took another swallow. "You don't deserve to live."

The crotch of the boy's pants darkened.

"Nasty little pig! You're pissing yourself!" She took as much alcohol into her mouth as she could manage, then swished and spit it onto the child's head and face. "Damn, what a little *Nancy-boy!*"

The child's tears flowed, mingled with blood, as mucus oozed down his soaked, soiled cheeks. He wondered why the woman lingered. It was out of character for her to look at him for more than a few seconds. It was always the girl who had interacted but to no more extent than to feed him or to take his clothes to be hand washed. They each had their behavioral patterns; staring was not among the woman's. The suspense generated a sense of fear the child had not experienced before. His bladder finished emptying into his jeans.

"You little devil child," the woman grumbled. "I don't know why in hell you do this kind of shit? Always gotta push the envelope and do your own thing!"

She glugged more alcohol. "Why do you have to be so damn difficult? We feed you. We clothe you. We put up with your little tantrums. You're full of Satan! That's why you do it, you dirty assed little brat!"

The woman took another drink then mumbled, "And then you walk around picking up copperheads and moccasins all the fuckin' time like you ain't got no damn better sense! They strike at us left and right, but they ignore you like you're their fuckin' leader or something? Nasty little devil child."

The obese woman shuffled toward the trailer. "Those damn dogs would eat you alive if I had my way, but no! I gotta keep puttin' up with you because of *him*!" She pointed toward the back of the trailer at the approximate location of the bathroom. The woman pawed the trailer door handle a few times, trying to get a firm grip. She opened the door, then wobbled up the steps and tripped on the doorsill.

"Damn it!" the obese woman howled on the way down. There was a loud thud as the small trailer shook when her knees hit the floor.

"Drunk assed cow!" the girl's voice escaped the open door.

The boy continued to lay on his stomach with his head turned to one side. The sun hammered on him as he stewed in the humidity and the warm, uncomfortable sogginess in his trousers. The pungent odor of urine reached his nostrils. There was no breeze. The sweltering summer air was heavy and stale.

Emptiness crawled into the boy's chest. Intense fear swam laps inside his brain. The feelings reminded him of the shadows, he thought he had seen moving in his room many times before, in the early evenings, and throughout the nights. The emptiness and fear converged and chewed on his soul. It overwhelmed him.

The child spoke in his private language again, sending unintelligible cries for help into the abyss that engulfed his mind. His tear-clouded eyes took on an appearance that resembled that of a corpse. Though drenched in water, sweat, alcohol, and urine in the heat of late July, he trembled, as if stricken with hypothermia. He heard the drunken woman complaining inside the trailer, and the girl laughing at her. The door slammed.

JULy 29: DUSk

The sun had begun to set as the campfire grew to an acceptable level. Crickets chirped, frogs sang, and other nocturnal creatures stirred. A wall of nearby trees amplified the fire's crackle. The isolated woodland heralded its dead silence. The smell of charred wood filled the air. Charlene and the man sat next to each other on a log. They stared into the orange blaze and watched small red embers rise toward the sky while tiny white and black ashes drifted away. A few flames leaped from the main fire and disappeared. The base of the fire hosted blue and white flames. An ice chest sat next to the woman and a bottle of whiskey beside the man.

Charlene lit a rolled cigarette and offered it. The man recognized the odor above the smell of the campfire. It was marijuana. He declined and asked whether she would mind if he smoked his tobacco instead.

"Smoke 'em if you got 'em. Hell, if they're good, I might ask you for one." Charlene tugged at the legs of her shorts to get a bit more comfortable. "Thank you for helping me get set up. It went a lot quicker than when I do it myself. I'm especially glad those bug lights still work." She motioned to one of the three dim purple-hued lights hanging from anchored metal posts. The lights buzzed, cracked, and sizzled, and emitted tiny sparks as insects were drawn in and electrocuted.

"Them things," there she went again, pronouncing an *i* like an *a*, "and the smoke from the fire ought to help with them skeeters. I'm sure a few are gonna chew on us anyway, but they ain't bad tonight. The humidity's easing up. They seem to get worse when it's real humid, especially right after it rains."

Charlene took a *drag* off her *joint* and chased it with a beer. "You hitched?"

"No," the man replied. "I was, twice, but it didn't work out. I used to think a third time would be a charm. I almost did it, but I chose to break her heart instead. Probably selfish on my part, but I just couldn't do it again. Too much pain from the first two."

"Believe me," Charlene placed a hand on the man's knee, "I been there! Were your exes witches?"

The man laughed. "No, they weren't witches."

"Whores?"

The man flashed an embarrassed, red-faced grin, "No, not whores, either, though I'd be lying if I said I didn't see them that way from time to time. Truth be told, I was just young, dumb, and full of *cum* the first time around. The second time, I was experienced in pain but not in love. I thought I had begun to understand love as time went by. When it seemed things were finally getting on track, my second wife left me for another man, right out of the blue, without any warning. It ruined me. I felt like I would die. I lost a truckload of confidence and self-esteem. I often wondered whether losing my military career had anything to do with her leaving, but then I realized it was only an excuse. Her plans had already been laid, and that was an easy out for her."

"Oh, that's sad! What happened? Were you thrown out of the military? Dishonorable discharge? Bad conduct?"

The man opened the whiskey and took a drink. "No, nothing like that. I was deployed to a combat zone. I got wounded by an explosion then processed out on a medical retirement with one hundred percent disability. I have scars all over me, under my clothes.

"I've recovered a great deal since then, but being rated at one hundred percent makes it tough for me to find the kind work I'm experienced and qualified for. I am plenty able-bodied but not on paper. So, I live off of military disability checks, and spend a lot of spare time at the gym, overcoming the effects of my physical impairments. It eats most of my days, but I don't have much of a life beyond that, so the time is well used the way I see it. It beats sitting around with my thumb up my ass, turning into a couch potato.

Charlene giggled. "If you ever want anything in your ass, I'll gladly do it!"

The man looked at her with feigned shock: eyes wide and mouth dropped open.

Charlene laughed and placed her hand on his shoulder. "I'm only funnin' again! I wouldn't stick anything in your ass! You're supposed to do that to mine!" She cupped her hand over her nose and mouth. "Did I say that? Oh, Lord, forgive me! Where are my manners?"

Charlene laughed again. "If my daddy were still alive, he'd pull his belt off and wear my ass out!" She cackled, humored by her own remark. "I ain't too far off the mark, either! Grown woman or not, I bet he would! My daddy sure did love me! Mama did, too. But me and daddy? We was tight! I was his little girl, no matter how old I got. That man tried so hard to help me along in my scrapes. I didn't actually get my shit together until long after he had passed away, God rest his soul. Mama tried to pick up the slack, but she just didn't have it in her. She's gone to be with him in The Great By-And-By."

Charlene inhaled more marijuana and took two more drinks from her beer. "I'm sorry. I got a little carried away. I didn't mean to interrupt. Please go on."

"No worries," the man replied, "I'm enjoying myself. We have all night. Interrupt me all you want."

"I'm enjoying myself too, cutie-pie!"

The man continued his story. "I nearly rebounded with a lady that seemed pretty awesome. Maybe she was, but I got cold feet and backed out. I mean, I just flat dropped her like a hot potato, without a word. Broke all contact overnight. I had never drop-kicked anyone I had feelings for. She was the first. She never chased after me, though. Probably sensed it was coming?"

The man took a drink then added, "I've dated, off-and-on since then, but never ran across anyone I thought I could endure long-term. It's not all about giddy emotions and romance, not like I used to think in my younger years. Relationships change. I thought I was on track in my second marriage. I thought we were on track. My wife thought differently. She left. I've felt a little dead inside ever since. I'm not prepared to make a leap like that again."

"Do you have any children?" Charlene asked.

The man took another drink of his whiskey. "No. My first wife was infertile. The second was a career woman. She didn't want any. It's been seven years since we divorced."

"I'm really sad to hear that."

Charlene slid over and leaned against the man and put her arm around his waist. She laid her head on his shoulder and took another *hit* off her joint. She reciprocated the man's stories by sharing her own.

"I dated this guy in high school in the twelfth grade. He was on the varsity football team. His hands were big and thick and strong! *My lands,* that boy was strong as an ox! Huge, strapping chest and big biceps! He took auto body shop and chopped a '49 Merc' then painted it purple. Hot lookin' car! He took woodshop, too. He was a man's man, inside and out, and quite gentlemanly! He opened doors for me and everything; real smooth talker, and he wasn't all grabby like other guys I'd dated. He didn't ever try to get in my pants, though he did like to pat my ass a lot. I appreciated that. He made me feel sexy. So anyways, we went out a few times on the weekends, and he wined-and-dined me.

"The time come that I was ready to share myself with him. We were in the back seat of his Mercury. I let him take off my top and unstrap my bra, and then these come out." Charlene snatched the front of her shirt, causing the fastened metal snaps to give way. She held it open. She was not wearing a bra.

"I ain't never bared them to no one before that day. I wasn't even gonna do it for him, but I was convinced he was *the one,* my first true love!" She stood and backed away, so the light of the fire could illuminate her chest. The setting sun was behind her.

"So, here you have it: one nipple the size of an old Kennedy half dollar and the other as big around as a damn beer bottle! And I don't know if you can tell, but this boob hangs just a little bit lower than the other."

Charlene cupped and jiggled her breasts. "That dude looked like he swallered his own asshole when he saw 'em!" She howled with laughter as she stumbled backward. "Whoa!"

The plucky woman did not notice she had dropped her marijuana, though she kept a firm grip on her beer. She took a drink then continued.

"He suddenly got all weird on me, acting like he done growed a conscience and wanted to save himself for marriage. He acted like he was afraid to kiss me! That ended the date real quick, let me tell you! When I went back to school on Monday, I noticed girls around campus whispering and pointing at me. I couldn't figure out why. They'd pretty much all seen me in the gym shower after P.E. at one time or other since middle school. Some of the jocks started cat callin' me and whisperin', too. A *lot* of kids got weird on me. That's when I realized he wasn't no man at all, just a smooth-talkin' little self-centered shit and a locker room gossip, just like all the rest of them immature little boys."

Charlene shuffled toward the man and dropped to her knees. She pulled her shoulders back and pushed her chest forward. "You wanna touch 'em?"

The look in Charlene's eyes was strange. The man did not know what to make of it. He accepted her offer and cupped each of her breasts from beneath. He rubbed her nipples with his thumbs. The dark red, terra cotta skin hardened and drew in. They took on a tough, leathery feel. Sporadic bumps arose, and her flat nipples extended. Goose pimples covered the woman's body. She closed her eyes, rocked her head back, and grinned with a light moan. Charlene rolled her head forward again then opened her eyes wide. She looked disoriented.

"Thank you," she whispered, then smiled.

Charlene raised her hand to take another drag off the marijuana but realized it was no longer between her fingers. She searched for a few seconds but did not see it lying mere inches away near the perimeter of the fire pit.

"Can I have one of those cigars you said you have?"

The man handed her one.

"Got a light?"

He glanced at the campfire with a wry grin. Charlene caught on right away. "I am not sticking my face or hand anywhere near that damn fire!" She laughed. "Give me a light, you booger!"

The man presented a disposable lighter and held it while Charlene nursed the flame into the end of the cigar.

"That's nice!" she remarked. "Smooth. What is it?"

"It's a peach...cigar-ello...," the man narrowed his eyes as he focused on the small cardboard package illuminated by the campfire, "siga-ree-yoh? However you pronounce it? Hard *l*'s? A long *e* with silent *r*'s? Who knows?"

"It's a what?"

"Peach mini cigar."

"Oh." Charlene rotated off her knees and sat on the ground then leaned back toward the man. He spread his knees apart. Charlene scooted back and rested her head on his abdomen. He was embarrassed, hoping she did not notice his kinked-up half erection.

Great, he thought, *I definitely need to adjust!*

The man squirmed to find some relief but decided to succumb to the discomfort in the hope Charlene would not notice. She did not react.

Good! Either she doesn't know, or she's just not saying anything!

Charlene continued to hold her beer with an iron grip. She puffed her cigar, then continued her story.

"I been married twice, like you. They were both bastards. Didn't have kids with either of 'em. I wasn't gonna breed with shit like that. The first one was a first-class jerk before we ever even married, but after being tricked by that smooth-talking high school jock, I figured a real upfront bad-boy had nothing to hide. Man, was I a fool! No sooner had we married than he decided it would be okay to beat the living hell out of me! He beat me worse when I told him there was no way I'd have a baby with a wife beater. I wasn't gonna bring no newborn into that kind of an environment! He kept insisting I better bear him a son, or else! No way, Jose! I wasn't gonna give that bastard a son! I shudder to think what that asshole might have done if I had let him knock me up, and I ended up giving him a daughter instead? I wasn't gonna put up with being beat, definitely not for refusing to be impregnated by a pig! I waited till he fell asleep naked one night, and I took a pair of pinking shears to his balls."

The man leaned forward and pressed against Charlene's back. "Oh, Lord, no!" he groaned. Charlene almost tipped her beer bottle. Though reacting to her story, the man took advantage of the opportunity to dig at his crotch in the hopes of finding a way to straighten his anatomy.

"Is everything okay back there?" Charlene chuckled.

Crap! She knows! "Yeah, I'm good."

"Mmm-hm!" Charlene snickered. She carried on, "He woke up and went to screamin' and hollerin'. His balls were still attached, but them jaggedy shears was dug in and hangin' on!" She inserted a single high-pitched, "Ha!" then kept going.

"He come at me bleedin' all over and sportin' his new jewelry, so I accessorized his face with an iron skillet, just like in them old shows. He fell backward in the bedroom doorway, howlin' like a banshee. I run on out the house and never looked back.

"I managed to get the marriage annulled after a while. We was legally married for just over two years but together for only about the first three months. Even with police reports, pictures, hospital records, and X-Rays of what he done to me in those three months, it took a long time to get it annulled. His arrest record wasn't enough. It helped that he was too embarrassed to say I nearly gave him a sex change. If he had, I probably woulda gone to jail for a lot longer than he ever did in them following two years. Knowin' him, he got drunk off his ass and stitched hisself up or got one of his nasty friends to do it for him? Whatever he done, there wasn't any record of it. That worked in my favor. I'm thankful for that."

Charlene puffed her cigar then shook her beer bottle. "I think it's almost empty. Can I have some of that whiskey?"

"Yeah. I don't mind, but you know what they say?"

"Honey, I was a hard-core alcoholic after them two husbands. That 'beer before liquor' shit don't affect me no more. And if it does, you're perfectly fine to stick your finger down my throat as long as you don't forget to hold my hair back. Hell, get me drunk enough, and I just might consider letting you stick somethin' else down my throat!"

The man laughed. Though tempted, he was not convinced of his companion's sincerity. Nevertheless, he played along.

"Deal!" He twisted off the lid and handed her the whiskey.

Charlene up-ended the bottle. Bubbles surfaced as she drank.

"Ah!" She handed it back to him. "My second husband was a thousand times worse. I made the mistake of catchin' him on the rebound. We dated while I was tryin' to annul, and we got hitched the week after it was finalized. For two years, he was very polite and cordial, and all. He had the patience of Job. We finally got married, and I'll be *damned* if I didn't find out he'd slept with like eight other women while we was dating! As soon as I confronted him about it, he beat the ever-lovin' *piss* out of me! I mean, he fucked me up, hard! I tried to fight back, but he was way too damn strong. He broke my arm and busted up my nose, and a handful of my ribs then jammed a pistol in my mouth. He told me he'd blow my brains out if I ever called the cops or dreamed of leaving him. He meant it!"

"I'm glad he didn't."

"Thank you!"

Charlene took the whiskey bottle from the man and turned it up again.

"The next thing I know, he's comin' home with a couple of big damn dogs that were mean as hell. He'd sleep alone with them in our bedroom and keep that pistol under his pillow. Made me sleep on the couch while he laid with his bitches. He took my cell phone, and everything even mounted a deadbolt backward and slept with the key. He isolated me from the rest of the world. I tried to get out through a window a few times, but he woke up, thanks to them dogs, and he dragged my ass back in by the ankles. He pulled my hair to hold me down while he used me for a punchin' bag."

Charlene stared into the fire. She grew distant.

"Are you okay?"

She didn't answer.

The man massaged her neck and shoulders.

"I don't know how the hell my ribs and arm ever healed? God was lookin' out for me, I guess? God at least gave me the brains to have learned First Aid. I don't know if you could tell my bones is a little crooked, but it turned out okay in the long run. I can still use everything the way it's intended."

The man coaxed the whiskey from Charlene, then took a drink and kissed the top of her head. She was quiet.

"Thank you," she whispered.

Charlene wiped her eyes with a fingertip then sniffled. The man offered the bottle again. She took a shorter drink than before. The two were quiet for a minute, then Charlene continued.

"A few times, I slipped out when he was at work, but he had eyes all over the place. He'd always find me before I could get anywhere. He lost a bunch of jobs 'cause he'd walk right off the site in the middle of work to come fetch me. Shit, he beat me for that, too."

Charlene puffed her peach flavored cigarillo.

"I finally wasn't gonna take his shit no more. As much as I loathe even the very idea of hurtin' God's creatures, even worthless wife-beating bastards, I asked God's forgiveness, then I did-in them two dogs with a box of rat poison I found in the pantry. He didn't know it was there because he never went in. He'd say the pantry and kitchen was a woman's place.

"When he come home and found them dawgs layin' dead, he about had a conniption fit. While he was panicking, he forgot he had that pistol tucked in the back of his britches, so I snatched it out and shot him square in the asshole. His knees buckled, and he went to squallerin' and beggin' for mercy, but I shot him again, in the balls, and put two more in the floor next to his head."

"Damn! Remind me to never get on your bad side! It sounds like things get a little *nutty* when someone crosses you!"

Charlene snorted.

"I see you caught the humor," the man said.

Charlene hyperventilated as she giggled. "Oh, Lord, have mercy! I haven't laugh-snorted in ages!" The female's hilarity intensified. The man joined his companion's glee.

The laughter subsided. "His pistol," Charlene continued, "was a little ole .22 his daddy had give him when he was a boy, so I don't know how bad he really got hurt except for his butthole? It was pretty tore up, I'm sure! I think I only grazed his balls through his jeans, but I'd put money that he was shittin' through a tube for a month! That bunghole shot made direct contact. Hemorrhoids from hell!"

The man laughed again.

"I might be deep country, but I ain't no dumb hick."

"What?" The man was startled and confused. "I don't get it?"

"I ain't dumb. I know I talk dumb, especially when I'm toasted from drinking, but I'm smart enough to take care of myself. I know what lines to never allow nobody to cross. Now, I might be opening up way too much to somebody I don't know, but somehow your vibe is totally different than any other man I ever met. You ain't got to worry about me turnin' you into no eunuch!"

"Well, thank you! You have no idea how relieved I am to hear that!" The man dropped his head and shook it then took a drink.

"Hey!" Charlene erupted. The man jerked, startled again. "You never told me your name! I told you mine was Charlene, but you ain't told me yours!"

"Pae," he replied.

"Pie? You mean like you want to eat some of my sweet ole cherry pie?" Charlene laughed. "I'm just funnin'! You know that!" She slapped Pae's leg. "That's a different name."

"It's pronounced more like, 'Pa-eh' kind of like you're talking to your dear ole pa and saying, eh? Close to pie but with a rapid pause after the *pa* sound, and a slight, almost long *e* sound at the end. Hard to explain and even harder to pronounce exactly right in English."

"Why did your parents name you that?"

"They didn't. It's a nickname that was given me when I was deployed to Thailand many years ago. It stuck. I think it means peace—I forget—but I remember the locals telling me it is a rough equivalent to Pete in that it is a tranquil sounding name. They said it fits me. Perhaps that's where I gleaned the peace meaning? They spelled the name P-a-e when they wrote it in English for me. The other Southeast Asian cultures spell it with an *i* instead of an *e*. I could never tell the difference in the inflection between Pa-e, Pai, and pie, but the native Thai could. I don't know what the word means in the other languages."

"That's right! You said you was in the service?"

"Yep."

"What branch?"

"Marines."

"Marines?" Charlene gasped. "Hubba-hubba! Well, you are big and strapping like a Marine, but you sure don't come across like a big ole ass! Oops! Don't get me wrong! I'm not saying Marines are asses. I love Marines, but you seem so calm and reserved? You're not pushy or overbearing, not a show-off or a dick. Oh! There I go again, sounding like I'm down on the Marines, but really, I'm not!"

Charlene turned and got on her knees again, facing Pae. "I can see why them people over there named you, Pie!" She grinned. "I sure got all pie-eyed when I saw your fine ass standing out there this afternoon! Is Pie what you want me to call you?"

Pae nodded and smiled. "Pie is fine."

"Pie is fine..." Charlene closed her eyes and turned her head, "fine-as-wine!" She leaned back and plopped onto her butt, looking behind to make sure her hand was not too close to the fire pit. Her shirt was still wide open and her breasts out.

"Look at me sittin' here, half-naked! But you know what? I don't mind. Do you mind? I don't mind. You have man boobs."

Charlene covered her mouth and grinned. She extended her other hand and raked her fingertips over Pae's chest. "Oh, please forgive me! I didn't mean that. I mean, your chest is so big and muscular! I was just sayin' boobs like a figure of speech. You got your man boobs, and I got these...weird-ass, lop-sided woman boobs with un-proportionate nipples."

Charlene rocked back and dropped her head forward. She pressed her chin against her collarbone and looked at her breasts as she tugged on one.

"*Nipples* sounds kinda cheap and skanky, don't it? *Areolas,* is the scientific word, I think? Well, not for the actual nipples but for these big round dark patches, right? These red oblong discs? I got these weird, mal-shapen areolas, and I also got sun freckles all over me. I sit around on that back-porch slab, topless, in a pair of cutoff jeans a lot. But you know what? I just don't care. Men and women? We all got boobs. We all got areolas. Why does society say I can't take off my shirt and get some sun like the boys do? Why can't I take off my shirt in the company of a man that I trust? A greasy, hairy, pale, toad-frog shaped man can take his shirt off any time he wants, but a woman can't? Not even a shapely, tanned, attractive one even if she ain't got no boobs at all? Why is this country like that, that they say men can go shirtless, but we can't? Piss on 'em! I do it anyway."

Pae mused at Charlene's pronunciation of the word *can't*. It sounded like she said, *cain't.*

Charlene stood and wobbled a bit. "You know what else? We got asses too, just like y'all men. Ain't no difference except for the shape."

Charlene turned around and bent over while she wagged her butt at Pae. "See? Here's my ass!" She slapped one of her butt cheeks. She wobbled as she fumbled with her shorts. She dropped them to her knees and spread her cheeks, then yelled, "Surprise!"

Charlene was not wearing any panties. She yanked her shorts back up then straightened herself.

"I used to shave my crack as best I could when I was young. It was the nastiest thing in the world to have to do that, but I couldn't stand having a hairy crack. It grows around my crater like a damn sasquatch! That was pretty scary to see, huh?"

The woman's guest was speechless.

"Don't even get me started on having an upset stomach day with all that."

"Ugh!" Pae moaned. He drank whiskey in desperate attempts to avoid dwelling on what he had seen, heard, and experienced tonight. Part of him wondered if the giddy female would willingly let him take her since her guard was obviously down. He also wanted to run off, screaming into the night.

Don't fall into temptation, he thought. *Fool! It's too late for that! You're in up to your eyeballs, brother! Just go for it, clown! Are you too stupid to see what she's doing here? Go for it, man!*

Pae's mind raced as his male biology suffered. The *little blue men* showed up to crash the party: his *nuggets* ached. Charlene, oblivious to his plight, kept rattling on.

"The girls in P.E. never noticed, because I started taking care of it when the first few sprigs showed up. Sorry. I'm sounding like a dirty skank again, ain't I?"

Charlene turned to face Pae again. "Anyways, I finally gave up grooming when I swore off men. The hair grew like wildfire. I ain't a nasty chick. I keep everything clean down there, so you don't got to worry about that. Ain't no chocolate bunnies hidin' in them weeds."

Yep. That's kind of killing the frustration. The mood is passing.

"I'm just thankful it didn't grow all over my cheeks, else I'd be getting 'em waxed if it had. I can live with a hairy crack but not gorilla buns."

Pae chortled. "Gorilla buns!"

"Well, it's true! I don't want no carpet on my ass! Bad enough I have thick shag in the crevice. Damn jungle crater! That's more hair than I've ever seen in anyone's butt crack! What about you? Have you ever seen that much?"

"Umm...well...no, I can't honestly say that I have. Sorry."

"No need to be sorry, sweetie pie! You didn't cause it. You ain't hurting my feelings none. I've been living with it most of my life. If I was self-conscious, I never would have said anything or shown you. I can't show you the good stuff, though. You're a mighty fine slice of pie, so I don't mind letting you cop a feel on my girls, but I just won't offer up my cooter anymore. You can grab on my boobs all you want and squeeze my ass if you'd like. We all got boobs and asses, but we ain't all got..."

Charlene paused and extended a finger. Her eyes lit up. She raised her brows. "Hey! You know what?" She stumbled forward into Pae. He caught her and held on as she sank to the ground with her eyes closed. She laughed.

"You and me both got *pie*!" Charlene howled. "I got my sweet cherry pie, and you got your name, Pie!"

Charlene snorted again. The snort was piggy-like, but it was music to Pae's ears. She opened her eyes.

"Oh, my God!" Charlene declared with glee, "I have not snort-laughed since forever, and here I've done it twice tonight!" She patted the dirt between Pae's feet then rolled onto her back in a hard, guttural laugh seasoned with a barrage of snorts.

"I'm sorry," Charlene managed between breaths, "I probably sound like a big flirt, don't I?"

Charlene's guffaw transformed into a high-pitched *hee-hee* sound as she sat up and placed a hand on her companion's thigh. Pae could not help but laugh right along with her. The joy was contagious, especially with alcohol swirling around in both their systems, amplifying the silliness.

"It's okay," Charlene panted. "We're out here in the middle of the woods. It ain't like nobody's gonna give a shit! Why not cut loose a little? Live life? That's what it's all about!"

JULy 29: MIDNIGHt

Pae sat at the foot of his bed. He gazed at a drawn curtain while he recounted the events of the day. A large box fan hummed from the opened window on an adjacent wall as it drew air into the room. Conventional wisdom declared the humid air should be pulled out, but he enjoyed sleeping in the breeze, so he oriented the flow in the opposite direction. An uncovered low watt light bulb in the center of the ceiling cast a dingy yellow hue across the room, perfect for his mood.

Pae drank from the whiskey bottle as beaded, fan-cooled sweat trickled down his torso. He curled his toes a few times and probed the texture of the dusty antique wood floor. A pint glass of water and an aspirin bottle sat near his feet. He sipped the whiskey and chased each swallow with a double portion of water.

Charlene had been a much-needed breath of fresh air. Pae had never met anyone quite like her outside the days when he used to frequent strip clubs. He was intrigued that she had no problem flashing him the way that she had. Thankfully, her wool had been so thick he could not see any details when she had bent over and spread herself. The night shadows had helped. Pae also thought it respectable that Charlene had salvaged a wisp of modesty by not offering all of her female goods.

Respectable enough in my book, he thought. *Precious few people have the morals that granny and grandpa had. She deserves at least a little credit, I guess?*

Pae had found Charlene's free spirit magnetic. She had proven herself, unlike every other self-proclaimed free spirit he had ever encountered save for one. He was glad she had not tossed herself at him like a piece of meat though it had initially appeared that way. As fun as he was sure it could have been, Pae appreciated Charlene's thin preservation of dignity through her drunken stupor. He was relieved he had also exercised restraint.

No one likes waking up with regrets.

Pae had picked up Charlene and carried her into her house when her consciousness had waned. He had removed her shirt but left her shorts on when he had laid her on the bed. She had been left on her side at the mattress' edge with her bathroom trashcan on the floor just below her head. The bathroom light had been left on, and a boxed window air conditioner set on low. Pae had leaned in and kissed Charlene on the forehead.

"Goodnight, you strange, wild, wonderfully unique creature, you," he had whispered before leaving her house, ensuring it had been locked on his way out.

Pae smiled at the recollection. All was well.

That little girl...why is she suddenly crossing my mind again? Why now? Tonight was perfect! Well, that's not a good way to be. Why wouldn't she cross my mind? Who am I to think I should just bask in the glory of the evening and shrug off that child as if she doesn't matter? What kind of a person am I to think that way?

I can't believe I was sunbathing naked in the backyard, great big privacy fence or not! It sure didn't seem like that big of a risk. I guess you just never can tell? Nothing I can do about it now. What's done is done. Come on, you need to stop thinking about this. It's time to get some shut-eye. Let it go. Hopefully, you'll wake up feeling refreshed tomorrow? Think about Charlene and the good time you had with her tonight.

Pae was exhausted, but his mind kept running away with him. He lifted the whiskey bottle from the floor and took one last drink. A few ounces remained. He was tempted to finish it off, but he'd had enough. The night was not getting any younger. No questions would be answered or mysteries solved before sunrise. Sleep beckoned.

Pae wobbled to his feet and swiped his hand toward the ceiling until he laid hold of the thin ball-chain that dangled from the ceramic light fixture above the bed. He yanked the metal strand. The room went dark. Pae flopped face down onto the mattress. Immediate snoring ensued.

A FORMEr AUTUMn

A woman tucked her son into bed. "Let's say our prayers, okay, sugar dumpling?"

The boy did not respond.

"Let's place our hands together and lace our fingers."

The boy complied without a word.

"Are you ready?"

The boy remained silent.

"Okay, here we go…"

The child's mother recited a famous, generations-old prayer from the 1750 edition of the New England Primer:

"Now I lay me down to sleep,
I pray the Lord my soul to keep,
If I should die before I 'wake,
I pray the Lord my soul to take."

The boy's mother finished the prayer with, "Amen." She kissed her son's forehead. "Sweet dreams, sugar dumpling." She left his room.

The boy rolled onto his side in a fetal position. He pulled his knees as close to his chest as he could and pulled the blankets over his head.

"Please don't take away my soul," the child whispered. "Please don't kill me in my sleep."

The boy sucked his thumb. He remained awake. His mind ran away while he tossed and turned for another three hours.

JULy 30: MORNINg

Rising humidity awoke Pae. The box fan was still humming away, but the cooling effect had diminished in the late morning sun. He rolled over and looked at his clock. It was 8:46. He pushed the bed sheet off and sat up. He could not recall covering himself during the night, but he was not surprised. Warm or not, he had a habit of covering himself when he bedded down for the night, even if only by a sheet. He looked around the room and remembered he had left a glass of water, a bottle of whiskey, and a bottle of blood thinners on the floor.

I'll deal with that later, Pae thought. He shuffled around the house, then bathed in the antique cast iron tub, got dressed, and cooked breakfast.

Pae was at Charlene's front door just before 11:30. He knocked three times and awaited a response then knocked again. A few seconds passed. He rapped on the oak fixture a third time, louder.

"Charlene? Are you okay in there?" After a short delay, there arose a metal click and slide from a deadbolt. The door opened a few inches, restricted by a chain lock.

"Hey," Charlene greeted Pae. She looked a little rough around the edges but appeared fine otherwise. She was wrapped in a silk bathrobe. Pink pajama bottoms, patterned in yellow cartoon pig skulls wearing black bows on their crowns, covered her legs.

Pae looked relieved. "I figured I'd come over and check up on you. You were a little wasted last night."

"Yeah," Charlene lowered her eyes, "I know." She looked back up at Pae. "Hey listen, I really am sorry about all that. I don't know what got into me?"

Although her southern accent was still thick, her speech was a little more proper, and it was not as slow and mushy.

"I'm really not that kind of a person, you know? Overly promiscuous? A sex hound? That's just not me."

"You don't have to apologize. I enjoyed every minute of it."

"Yeah. I should not have offered so much for you to enjoy. It just wasn't right."

"That's okay. Don't beat yourself up over it. I hope you know I didn't take any unfair advantage of you."

"I know you didn't. I was drifting in and out of reality, but I remember you tucking me in and making sure I wouldn't drown in my own puke." She withheld that she remembered him kissing her forehead and the words he had spoken. "Well, I've got things to do. Thank you for checkin' in on me."

"You're welcome."

Charlene closed the door. Pae heard the deadbolt turn again. He stood for a moment, a little confused and concerned. He watched the door for a minute then walked to his car.

Pae drove to the Paq-Ur-Saq convenience store to pick up a few items he had forgotten the day before. After shopping, he approached a payphone he had noticed on an outside corner of the storefront. He picked up the handset and was surprised to discover a dial tone.

I thought these things were extinct?

Pae extended the metal-sheathed cord and raised a leg to wipe the handset on the knee of his pants. There was too much *ear cheese* on the receiver to risk wiping it with his shirt. A silver, stranded-metal cable suspended a plastic binder beneath the phone. He opened it. The cover contained a paper phonebook. It almost looked too thin. Pae thought vandals might have ripped out most of the pages.

Nope. It's complete. Not a whole lot of people around here, I guess?

Pae thumbed through the blue pages then checked to see what coinage the phone accepted.

Oh! That's different!

The phone had a magnetic slot for reading charge cards. Pae debated using a card then decided to fish his pockets. He had plenty of coins. He dialed then awaited an automated prompt for the expected deposit. He inserted the required currency. The phone clicked and popped then delivered a ringing signal after he dialed.

"Empire County Sheriff's Department, non-emergency number," a southern female voice answered, "If this is an emergency, please hang up and dial nine-one-one. If not, then how may I help you?"

Pae hesitated. "I'd like to report a possible case of child neglect that might be bordering on abuse?"

"Alright, sir, may I have the number you're calling from?"

He looked over the metal telephone chassis. "I don't see one. There might have been a number on it, but the plastic's been popped out, and the paper removed. I'm at a public payphone."

"I see. And where is this payphone located, sir?"

"At the Paq-Ur-Saq convenience store off the northbound lane of State Route 221, about ten miles southwest of Palafox, near Knollwood. Hold on, let me see if there's an address on the storefront."

"That's okay sir, I have the address. Now, you said you'd like to report a possible case of child abuse? Is the child in any immediate danger that you're aware? Have you contacted the state Child Protective Services?"

"No, ma'am, she isn't, and I have not. Given what I'd observed, I think the police might be better to look into it."

"And, why is that, sir? What have you observed?"

"A little girl, maybe five years old, give or take, was out wandering alone on Busby Place without any supervision. She was bundled up heavy like it's the dead of winter and covered in dirt. I think she might have been dumped off?"

"Out on Busby Place, you say? How long ago was this, sir? Did it just happen?"

"No, ma'am, this was yesterday, late afternoon, somewhere around four or five p.m., I suppose?"

"If it was yesterday, sir, how come you're only reporting it now?"

"The child disappeared too quickly. I couldn't see where she went. I wasn't sure if it was worth me calling since I don't know where she went or where she lives."

"Did you try to find her, sir?"

"No, ma'am. I'm not familiar with the woods around there. I wouldn't know where to start. Besides, I wasn't properly dressed. I was wearing gym clothes and didn't have any shoes on. By the time I looked to see where she was headed, she was gone."

"I see. Please hold while I patch you through to Sheriff Busbee."

Pae did not carefully consider what the dispatcher had just told him. The phone went silent for a moment. An older male voice, also with a deep southern accent, picked up the line.

"This is Sheriff Busbee. How may I help you, sir?"

"Good morning, deputy. How are you today?"

The voice on the other end became tense. "Son, this is Sheriff Busbee, not Deputy. Now, what can I do for you?"

"My apologies, sir. I've never been patched directly through to a sheriff before. I guess I just took it for granted that your department had deputies on staff?"

The voice on the other end, bordered on anger. "I do have deputies on staff, but they are not handling this call, I am! Now, please get to the point!"

"Apologies again, sheriff." *Uptight turd.* "I saw a little girl out wandering around yesterday afternoon on a road called Busby Place. She was wearing heavy winter clothing and was pretty dirty from head to toe. She must have been about five or six years old, but she didn't have any adult supervision or older children with her. I can't help but wonder if maybe she's being neglected or might have been dumped off?"

"Uh-huh?" the sheriff responded in a curious tone. "And where is she now? Is she with you?"

"No, sir. I was inside the house when she disappeared from my view. I didn't have any shoes on so I couldn't go looking for her. I think she might have gone off into the woods? I didn't see any cars pass by."

"What did you say your name was, son?"

Something didn't feel right. The hair rose on the back of Pae's neck. "I didn't give you my..."

"So, you're a smartass, are you?"

"Sir?"

"Don't want to give me your name, and calling from a payphone a day after spotting the kid? Spineless little weasel! Well listen here, mister smartass weasel, there ain't but four residential homes out there on Busby Place, but only three are occupied. I'm betting, yours is one of them? One has a woman living in it, one an elderly couple, and the other is vacant. And then there's some folk on that private dirt road off the end of Busby. I know you ain't related to those folks, so you couldn't possibly be staying there.

"So, here's how it works around here, son. We're quiet out this way. We don't go around stirring up shit, and we damn sure don't go around calling the law based on random sightings that we can't explain. Folks out here have a way of life that most outsiders can't understand. They keep to themselves. They handle their own problems, and the law doesn't get involved unless it absolutely has to. How we choose to enjoy ourselves is our business and no one else's. Now, if you ever have a legitimate, honest-to-goodness, undeniable crime to report, then, by all means, give us a call. Otherwise, you would do well to let people be. You understand me, son?"

Pae was floored. He did not know what to think. He delayed too long, so the man repeated, "Do you understand me, boy?"

"Yes sir, sheriff, I understand clearly."

"Good! Now, you go on and have yourself a great day and stay safe." The line clicked, then went dead.

I don't believe it! He hung up on me! Something's seriously wrong with this place. Why did I think it would be a good idea to move here?

Pae remained in place, dumbfounded for a moment, with his back to the phone. He observed the parking lot. No one else was around and no other vehicles except for the one belonging to the store's employee. There was no traffic on the state route. He wondered what to do next. He thought about rubbing his prints off the phone, but the Sheriff had already connected the dots and figured out where he lived; it was not rocket science. He returned the handset to its cradle then left.

Pae turned off of the state highway and headed up Busby Place. In the distance, he saw an old, blue, nineteen-seventies era pickup truck sitting in the middle of the road in front of his property, facing him. As Pae drove nearer, he could see two men sitting in it. He cut the corner into his driveway to avoid the unfamiliar vehicle, then parked and walked out to meet his visitors. He approached from the passenger's side and stopped three feet from the door.

"Good afternoon," Pae looked past the heavy-set, bearded male passenger in a baseball cap, to address the driver. "May I help you?"

"Well, I sure as hell hope so," the driver replied, then grinned at his much larger passenger, who turned to reciprocate. The driver was thin and stringy with a thick barbell mustache, a triangle-shaped tuft of hair on his chin, and long, wavy, black hair with an equal mix of gray. He had poor quality, faded green tattoos on his neck, arms, and knuckles.

"It's a real easy thing to do," like Charlene, the pickup truck driver pronounced his -ing's like -ang's. "Now listen closely because I'm only going to explain it once."

The passenger's eyes widened. He raised his brows while gesturing toward the driver with his thumb. He grinned and nodded, then winked at Pae.

The driver continued, "We ain't all Jethro and Daisy-May neighborly out here, delivering sweet cornbread and casserole dishes to each other like you're probably used to seeing on TV. We mind our own damn business!"

The last sentence caught Pae off guard. His blood ran cold. The men in the truck could see it written all over him.

"I see I have your attention. Good! Now, my daughter comes up and down this road from time to time. You might have seen her lately? Pretty little young thang: long, luscious blonde hair, with dark eyes and full, pouty lips...fine little ass, too!"

The driver paused to observe Pae's body language. Pae held steady. He sensed the skinny, wild-eyed man had selected those words on purpose. He could tell both men were scrutinizing every move, expression, and involuntary twitch.

"No?" the driver asked. He tapped his chin with two fingers then sat his hand atop a pistol between him and his passenger on the truck's bench seat. Pae noticed another firearm on the dashboard.

"Well, if you do, don't walk up to her. Don't talk to her."

The driver paused. He radiated a peculiar expression that bordered on glee.

"Don't cake up her pretty little pearly whites with no doughy shit."

Both men's eyes burrowed through Pae, wondering whether he might reveal his sin of having already interfered. He remained steadfast, unshaken. After a tense moment of silence, the driver resumed his warning.

"Don't even wave at her. I am highly protective of my kin, especially my little girl. Believe you me, I'll know it if you do anything at all with her.

"And I know you been livin' in that house since late May. You moved in on the twenty-first. I know when you leave, and I know when you come home. I know a few other things about you, too. Like I said, we mind our own business out here. The last thing either of us needs is an old-fashioned feud. Those don't turn out well for nobody.

"Now, you go on doin' your little thing like you always have, and we'll go on doin' ours. Our paths shall never meet. We'll live in harmony just like ole Jethro and whatever the hell that twat's name is? Now, see how easy that is?"

The driver grinned and nodded at Pae and then at his passenger. "What do you think, Bubba? Does that sound easy to you?"

The passenger looked at the driver and reciprocated his expression. He held the grin as he turned to face Pae. "Sounds easy as takin' a jailhouse shit, brother!"

"Now, Bubba, you know that takes a little effort in the common area, what with all them hungry eyes watchin' and waitin' to plow in!"

"Yeah, you got me there, baws-man," the large passenger replied without breaking his mutual gaze with Pae. He continued to grin. "I reckon it's only as easy as you make it." The man turned toward the driver. "Gotta shake out the luggage and rub on a little snot just to be ready." He looked at Pae again. "Never can tell when the balloon knot's gonna get tore."

The driver patted his passenger on the shoulder. "Yeah, that's one hell of a sting goin' in, ain't it, brotha-man?"

"You damn sure got that right, baws-man! One hell of an eye-poppin' surprise!"

"Bustin' that rubber O-ring!" The driver grinned, shut his eyes, and shook his head. "Damn! Lawd have mercy, what a burn!"

The driver removed his hand from his passenger's shoulder and gripped the truck's column shifter. "I think ole Jethro here understands, don't you, Jethro?"

Pae did not respond. He took a step back and nodded once, fixing his eyes on the driver.

The driver nodded, then added, "Yeah, he gets it. You have yourself a fine day, good neighbor!" He shifted the vehicle into drive then turned left off of the roadway. The truck kicked dirt, blades of grass, and loose gravel onto Pae as it continued turning in the opposite direction then speeded away up the private red clay road. It disappeared into the woods, shrouded by a drifting bank of stirred, red-orange dust.

d. bRENT iSBELL
SICKS

JULy 31: MORNINg, THe WEe HOURs

Pae awoke in a heavy sweat. It was a rare occurrence with the box fan on full blast, even in July, but this time he was drenched. He sat up. He could feel and hear the fan and could see its silhouette in the window. The air was refreshing. The sweat dried after he removed the bedsheet. His dreams had wrecked him again, as they once had many years prior. He had no doubt that it was his troubled soul--triggered by the little girl and her father, and not the southern heat--that had caused him to perspire. He looked at the soft, green LED display on his alarm clock: it was 2:58 a.m.

"Shit," Pae whispered. He drew his feet close and sat naked and frog-legged in the flow from the fan blades.

His mind lingered on the images that had stirred him:

He had seen a butterfly and some squirrels carrying hammers. He had seen bicycles with no riders traveling in a circle around a colorfully decorated Christmas tree. He had heard an old, familiar female voice and had smelled a mix of tobacco, nicotine, and coffee on her breath. The earthy scent had always appealed to him.

The dream had faded into images of many hands, pulling and twisting a piece of putty. The squirrels hammered on the putty while the hands pulled. The tensile strength failed. The putty had ripped. The ornaments had fallen off the Christmas tree, and all but a few colored lights had popped. The dream had ended in a sudden black, empty feeling.

"Damn it, damn it, damn it!" Pae muttered.

He arose and crept into the kitchen. He opened a jar of commercial moonshine and took a drink, hoping the alcohol would relax what he thought must be a muscle spasm. He fumbled around in the moonlight and located his box of mini cigars, then withdrew one and peeled the foil wrapper. The dizzying smell of butane filled his nostrils as he lit it with a short blue flame from the stovetop.

Pae walked outside onto the steps behind the kitchen and sat. The night was black. A few stars twinkled, but clouds concealed the majority. There was no moon. A mosquito's wings sang in a high, annoying pitch, followed by silence. Not long afterward, Pae felt a sting. He ignored his instinct to swat.

I'm just not in the mood for harming anything, not even you. Everyone has someone they care for. Skeeters do, too, I suppose? Take what you need for your young 'uns then be on your way. At least you're not singing in my ears.

Pae took a drink and puffed his cigar. He exhaled smoke and sighed. He spoke in a low voice, a little above a whisper, "Lord, I'm troubled. That dream messed with my head, and my body's having another one of those weird spasms. It's making me recall those times and causing me to think of that little girl I met yesterday. She's been on my mind constantly! It's making me half crazy. I can't help but wonder what on earth she's having to live with at home?"

Pae took another sip of moonshine. His mind ran in circles. He spoke again, "These spasms are horrible. They make me wish I were paralyzed."

He raised his jar of moonshine. "I know I shouldn't run to this, but I really do need a great big larapin swig of it tonight." He drew a puff from the cigar then exhaled. "And, of course, I feel like I need one of these, too. What can I say? It helps calm me. You know as well as I do, Lord that this physical pain is a killer. It ain't fun, especially where it's at."

Pae took another drink and a drag off of the cigar.

"So, what can I do about that little girl, if anything? What about that bone head sheriff? Those men in that truck? What can I do? Is there anything at all?"

The groggy man finished his cigar. He put the butt out on the steps then pitched it into the dirt underneath the house. He stayed on the smooth formed cement steps. A few more mosquitos had commenced drilling for blood, but Pae did not care. He was tired and tipsy. He waited to see if any ideas would come to mind regarding how to handle his concerns.

Pae's thoughts drifted. *I sure wish I knew what caused that pain*, he thought. He was quite certain he knew. He just did not want to remember. Denial was easier.

The man considered the little platinum-haired girl some more, but she caused his mind to race in too many directions. He knew he would have difficulty going back to sleep if his brain did not settle.

Pae stood up and leaned against the doorframe then took a few more sips of the blackberry flavored 130-proof alcohol. He fished a piece of fruit from the jar and chewed on it. The man closed his eyes. He had not drunk anything that potent in ages. The whiskey from two nights prior was caramel water in comparison. The chewed, alcohol-saturated berry went straight to Pae's head. The slosh in his brain and his rubbery legs reminded him that the four-foot drop off the cement steps would not be fun. Even if he were too tipsy to feel it, Pae was not in the mood for waking up with a mouthful of lawn, covered in ants.

Pae started to sway like a Gulf Coast palm in a stiff wind.

I think my body already has this one taken care of? He exhaled in relief when he realized the spasmodic tension had passed.

The woozy man struggled to twist the lid onto the moonshine jar. He succeeded, then went inside and set it on the kitchen table. He shuffled into the bathroom. Too tired and unstable to risk standing, he sat to urinate. Pae felt himself drifting away.

Just let me sit here and die.

It took some effort, but he managed to get back into the bedroom. Pae hit the bed like a sack of potatoes at 3:33 a.m.

A FORMEr AUTUMn

" Are you okay, sugar dumpling?" A woman asked her seven-year-old son as she undressed him for his bath. The boy clinched the tail of his T-shirt with one hand and cupped the crotch of his cotton briefs with the other.

"Don't look!" the boy said.

"Are you sure you're okay?"

"I'm fine, mama. I know how to do it. I'm seven!"

"I understand. You're a growing boy. Don't want your mama to see your little dingle-dangles anymore?"

"Mom!"

"Okay. I'll leave you to it, then. Let me know when you're finished."

"I can let the water out of the tub when I'm done, mama. I can turn off the light, too."

"Do you want your bathtub toys?"

"No, ma'am, not tonight."

"Alrighty. This is the fourth night in a row. I hope you're feeling okay?"

"I am. I need you to leave so I can get in."

"Well, okay, then. Enjoy your time."

The boy did not respond. He followed his mother, then closed the bathroom door behind her and locked it.

JULy 31: AFTEr SUNRISe

Pae sat on his front steps with a piping hot cup of coffee. As usual, the road in front of his house was empty. The people from the private dirt road passed through once or twice a day. There did not appear to be any particular pattern, but then he had not paid attention before. Necessity had changed that.

After a few sips of coffee and random checking of the time on his phone, Pae dialed. A hint of anticipation stirred in his chest. The phone started ringing. *I waited an extra ten minutes,* he thought. *They should be there.* The ringing stopped.

An older-sounding female voice greeted Pae with a thick southern drawl, "Light on the Hill Christian Church; this is Emily, how may we be a blessing to you today?"

"Good morning, ma'am. I need to speak to someone about getting help for a child I think might be getting physically and sexually abused?"

"Oh! Oh, dear! Have you tried talking to the parents, sir?"

"Yes, ma'am, I have. That interaction greatly enhanced my suspicions."

"I see. Well, have you directly observed any such behavior, sir?"

"No, not directly. The child was dirty and in filthy clothes. She was out wandering around by herself. She's maybe five or six years old, doesn't talk, and uses obscene hand gestures."

"Obscene hand gestures, sir?"

"Yes: flipping the bird, the middle finger."

"Is the child a relative, sir?"

"No, ma'am. She belongs to my neighbor."

"Hold, please, sir. Let me patch you through to Pastor Strickland."

"Yes, ma'am. Thank you."

Pae's anticipation built as he awaited the transfer. The delay was momentary, but it felt like an eternity. The line was picked up.

"This is Pastor Strickland," a male voice said in a cleaner southern accent. "How may I be of service?"

"Good morning, Pastor Strickland, my name is Pae. I'm trying to get help for a little girl that I have strong reason to believe is being neglected and abused, and possibly being sexually molested?"

"Are you a member of the Church, Mr. Pae?"

Pae's brows raised. He hesitated, surprised by the question. "No, sir, I am not."

"Well, Mr. Pae, the Church would be glad to help, except that we don't make a practice of providing services to folk who are not members of the congregation in good standing. That ordinarily means someone who has been in regular attendance for at least six months and tithes at least ten percent of their income regularly."

"What? Why? I don't understand?"

"You see, Mr. Pae, we've learned that when you get a reputation for being indiscriminate with providing Church resources to assist the public, it tends to attract all kinds of unsavory types. The next thing you know, the Church starts receiving all kinds of odd people, and the well quickly runs dry. We believe in helping, Mr. Pae, but we also believe in running the Lord's house decently and in order."

"But pastor, we're not talking about decency or order in the Church, we're talking about a little girl's life. An under-aged child might be in some genuinely serious trouble here! Besides, I have lived out here for only a few months. I haven't had that much time to get established in any church."

"Are you currently in attendance elsewhere, sir?"

"No, sir. I am not."

"Well, with all due respect, Mr. Pae, God's resources are not here for men to plunder."

"Plunder? What do you mean, 'plunder'?" Pae's left ear burned; it scorched. Tension arose in his voice. "I'm not looking to plunder anything! I'm looking for help for a little girl!"

"If you're serious about the Church's help, sir, I recommend you establish yourself, so that you may show yourself trustworthy, and prove yourself a good steward of your resources before we entrust you with the Church's. If not here, then do so at a church of your choosing."

"Thank you for your time, pastor."

Pae hung up. He stood and glugged the rest of his coffee. Though the liquid had cooled a little while waiting to make the call, it still burned on the way down. The anxious male paced in front of his house.

After all these years, those kinds of churches are still out there! Not willing to lift a finger unless you're a member of the good ole boy club!

Pae knew of several churches in other states and towns that would have helped, but he was not familiar with any in this region. He did not know where they were. He called a few others of varying denominations. They were all too similar in their prerequisites for offering assistance. One had asked whether he had any tattoos and if he drank, or smoked, or used drugs, and another whether he was divorced. Another had asked if he had ever spoken in tongues and yet another whether he believed the Bible was still viable in modern society. They all asked questions that were irrelevant to the help he was seeking. Their questions reminded him of the churches he had been raised around. Each had dodged essential issues for the sake of bizarre ritualistic rules and appearances.

Thirty minutes passed. Pae had called twelve churches, including three in other counties. The only one that was more than willing to help was too far away. He did not expect assistance from that particular one. He was relieved to find assurance that he was not fooling himself. Alas, three hours' driving distance was not feasible. *There goes that idea.*

Pae was shaking with frustration. He wanted to punch some church people. He wanted to destroy something, and he wanted to cry. *Self-righteous, legalistic Pharisees!* the man thought. He prayed as he paced, then stepped inside for more coffee. After pouring, Pae swiped through the county telephone directory on his mobile phone. He ran across one church he had overlooked. It was in Palafox.

"Hmm," Pae mumbled. "I really don't want to go there." *That town gives me the creeps. Oh well. That little girl is more important than my creeps. Perhaps it will help if I show up in person instead of making a call? Might as well do this right, even if they do send me packing for whatever ridiculous reason?*

Pae dressed in a pair of silk blended cotton slacks and a fine cotton dress shirt with a necktie fastened in a Full Windsor knot. He slipped into a pair of polished dress shoes and a matching belt. By then, he was half soaked in sweat. *Oh well, what can I do?* Pae's house had no central air conditioning.

Not long afterward, the determined male entered his car, rolled up the windows, and cranked up the air conditioner. He tuned the radio to an eighties and nineties rock station. An electronically enhanced death metal song blasted across the speakers. Pae recognized it right away. The lyrics were saturated in rebellion against insincere and hypocritical church-going people and corporate greed. He understood the song's sarcasm. "Appropriate," he grumbled.

Pae recalled a late-twentieth-century hymn from his childhood that he refused to tolerate. "There's nothing *'wonderful'* about them," he complained, "except for precious few. They are rare. Let's see if I can find one in a place like Palafox?" He turned up the radio's volume then went on his way.

Pae arrived at a large, impressive looking tan brick church in Palafox. It was a beautiful building, but it bothered him. It triggered too many negative childhood memories. He parked beside other cars in the paved lot then strolled to the double doors of the main sanctuary. They were locked. He walked around the right side of the building, then around the back to the other side. There it was, a few feet to the left of his car: the office door.

"If it were a snake, it would have bitten me," he whispered. He went inside.

The office smelled of polished wood, shampooed carpet, and reams of paper. It was a pleasant aroma that would have been fine in a public library, but in this setting, it stirred more unsavory memories.

Why do so many churches have to smell like this? Do they all buy their materlals from the same place?

Though different from the interiors of mobile homes, the odor was just as distinctive as when trailers had been built with thin, synthetic wood panels. It was much cleaner and more robust but still as cringe-worthy in Pae's mind. His insides squirmed.

This place smells as varnished and fake as those people on the phone. Well, I'm not here to smell it.

A pale, elderly woman wearing dark maroon lipstick greeted him. Never mind that she had no lips. The lipstick had seeped into the deep, cracked wrinkles around her frail drawn up mouth. Huge, jeweled earrings stretched her lobes. *The Gautama Buddha,* Pae thought. A bulky stone necklace lay around the woman's neck. She wore a floral dress with a high Victorian style collar.

"Good morning, sir," the receptionist greeted Pae with a cynical smile. "Do you have an appointment with us today?"

"Good day, ma'am. It is a wonderful day the Lord has made, is it not?" Pae replied. *Ugh! That sounded lame!* He hated being fake but figured perhaps if he came across a little more like one of them, they might be more willing to listen?

"Yes, indeed it is, sir. Do you have an appointment?"

"I was hoping to speak to someone about finding help for a dear, small child who is in an abusive home." Still a hint of *church-speak* with that *dear, small child* bit. *Maybe it will work?*

"Do you have an appointment, sir?"

She's not letting it go. "No, ma'am, I'm sorry, I do not."

"One moment, please." The receptionist stood and walked across the room to another door. The nameplate on it read REVEREND SMALLS. She tapped on the door. "Reverend Smalls? We have a walk-in who would like to speak to someone about a, 'dear, small child who is in an abusive home.'" The receptionist's tone was almost sarcastic.

"Send him in," a male voice called from behind the door.

The elderly woman walked back to her desk and sat. She picked up a stack of folders and straightened them. *Funny,* Pae thought, *they didn't need straightening.* Without lifting her eyes, the receptionist told Pae, "Reverend Smalls will see you now."

"Thank you, ma'am."

As Pae opened the reverend's door, a towering, barrel-chested, dark-skinned man stood from behind a desk. Pae froze in his tracks. *Reverend "Smalls," indeed! There's nothing small about this fellow! He's huge!* The reverend was at least seven feet tall and wearing the largest pair of blue denim suspended coveralls he had ever seen, with a plain white T-shirt beneath. Pae wondered whether the clothing had been custom-tailored. The reverend had to have been 6x in size if not greater, and four or five hundred pounds of corn-fed carcass. He had never seen a man this large in person. He was a beast! He also had the most inviting expression Pae had seen since moving into the sticks. The reverend extended a meaty hand with thick, sausage fingers.

"Good day, I'm Reverend Smalls." The reverend smiled.

"My name is Pae." The reverend's shake was plenty firm but not the iron vice Pae had expected. He was grateful his hand was not crushed.

The reverend walked back to his desk. "Please, have a seat, Mr. Pae." He settled in. "How may I be of service to you?"

"Forgive me for not getting right to the point just yet, but I *really* didn't expect to see a pastor in coveralls."

"Ah, yes!" the reverend smiled. "Half my congregation didn't expect it, either. Half of that half left our assembly to attend elsewhere. Some of the remainder still grumble, but they take their chill pills when I show up on Sunday, dressed appropriately. The times they are a-changing, Mr. Pae. But then the times have always changed. There's nothing new under the sun. Change is constant. That being said, a black minister has been easy for them to accept over the past two months but a black minister who is an average, everyday guy? One who likes to be comfortable at work, and who leaves at lunchtime to go do *real* work in the community for the remainder of the day? That, my dear Mr. Pae, is what sticks in their traditional old-ways craw. Mr. Pae. I am not here to play church or to put on a show. This town is in shambles, and so is this congregation. There is a lot of work to be done out there, real work."

Reverend Smalls leaned back in his chair. "Now, Mr. Pae," the reverend's countenance seemed all the more inviting, "how may I serve you, my friend?"

That short speech had been music to Pae's ears. "Well, sir, I'm seeking help for a little girl that I am quite certain is being neglected. She might also be getting sexually abused?"

The reverend leaned forward and rested his forearms on his desk. His brow furled. "Who is this child? Does she live nearby?"

"No, sir. I think she lives near me out in Knollwood."

"Do you know whether her family attends here, or somewhere else within the community, so that perhaps I may sit with them and discuss your concerns?"

"I do not know her personally or her kin. I met her daddy yesterday. He was unpleasant."

The reverend leaned back and rotated his chair perpendicular to Pae's. Sunlight radiated from the open binds to the left of the minister, casting lines across his body. He looked toward the wall and rubbed his chin. "Describe this girl."

"She's maybe six years old but looks closer to five; small child; wears a heavy, pink-colored winter coat in the blazing heat; wanders around without any supervision. She has dirty, unwashed, long, platinum blonde hair pulled up in a ponytail--at least when I saw her--and dark brown eyes. They reminded me of Brazil nuts but not quite that dark; beautiful little girl."

The reverend's mouth twitched. He glanced at his guest without turning his head. Pae did not notice. The clergyman kept rubbing his chin. "Knollwood, you say? Busby Place is the only road out there. There are no children out that way that I've ever been told."

"You're familiar with the folks out that way, and you've only been here two months?"

"Palafox is a small town. Word gets around quickly. I get out there in the community. I roll my sleeves up and work. I've learned a lot of things about a lot of people, and about how this town and the outlying rural communities work, both the good and the bad. I stay involved, so I see and hear a lot. Two months can be much longer than one might think. But children in Knollwood? That's a new one on me. I know of six adults who live out there. You are undoubtedly among those six. Two of them come in and out of town almost daily, but they keep to themselves. They never have any children with them. My knowledge is not all-inclusive, mind you. A lot of it is second-hand. I take what I hear at face value until I learn otherwise, and I don't entertain what folks say about each other personally. I won't indulge gossip. Eat the meat and spit out the bones."

"So, is there anything you can do, reverend? I have kind of an awful feeling about that little girl. I've been praying for her. I've also been threatened by the man that claims to be her father and by a friend of his, too. I called the sheriff's department, and they basically told me to steer clear, in no uncertain terms."

"Blue pickup truck?"

Pae looked like he had seen a ghost. "Yes."

"I see." The reverend rotated, then leaned forward again and placed his forearms on his desk, with his fingers laced. "This sounds like a tricky situation, Mr. Pae. It definitely sounds like one that requires action. I will see what I can do."

"Would you mind praying with me for the little girl, well, that whole family, before I go?"

"It would be my pleasure, my friend!" The reverend stood and walked to the front of his desk. He took Pae's hands into his huge meaty paws and began to pray. Pae was pleased to hear another pray the way he did, in average, everyday language, not loaded with *thees* and *thous* and other traditional Christian jargon. Pae grinned and nodded with a smile. *A preacher who doesn't pray in King James!* This pastor, this *reverend*, was the most down-to-earth Pae had ever met. He felt good about this man.

When they finished taking turns praying, the massive reverend hugged him. "You take care now, Mr. Pae. God's doors are always open if you'd like to come worship with us, and you're definitely welcome to join us in the field. No pressure. No obligation. No membership required."

Pae's eyes were puffy from the build-up of emotion. The bags were a light shade of purple as his eye sockets darkened. He was unaware of how much he resembled a raccoon. The reverend's words had touched his heart.

"Thank you, Reverend Smalls. I just might take you up on that. You have a great day, sir."

"Take care now, Mr. Pae."

Pae departed, ensuring he offered a parting courtesy to the receptionist. She returned the courtesy with her eyes averted. As Pae stepped outside, he saw an elderly man walking. The man's polyester slacks were hiked above his navel.

A FORMEr AUTUMn

"**W**ake up, sleepyhead! Rise and shine! It's time to get ready for school." Mrs. Moffat turned on the bedroom light. She kissed her son on the forehead, then peeled the blankets.

"Sweetie!" the woman said, "Don't tell me you put your clothes back on and slept in them all night? They're dirty from yesterday! You had a bath, sugar, now, you're all funky again!"

The child groaned. His mother helped him sit up.

"Your shoes are on, too? Sweetie, what were you thinking? Are you trying to come up with an easier way to get ready for school? If you are, at least put on some clean clothes, but why wear your shoes to bed? That's got to be uncomfortable?"

The boy groaned again.

"Come on. We've gotta get you into some clean clothes."

The boy insisted his mother leave the room and let him have his privacy while he changed. When she returned several minutes later, she found her son fully dressed. She was impressed except for one small detail.

"Sugar dumpling, you can't hike your pants up to your neck, honey! You look like Paw-Paw Sinclair! Here, let's pull them down where they belong."

AUGUSt 7: EARLy AfTERNOOn

The pleasing scent of fresh-cut lawns teased the early August wind. Silver-lined patches of cumulonimbus clouds drifted across the sky. A bright environmental haze blanketed the air and dimmed the colors of the evergreen trees with a faint yellowish hue that washed out the horizon.

Pae sat in his car as it idled. His window was down. He relished the smell of cut grass. It reminded him of watermelon rinds. He also enjoyed the scents of wild vegetation. The combination of the two was heavenly! He could not resist the aromas, so he used the air conditioner to counteract the humidity while he savored them through the opened window.

Pae was parked across the street from the public K-12 school in Palafox. He had parked there every day that week in the mornings and again in the afternoons, hoping to see the little girl or at least the blue truck. She had to have been in kindergarten or first grade. The dismissal bell rang. A few packs of children exited the school. About a dozen climbed aboard a public school bus and a few onto the county's rural transit. Several others got into waiting cars. The majority walked toward town. Within five short minutes, the school grounds were empty. Another day had passed with no sign of the child.

Either she's homeschooled or not attending at all, Pae figured. He remained a while longer and stared at the school building as he recalled his frequent, peculiar, and unsettling dreams from the past week. Before July 30th, his sleep had been blissful for at least the past three years that he could remember.

A fORMEr AUTUMn

The child embarked upon his three-block walk to school after breakfast. Prompted by intuition, his mother watched through a window. He walked up the road in the direction opposite the way he had walked every school day since the first grade. His pants were hiked above his navel again. Mrs. Moffat wondered why her son walked in the direction he had previously avoided because of the threat of neighborhood dogs. He had followed the altered path, enduring the dogs every day for a week. She also wondered why he had started pulling his pants so high.

"What's wrong, honey?" the seven-year-old's mother eventually asked. "Why don't you want me to pay for the charter bus? It picks up all kinds of kids, even the high school and middle school kids. There will be lots of interesting and exciting people for you to talk to. At least you won't have to be alone or walk past those mean dogs every day. Why don't you walk the way you used to or stop to play in the woods after school anymore?"

"I already told you, woman," the child erupted, "I just don't want to! Leave me alone!"

Mrs. Moffat snatched one of her son's arms near the shoulder. "Don't you talk down on me like that, you little scudder!" she wagged her finger in his face. "I've been mighty patient with your weird quirks lately, but I won't hesitate to tan your little hide! I am still your mother, whether you think you're all grown up or not!"

"I'm sorry, mama," the child whined. His wide eyes were glossed over in distress. He would not look at his mother.

Mrs. Moffat released her son. She squatted to meet him, eye-to-eye. He avoided her stare. "Honey, I love you! I just don't know what's gotten into you lately? I can tell those dogs are really stressing you out. You've been wetting the bed and having nightmares ever since you started walking that other way. I'm just trying to help you, sugar dumpling. Can't you understand that?"

The boy lowered his head. He trotted into his bedroom and locked the door. He burst into tears and started rubbing his eyes with the backs of his hands. He made noises that sounded like he was chewing his tongue while he sobbed.

AUGUSt 7: EARLy AFTERNOOn

Pae's car still idled with the air conditioner on and the window down. He put it into gear then headed home. Twenty minutes later, the troubled male pulled off at the mouth of his road and parked in the weeds. He sat with the engine running for an additional minute, then shut it off and stepped out. The man paced back and forth along the state highway, on either side of the entrance to Busby Place, curious to see whether any trails led into the woods. He discovered several. Some appeared well worn. One was overgrown.

A chill ran up Pae's spine, causing the hair on his neck to rise. He felt the same sensations on his forearms. He paused at the tree line. His pulse quickened. The longer Pae hesitated, the more his mind reached into the past. The man's gaze intensified. A light bead of perspiration built on his forehead. He shook off his jitters, then breached the first trail. Pae explored for at least three-dozen yards. The further in he went, the more obscured, narrow paths he came across, and the thicker the surrounding vegetation. The place was a labyrinth. Each new step was psychologically more challenging than the last. Pae wanted to abandon his search, but he knew he had to press forward. He heard the trickle of a creek in the distance. He explored until he found it.

There was no sign of the girl and no indications she had been there, though there were plenty of cleared areas and trails leading away. The child could easily be close by, and Pae would never know. She could evade the large male with little effort if he were to draw too close. Pae decided he had gone far enough. He did not want to risk getting lost. The man turned and increased his pace, the closer he moved toward the wooded perimeter. Once out, the massive adult plopped onto the driver's seat in his car. His hands trembled. He started the engine and took a few deep breaths then drove home.

SICKS

AUGUSt 8: BEFORe SUNRISe

She lay naked upon Pae's chest. She was warm, and her skin was clammy from the sultry summer heat. He stroked her hair with one hand and rubbed her lean, petite back with the other. His eyes were closed. She started humming while she played with his short, thick locks. Pae smiled. He slid both hands to her buttocks. They were clammy, firm, and covered in goose pimples. She hummed louder. Pae opened his eyes and kissed the tip of the female's nose. He smiled. The little platinum blonde girl reciprocated. Pae's eyes bulged. The child shot backward like a deflating party balloon.

"Little cunt!" a boy's voice yelled.

Pae heard laughter from several other boys. He started gagging. His throat was clogged. His hands flailed in darkness. One of his palms slapped an object that felt like a firm mound of flesh. Terrified screams erupted in his head, but none escaped his mouth. Pae heard a little boy's muffled groans. Something took hold of his wrists and ankles.

"Bitch!" another boy screamed.

The platinum blonde girl pushed against Pae's abdomen. "No!" she wailed. "No, stop!" Her ponytail was tightly clinched in Pae's fist.

"See?" Pae heard a whisper. "You're no different!" He heard a quiet laugh. "You know you want it! It can't fight back! Take it!"

Pae looked down at the image of the little girl. The word *innocence* entered his mind. He wrapped the naked child in a hug. His heart pounded as a hot tidal wave of adrenaline roared through his arteries.

"You are us," a young male voice whispered.

The little girl shrieked. Taunting laughs emanated from a small crowd of boys.

"Little cock sucking faggot!" someone whispered in Pae's ear. A heavy odor, reminiscent of chlorine, filled his nostrils. He started to choke again.

A pale, serpent-like mist with empty, grotesque eyes appeared and shot into his chest.

Pae screamed as his head left his pillow. He sat up and dropped his legs over the side of the bed.

"Damn it!" he whispered while he clutched his chest. Pae trembled violently, trying to calm himself. "Please forgive me," his voice wobbled in a quick prayer after he came to his senses. "Forgive me! I'm sorry! Please forgive me!" Sweat trickled down his forehead and dripped off his brows. His back, chest, and abdomen were drenched. "I'm not as strong as I thought I was. Please help me!"

Pae continued to shake like a leaf, patting his chest and wondering whether the serpentine mist had actually been a dream? The icy sensation of the spirit's contact had been too visceral. Pae's heartbeat was rapid and irregular. His mind filled with doubt as he tried to convince himself it had indeed been an imagined, subconscious visage.

"I am not!" Pae whispered. "I am not! I am not! I am not! Get out of my head!"

Guilt and self-condemnation ran rampant through the man's soul. He felt more disconnected from himself, from reality, and from God than he had in years. Pae dropped to his hands and knees on the antique hardwood floor. He lowered his forehead and prayed through a flood of tears.

No light sifted through the window. The pre-dawn August sky was cloaked in a thick pelt of clouds that suffocated the stars. Long had the moon settled, buried deep within a celestial grave. The plastic blades of the aged box fan sang its gentle melody as it pushed humidity from Pae's sheet-covered torso. It was the only sound in the tiny country house.

AUGUSt 8: EARLy EVENINg

He heard laughter from the living room and kitchen through the trailer wall. The wafer-thin panels were not insulated well enough to suppress much noise. Laughter was rare. Most times, petty bickering sifted through, and some profanity, followed by occasional yelling and objects hitting the walls and floor. Though he recognized the words, he often did not comprehend their context unless directed at him. He had never been allowed to converse with another living soul. He had been conditioned to follow orders and nothing more.

The child gazed at the plate near his feet on the padded blue trifold mat upon which he spent most of his days. He did not know what to call the food. He did not know how to use flatware. He had none. He used his hands exclusively. The child did not know that those in the forward part of the trailer used such things. The thought had never occurred to him.

He was careful to not spill his cup of water. He had done this before, but refills had rarely been prompt, even when the adults had been aware. Accidental knock-overs and drops had not been a problem until the lid of the sipping cup had been split. The child had hit the mini tumbler during the night then rolled over on it, cracking the hard, plastic cap as it lay upon its side. The vessel had warped, making lid placement difficult and unreliable. Though spillage was unlikely due to the child's increased caution, replenishment usually occurred at strict intervals. The water had to last. He could not afford to waste even a few drops.

The youngster continued to stare at his plate. The food was difficult to stomach. It tasted fine as far as he was concerned, but the servings were repetitive. He ate the same kind of meal daily. There was seldom any variety as far back as he could remember, and never for holidays, birthdays, or special occasions. Those did not exist in his world. At least the texture was soft and easy to manage. It sometimes had a funny shape like a ribbed tower when the girl shook it from the container. Most times, it clumped in segments. He did not know the words for cylinder or can, but he did enjoy the picture of the dog on the label. It looked like it was smiling at him.

He enjoyed days like this when the girl had been distracted enough to leave the can on the floor with the label facing him. It warmed the child's heart. He would eat then fall asleep with his thumb in his mouth. The boy despised flies, but when he focused on his paper canine friend and pulled the blanket over his ears, he could block them out.

Today, the little boy remembered the three others as he sucked his thumb and stared at his plate. They had been a little younger from what he could remember, and they could not talk. He missed them. Though he had been exposed to them for short periods during the cold seasons, their presence had grown on him. The child had no concept of time. It seemed they had been gone forever. He wondered where they had been taken and if they would return.

The youth's mind drifted back to the laughter in the other room. He desired inclusion in the whimsy. Laughter was an inviting emotion. He was familiar with such expressions to the extent of having experienced spontaneous bursts while observing woodland creatures. Adult laughter was a different story. It had always been used against him in ridicule, without exception. He was not a part of them, and they were quite adept at expressing that fact. His limited inclusions in their presence reminded him of the benefits of his otherwise perpetual isolation. Still, laughter felt good. He longed to engage others in playful joy.

The boy looked forward to being fetched for work. Customers were free to handle him as they pleased as long as they did not threaten life or limb, but they were strictly forbidden against training him. One had. The boy had not been sent back to that customer. Instead, he witnessed the price one pays for willful disrespect through interference.

Though usually treated better by customers than the people who kept him, they were incidental where the boy was concerned. The actual thrill of work was in being dropped off afterward. The child had the opportunity to stroll the woods before returning to the trailer if released before sunset. He could enter his true reality. No one was out there to correct, scold, or mistreat him for errors in etiquette or breaches in protocol, or for his emotional meltdowns. The youngster knew how to hide and how to be as silent as the animals. He had learned from watching them. Sundown was curfew, and that was plenty of time--at least in the warmer seasons--to vent his frustrations and to find his strength in the simple joys of life away from human contact.

When the boy arrived from a job, he would occasionally find the large woman, and some of the adult men passed out in the mobile home smelling awful from whatever they had been drinking. The tall, slim, tattooed man with long, salt-and-pepper hair and the girl would often be absent. The man seldom consumed alcohol to the point of intoxication and, therefore, would not be among the snoozing. Once in a while, there would be strange-smelling, pulverized plants in a bowl, or in plastic bags and ashtrays near the sleeping adults. Wild mushrooms would also be present. The boy knew better than to sample anything he saw lying around. He had attempted once but had been caught. The longhaired man ensured it would be a lesson he would not soon forget. He avoided mushrooms like the plague, even the ones he ran across in the woods. Inside the trailer, the boy had learned to mind his business, even if the adults were asleep.

On the other hand, the girl would usually be in the broken-down panel van behind the trailer or tending chores around the property if she were not with the longhaired man. At times, she would announce the boy's arrival, but she would not communicate with him directly, except to bark orders.

Regardless of who addressed the child or why, direct instruction was minimal. He had adapted to unspoken behavioral norms through experimentation. During one such experiment, he had picked up an empty bottle and thrown it onto the floor to announce his arrival. The test was ineffective. During another, he had pushed the TV set off the stand, and at another time, he had hurled a bottle against a window. The overzealous youth discovered he had erred. The adults did not seem to mind him pounding on the interior wall once inside or yelping as loud as he could. The chained dogs would never alert to his presence, though they would go completely *haywire*--as the adults would often say--when anyone else approached, including them. It frustrated them to no end that the dogs would not react to the boy, but since he was the only one the dogs held their peace around, they figured it was not worth getting *wrapped around the axle*. They had decided to let the dogs and the boy be. The boy would slip like a burglar onto the property and into the small, twelve-by-fifty-foot mobile home. He would abruptly announce himself if the adults were asleep or distracted, then walk straight to his room.

The small boy continued to ponder his life as he looked at his plate and the picture of the dog on the can. He reminisced about other foods: delicious treats he could not name except bananas. That word he knew. He had to be taught to chew them. That was not a fun experience. Because of prior conditioning for work, he did not think it natural to chew bananas. He would try to swallow them. He eventually caught on. He loved bananas.

A plastic toy sat near the child. It had a drawstring and push buttons below photographs of animals. He pulled the toy close and pressed the button below the picture of a dog. He yanked the string. The speaker announced the creature then emitted an electronic bark. The boy looked at the picture on the toy and then at the one on the can. "Dog!" he said, copying what he had heard. He tried to mimic the bark. The toy had taught him the names and sounds of several common animals, and the names of basic vegetation like trees, bushes, and grass. He pushed a button below another image. "Horse!" he said. He imitated the neigh as best he could. The boy did the same with the lamb. The youth was intrigued by the lamb's wavy, lumpy-looking fleece. It reminded him of the wild cotton he had seen growing in an abandoned field nearby, and of the clouds. "Lamb!" the little one said, followed by what he interpreted as the sound. "Ma-a-a-a-a-a!"

AUGUSt 12: MORNINg, THe wEe HOURs

Pae had begun attending the church in Palafox the Sunday morning following his meeting with Reverend Smalls. His dream life had been active every night since meeting the little platinum blonde girl. He could not recall any distressing dreams in the years following his second divorce until that first one while he sunbathed in July. The greater his concern for the child, the more intense his dreams became. This morning would be no different.

A woman with short brown hair and a distorted green face, held two hands over Pae's mouth as she lay beneath him. She tried to push her long, spider-like fingers past his teeth. She beat him with two other hands. Pae felt a lump in his throat when he heard the woman utter unintelligible, primal sounds. The image disturbed him when the utterances sank into deep, guttural moans. They were haunting. Pae grunted in his sleep and rolled over.

Several great white sharks and one large tiger shark began circling. They swam in crystal blue water. A viper repeatedly struck the bottoms of Pae's feet, but its fangs did not make contact. He felt the light thump-thump-thumping of the serpent's snout on his soles. Pae kicked his feet as he slept though they remained still and almost paralytic in his dream. The snake's strikes and the circling sharks persisted while foreboding black clouds formed over the ocean's surface. The brewing storm was too distant for Pae to see any turbulence. Multiple lightning strikes were visible as patches of clouds illuminated. He heard the low, continuous growl of thunder and sensed its vibrations moving through his chest.

The specters of four young boys replaced those images. All appeared deceased as they drifted together upon an abyss. Pae's heart rhythm increased. He grunted and moaned. He saw a motel room and thought he heard a woman's voice cry, "My baby! Oh, God, my baby!"

A tear escaped and dripped onto Pae's pillow. He wallowed under the sheet. Three of the boys floating upon the abyss spun as if turned by eddies in a river. The fourth, in the middle of the group, remained oriented in a static trajectory. Low sounds arose that resembled distant owl screeches and exotic birdcalls. None were recognizable. The sounds had an almost electronic pitch. They were peculiar and disturbing. Whispers from many voices filled the ears of Pae's subconscious mind, voices he could not decipher. His soul was distressed. He rolled over again.

The shift did not break the dream sequence. The lips of the fourth boy extended outward as if puckering for a kiss. Unintelligible voices, screeches, haunting moans, and whispers grew louder. The boy's mouth continued to stretch forward, and the surrounding noises increased. The child's lips became larger and more circular until they transformed into a trumpet's bell. It made no sound. There were no sounds at all. Everything had ceased. It was as if Pae were floating with the boy in the quiet vacuum of space. A vapor drifted upward from the bell of the trumpet. Pae thought he smelled burning cloves, but he was not certain. The odor was pleasant. Reverend Smalls' face faded in. He appeared to be speaking, but his voice was not audible. The air continued to sweeten. The images of the boy and Reverend Smalls faded, obscured by intense flashes. The flashes halted. Wolves howled then erupted into frenzied yelps as if they had closed in on prey. A feminine voice shrieked, *"SAVE ME!"*

Pae leaped from his bed. "Damn it!" he yelled, then pounded on the wall with the edge of one fist. He was standing, rattled to the core, with the bedsheet wrapped around his shins and feet. That cry had been too loud and too real. Pae trembled. His eyes were opened wide, already adjusted to the darkness.

It's a wonder I didn't fall and break my neck!

Pae propped himself against the bedroom wall with both hands. His body still shuddered from the effects of the rude awakening.

"Lord, forgive my words, "he mumbled in prayer, "I was startled." Pae was drained. The sweat on his back felt like melting icicles as the box fan cooled it. He remained propped for another minute. The little girl's face ran through his mind. His strength increased, but he was still groggy. He rubbed his tired, fogged eyes and stared at his alarm clock until the display came into focus. The characters "3:11 AM" stared back.

Pae stepped free of the tangled linen then turned and swatted the air above his bed. He caught the long, beaded metal chain and pulled it. The dim yellow bedroom light came on. He wobbled into the kitchen, feeling like a wet noodle. He pulled the jar of peanut butter from the cupboard and scooped it with a spoon. He looked out the window that faced Charlene's house.

In the distance, Pae saw a set of amber automotive parking lights. They flickered as something passed in front of them. Seconds later, a pair of red brake lights and white reverse lights appeared to the left of the amber ones. There was no license plate illumination. He continued to watch. It was obvious to Pae that another vehicle had backed up and turned around to travel in his direction. He walked into his bedroom and turned off the light. He left the bedroom and peeked through the curtain that covered the large, plate-glass living room window facing the road. As he had suspected, the moonlight revealed the silhouette of a classic pickup truck as it eased past on its way toward the dirt road. Its headlights were still off. The first vehicle had turned in the direction of the state highway. Its driving lights were also off. It navigated via dull amber fog lights.

After the truck's gloomy silhouette disappeared into the woods, the words *Love your enemies, pray for those who hate you,* entered Pae's mind.

"But it's three o'clock in the morning," he grumbled.

Those words went through his brain again, and again he quibbled, "I don't feel like it. I'm tired, and I'm sorry, but I just don't feel any love at all toward those people."

Pae sensed a new impression. *Feels' got nothing to do with it. Love your neighbors.*

He exhaled in frustration. *It's way too early to deal with this!* "Damn it," he whispered.

No, the next impression came. *I will not damn this situation. It is not about you.*

Pae bobbed his head in a shallow, rapid nod as his exhausted mind recalled the little girl. "No," he mumbled, "I reckon it's not about me at all."

He sat on his sofa and continued to scoop peanut butter in the dark. Though reluctant to begin, he ended up praying until 4:38.

AUGUSt 16: EARLy AFTERNOOn

Reverend Smalls drove his sport utility vehicle to within several dozen yards from a small white trailer tucked away in the woods. A locked metal gate prohibited the vehicle from proceeding further. A sign stating, PRIVATE PROPERTY: KEEP OUT hung from the gate. Reverend Smalls parked and walked around.

Three chained pit bull terriers started barking. The reverend was a few dozen feet from the trailer when the front door swung open. A tall, slim, salt-and-pepper haired man with a handlebar mustache and triangle-cut chin whiskers stepped out and aimed a shotgun the Reverend.

"It's broad daylight, boy! Is you able to read?" the man mocked the reverend.

"Begging your pardon, sir. I just have one question, then I'll be on my way."

"You escaped from your cage at the *Monkey Town* Zoo, didn't you, boy?" the man said, using a dated Citizen's Band radio reference to Montgomery, Alabama, as an insult. "Probably explains why you can't read? Go ask your questions somewhere else, jungle bunny! You don't belong here!"

"Are you Mr. Busbee?"

The man spit. "None of your damn business! You're on private property. You need to leave."

"Mr. Busbee, I'm Reverend Smalls. I pastor the First Assembly Church out in Palafox. Sir, I wouldn't intrude except that I received a concern two weeks ago about a little girl who was out wandering alone right up the way on Busby Place. I've heard she's about five or six years old and has platinum blonde hair. I was wondering if you might know who she is or where she lives? Folks are concerned about her welfare."

"Ain't no young'n's here, lobber-lip. You're intruding on private property. Now, you're gonna leave on your feet or in a box, but either way, you're gonna leave."

The clacking sound of sliding metal rang out as the man pumped the shotgun, racking a round into the chamber.

Reverend Smalls smiled and waved. "You good folks are welcome to attend the First Assembly Church in Palafox if you ever get the notion. Everyone is welcome. I apologize for the intrusion, sir. That little girl must live someplace else. You have a great day, now, and God bless you. I'll be praying for y'all." The reverend turned and started walking away.

"Yeah, you do that! Pray all your big ass wants as long as you keep movin' while you're doing it! Get on up outa here, now! Git!"

The longhaired man noticed the pit bulls had gathered and lain in the shade of the oak tree. "Lazy-ass, good for nothin' mutts!" He walked to the dogs and nudged the hindquarter of one. It did not stir. None of them did. Their eyes were closed. "The hell?" the man mumbled. He did not notice Reverend Smalls enter his SUV and back away.

AUGUSt 16: LATe AFTERNOOn

Pae was driving home from the Paq-Ur-Saq along State Route 221 when he came upon a familiar blue pickup with the hood raised on the side of the road. Someone was leaning over the fender into the engine bay. Pae remembered the morning of August 12th: *Love your enemies.*

Well, he thought, *I've been praying for them for a few days. Let's see how this goes.* He checked his mirrors, then slowed and straddled the lane and the grassy shoulder. He stopped alongside the truck and checked his mirrors again then rolled down his front passenger window.

"You need any help?"

The person moved out from under the hood and turned toward Pae's car. It was the longhaired, tattooed man with the black mustache and triangle chin whiskers. "Does it look like I need any damn help?"

Pae leaned toward his passenger's seat and looked into the man's eyes. "Yeah. It kinda docs."

The man spat a long, thick trail of saliva. It hit Pae's car door. A few drops hopped over the windowsill and rained inside. "Well, I don't."

"Okay, then," Pae replied. "Take it easy."

"Pussy."

Pae ignored the insult. He checked his mirrors, then eased onto the tarmac, and continued on his way. The man leaned over his truck fender and resumed tinkering.

AUGUSt 17: THe WEe HOURs

"RUN!" a child's shriek pierced the black night air.

Pae scrambled from his bed. He knocked the clock radio from the nightstand and dumped the contents of the drawer while struggling to get a grip on his pistol. He kicked to free himself from the sheet and bedspread that had twisted around his ankle. Pae's heartbeat thundered while he ran naked out the front door with his weapon drawn.

Pae stopped in the middle of the torn-up old country road. He heard nothing but the sound of his pounding heart and the air coursing through his nostrils. His hands trembled. He looked in every direction and listened intently, but he could see and hear nothing but the surrounding night.

As Pae's adrenaline subsided, he realized he had dreamed hearing the scream. *Did I, though?* He remained in place, fighting his doubts.

A life-sized companion type doll with cinnamon hair lay in a bed next to a young boy. It was stripped naked except for a pair of canvas sneakers that were too big for its feet. The plastic image's mesmerizing diamond eyes sprang to life. She leaped from where she lay. Pine treetops started shaking wildly. The boy had seen nothing like it before. Giants held the trunks of the trees. They laughed while they rattled them with intense vigor. Two other giants appeared. Each held one human male likeness: only one was anatomically detailed; the other had a small, single lump molded into its vinyl crotch. One giant slid a long, needle-like fingernail into the tiny hole in the anatomically correct baby doll's lips and another into the factory weep hole between its legs. He twisted both nails. The other pulled the arms and legs from the figure he held, then stapled the lips and breathed on its eyes, leaving a permanent fog. A crowd formed in the distance. They started rushing toward the young boy. No one among the charging horde had distinct features. Each member was about the same height as the baby dolls, but the details of their faces were blurred like smeared graphite. With bewildered eyes, the young boy screamed in an ear-splitting pitch to his cinnamon-haired companion, "RUN!"

"Damn it!" Pae grumbled. "It was a dream!"

Pae tapped the topside of the pistol against his lips with his trigger finger extended along the chamber's edge. The male stopped moving when he realized he was not tapping it at all. His finger was on the trigger, and the safety was off. The barrel was angled upward, and the tip was resting against the man's teeth.

"No!" Pae mumbled. "I already went through this song and dance on once before! You tricked me into it this time around, but I'm done playing with you!"

Pae released the magazine then pulled the upper receiver back, ejecting the live round from the chamber. He dropped the empty pistol onto the road then brushed his left ear three times with his hand.

"You lose again!" Pae said. "You don't get to win anymore! Go away!" Pae returned to his bedroom and prayed.

AUGUSt 17: MORNINg

Pae left the gym a little before noon. As he backed from the parking space, the car's steering wheel pulled to the right. He ignored it for a few seconds, thinking it was his imagination then thought it best to investigate. He placed the gear selector into Park then got out to check the tires. Sure enough, the right front tire was flat. He changed it and drove home. He followed his compulsion to avoid the café so he could fast from his post-workout meal on the way home. He said generic prayers at intervals throughout the trip, not sure of what he should pray, though sensing an urge regardless.

As Pae headed up Busby Place, he saw his neighbor's blue pickup truck parked in the middle of the road in front of his house. He could see the driver through the rear window. As during their initial meeting, Pae pulled into his gravel driveway at an angle to avoid the truck. He parked and walked toward the house.

The truck's driver called out from the cab, "Looks like you didn't need any help either, did you, sissy boy?"

Pae stopped walking and turned his head toward the truck. "No, sir. None at all."

"Sir?" The man chuckled. "I like the sound of that coming from your pretty mouth! It sounds sweet!" He hung his left arm out the window, wielding a snub-nosed .38 revolver. "I told you one warning is all you're gonna get."

"I haven't gotten anywhere near your kid!" Pae fired back, feeling a twinge of irritation.

"I didn't say you did. But what you apparently don't seem to comprehend, pretty boy is that when I told you to keep your nose out of my business, I meant, keep your nose out of my damn business! All of it! That includes a little car trouble on the side of the road. But I will let you slide on stupidity this one time. Hell, what can I say? I never thought about it, but maybe I just got a soft spot for big bitches like you who look a little spaced-out in the eyes? You must be a fuckin' retard or somethin'?"

Pae did not respond. He was too busy suppressing his anger. *God, I need some help here! I kinda figured you were up to something when I left the gym!*

"One more thing, sissy boy: I know you're going to that church up there in Palafox. If I find out you had anything at all to do with that giant ape trying to invade my territory, you won't get a next time."

A new feeling overcame Pae. It was not anger, and it was not adrenaline. It was invigorating, regardless. "He's not an ape!" His eyes were aflame. "He is a man like you and me, a child of our creator, the living God!"

The man laughed and shook his head with a dark look in his eyes. He concealed his nervousness. "You have got to be one of the queerest mother fuckers I have ever met in my whole damn life!"

"Are you finished?"

The man could feel Pae's gaze boring into his soul. Something within Pae terrified him. He tried to hide his sudden fear. His left eye twitched. "You got some balls, don't you, boy?" The man cocked the pistol's hammer with his thumb.

"I got what God equipped me with, yes." Pae turned and faced the man, with his shoulders squared off against him.

Whatever was in Pae's spirit blazed in his eyes and shook the man's core. The man turned his head and pushed on the insides of his lips with his tongue. The muscles rippled in his left jaw. He turned back to Pae. His top lip quivered as he spoke. "You ain't got no damn brain, faggot!"

"I have enough of a brain to listen to God when he instructs me to pray for you and your family." Pae's voice had been calm but firm, and his stare unyielding.

"Fruity-assed, pussy, mother fucker!" Pae's adversary hissed. The man de-cocked the pistol then pulled his hand back into the cab. He stomped the accelerator pedal and burned a black pattern into the weathered asphalt. The truck kicked up a thick cloud of red-orange dust once it hit the private road. The back end fishtailed as it tried to gain traction.

Pae watched the continuous plume of dust for a few seconds then looked at Charlene's house. *Love your enemies? Hmmm. It seems to me restraint is the better part of love when your back is against the wall? I sure wanted to monkey-stomp the pistol out of his hand and drag him through that window, then cave his head in! It would not have solved anything, though. I'm glad you showed up, Lord, else I might be a goner by now?*

Pae continued to contemplate. He wondered why the concept of laying down one's life for another crossed his mind.

"Okay," he mumbled. "I'll bite. Besides my dignity, self-respect, and manhood, what did I lay down? And how does that equate with laying down my life for someone, especially in this situation?"

He waited.

You laid down none of those. You laid down dangerous pride: the desire to get your way in a situation where your way will not accomplish the desired work. You laid down anger. You laid down resentment. You laid down a thirst for revenge. You feel like you lost, and that's okay because, again, it is not about you. You are not the center of the universe. And you're still breathing. He's still breathing. That child is still breathing. Though you lack understanding, you are loving your enemy. See the gift for what it is and keep moving forward.

Pae meditated on this for a bit then inhaled the muggy August air. He closed his eyes. The scents of evergreen trees and tar coated telephone poles filled his nostrils. He became aware of blue jay calls, the sounds of scampering squirrel feet, and noisy cicadas.

A fORMEr AUTUMn

"Mama!"

"Yes, Beverly?" Mrs. Moffat replied to her daughter.

"The little freak is sucking his thumb again! He's sleeping with my doll, too, and he's wearing his clothes in bed!"

Mrs. Moffat went to her son's bedroom. Her eleven-year-old daughter stood beside her brother's bed. When the children's mother entered the room, the girl attempted to retrieve her life-sized doll from her brother. He scowled and wrapped the naked figure tightly in his arms.

"You have others!" the boy protested in his sister's *tug of war*. "Leave me alone!"

"Honey," Mrs. Moffat urged her son, "please give your sister's doll back!"

"Mama, tell the little creep to take those stupid homemade fairy wings off of her and to put her clothes back on!" the girl demanded. "I don't want my doll sleeping naked with him! That's nasty! He put his dirty little hack-about sneakers on her: those grubby things he was wearing in the woods after school a few weeks ago!"

"No!" the boy yelled. "You have other dolls! Leave this one alone!"

Mrs. Moffat tried to help her daughter pry the toy from her son. He kicked the covers off the bed during the struggle. A pungent odor arose.

"Mama, he peed the bed! Never mind! I don't want Rebecca back if she's been lying naked with him in a puddle of pee!"

"Suck it, bitch!" the seven-year-old hurled his venom at his sister. The wide-eyed eleven-year-old girl covered her mouth. She backed away.

AUGUSt 17: AFTERNOOn

It had been two weeks since Pae had talked to Charlene. He wondered whether the men in the pickup truck had had anything to do with it, but he dismissed the idea once he thought it through.

I guess she pounced too far too soon, then panicked once she sobered up? Now, she's putting up a wall to protect herself? Oh well, it's not like I haven't had to cut my losses before. Charlene was fun and just the right kind of crazy, but maybe it's best if she keeps her distance for now?

Pae had not seen the little platinum blonde-haired girl, either. He feared the worst but realized there wasn't much, if anything, he could do. Reverend Smalls had put the word out to a few trustworthy people in Palafox and to some in the unincorporated villages within the surrounding area to keep an eye open for the little girl.

Three men and a sheriff's deputy had approached the reverend at the church office. The longhaired man had not been among them. Reverend Smalls had been ordered to stay away from posted private property or face arrest for unlawful trespass. He had been told he could proselytize in town all he wanted, but private rural land was off-limits.

The town was sealed up. Everyone who knew anything at all was dead silent, and the rest were locked out by an invisible iron curtain. No one could provide any information. It was as if the little blonde girl did not exist at all. Reverend Smalls had called Pae to inform him.

Pae had considered calling the state police or the FBI, but he knew he lacked a sufficient argument to pique their interest. Besides, he could not help but wonder whether the locals had corrupted connections in other agencies. He felt it best to tread lightly.

As a last-ditch effort, Pae set out to explore the wooded trails around his neighborhood in hopes of finding the long-missing little blonde-haired girl. He feared the worst. The trails were becoming familiar. He had suppressed his anxiety and explored them many times over the past ten days. He had come across a few signs of human presence by way of snapped twigs and troubled soil, but nothing indicated who might have been responsible. Pae carefully eased up a trail he had missed before. He discovered footprints that matched the girl's boot size. Other prints, the same size, had been left by bare feet. There were no adult footprints. Pae found a pair of weathered, rotting, little boy's cotton briefs lying beside the trail beneath a thicket. His brows narrowed, and his nostrils flared as he raised his chin and locked a gaze upon the soiled underwear.

A fORMEr AUTUMn

"Margot, we just don't know what to do with him. He's been so weird lately. I hate saying such an awful thing about my own son, but he's so different all of a sudden! Frankly, it's starting to scare me!"

Nelda Moffat sat with her neighbor on a sofa. The women shared a pot of tea. Nelda's husband sat in a high-backed, fabric-covered chair, and Margot's husband in a recliner. The men sipped pale draught beers from chilled mugs.

"Nelda, honey, I hate to break it to you," her friend said, "but that one's always been weird. It comes with the territory. My Michelle is an artist, too. She did plenty of strange things when she was your son's age—albeit not quite as strange as he—but strange none-the-less."

"No, this is different. He's been bathing in his underwear. I didn't know at first because he'd been stashing it in the back of his bedroom closet then tossing it into the dirty clothes hamper when I wasn't looking. I figured it out when I smelled the mildew."

"So? What's so weird about that? Boys do all kinds of screwball things. Girls do, too. If I could count the times, Michelle had tried to hide her used tampons instead of just throwing them in the trash."

The men looked at each other and then at their wives then at each other again.

"Want to see my new outboard motor?" Margot's husband asked.

"That's right! You did just buy one? Sure, let's take a look!"

"It's in the shed behind the house. Come on, I'll show it to you. I'll show you what I've done to the project car, too. Bring your beer. We'll take a few extra bottles with us."

The men grabbed their mugs and hastily retreated.

"Men!" Margot rolled her eyes.

"God bless 'em," Nelda replied.

"So, what other strange and mysterious things is your boy getting into?" Margot asked with a smug grin as she tilted her teacup.

"He's been sleeping with one of his sister's companion dolls."

The woman sprayed tea across the coffee table and coughed. She set her cup down and wiped her chin.

"Here, let me help you clean that." Mrs. Moffat stood from the sofa.

"No, honey, no. I've got it. You just keep on talking. Believe me, I'm all ears." The woman retrieved a rag from the linen closet and wiped the table. "Sleeping with dolls, you say?

"Not just any doll, one of those life-size ones that almost looks real. I caught him petting its hair and talking to it one night."

"Well, hon, that is a bit peculiar, but it's common for children to have imaginary friends. It's a little unusual that they have ones of the opposite sex, especially ones they can see and hold in real life, but if that's what the child thinks he needs for whatever unknown reason, then I guess that's what he needs? Our little Butch used to tear the heads, arms, and legs off of Michelle's dolls. He'd catch them on fire, too. Be thankful yours makes love to them!"

Mrs. Moffat's eyes *bugged*. "Margot!"

The other woman laughed. "Well, hon, what did you expect? That was just too juicy! I couldn't let it go without poking at least a little fun! You should see the look on your face! Seriously, though, don't let it eat you. You really are better off having a boy who enjoys the company of girls even if they're not real. What else does he do?"

Nelda Moffat rolled her eyes and took a sip of tea. "I catch him sucking his thumb now and then. He never did it before. He's been mumbling and moaning in his sleep and wetting the bed every night, too. We had to buy extra linens to keep from doing so much laundry, and some of those fitted rubber mattress covers, too."

"Well, honey, that's not too strange. Cut him back from water after six. And if he gets thirsty, allow him only a swallow or two. As for the thumb sucking, well, maybe he's been doing it all along, and you just never caught him before?

"Now, about that doll? I don't know what to say except to let it run its course. My Michelle has been going through some weird phases ever since her hormones started changing. Her artistic side pushed her a bit further than other girls her age. Please don't breathe this to another living soul, but I caught her diddling herself—you know, *down there*—with her fingers full of different colored oil paints on the shed floor two weeks ago! Let me tell you, I had a cow! I just nearly flat-out died of a stroke right there on the spot! She's fourteen, but I swear sometimes she acts like she's four? She was painting flowers on it, of all things! The doctors have always said she's a little 'slow.' We had a heart-to-heart talk, and she's doing fine. Sure, we'll be more than relieved once we finally get that poor child out of the house, but for now, we deal with it. It's bumpy, but we get by. Honey, it's all a part of growing up. Kids, especially the extra sharp, gifted, and mildly retarded ones like my poor little Michelle, need creative outlets, even if we can't let anyone else know about it."

Nelda Moffat still looked troubled. "Margot, he's been walking the long way to school. He absolutely refuses to let me pay a dollar a week for him to ride the charter bus that picks up kids who live outside the district. I wish this place wasn't zoned so funny. I realize it's only three blocks, and he's been walking it since the first grade, but he has never walked in the direction that takes him by all those crazy dogs. He's been doing it every day for a few weeks now. That's when he started wetting the bed."

"How is he when he's at home? Does he still go outside and play with his friends?"

"He's fine at home and outside. None of that has really changed as far as I can tell, except that he's been a little irritable, off-and-on."

"Then stop fretting. Let him be."

"There is one more, little thing: he hasn't gone shirtless on the warmer days like he used to, and he insists on hiking his britches over his belly button, claiming he feels naked if he doesn't."

"Well, the poor dear is as skinny as a rail. Maybe some of the kids at school are making him feel a little self-conscious about it? If he's not getting into fights over it, then leave him be. You'll both be better for it."

Mrs. Moffat sighed. "Okay, then. It won't be easy, but what can I say? My son is a little weirdo. Like his first and second-grade teachers have both told me: he's touched in the head."

Mrs. Moffat had no idea the extent to which her son had been touched. She and her husband failed to notice he no longer looked anyone in the eyes, neither would he face or smile at a camera's lens. Their son's light had gone out.

AUGUSt 18: MORNINg

Three men stood on a street corner near a mechanics' shop, smoking. A fourth approached them.

"Whatcha got, Bruno?" a slim, salt-and-pepper-haired man with a thick barbell mustache and a triangular tuft of chin hair asked.

"Big boy's congregation ain't talkin', Mark," Bruno replied, "but a few that left him have their eyes peeled for us. They want him run out of town."

"Their business, not ours. We can't afford to rock the boat any more than we have to. Let those pathetic, back-stabbing churchgoers do their own dirty work. They always have."

"He ain't nothin' to worry about, anyhow," Bruno continued. "We went up there with one of your brother's deputy dawgs and told him to shut his yap and stop shakin' the bushes, just like you instructed. It looks like he's listenin'. He's more interested in trying to reform folks than he is in chasing little blonde-haired ghosts. He ain't got much of a clue what he's lookin' for, anyway. You cut off his only lead when you ran him off your property."

"Yeah," Mark muttered. The look in his eyes was a little odd.

Bruno could see it. He spoke up. "I got no shame in sayin' I'd be afraid of him, too, brother. He's the biggest damn farm boy I ever laid eyes on."

The salt-and-pepper-haired man *slugged* the larger one square in the face. The six-foot-eight, two-hundred forty-pound man fell backward like a sack of bricks. His head bounced off the edge of the sidewalk. He lay still for a moment, cussing under his breath before he sat-up, on the parking lot asphalt. He rubbed the back of his head and looked at his hand a few times, then placed a hand over his nose.

"Damn it, Mark! You broke my fuckin' nose! Son...of...a...bitch!"

Mark stated in a casual, controlled tone, "Don't you ever accuse me of havin' any fear again, Bruno! I just leveled your gigantic ass. I dealt with bigger and meaner than you in the county lockup. Some hard mother fuckers in there. I can damn sure handle that preacher!"

Mark lied about his fear. He was terrified of Reverend Smalls, but it was not the man's size that rattled him. There was something else. Something intangible had preceded the reverend's arrival on the property. Mark had felt every hair stand up on his body several seconds before the dogs had been alerted. Reverend Smalls had appeared as calm as could be, even with a shotgun bearing down on him and three chained pit bulls waiting to be released. The dogs had fallen languid after Reverend Smalls had departed. Mark wondered whether the reverend had drugged them but remembered they were still energetic and continued barking when he had walked outside with the gun. Reverend Smalls had not come any closer than thirty feet from the trailer or the dogs. The August heat could easily have suppressed the animals. Mark was a bit too superstitious to consider the possibility. They had recovered from their lethargy overnight, but Mark's fear had not subsided. It gnawed on him around the clock. It was the same fear he had experienced during his last interaction with Pae.

Mark had sensed nothing during his initial confrontation with Pae. His confidence had been as high as ever. Their second meeting by the roadside had been uneventful. Mark had convinced himself that he was the ruler of the roost, the supreme alpha male. Even so, he knew Pae could have exited his vehicle and snapped his bones like a pile of brittle twigs, but he had pegged the larger man as an overgrown jellyfish, having no spine at all.

Mark and Pae's third meeting had begun the same as the first two but had taken a hard turn. Mark could not figure it. He had looked into the eyes of many evil men throughout his life. His father had been the worst. Pae's gaze had been the polar opposite. Mark had viewed him as a weakling, but then something indescribable had come through the windows of the other man's soul. It was not the same nervous and artificial boldness he had witnessed from tough talkers. It was like a supernatural presence. It continued to weigh him down. The lingering psychological drain was penetrating and unsettling. Mark felt genuine fear as if he had brushed absolute and irreversible judgment. His confidence was unraveling.

Mark wanted nothing more to do with Pae or with Reverend Smalls. He was terrified and was not about to willingly express that fear in the presence of his partners in crime. He figured the best way to deal with it was to mask it with violence as he had since his youth, a behavior he had learned from his father.

"I talked to my brother," Mark told the other men. "He spread the word to a few state troopers and to some of the other fuck-stick law dogs he has in his corrupt little circle. If anyone gets blabbery about anything, he'll make sure his boys harass the livin' hell out of 'em. Meanwhile, have your crews keep their eyes open around town and out in the county, but make sure none of 'em do anything out of the ordinary. Clayle will take care of whatever dirty work needs to be done so that no heat comes back on us.

"As I've said a thousand times over the years, make damn sure your contacts and your contacts' contacts don't ever find out who each other is. Communicate by disposable phone or coded written message, only. Use your drop off points. No computer communications and no electronic fund transfers; cash only, period! We'd use carrier pigeons if we had 'em. Make sure you're not followed. Don't let the little rug rats in your divisions talk to each other. Keep their asses separated when they're not out on a job. If they're too young to talk, who gives a shit? Whatever you do, don't let 'em out of your sight!"

"What about yours?" Lance asked. "You let 'em run all over creation."

"Only in the woods out in the back forty, and up and down the road once in a while. They don't go near nobody, except customers."

"What about that big pretty boy you told us about?" another man asked. "Didn't one of yours trot on up to his place and get a mouthful of grub?"

"So? What about it, Bobby? Wasn't a damn word spoken! You can't talk if you're too busy stuffin' your face. If anything had been said, I imagine more than an eight-hundred-pound silverback gorilla would have showed up at my place? I know how to tighten up the little lollipop lickers like I just tightened up ole Bruno's ass. One of the key things that keeps this operation afloat is cover and concealment. Make sure the cash keeps flowin' in our direction. The brains of this shindig is way above my head. He'll make us all disappear overnight if we fuck it up! Keep the town quiet, don't stray outside the county lines, and we'll keep sharin' the kiddies. We'll get our cuts, and we'll forward the rest to the bigwigs. Everything will be fine.

"One more thing," Mark added, "I damn well better not find out any one of you or anyone in your circles is getting drunk off their ass or doing any shit, whether swallowing, snorting, shooting, or otherwise. Leave that to your old ladies and whores. You keep your own heads clear. Don't say *dick* around your bitches. Our business is not their business, except where Sasha is concerned. Mother Superior knows how to keep her yap shut, and she won't think twice about bleeding an old lady or a *doorknob* if one of 'em squawks. I ain't got to tell you what she did to Possert's little *squeeze*. Damn *rattle trap*! You gents have been toeing the line for a few years now. Keep it up. I don't give a shit about weed, just don't over-do it. But I cannot remind y'all enough to stay away from the hard drugs and too much alcohol! If you gotta drink, do it at home and sleep it off. Don't go out *jukin'*! Nothin' makes *slack jaws* quicker than booze! Any of those damn chemicals will send us *up the river* in a heartbeat if we're not careful!"

Mark looked at the mechanic's shop near where the men stood. "Speaking of slack jaws, let's get a bite to eat. I can tell that damn truck's gonna be in there all day. We'll walk. It's close enough. Leave Lance's SUV here."

The men started walking.

"I can't believe I was dumb enough to wear out that whore over in Henshaw County a handful of years ago then run off with her little titty sucker," Mark complained. "I had to wrap up that little bundle of misery in my jacket and ditch it by the river in a drainage pipe. Couldn't run fast enough hanging onto it. Besides, a kidnapping charge would have really shit on my day. It's a good thing Sasha understands loyalty. I called her from booking. She went and picked it up before a damn 'possum, or a 'coon got a hold of it. Turned out, the cops weren't after me at all. They weren't even out looking for the brat. Those bastards that run me off from the motel had to have been buddies of that whore? Somebody keeping an eye out for her?

Maybe she had a brother or something? Hell, I don't know. Don't matter no ways, anyhow.

"A couple o' pigs swilling coffee and donuts saw me hauling ass down the road without a jacket on in fifty-degree weather. One of my damn shoes had come off. They figured I looked like I had done something, so they ran me down and face-planted me on the side of the road. When they searched me, they found a snapshot of Candy in my wallet. I had forgot it was there. I told 'em she was my niece. They asked me, 'So, why the hell do you have a snapshot of your underage niece posing like that in the shower?' Sasha cooked up a story for the public defender. The judge bought it, but he still sent my ass up the river for two years. Drug treatments and damn electro-shock therapy. Fuckin' Henshaw County lockup! At least the big bosses on the outside didn't let me get mowed down while I was in there. Didn't stop me from getting turned-out all the damn time, but hell, you can't win 'em all. It'll be a cold day in hell before I ever smell the mix of wet cement and deodorant soap again...get my ass jackhammered if I can't cough up enough of that cheap-assed bagged tobacco shit or bags of fruit, sugar, and bread from the kitchen!

"Sasha kept that milk pukin' little shit stain for me. Candy was fine with it until I got out and started training it. Her yappy little mouth didn't much matter no-how. The runt turned out to be my prime money maker. Never gave me anywhere near the hell as the others, especially her. That one...I am damn sure glad I snatched it up from that two-timing whore."

"Speaking of Sasha," one of the other men asked, "where'd Mother Superior slip off to?"

"She hauled her big ass around the corner. Got word that one of her adult film friends was passing through town on her way back to California. She wanted to hook up for some trouser trout. She's been cravin' the taste of tuna ever since one of you knocked her up."

"Well, hell, Mark, I'm sorry about that, brother," Bobby piped up. "I mean, what's mine is yours, and what's yours is mine, right? You know, the code? She's big and pale and kinda shapeless, but she's still one hell of a looker right in the face. She dolls up nice when she wants to!"

"I ain't mad about it. You two have been banging each other for years. Hell, you saved me the headache! Stuffed her with triplets: three more money makers on the way. I'd call that one hell of a bonus! Too bad, you couldn't give her more. Got that fourth one comin', too. Unexpected surprises around every corner! Train 'em right up into it. Ain't got to fight with someone else's belligerent little shit. Ole Big Bertha has been yowlin' for some clam forever. Candy sure as hell won't give it up to her, and I ain't going to make her. The code don't apply to everyone.

"As soon as she found out that friend of hers was in town, she got all prissied up the best I've seen her since before she packed on all the tonnage. Hell, this was the first in years I was tempted to throw her down and bang the living daylights out of her, but I knew she had her heart set on this, and we've got business to tend. So, I cut her loose, and she hooked up with her fancy Hollywood friend, then off they went, *lickety-split!*"

"*Lickety-split!*" Wade chuckled. "Your jagged jailhouse ass just ain't right, brother."

SEPTEMBEr 1: MORNINg

September brought a soft whisper of autumn. The air was dry and crisp, and the temperature pleasant, in the mid-sixties Fahrenheit, a refreshing departure from the mid-nineties and sweltering humidity the day before. The post-daybreak breeze was stronger and more consistent. Intermittent patches of white and gray cumulus clouds eased across a contrasted canvas of majestic, sunlit azure sky. The air was saturated with the sweet fragrance of wild blooms.

Pae sat on his front steps, sampling the fresh air. *What kind of blooms are those? Apricots? Cherries? Do blueberries smell like that? Do any of those bloom this time of year? I can't remember.* Whatever fragrance Pae sensed in the breeze, it was pure olfactory heaven! He had encountered the same magnificent odor during his childhood in southern Alabama but had never figured out the source. *Some mysteries are best unsolved, I suppose? It's plenty, just to enjoy it!*

The man closed his eyes, inhaled through his nose, and smiled. He considered having a drink and a cigar, but the moment was too perfect. A glass of merlot would have been fine, but a cigar might ruin the ambiance. Then again...

He looked at Charlene's house. She was on her front porch, smoking a cigarette and drinking something from a tall glass. She sat with her hips as far forward as she could in a folding lawn chair with her back arched. Her posture reminded Pae of a kidney bean. Charlene's right foot was raised about eye level and propped flat against one of the narrow wooden columns that supported the porch roof. She wore cutoff shorts that were split up the sides. She also wore a medium jacket in response to the temperature drop.

Pae waved a few times over the space of about fifteen minutes, but Charlene either did not see, or she ignored him. He could have shouted to catch her attention but decided instead to have that drink with a *smoke*. He went into the house then returned with a bottle of shiraz, a wine glass, a box of mini cigars, a lighter, and a thick ham sandwich. *The classy hillbilly,*

Pae thought. He glanced toward Charlene's house again. She had left her porch. He ignored his disappointment and sat upon the shallow, two-run stack of four-inch-tall, smooth cement front steps, prepared to enjoy the morning.

Man, what a gorgeous day!

Pae changed his mind about the alcohol and decided instead that he would drive to the gym after finishing the sandwich and cigar. The drive would be a little over fifteen miles, but it was already a part of his routine. Medically retired and unemployed, he had plenty of time to burn. Besides, it was a worthwhile escape from the negative vibes from his sparsely scattered neighbors. The less he idly loafed around the house, the better. Twenty minutes passed. He stood, then walked inside to put away his things in preparation for the gym.

After working out, Pae showered, changed clothes, and took a route further away from home to explore the outlying county. He came across a topless bar about thirty miles from the gym. It was early for such an establishment to be open--almost noon--but the neon sign was illuminated. He passed the bar but decided to turn around and check it out anyway.

Pae pulled into the white shell and gravel parking lot and waited for a minute with the engine running. Two large custom-built touring motorcycles were parked together near the main entrance. A factory-produced trike sat about ten feet to the left of them, away from the building. Seven automobiles spanning five decades were loosely scattered around the lot. Only three of them were parked directly in front of the business. The two oldest were from the early nineteen-fifties and mid-sixties and in pristine condition. The remainder were clean, with spiffy paint and no body damage. Well-kempt vehicles in an isolated wooded location were a good sign. Even the building and grounds were pristine for their apparent age.

Now, why would I feel compelled to stop here? Pae was apprehensive, unsure whether to go inside. He had been in plenty of nudie bars in his younger adult years, so this would be nothing new, but his state of mind had changed.

I shouldn't be anywhere near a place like this. Those days are gone. I shouldn't indulge in booze or cigars, either. Some things prayer solves right away, but most take time. Others, we just make excuses and hang onto because of weaknesses and fears that we are unwilling to face. But this? This is a little weird. What's the draw?

Pae chose to err on the side of caution by praying. Ten minutes passed. No clear impressions entered his mind or stirred his heart rhythm. He experienced neither a *warm and fuzzy feeling* nor fear. As far as he could tell, he had no clear direction. It was just him and the car. Though often difficult to distinguish, he concluded that it was not his conscience that hindered him but his intellectual reasoning. He sat for a few more minutes, listening to eighties new wave pop music on the classic rock station while he pondered whether to stay.

Pae sat a few minutes longer. *Well, Lord, if you're going to be silent on this one, I'll take it as a sign that you're telling me to be a big boy and make my own decisions. After all, that's where life's lessons reside.* He turned the car off, walked across the shell lot, and entered the building.

A woman in her early to mid-forties greeted Pae with a smile. "Well, good morning, sugar!" Pae stopped to allow his eyes to adjust to the low light. As the greeter's details came into focus, he immediately noticed her bangs were combed straight, and they covered her brows. They reminded him of the little girl he had encountered a little more than a month prior.

Pae approached the podium where the woman sat then stopped dead in his tracks. The greeter's eyes were nothing short of striking: her irises were saturated in a brighter, greener hue than any Pae had ever seen. To describe them as emerald crystals would be an understatement as far as he was concerned. He could not help but wonder whether she wore colored contacts. He was mesmerized.

"Welcome to Spanky's!" The woman pointed toward the cash register behind the bar. Pae remained transfixed in her eyes, but she did not seem to mind. He snapped out of his trance and looked in the direction she was pointing. A tall, middle-aged man, about six-foot-five, was inventorying the register. He had a beer gut, tattoos, and a full head of thick, greying, swept-back hair, with Elvis Presley style *mutton chop* sideburns.

"That there's Spanky. My name is Sherri-Lynn." The woman extended her hand. Pae shook it. Her grip was firm, warm, and electrifying. Pae's stomach turned to jelly and his knees to wet noodles. He gazed into the greeter's eyes again. She flashed a broad smile accentuated by long, cavernous dimples. "Folks usually just call me by my stage name, Fabulous Feline."

Pae stood as if rooted in place. His mouth started to drop open. *Idiot,* he thought. *Don't stand here with your jaw dropping to the floor! She's gonna think you're afflicted or something!* Pae returned to his senses. "You don't say?" he hoped the woman did not already think ill of him for his dopey reaction.

"And yes, I *am* a part of the scenery here!" The woman grinned and winked.

If she thinks I'm a goof, at least she isn't showing it!

"We opened at eleven, so I'm not in costume yet. We're still getting situated, but two of our other girls are here and ready. We serve finger foods and burgers in case you're hungry? We ask that you please, be responsible, and don't drink and drive, but if you feel you must, then, by all means, be extra careful. We don't want anyone getting caught for DUI, and we sure don't want anyone getting hurt or killed out there. God forbid you should have an accident in the middle of nowhere. It might be a while before anyone runs across you.

"Make yourself at home, anywhere you want to sit. There is no cover charge. We have an ATM right over there. It charges a dollar-fifty fee on top of whatever your bank charges. Most financial institutions will refund the fee if you keep your receipt and send it to them.

"We ask that you treat our girls right for their willingness to show you their bodies, but you're not under any obligation, as we do have a twenty percent surcharge on food and non-alcoholic beverages, and a ten-dollar minimum on alcohol. We do this to make sure the girls don't get stiffed on tips. As far out in the boonies as we are, it also helps us to stay in business. We don't expect any extra, as far as that goes, but you're always welcome to leave a little extra if you feel inclined. Some folks come in and loiter for a while then leave without paying a single red cent. We don't like it, but we don't chase anybody away for that, either. We can't afford to get a reputation for runnin' people off. Troublemakers are an exception."

Sherri-Lynn squeezed Pae's forearm. His heart leaped as a hot rush of blood swept through. He thought he would melt. There was something magnetic about this woman, much more than her eyes, dimples, and smile. Pae was glad he had trusted his gut by entering the place.

"You are our new customer today. The others you see here are regulars."

Pae saw two other men to his left, likely the bikers he figured, sitting in a corner at the back of an elevated area adjacent to the bar. They were drinking beer and eating near a pool table. Two denim and leather-clad women sat together at his right in the middle of the main room near the stage. They were leaning against each other and sharing appetizers off a single plate.

Sherri-Lynn stood and moved her hand to the back of Pae's arm. "One other thing, shug," she shortened the pronunciation of sugar, "the sign out front says *topless* for legal reasons, but the girls will show you everything in one of the private rooms for an up-front hundred-dollar tip. That gets you a half hour's time to watch your own private peepshow and get treated to a lap dance or two. We can't legally charge it, but then you can't get the peep show if you don't pay. The price is a little steep, but it's worked for us so far. They get plenty of business.

"You can get regular, ten-minute lap dances for twenty bucks, not fully nude though. None of the girls' clients complain outside our doors. When you've got a good thing going, folks just don't want to ruin it. All that we ask is that you *not* try to touch the girls if they don't want to be touched. Let them do the work unless they say otherwise, and keep in mind they are not prostitutes.

"If you want a happy ending, you'll have to do that yourself in the bathroom stall, but we'd prefer you do it in your car, or wait till you get home, or maybe take your chances in the woods? Anyhow, make yourself comfy, and one of the girls will bring you a menu."

Pae made a withdrawal from the ATM and sat at a table close to the stage. A slender girl in her late teens or early twenties with a porcelain complexion and dyed black hair approached and laid a menu on the table in front of him. She was topless, with a purple, studded choker around her neck. Purple, jeweled pasties covered her nipples. Black tassels dangled from them. Silver chains connected the pasties and the choker in a triangular pattern. She wore purple and black gloss latex shorts and black, studded, side-laced, over-the-calf, stiletto-heeled boots that were cut like open-toed sandals. The young lady also wore spiked bracelets and had an assortment of small tattoos, displaying birds and decorative Calavera sugar skulls, cartoon kittens, a unicorn, and a few pinup girls. She had short, rolled bangs and pigtails.

"Would you like something from the bar?" the young lady asked, with an odd smile that did not quite look genuine.

Pae made eye contact. "Not just yet. I'll need a minute, please."

The girl walked away.

Pae looked over the menu then browsed the laminated cocktail list in the condiment tray at the center of the table.

Sherri-Lynn arrived a few minutes later. "Are you ready to order, hon?"

Pae smiled then looked around. "What happened to the other girl?"

"She's a little cranky because she didn't want to come in this early. She had her heart set on doin' other things today, poor thing, especially with the weather being so nice and all. Don't take it personal. What can I get for you, sugar?"

"That three meat burger looks pretty darn tasty."

"How would you like the burger portion cooked, hon?"

"I get a choice? Nice! Medium, please. Only a little pink in the middle."

"You like *pink* in the middle, do you?" Sherri-Lynn joked.

Pae's heart leaped. He blushed. He had a witty reply but chose to hold his tongue.

Sherri-Lynn's face seemed to glow. "Curly fries or tater logs?"

"Tater logs, please."

"Alrighty. And to drink?"

Pae thought for a moment. "Bloody Mary, I guess? Double-shot. Why not?"

"Double-shot it is, hon." Sherri-Lynn took the food menu. "It'll be right up in a few minutes."

Sherri-Lynn winked at Pae then walked away. He turned to watch her go. It was then that he saw the full length of her straight hair all the way down to her waist just above her buttocks. Her hips were wide, her waist narrow, butt full, and thighs thick. It looked as if she had a fair bit of muscle beneath the fat. She did not look squishy. Though heavy and old by most topless bar standards to which Pae had been exposed, he found her refreshing. *Real curves!* He smiled as he watched Sherri-Lynn sashay up the two steps from the dining floor toward the bar and kitchen. He thought her shape was glorious! Sherri-Lynn glanced over her shoulder as she walked past the bar. She caught Pae watching. She smiled and winked again.

About ten minutes later, Pae heard Sherri-Lynn bickering with one of the other ladies. Their voices were low but distinct. The younger girl quibbled, "Why can't *you* take it to him? You took his order!"

"Because I have to change clothes, that's why! And it's your job! That man out there is not going to eat you, for crying out loud! He wants to eat the food! Hell, he was looking like he wanted to eat me! I'd say you're in the clear on this one, hon!"

"Yeah, but I just don't want to be around him! I don't know why? It's...I don't know? He creeps me out like he's reading my mind or something?"

"Well, I've gotta get dressed, and Kayla is still doing inventory in the supply room. Just take it to him then go do something else! It won't take but a second. Jiminy flippin' bees' wax!"

Pae saw Spanky look in the direction of the arguing women. "Fine!" he heard the younger one relent. He returned his attention to the empty stage just before the pale skinned girl with black hair trotted around the corner. She plopped the dish and the Bloody Mary on Pae's table.

"Here. Enjoy." The girl forced a partial grin before she diverted her eyes. She lingered by the table. Pae took the hint and removed some cash from his pocket. He had not exchanged any of the larger bills for Ones, so he offered her a Five. "This is for you."

The server took the cash. "Thank you, sir," she yanked the money with a hint of rudeness then walked up the steps to tend to the men in the far corner. Pae did not bother to watch her go. He did not know Sherri-Lynn had observed their exchange.

Pae had eaten half the burger and several fries by the time Sherri-Lynn returned. His stomach had been marginally satisfied, but his eyes feasted! She wore skin-tight, light tan leggings tucked into dark brown, low-cut suede boots. The leggings had diamond-shaped cuts up the sides, exposing flesh from ankles to hips.

Pae could not help but notice Sherri-Lynn's crotch. He recalled an old bra commercial that used the words *divide, lift, and separate.* An image of a desert-dwelling beast of burden flashed through his mind. It was a plump critter, too! He was glad he was sitting behind a table.

Sherri-Lynn, the Fabulous Feline, was not wearing a top. She had a dark brown leather choker around her neck with a large, oval, diamond-cut, crystal medallion hanging from it, flanked by two smaller crystals. Dark brown velvet gloves extended the length of her forearms to a few inches above her elbows. The costume blended well with her skin. Contrasts were minimal. They projected a nearly nude quality.

Sherri-Lynn's body was covered in tiny, black sun freckles that were larger and more concentrated below her collarbone. Her stomach was flat with a small *pooch* of lower belly fat below her navel that reminded Pae of a woman around three months pregnant.

Across the Fabulous Feline's chest was a tattoo of a tall, slim, black cat, sitting and wearing a top hat and a monocle. The lower portion of a crescent moon was obstructed by the hat. About a half-dozen stars were sprinkled around the moon and the cat's head. It reminded Pae of classic die-cut Halloween decorations. Cradling the bottom end of the cat in a semi-circular, rocker-style pattern was olde English script that read: *Magic Begets Design Begets Magic.* Pae pondered the meaning.

The Fabulous Feline had pulled her hair back into a high ponytail near the crown of her head. The length hung below the center of her back. *But those eyes!* Pae thought, *those sparkling, bejeweled, bright green eyes!* The Fabulous Feline's dark brown mask enhanced them. Her straight-combed bangs covered the top of the disguise. They met her eyes in a perfect conspiracy to give Pae a few heart palpitations.

"Mama Mia!" he gasped. The Fabulous Feline heard him.

"Mrwoowrrr!" she replied. She crooked the fingers on both hands and made slow, scratching gestures.

Pae was cotton-mouthed. He took two drinks from his Bloody Mary.

"I see you like my alter ego!" The Fabulous Feline said with a smile. "Do you have a little catnip for me?"

"Actually, I do, but where shall I put it?"

"Mmmmm...meow...how about pinning it on kitty's tail?" The Fabulous Feline turned around and pushed her butt toward him. The waist of her leggings was fastened by a velvet cord tied in a bow on the back. A second lace ran in a zigzag pattern, a little lower than midway down her buttocks. The laced area was open about six inches across, exposing the cleavage of her full buns.

Pae felt his blood rush. "Hold on, this will take a second. I'm having a little bit of a problem."

Fabulous Feline giggled. "No worries, shug, it happens a lot." She watched as Pae straightened his leg so he could fish his pocket. He pulled out a small stack of folded bills and counted one hundred dollars in twenties.

The Fabulous Feline erected herself. "Hold on, hon! That's an awful lot right up front! Did I forget to mention that the full show in the back is with the younger ladies, only?"

"It's okay," Pae assured her. "This isn't a bid for that. I've been living like a hermit for a mighty long time, and it's just good to treat other people to a little kindness." Pae felt guilty for not having treated the younger lady as generously.

"Here," he handed an extra eighty dollars to the Fabulous Feline. "This is for the girl who served me and for your third lady, an even split between them. No sense in me being a stick in the mud."

"Are you sure, hon? That's an awful lot of money for nothing."

"It's not nothing. It's kindness, generosity. And yes, I'm sure. No worries."

"Well, if that's what you really wanna do?"

"Trust me, your machine let me take out plenty. And no, I'm not drunk or up to anything."

"In that case, don't slide it under my laces. You can go ahead and sandwich mine between my cheeks if you want to? I'll take the rest in my hand." She bent over and whispered, "You can grab a little feel, too!"

Pae wedged the money between the Feline's buns then squeezed and patted one. "Purr, purr, purr." The Fabulous Feline grinned, then smiled and thanked him. She kissed Pae on the forehead, then took the extra eighty dollars in her hand and walked to the table where the two female customers shared an appetizer.

Pae observed the ladies' interactions then turned his attention toward the stage. It was a typical setup: small, draped in red velour, and lined with strings of red-orange lights; a pole stood in the middle; a diamond pleated, purple velour bench was against the wall, behind the mast. A compact disc jockey station sat in one corner, a few feet from the stage, and a karaoke machine in the opposite corner. Pae looked at the floor beneath his feet. *Yep: dance floor tile.*

Fabulous Feline passed by on her way to the bar. She met another female, about the same age as the younger, black-haired dancer. She handed a portion of cash to the young lady and nodded in Pae's direction as she talked with her. The younger lady smiled and waved at Pae. She walked to his table and kissed him on the cheek then sat with the two women who were seated at the other table. Her costume was tailored in country-western fashion with boots, pink cutoff jeans, a rhinestone vest, and a cowgirl hat. She wore nothing beneath the sleeveless garment.

No doubt that's Kayla, the other employee, Pae thought. The younger lady offered the two female customers a cigarette. All three lit up then conversed.

Pae hummed for a few minutes while he finished his lunch. He felt a hand on his shoulder. It was the Fabulous Feline. "Come with me, shug. You can bring your drink with you."

Pae hesitated, surprised by the Feline's invitation, then stood. She took him by the hand and led him past the bar into one of the private rooms.

"I'm a little confused," Pae said, as he and the Fabulous Feline entered a small room in the hallway. "I thought you said you don't do this?"

"Don't worry about it, hon. Very few men in this world would treat me that well, knowing they won't get anything in return. In fact, you're the first that I can honestly remember."

She closed the door. "Have a seat. Make yourself comfortable."

Pae stepped toward a chair that was in a corner near the door. Fabulous Feline sat facing him on the end of a small, padded platform that was covered with pillows.

"There's a high definition camera with night vision in that dark corner at the ceiling, so we can keep an eye on things in case a guest tries to get too rowdy. We have security on staff. He's a big guy that makes Spanky look like a fat little schoolboy. He normally works in another room watching the monitors when he isn't bouncing. Like everyone else, he chips in and does other stuff when business is slow, and when it's in full swing, the girls take turns watching the cameras while he roves around.

"Sometimes, people get a little too drunk and start thinking we're running a whorehouse. We might not be all squeaky clean the way society sees us, but we are *not* whores!

"Anyway, before I came to get you, I talked to Spanky and to our bouncer to let them know I turned the camera off in here. I also left a note on the monitor. They'll make sure the girls stay honest. They'll lose their jobs if they don't. We've always run a tight ship. That's part of the reason we've been here for decades. You don't have to worry. Nobody's gonna spy on us." The Fabulous Feline smiled and winked.

Pae was content to sit and listen.

The Fabulous Feline continued. "I've been at this, in this place right here since I was sixteen. The previous owners set me up with a fake I.D. so they could hire me on. I looked older than my age back then. It was a lot easier to get around the law in those days.

"I've seen a lot of different types over the years. I've learned to read people. I could tell from the minute you showed up that you were different. You're not the kind of guy we normally see in here. The ones like you, exuding a kind of natural, innocent charm, are often a lot younger, and they look like their eyes are going to pop out of their heads. But you strolled in and mellowed out like you're a regular. I could tell the younger ladies didn't do a thing for you, but I saw that twinkle in your eyes every time you looked at me." The Fabulous Feline smiled again.

"Well, you are closer to my age," Pae responded, "and I do enjoy a woman with a little meat on her bones."

"I appreciate that," the Fabulous Feline tilted her head, "but there's something else going on? You got a little *wood* out there, but that's not why you stopped in. That was just a side effect. You're not here for titties or asses. You've got a lot on your mind. It's written all over you. That's why I brought you in here."

"Well, yeah, you pegged me on that one, but I'm not positive I get what you're saying about why we're in here? I think I do?"

"We're in here so you can talk if you'd like? Get it off your chest, whatever it is? No judgment, hon. Spill as much as you'd like. Do you mind if I get a little more comfortable?"

Pae's mind drifted. He took a drink of his Bloody Mary then delayed a few seconds before he replied. "No, not at all. Please, do."

The Fabulous Feline crawled further up on the padded platform. She remained on her hands and knees with her back facing Pae. He thought he would explode. Those brown, diamond-cut leggings left little to the imagination. Everything was outlined beneath her caboose. Pae looked up at the ceiling after he spied a small wet spot in the crotch of her tights. He tried thinking of college football to get his mind off of it.

Fabulous Feline pressed the play button on a portable sound dock then turned the volume down. An older, electronic alternative song started playing. Pae thought he recognized it. The Fabulous Feline remained on her knees and leaned back to straighten herself then untied her laces. She pulled the tights down just below her buttocks and wagged her hips while she flexed her cheeks. Not long afterward, she lay on her back and performed a few additional moves. She removed her boots and dropped them on the floor, then peeled her leggings and tossed them into Pae's lap.

"So, what's troubling you, hon?" The Fabulous Feline moved like a cat but out of sync with the slow rhythm of the dark, synthesizer-enhanced music.

The man sighed. "Girl troubles, I guess you could say?"

Fabulous Feline nodded toward Pae's lap. "Unzip, hon. Give him a little room. Don't let him out, though. I'm not trying to be rude, I just don't need to see it. Every now and then, a horndog will try to launch his rocket. We politely ask them to put it away, or they'll get thrown out. Sometimes they listen, and sometimes they don't. They get tossed without a warning when they do it on the main floor. Our regulars ain't that dumb. Anyway, I've seen more than my fair share of those things bounce out in here. I don't doubt yours is a beauty. I just don't want to see it. You shouldn't be uncomfy, though. Unzip. Give him some breathing room."

Pae nodded. He unfastened his belt and the top button of his jeans, then pulled the zipper halfway down. He welcomed the relief.

The Fabulous Feline continued. "No offense toward you, personally. So, you're having girl troubles? Girl or woman? You have a teenage daughter who's giving you hell? Are you trying to date outside your age group, or are you just using the word 'girl' figuratively?"

"Literally, not figuratively, but nothing like any of that. I've just been a little heavy-hearted thinking about a child I saw out wandering around a little over a month ago. I'm pretty sure she lives on the same road as me, up in the woods. Poor thing walks around like a zombie, all bundled up like it's snowing."

"Child abuse, hon, maybe even sexual." The Fabulous Feline sounded sure of herself. She stopped entertaining and sat on the edge of the platform, nude except for her mask and gloves.

"Where do you live, if you don't mind my askin'?"

"About forty-five miles northeast of here, out in the county, in Knollwood."

"Oh, that shit hole? What are you doing out there?"

"I live on disability. It's the only place I can afford and still have money in my pocket while I look for work."

"Well damn, hon, why did you give me all that cash then? I'll gladly give it back!"

"No, you keep it. Really, it's not a problem. I have a pile of it in my credit union, more than enough to live off of for the next five years or so. It's military reenlistment bonus money that I never spent. I've been sitting on it and budgeting for a while. I invested a portion of it, too, so it's earning a little extra for me. I draw a decent monthly pension on top of it and get free medical care, so it's not too bad. I only use it when I have to or when I want to treat myself. Today, I get to treat myself and you, ladies, too."

"Well, bless your heart, hon, and I sincerely mean that! Thank you! The Fabulous Feline certainly appreciates it! So, what's the story on this little girl? Do you know anything about her?"

"No, but I did meet her daddy. He is not a pleasant individual. More or less threatened my life if I so much as look at her."

"Why do you suppose that is?"

"I don't know for certain. I called the Sheriff and reported that I thought she was neglected and possibly abused. That fellow showed up right after the call. Either the dispatcher or the sheriff squawked."

"Oh, hell! You must have called Sheriff Busbee's office? Knollwood is just across the line in Empire County, ain't it?"

"Yes, ma'am."

"Well, damn, hon, all them people up in there's bat-shit crazy! Three main families occupy that area up near Palafox: Tillman, Busbee, and Erdman. They are good people everywhere else I've run across 'em. Many of them are wealthy and influential, and a handful are married into my family but that teensy little pocket of Empire County? It's like all the crab apples got piled together right there, and the worms moved in with 'em. The rest of the county is pretty decent for what little's out there, but right across the line in Knollwood and Palafox? There's a reason that property is dirt-cheap. No one else wants to live there. I can imagine! I've heard a bunch of rumors over the years, but I don't know if any of 'em's true."

"What kind of rumors?"

"That it's ate up with petty, organized crime. It's all word of mouth, though. No one's ever proven anything one way or another. There's never anything on the news. It's almost like they don't exist. People get the impression that it's one of the safest places on earth because of the silence, but there's just too many whispered stories of unreported crime. People don't usually move there because there's not much available. They haven't let that little flea speck of an area grow for decades."

"You ever hear any rumors of the sex trade out there? Prostitution?"

"No." Fabulous Feline was silent for a moment, pensive. "I can't say I recall anything like that. It's all drug-related rumors where the organized crime is concerned. I hear more about domestic spats than anything else, but again, it's so hushed out there that even the domestic squabbles seem to be few and far between. There's been an awful lot of teen pregnancy in their school over the years for how small their overall student body is. I've always just chalked it up to horny, bored teenagers and parents who don't much give a shit."

"So, Miss Feline, what made you think the little girl might be sexually abused?"

"It seems to me she's wearing that jacket like a security blanket."

"Yeah, I had that same impression."

"She might be physically abused and hiding the bruises? How old do you think she is?"

"Five. Could be six? She's a little smaller than most six-year-olds. Hard to say."

"Oh Lord, bless her poor little soul! You said you called the Sheriff, and then her daddy showed up?"

"Yep. Same day, a few minutes later. He said he was highly protective and that I shouldn't even consider saying hi to her, much less anything else. But the way she was dressed and as dirty as she was from head to toe, there's no way anyone could be that protective of her for her sake? My gut tells me there's a different motive."

"They're hiding something for sure, shug, and that Sheriff's helping 'em do it. Likely blood-related. Don't want family secrets getting out?"

"Yeah, well, he did say something about her having a fine little ass, so I'm willing to bet you're right on target. Normal men don't go around saying that about their daughters, not even stepdaughters or fosters."

"Damn!" Fabulous Feline shook her head with her eyes closed. "He didn't?"

"He did."

"What the hell?"

"I think he was just trying to provoke me for some reason? Trying to get a rise out of me? It was clear he wanted me to stay away from her. He was armed, too. I hope he wasn't serious. There's too much mental, emotional, and spiritual sickness in this world, way too much. I grew up around it."

"So, did I." The Fabulous Feline leaned back and kicked up her legs then opened them like scissors. "Surprise, surprise!" She sat up again.

"Scoot on up, hon. Bring your chair over here." Fabulous Feline's legs were still opened as she lowered them and sat up. She patted on the platform between them. "Sorry, I caught you off guard. I can tell this is weighing heavy on you, so I tossed in that little cheer to help pick you up."

Pae gripped his Bloody Mary while he pulled his chair as close as he could.

"Feel this." The Fabulous Feline took Pae's hand and placed it upon her vaginal triangle. Her skin was clean-shaven but tough. It felt leathery, not baby soft as he had imagined.

"I've been shaving it my whole life." Pae sensed there was a legitimate story behind her statement. It sounded more like a preface than a brag. The Fabulous Feline confirmed Pae's suspicion.

SEPTEMBEr 1: LAMENTATIOn

"I was sexually molested by my stepfather," the Fabulous Feline told Pae, "It started when I was eight years old, right after he married my mama. He did it regularly, right up under her nose, often when she was right there in the house with us. Because of my skin color, the bastard nicknamed me his little savage princess."

The Fabulous Feline closed her eyes and shook her head. She continued, "This went on for a few years until one day when he got too brave and thought he would penetrate me with more than a two-finger salute and a stink-finger *shocker*. My hymen was already history. I must have been eleven or twelve when he decided to go all the way? Hard to remember, because I've tried to block it out. Whatever my age, I hadn't had my period yet.

"He threw a folding mat on the garage floor, then pushed me down and pinned my shoulders. He had already tied down the trigger of his buzz saw, I guess so mama would think he was working on a project, but more likely to drown out any noise from us? He threatened me with a hammer, then yanked my jeans off and threw my ankles over my head. He tried to dive right in. He was up just a little too high. He missed and banged his nasty ole dick head on that ridge just above the opening. That hurt like hell! Wasn't a picnic for him, either? He jumped, and I screamed, *bloody murder*. I couldn't tell, but it felt like he bruised the shit out me!

"Somehow, mama heard me over the noise of the saw. She had to have been right outside the door at the time? She came in and caught him pressing his hand over my mouth, still trying to force himself inside, but I was squirmin' and kickin' too much. That, and his filthy pecker wasn't quite stiff enough, probably because he had banged it too hard? He could have been a little tipsy, too? Mama knocked his brains half out with an aluminum baseball bat, then snatched me up and ran in the house to call the police. She filed for divorce the next day while he was still laid up in the hospital with stitches in his skull. She damn near killed him."

Pae wished he could read the Fabulous Feline's full expression through the partial mask. She looked as if she were a thousand miles away.

"His breath smelled rotted like garlic and tabasco peppers mixed with sweaty asshole and cinnamon gum. I can't shake the memory of how hot it felt on my ears."

The Fabulous Feline continued to drift for several more seconds then resumed her story. "I had a few sprouts growing down there at the time. I reckon he thought it was okay to plow the field when he saw the weeds growing in it? I was old enough to get deflowered since I finally had some sprigs? Filthy prick! He hadn't seen the hairs before that day because he had been out in the gulf working on a rig for a handful of months. That was most likely his first day back, as I can't remember him ever waiting to get his hands on me unless something stopped him. After that, I felt dirty every time I looked in the mirror. Being felt-up, licked, and sucked on as a prepubescent girl was hard enough on me, but that sent me over the edge.

"I tweezed the hairs until they grew in too thick, then I started shaving. I tried a chemical hair remover once and scalded the living shit out of myself. I sure as hell learned that lesson! I shaved pussycat for years after that, and then I started waxing after the skin toughened up. I've never allowed more than a couple of days of stubble. Keeping it slick is sort of my way of preserving a reminder of innocence before he came into the picture. So, no *whisker biscuit* for me. I realize it's a psychological problem, connecting to my childhood innocence by maintaining a bald beaver, but as they used to say all the time, it is what it is."

Fabulous Feline saw a tear run down Pae's face. "Oh, honey, are you okay?"

SEPTEMBEr 1: SI6Ks

Fabulous Feline leaned toward Pae. He followed her lead and leaned toward her. They embraced. A tear ran down Pae's other cheek. He released the Fabulous Feline and leaned back in his chair.

"I understand what you went through," Pae said. "I was raped by a group of boys when I was in Second Grade. I remember it like it was yesterday."

"Oh, sweetheart, no!"

"I have a pretty damn good idea what you're talking about. That little girl? The memories came flooding back when I saw her wandering around alone wearing that heavy jacket. I was a little older than her."

Fabulous Feline's mask was still on, but it was apparent her eyes were watering. "Those other boys raped you? Does that mean they penetrated you?"

"Yes, all six of them, between the ages of eleven and fifteen. They tore me up pretty bad."

"God, no!" Fabulous Feline gasped.

Pae's expression went blank as he stared into the Fabulous Feline's eyes. "They took turns forcing oral and anal on me, one up-front while another was out-back. They held my legs up like wheelbarrow handles and used a bottle of baby oil. I'm glad I lived through it. I think I almost died. I blacked out a couple of times."

Fabulous Feline turned her head. She lifted the mask and wiped her eyes. "I'm sorry, hon. Give me a minute."

Pae waited for her emotions to settle.

"I'm okay, now," the Fabulous Feline said. "You can continue." She re-established eye contact.

"Those boys looked like giants to me, like adult men. The oldest one showed me a knife and said he'd gut me like a fish if I tried to scream or ever told anyone."

"I'm surprised you can even talk about it with this much composure?"

"Years of therapy helped me reach this point. It still hurts, but thankfully, it does not have as firm a hold as it once did."

"If it's not too personal for me to ask, you said they penetrated you? Did any of them...you know?"

"Yes. Three of the oldest boys finished in back, one up-front, one across my back, and one on my neck. I can still remember the taste. As old as I am, I can still remember."

Pae shifted his glance and bit his bottom lip while he expanded and contracted the upper. He emitted saliva-moistened squeaks as he inhaled and tapped an index finger on his knee. He stopped the audible sound effects but continued to drum his finger.

"I remember the feel of their clammy asses in my hands, and the feel of baby oil slopped all over my tail end while they forced their way in." Pae resumed eye contact with the Fabulous Feline. "I had nothing else to hang onto while they held me up with my legs parted like a wishbone."

Fabulous Feline covered her mouth, "Oh, baby doll!" Her voice was filled with sympathy.

Pae nodded with his eyes toward the floor. "I remember the first time I ejaculated several years later. I thought I was incurring the wrath of God. My body had never done anything like that before. It scared me out of my mind! It happened by complete accident. I was twelve. I had no idea what had happened. I thought God was punishing me for getting excited over a dirty magazine for the very first time. I thought my prepubescent blank rounds were his way of telling me I had turned into a monster like those other boys. It was simultaneously the greatest and most horrifying feeling in the world."

Fabulous Feline paid close attention to Pae's mannerisms as he spoke.

"Sorry," Pae said, "I got off track."

Pae rubbed his hand across his face and through his hair. He sighed.

"Those boys raped me in the woods. I would stop in there and play after walking home from school. They stopped when they thought they had heard someone else walking around out there. They all ran, but not before the oldest dumped his load down my throat."

Pae disconnected.

"Are you gonna be alright, hon?"

"Yeah."

"Take your time, sweetie."

Pae took a few drinks from his Bloody Mary. He sighed again then reengaged.

"Funny thing is, I clearly remember hearing footsteps. They were pretty loud, crunching on the leaves and twigs, but there was no one else out there. It was probably an animal?"

Pae looked into Fabulous Feline's eyes. "I'm glad none of those boys were *hung like horses*. That's probably the one thing that kept my heart from stopping. I vividly remember that sensation. It was like green pinecones being rammed up my ass: thousands of needles."

Pae paused, unable to read his companion's body language. She appeared relaxed, but he thought he sensed tension.

"Forgive me. I'm sorry for giving so many details." Pae's gaze went blank again.

The corners of the Fabulous Feline's mouth drew tight. She was silent for a moment. Her eyes were difficult to read through the holes in her mask, and the shadows cast by her long bangs in the poor lighting. It struck her odd how Pae had shut off his emotions, slipping from tears to an apparent disconnect within a matter of seconds.

"You're good, hon." The Fabulous Feline drew a breath. "Don't hold back on my account."

"I remember it like it was yesterday: getting pumped by sloppy little greased-up poles, while the pulse in my neck hammered away." Pae's expression grew dark and more distant. "That grueling, intense pressure while the first one was trying to force his way in...my ears scalding and my forehead feeling like it was going to bust...and then that horrible sensation, like an insane pop! I could tell my rubber band had broken."

And now he's using humor? Fabulous Feline wondered what kind of a man she had invited into the room. She had never spoken to a male who had confessed to being sexually assaulted in his youth. It was familiar yet completely foreign. Though his memories ignited the hellish fires of her own, she chose to bear with him. *It's only fair.*

"That was the first moment I had blacked out. When I came to, they were going to town on me. I was still hanging on, so I hadn't actually fainted. The blackout was like I had left my body, but I couldn't see anything. It happened several times." Pae stopped talking. He tilted his head back and closed his eyes. Tears fell again.

"Damn it," Pae grunted.

Fabulous Feline took one of his hands and caressed it.

"I've had muscle spasms down there ever since. Sometimes, it feels like I'm being pried open again. Psychosomatic, I guess? I laid there in the woods, for I don't know long before I was strong enough to hobble out. It was hell, but I managed to clean myself with a garden hose in a neighbor's backyard before walking the rest of the way home. The neighbor wasn't there; that's why I chose their property to wash up. My parents saw how red and swollen my face and neck were. I managed to convince them I had been stung by something while playing and had suffered an allergic reaction. Mom could tell I was breathing fine, so she gave me an antihistamine and a cold compress. I looked okay the next morning, so she didn't think any more of it. I had problems downstairs for a few days, but I downplayed it as having an upset stomach. Mom thought it was more allergic fallout from an insect.

"My hair stood on end having to sit in the bathtub every night, but I wasn't about to let on that my butthole had been ripped. I wouldn't let mom tend me anymore. I was old enough to handle my own baths. The residual bleeding scared me, but I dared not say a word. Fortunately, I was sharp enough to wear my undies in the tub, so no blood stayed in them. It dissolved in the bathwater. I packed my crack with toilet paper for a few days until it stopped spotting. My behavior had to have been strange? Forcing myself to wear a false face was not easy, but I thought it was necessary."

Pae stopped. He opened his eyes, then dropped his head and looked into the Fabulous Feline's. "I never said a word to anyone about what those boys had done. I was prepared to take that secret to my grave until the shame got too heavy to carry."

"So, you never even told your parents?"

"No. I still haven't. We went to church every Sunday morning and night and on Wednesdays. It was an old-fashioned church, very strict, and reserved. They acted like you'd burn for eternity just for wearing blue jeans into the sanctuary. God help you if one of the congregation or the pastor caught you buying a pack of cigarettes or heard you cuss! I didn't dare mention what had happened to me."

Pae chuckled with a distant expression. Fabulous Feline cocked her head, puzzled. Pae could read her curiosity.

"It never really dawned on me that they referred to the main building as the *sanctuary*, but in all honesty? I never felt safe in there. A sanctuary is supposed to be a place you enter to escape the storms in life, a safe haven from the outside world. I suppose it was in one sense, as people were always on their *p's-and-q's*. Nothing bad ever happened in the sanctuary. But inside of me? I never had any peace. I always felt like I was endlessly being watched and scrutinized, like they were all just waiting for me to slip up. They seemed to be well-meaning, but they criticized and gossiped, and stabbed each other in the back like you would not believe."

"Try me," Fabulous Feline challenged him.

"Indeed!" Pae nodded. "And then they had the nerve to tell the rest of the world how screwed up it was. As a result, I was terrified that if I had said anything to my parents, they might tell me I would go to hell for having unmarried sex, especially with other boys. I didn't know much about the Bible, but I was quite familiar with all the big taboos. The Sunday School teachers assumed we comprehended more than we did, and I doubt the preachers ever gave it any thought at all. They were full of fire and brimstone, and none of their sermons were tailored for small children. Even Sunday school talked over our heads most times or watered things down so bad with puppets that nothing really stuck."

"Do you hate the Church because of that? Do you hate God?"

"I did for a long time. I hated both. I still have a chip on my shoulder toward the Church at large, and I still have trust issues toward God. But in time, I realized the ones to blame were the ones who raped me, not the Church, and not God. That took a while. Originally, I was ungrateful that he had preserved me because I could not come to grips with why he would allow such a thing in the first place? It was not easy to sort through, but I did. It took decades for me to change my perspective, well, for God to change it while I acquired what little trust I have."

"You're quite a man, Mister Pae! Shit, I don't know if I could do that? I mean, *damn*!"

"That's alright. You don't have to. We all have our own paths to walk. I've grown a lot. But back then? Being a second-grader? I lacked a great deal of understanding that adults took for granted. After all, I was only seven years old. I didn't comprehend much, especially in church. Because of television, I thought my parents might send me away to live with someone else or to a military boarding school if they didn't outright kill me?

"For years, I wondered when God was going to strike me dead over the filth of my second-grade homosexual acts? Never mind that I was gang-raped at knifepoint. I don't think that way anymore, but I did live in deep-seated fear for a long, long time. It didn't help that I began to struggle with my sexuality. The worst part was when I started having difficulty being in the presence of children. It lingered into adulthood."

Sherri-Lynn felt a chill. "What do you mean about difficulty being in the presence of children?"

"It became difficult for me to be in the same room with small boys. I still have trouble looking them in the eyes most times. It is a direct side effect of having been sodomized. I developed an aversion to boys of all ages, even toddlers and infants. The exceptions were the friends I'd already had at the time. I had begun to view girls differently. I've struggled with a lot of bizarre imaginations."

"Do you have predatory tendencies toward children?"

"Are you asking if I'm still damaged and occasionally struggle with unnatural thoughts and emotions or if I actively pursue predatory behaviors? If the latter, then no."

Pae's choice of words did not sit well with the Fabulous Feline. "So, what are you saying, exactly?"

"What I am saying is that I put a loaded gun in my mouth one night and cocked it. I squeezed the trigger, telling myself that I would not become the kind of a monster that did those things to me."

"You squeezed the trigger?"

"Another hair and I would not be here today."

"What stopped you?"

"I'm not sure. I guess you could say God intervened? I realized I am not a monster. I wasn't like those boys, Sherri-Lynn. Although I had been terminally scarred, I was not the same as them. I have no doubt that something unnatural had twisted the minds of those boys long before they ever caught up to me. I mean really, what kind of a child that age thinks that way without some kind of extreme influence? The ringleader could have been a victim of sexual abuse himself? That, or he had some seriously damaged role models that influenced him in other ways? Depraved household? The difference is that I could never harm another living soul the way I had been harmed. So yes, I struggle with thoughts no sane adult male should ever have--I'd rather not discuss it--but no, I am not a predator, though I have little doubt I fit the psychological profile."

Sherri-Lynn wanted to dig deeper, but she was afraid of what might turn up.

Pae looked away. His soul clouded with self-condemnation and shame for having been this open to a stranger. "I've said way too much."

"Come here, honey." Fabulous Feline ran her fingers through Pae's hair then moved her hand to his cheek. "Get up here with me." She twisted her torso then pressed a button on a wall-mounted intercom.

A deep male voice came through the speaker. "Yo, this is Tiny."

"Tiny, I'm gonna be in here for a while. I'm fine; I just don't want to be disturbed. Make sure nobody turns that damn camera on or opens the door! I'm spending time with an old and dear friend. We go way, way back, shug. Could you do that for me, please?" Sherri-Lynn had lied. She had never met Pae before.

"You got it, Sherri-Lynn."

"Mrrroowwwwr!" She released the intercom button then pulled off her gloves. The mask stayed on.

Pae felt as if a bus had hit him. The emotional dump reminded him of former therapy sessions. He continued to sit in the chair for the moment, not responding to Fabulous Feline's invitation.

"Don't beat yourself up, shug. I told you I brought you in here to unload. I'm not backing out. If you need to let go of more, then let it go."

Pae wanted to smile, but a grimace was the best he could muster. He took another drink of his Bloody Mary. "I was hypersexual for many years," he added, "trying to validate myself as a male. The irony is I've had very few sexual partners. I do not attract many women at all, at least not in a romantic way. Fortunately, I've learned to suppress the sexual tension. I find more profitable outlets."

"What about men, hon? You said you've struggled with your sexuality? If you say you don't like to be around boys, but you've struggled with your sexuality, then what does that mean?"

"Not what you might think? I've never sought a homosexual relationship. Never desired one. But...I've struggled with all kinds of imaginations that don't add up; things that are a bit too personal, even in light of what I've already stated. None of it makes sense to a rational mind. The best I can figure is that it comes with the territory?

"I believe a soul leaves behind and also inherits things when sexually bonded to another one, good or bad, right or wrong. Pre-existing emotional attachments need not be present. Sexual trauma causes damage in ways the unaffected do not expect and often do not want to understand. I want to understand it, but I cannot. Therapy helped, but it could not cure me of the thoughts. It's a lifelong battle between what I know is right and wrong and what I crave despite it all. Who knows how I'd be had teenaged girls sodomized me with a stick, instead? I often daydream of how I might have turned out had nothing happened at all?"

Pae changed the subject. "You can't tell because I'm all covered up, but I get my whole body waxed regularly. There I go, spilling more of my guts to a stranger."

Fabulous Feline sensed Pae was growing uncomfortable. She went along with the shift. "No, it's okay. Say what's on your mind."

"I work out all the time and carefully watch what I eat. I don't have an ounce of fat anywhere. I gotta watch it though, as I've been slipping a little lately. I get my body waxed from the neck down, but I don't do it for the sake of the classic bodybuilder look. The hair removal is not vanity. Like you, it helps me feel clean, psychologically. It helps me stay connected to my inner child."

"Do you wax your beautiful place, too?"

Pae smiled. "My beautiful place? That's a first! No one's ever called it that before. One of my exes ridiculed it half the time because I am below average, and the other didn't seem to care one way or the other."

"Why did you divorce?"

"My first wife was like me, a victim of early childhood. We both lacked the mental faculties to make wise decisions. We were driven by emotions, and by escapist mentalities. I was excessively clingy, and she was largely detached. It fell apart quickly when the emotions faded, and the realities of life settled in."

"And the second?"

"We weren't in love. It took a long time to admit to myself that it was mutual. I used to blame her exclusively, but I've learned to recognize my faults and differences and accept my share of the responsibility for the dead relationship. I have no children from either of them."

Pae did not notice the Fabulous Feline's nipples harden. He was too drawn by the intense fascination that radiated from her crystal, emerald green eyes.

"My first and second marriages were about five years apart. My second wife was at least four years off of her first marriage when she met me."

"So then, neither of you were rebounds?"

"No."

"How long have you been divorced this time around?"

"Seven years. I haven't dated since then. I've had a few nice lady friends with no formal dating involved and no physical intimacy of any kind. Emotional intimacy was also lacking in those friendships. They were fun but pretty shallow."

"That must have been rough?"

"At first, yes. I was whacking my Willy every time I turned around."

"*Ugh!*" Sherri-Lynn rolled her eyes and stuck out her tongue.

"Oops! Sorry. It had less to do with being horny and more with just being frustrated with life. It was my pressure relief valve. I don't know if it was a man thing or a *me* thing, but that's just how it was. Eventually, I got used to the alone time and began to view it less as loneliness and more as a refuge. I got used to the single life. In a very real sense, it became the sanctuary I had always thought church was supposed to be."

Pae decided to accept the Fabulous Feline's offer to join her on the platform. He left his Bloody Mary on the floor and stood.

SEPTEMBEr 1: TIMe STANDs STILl

" **M**ay I take a peek before you settle in with me?" the Fabulous Feline asked Pae as she sat upon a padded, quilted platform inside a private room. Pae stood before her. He was confused by her request, but he caught on. "Be my guest."

Pae's jeans were unbuttoned, and the fly partially open. The zipper eased further down the track as the Fabulous Feline pulled the sides of the fly. Pae wished he could read her expression through her mask. He thought her cheeks looked a little darker from a blush, but it was too tough to tell from her skin tone in the low light. She stopped cold.

"What the hell?" The Fabulous Feline grinned. "Purple undies? Are these silk?" She looked up at Pae and giggled then dropped her focus to his waist. "There's a cute little bow on 'em, too!"

"Yeah, they're women's. I'm a little freakier than your average bear. This is the fun side of the lingering psychological damage to which I had alluded. Men used to stare at me in the gym locker room as if horrified, and they'd keep their distance in the weight room knowing these kinds of panties were under my sweats. But they eventually figured out I was safe. Now, they don't even bat an eye. Two of them even started wearing G-strings, and one started going *commando*. Go figure?"

"Well, that's...um...a little creepy, but this I like! Purple man panties! You're obviously secure in whatever it is you've decided you are?" The Fabulous Feline pulled Pae's underwear down, keeping his manhood covered as she pushed it aside with the thin silk garment.

Pae could not sense the Fabulous Feline's rapid heartbeat. His own was undeniable. Both wandering souls shook like leaves in a windstorm as they slipped into the honeydew sweetness of eager imagination. Pae caught intermittent glimpses of the Fabulous Feline's swollen, ebony nipples. He tried to avoid dwelling while his anatomy reached upward. The Fabulous Feline gently squeezed it through the silk. She remained silent. She was careful to not uncover too much while she pulled the waistband of his underwear downward. Fabulous Feline smiled as she examined Pae's lean, muscular, hairless groin then pulled his underwear back up.

"Oh! I caused some trouble!" the Fabulous Feline remarked. A dark mass formed in Pae's underwear followed by a thick liquid that oozed through the silk. The tangy, chlorine-like odor was unmistakable. Pae looked at the ceiling. "Sorry. I didn't expect that to happen. I've been divorced for seven years, but it's been at least ten since a woman got that close."

"You're okay, hon. That was my fault." The Fabulous Feline closed her legs and shifted her position. She could hear her heartbeat and feel it thunder in her burning ears and at the base of her neck.

Sherri-Lynn fought her way through the awkward silence. "What's the story on all those scars, shug?"

"The war," Pae answered, still looking at the ceiling. "I was a Marine. Everything's there. It works like it's supposed to."

"Obviously," the Fabulous Feline replied. "May I?"

"Huh?"

The Fabulous Feline could see that Pae was disoriented. She did not respond but took a chance on uncovering him instead. Pae's manhood was shorter than the female had expected, but the size was irrelevant, as she had not allowed any penetration since her stepfather's fingers had intruded during her youth. The excited woman sat in silence for a moment.

"Beautiful!" the Fabulous Feline whispered. She grinned with delight. "Is it okay if I say hi to him?"

Pae's breaths were slow and heavy. He could not figure out what had caused the Fabulous Feline to violate previously stated boundaries. He broke a sweat and swallowed air. He could not remember the last time he had felt so *cotton-mouthed*. His pulse hammered. Veins protruded while his anatomy bobbed, and the color deepened to a dark, red-violet hue. Pae stood in awkward silence, not responding to the Fabulous Feline's question. He sensed her unease after a few eternal seconds.

"Please, do!" Pae urged when he thought the Fabulous Feline might withdraw. He heard a faint gasp when she gripped him. Her palm was hot. He closed his eyes.

"Are you sure about this, Pae?" the Fabulous Feline's voice sounded labored. "I don't want to give you any bad first impressions. I assure you I do not do this for just anyone. In fact, I've never done this on a first meeting. It's usually a third or fourth date kind of a thing, real dates."

Pae fumbled through his response, "I'm pretty sure we're a wee hair past first impressions? The question, I think, is whether you really want to commit to this? Please don't do it if you think you'll regret it. As I said a while ago, I fully expect our souls will attach to each other as a result. Don't lose a piece of yourself on me if you truly cannot live without it, or more importantly, if you can't live with it. I've lasted this long without a woman's touch. I can keep going."

The Fabulous Feline waited. Pae glanced at her, but he could not see her eyes.

"No matter your decision, you're an incredibly beautiful woman, Sherri-Lynn, and your heart is pure gold!"

"Oh, hell," she said, "neither of us is getting any younger."

Pae had leaked a fair amount, and he continued to ooze, but he had not fully discharged. The Fabulous Feline spread the liquid with the fingers of her right hand then squeezed him twice with the left. A thick stream shot into her bangs and across her mask. Pae jerked and almost fell onto her. His knees were butter. He leaned forward and placed his hands atop her shoulders. The Fabulous Feline giggled as Pae splashed her breasts, abdomen, and thighs.

The Fabulous Feline cooed, "Ten years is too long for any man, Mister Pae! That took no effort at all!"

Pae was still zoned out on the ceiling. His biology continued to pump. His ejection splattered the Feline's triangle. He moaned. Sherri-Lynn wondered whether his brain had registered what she had said. She stroked him slowly and reached behind with her right hand then intermittently squeezed one of his thick, iron buttocks.

"Don't say anything," she said. "Enjoy the moment."

Pae swallowed dry air again. His chest heaved. His breathing echoed off the walls and ceiling of the tiny room. Thick drops continued to fall. He remained as hard as carbon steel. The Fabulous Feline pawed the entirety of Pae's war-scarred groin and ran her fingertips between his cheeks.

"Pae?" the Fabulous Feline asked.

"Yeah?" his voice wobbled.

"Please don't be upset at me for asking, but has it really been ten years?"

"Aside from me choking the chicken once in a while to relieve the frustration, yes. Most times, I just let nature take its course and end up with wet dreams. No women in ten years, though."

"I'm willing to bet you're clean?"

Pae exhaled through pursed lips. He closed his eyes when he felt a light pressure swirling around his bum port. He drifted into oblivion when it received a trimmed and manicured intruder. Sloppy wet heat engulfed him from the front. Moans arose from the Fabulous Feline. Her fingers went to work fore and aft. Pae blasted off a second time. He gripped the sides of her head and uttered a tumultuous groan. Electricity shot through his body. His muscles tensed, and his sphincter clinched the Fabulous Feline's finger like a vice. Aside from his initial howl, Pae remained as quiet as a mouse while his partner lapped up the remainder of his donation and eased her finger from his bum.

Pae's erection did not relax.

"Forgive me," Pae panted, "but this is really starting to hurt."

The Fabulous Feline stopped and wiped the edges of her mouth. "I'm sorry, hon. What's going on?" She looked up at his face.

This might sound crass, but my butthole is aching like mad, and my balls feel like they're being squeezed and pulled to the floor."

"Oh, doll, I'm sorry! I didn't mean to hurt you!"

"It's alright, really It Is. I loved it! The problem is that men love to brag about having multiple orgasms, but I can almost guarantee you they're lying. I've had multiple orgasms, only two other times in my life, and each time the second one produced physical pain. Only once have I cum a third time. That took almost an hour to build up after the second. I immediately regretted it. That was some of the most intense, dull, nagging pain I'd ever experienced. I almost wanted to die, and for two days, I felt like I'd been flattened by a steamroller. I don't think men are built for multiple orgasms like women are? It could just be me?"

"I'm sorry, hon. Please forgive me."

"No, no, you're fine, Miss Feline, believe me! What you just did was well worth it! We just need to stop, is all. It feels like blue balls and squashed balls at the same time, not to mention what's going on out-back."

"Oh! I'm sorry!"

"Again, no need to apologize. I loved it! It's just been so long that my body is in a bit of shock, is all."

"Well, I can understand that. It has been my pleasure to make you happy, hon."

"I've only ever dreamed of something like this, Sherri-Lynn. I've had sex plenty of times in years past, but not on this level. Can you believe that? Nothing even close to comparing to this kind of freedom, especially being treated for no reason at all and without having to make the first move. You are a magnificent woman, Sherri-Lynn!"

"Thank you, kind sir! I can see your little fellow is not going to relax any time soon. It has indeed been a mighty long time, hasn't it?"

"Yes, it has."

"The poor dear is turning purple. He looks like his head is going to bust."

Pae chuckled. "I don't mean to be rude, but please stop. You're killing me, here!" He stuck his tongue out.

"Will you turn around for me, shug? I won't keep fiddlin', I promise. I'm just dying to see your granite ass, is all. It felt amazing! I've gotta lay eyes on it!"

Pae rotated his body by shuffling his feet. His trousers had slipped and were suspended above his knees.

Fabulous Feline grinned then pulled Pae's underwear up to his waist. "Oh, my flippin' God!" She giggled. "I'm not imagining things! These do have laces on the back! You have no idea how turned on I still am! I do love these purple panties! This fantastic, rock-hard ass, though!" Her hands shook as she pulled his underwear toward his knees. She grasped each cheek. "Clean and smooth as a baby's bottom! Fan-flippin-tastic! Pae, you're one hell of a beautiful man!" She squeezed a couple of times, then withdrew. "I need to stop."

Pae turned around to face the Fabulous Feline.

"Your little soldier's gonna be standing at attention all day, isn't he?"

Pae rolled his eyes and grinned. "It kinda looks that way, huh? Oh! And he's a Marine, not a soldier. He has a bigger helmet!" Pae chuckled. "Just a little military humor there. Nothing serious."

"Well, his helmet is big! There's no doubt about that! Take off your pants and your cute purple man panties. Come up here and join me."

Pae noticed he had kicked over his Bloody Mary at some point. *Oh well,* he thought, *it was more than worth it!* The man removed his black leather tactical boots and slipped from his garments. He sat beside the Fabulous Feline on the edge of the platform and shivered as he contemplated the possible consequences of his actions. Pae felt a mix of shame and elation. He tried desperately to not overthink the situation.

"Are you alright, shug?"

"Yeah. I'm good."

The Fabulous Feline massaged Pae's neck and shoulders. "Damn, these are some of the biggest muscles I've ever seen up close and personal!"

"Sherri-Lynn?

"Yes, hon?"

"You've never had sex with a man?"

"I've had lots of sex, hon, but only handjobs, oral, and anal. I've never had vaginal intercourse. Why?"

"You finished me off like a pro. Is that normal for you?"

"No. I usually ask them to tell me when they're getting ready to cum. I'm selective. I won't lie: I love to swallow! It can be quite tasty, especially if he eats a lot of chocolates and other sweets. Too bad, you don't have more to donate. I don't know what you eat, but it made you taste awesome! No, wait! I think I *do* know what you eat?" The Fabulous Feline laughed. "Sorry! I hope that didn't sound too gross?"

"Not gross at all. I'm thankful! I've never been with a woman who actually enjoyed getting a mouthful. The few I'd been with, including one of my wives, had pretended they enjoyed it, but they always panicked at the last minute. So, what made you dive in the way you did? No woman I have ever met has behaved that way. None has ever just gone for it without being coaxed. I was under the impression you weren't about to touch me with a ten-foot pole?"

"You didn't push, that's why. You didn't stick it in my face and expect me to act. I wanted it as much as you, and you allowed me the freedom to decide for myself."

"When is the last time you finished off another man like that?"

"Seven years."

"Wow! You threw that out there quick!"

"Because I didn't have to think about it, hon. It's true. That was also the last time I'd touched a man outside of a little hand-holding and some kissing. I am not looking for fulfillment in a man, not even from you. I hate to sound rude. It's nothing personal against you. I am already fulfilled. But, just as you wanted to give me that cash, I wanted to give you something. And…I wanted relief from my sexual frustration, too. Seven years was an eternity. I can't imagine ten. So, I guess there was a little selfishness on my part? Why the concern over my last time, shug?"

Pae looked into the Fabulous Feline's eyes. The heavyset, curvy woman with milk chocolate skin, flowing, natural auburn hair, and crystal, emerald green eyes made him crazy. He said not a word but instead snatched the base of Sherri-Lynn's ponytail. Her eyes widened, and her mouth dropped open with a sharp gasp. Pae opened up and laid into her with an aggressive but soft kiss. He cupped her left jaw with his other hand.

The Fabulous Feline whimpered. Her heart did somersaults as she dug her short, manicured fingertips into Pae's thick, sweat covered back. The Feline's breaths grew more encumbered as they kissed.

"Shock me!" the Fabulous Feline panted.

"What?"

"Shock me! Plant a finger in my dumper!"

"Are you sure?"

"Do it!"

"Do you have any lubricant?"

"Lick your finger! I don't care, just do it! Please!"

The Fabulous Feline whimpered when Pae's finger entered her.

"Please don't take away my girlhood," she whispered. "Please don't invade my pretty little girl. Play in my bum all you want, but please don't steal my little girl's virginity! Shock me!"

Pae's conscience took a dive into a whirlpool; its head dipped below the surface several times, but it continued to swim madly, sometimes against the current and sometimes with. His conscience turned topsy-turvy, with feet kicking the air as it capsized. It rolled over and bobbed upright then started flailing again. His mind cluttered with conflicting thoughts. Compassion urged him to silently pray for Sherri-Lynn while they continued to share each other's bodies. Guilt and elation tugged at his heart.

"Shock me more!" the Fabulous Feline demanded. "Two fingers! Be easy, but give me two! It's been a long time, but I can take it! Go all the way to the last knuckle if you can! Oh, God, yes!"

Pae kissed, nibbled, and gently sucked on the Feline's neck and collar bone. He bit and licked her left ear. The enticed female panted, sighed, and moaned. Her eyes widened when Pae started pressing on the wall behind her vagina.

"Oh, my God! Pae, what are you doing in there? That's incredible!"

"Lay down," Pae told the Fabulous Feline.

"Come up here with me!" Fabulous Feline urged, "Don't slip out! Follow me!" The Fabulous Feline scooted backward on the platform. Pae moved with her keeping his fingers in place. The Feline raised her legs and bent her knees. Pae started massaging her clitoris with two fingers from his other hand. He applied firm pressure to either side as he slid them back and forth and probed intermittently.

The Fabulous Feline's emerald eyes blazed through her mask as she lifted her head. "Give me a third! Shock me harder!" she huffed. "Three fingers!"

Pae stopped massaging the Feline long enough to dip a finger into the thick, milky flow that oozed from her womanhood. He applied it to the rim of her backside and to his ring finger, then eased in. She yelped. Her eyes rolled back, then slammed shut. She panted and arched her back.

The Fabulous Feline gripped the patchwork blanket in both hands as Pae massaged the surface of her vagina while he pleasured her bum. Pae drew close. The Fabulous Feline crossed her ankles and rested them on his upper back.

"Please don't take away my prize!" Sherri-Lynn pleaded.

"I am not here to steal your treasure," Pae told her. "I am here to give you more."

SEPTEMBEr 1: ETERNITy FADEs To NOOn

"Wow! Fabulous Feline, I didn't know a woman was biologically capable of doing that!" Pae sat beside her on the edge of the platform. Both looked dazed.

The Fabulous Feline replied, "I've heard about it, but I've never experienced it first-hand or talked to any other woman who has. I didn't think it possible either, much less from me! You made my head spin in circles! You would be an unbelievable lesbian!" The Fabulous Feline laughed at her own comment.

"Heterosexual men are lesbians trapped in male bodies, are we not?"

"Whoa!" The Fabulous Feline covered her grin and slapped her knee. "I didn't see that coming! But now that I think about it, you are absolutely correct, sir, if not a tad strange for coming up with it?"

The man and woman chuckled in unison.

The Fabulous Feline added, "On second thought, scratch that. Most men are dogs, not lesbians. They'll cause wounds then want to lick them, and they'll gladly lick others. They'll pretend they care, and they'll play the game of romance until they get what they want, and if you're lucky, you'll get the leftovers. But very few are lesbians in male bodies. They lack the female connection in their brains. I think they're perfectly capable, but they're terrified of tapping into it. You, my dear Pae, take the lesbian honor in spades!"

"Well, I do wear women's silk panties, so there's that. I'm glad you think I would have been a great lesbian! High praise from a lady, especially one as gorgeous as you!"

"Hey, now! You're already in! You don't need to keep up the flattery, but I do appreciate it. Seriously, though, it's not the panties or even the actions. Any man can do what you did. It's the psychology, Pae." Sherri-Lynn shook her head. "Damn, you're on a whole other plane! You're in touch. I am amazed that any woman would dare throw you away."

"Well, no one has ever had this version of Pae. I didn't exist in my current form back then. I was working on it. I guess life had to kick me in the teeth some more to draw it all out?"

"Speaking of drawing things out, you caused me to make a bigger mess than you! That's... Man! That's... Mm!" Fabulous Feline closed her eyes and shook her head. "That three-finger shocker got me most of the way there. I'm glad you eased your little Marine into my foxhole once you got it nice and dug-out. That backdoor action..." she shook her head again.

"It cured him. He finally fell asleep." Pae grinned.

"That he did."

"I'm glad you have hand sanitizer in here."

"Are you kidding me? In a place like this? We can't afford to go without it."

"It feels good to get clean after taking a dive, that's for sure. Too bad, we fouled up the blanket."

"We have other blankets. It's kind of nasty that we had to use it as a rag, but that's how it goes, I reckon? The sanitizer gave me a run for my money, and I'm sure I'll be feeling the stretch in my bum for the next few days, but it was damn well worth it!"

"That was an understatement and a half."

"I dream of what vaginal sex might be like. I won't compromise, though. The last remaining strand of my virginity will either go to an honest-to-goodness true love, or I will die with it. There are at least four men in my past who probably still walk funny because they tried to charm me out of it and refused to take no for an answer. Believe me, they took no for an answer! This southern girl don't play around!"

Fabulous Feline inhaled deeply through her nostrils then looked at Pae. "Those men don't count. But you? Like I said, I didn't think that possible. I never would have dreamed I could ejaculate like a man, much less gush the way I did. You're magic, Mr. Pae! And I thank you for honoring me by not getting carried away. My *girl* is probably slammed as tight as a bear trap after more than three decades of growing cobwebs, but you took fantastic care in working around her! Obviously, you bypassed the gold and went straight for the diamond mine! Thank you."

"My pleasure, Miss Feline. Thank you for inviting me down."

"Pae, this is probably the most awkward question in the world considering what we've just done," the Fabulous Feline switched tracks, "but do you think you might ever open your heart to another woman, for more than a *friends with benefits* kind of a thing? Maybe a little more than what we've done here? You know? A steady commitment?"

"I thought I had met someone with some potential when I was returning from the store the same day I saw that little girl. It was a woman who lives next door to me. She invited me to a private bonfire. She got drunk and flashed her boobs and her bum. She also told me about her two ex-husbands. Really spilled her guts, kinda like we've been doing here. She was a free-spirited kind of a person. It was obvious she'd led a hard life, but even as rough as she appeared, she was still attractive as all get-out as far as I am concerned. But then she barely said two words to me the next day and has been avoiding me ever since."

"Besides the drunk flashing, did you two have a sexual encounter?"

"Yes, and no. She asked me to touch her breasts, but that was the extent of it. She just ripped open her shirt and flopped 'em out. She wasn't wearing a bra. In all honesty, I think she enjoyed it more than I did? She made me nervous."

"I hope I haven't made you nervous?"

Pae chuckled. His eyes beamed. "Not even close!"

"Thank you, hon. This other woman sounds lonely and confused, and afraid that she may have come at you too quickly?"

"Well, she did, so..."

"So, give her time if you want a friendship to come of it? It's possible she doesn't even want a man, or she could already be seeing one and is just holding her cards close? If she flashed you, I sincerely doubt it, unless she has deep-seated issues and is a social butterfly? There are not a whole lot of women in the world who will just throw their tits and asses in the face of a man outside of this kind of a joint, so my money's on her having daddy issues. It could just be that she loses her inhibitions when she drinks? There are folks like that. Odds are she's just super lonely, and now she's kicking herself for acting like an eager puppy dog? You know, a person can get a little stir-crazy living that far out in the sticks. Let her be. She'll either come around or she won't. If she doesn't, you'll always have that memory. Strange or not, it sounds like it was a pretty decent time?"

"It was great, actually. I guess we were what each other needed at that moment?"

"And now you're here, and you need me. And obviously, I need you, too."

"So, what about you, Sherri-Lynn? Will you ever fully open your heart to a man?"

"I don't know, to be honest. It's awfully hard for me to do what we've done and not form an attachment. That's why it's been seven years since my last. I got tired of leaving a piece of my soul with men who weren't serious about me. I suppose I could open my heart enough to commit, but he would have to be one hell of a man and a true friend, not a user."

"There are not many true friends out there in this world. There are plenty of takers but few givers. I was married to two takers. Whoever you might eventually settle down with, if anyone, I hope that he will truly be someone who satisfies your soul. You have most certainly satisfied mine, and I am not referring to the sex alone. It was a pleasure being able to share you and still preserve your dignity. I hope my gifts to you have been as meaningful as yours have been to me."

The Fabulous Feline and Pae sat shoulder to shoulder. Pae thought he heard her sniffle. He looked but saw no tears run from beneath her mask. Her eyes were fixed on the wall. She turned and saw him watching.

"If you don't mind, let's get a little more comfortable, shug? Lay down facing that wall, if you will?"

Pae took a pillow and lay down, facing the wall as the Fabulous Feline had requested. She eased herself onto the bed and pressed herself against her partner's back. "You okay, hon?"

Pae smiled. "I'm good. I can't remember the last time I was cuddled, especially from behind. My wives wouldn't do that. Sorry. I shouldn't make comparisons."

"Don't fret, hon. Those days are over. Let 'em go."

"Thank you, Fabulous Feline."

"Fabulous Feline is just a character, a stage name, hon. You are being treated by the real Sherri-Lynn today. She pulled off her mask and tossed it toward the wall. "I could tell you needed a little closeness when you gave me that huge tip without expecting anything in return. It's not all about generosity, as you had tried to let on. You needed something."

"Deja vu."

"It bore repeating."

"You mean my hungry eyes weren't a dead giveaway?"

"Shug, that googly-eyed look you gave me when you walked in was because of *my* eyes. I've seen and heard men say things about them way too many times to think otherwise. You didn't look hungry or horny, just startled, until I showed up in costume. Then, yeah, your expression changed. I saw the blood drain from your face. It went somewhere else!" Sherri-Lynn laughed. "And yes, the green is natural. About two percent of the planet has green eyes, and even fewer are as green as mine. Nearly no one has these peepers. I usually lie and say they're contacts though because men do try to pick up on me when they see them. You'd be surprised at how many I run off just by telling them they're really brown. Most of 'em are too dumb to know any better. My dark skin helps in that regard. It comes from the Australian Aboriginal side of my bloodline—my biological father--and the green eyes, dark auburn hair, and freckles from the Irish."

"Aboriginal? That explains it. I was wondering where your unique blend of skin tone and features came from? That's interesting!"

"It would be more interesting if I knew anything about my Australian roots. I was born and raised here. I'm just another among the Alabama GRITS (Girls Raised In The South). Daddy was killed around the time I was born. He was in the wrong place at the wrong time. Mama never told me exactly what happened, and she never said a thing about her times with him in Australia. It's all a mystery to me. She didn't remarry until I was eight."

"Well, just another of the GRITS or not, you're probably the most unique woman I've ever laid eyes on. You are nothing short of absolutely stunning! I've been dying to tell you since I walked in the door. Now that we've shared each other, I figure why not?"

"Thank you, sweetie. You already know how I feel about you."

Pae blushed, but his back was to Sherri-Lynn. She could not see. "So, how did you come to be in this line of work? It seems a little strange to me that someone who's been through what you did with your stepdad would want to be anywhere near a strip club?"

"Stepfather, not stepdad. There was nothing dad about that man."

"I'm sorry. I didn't mean to be insulting."

"You're fine, hon. Don't sweat it. I was pretty messed up from that childhood ordeal. I can't deny that. After my mama had my stepfather arrested, she tried to get me help through our church, but once they heard what she had done to him, they more or less blackballed us."

"I'm not surprised. It sounds like the churches my family attended. What happened?"

"Too old fashioned, I guess? Too religious and judgmental, just like yours? They looked down on us, gossiped and whispered, and started avoiding us as if we were the ones who had done something wrong? Every now and then one of them would try to act like they gave two cents by saying they'd be praying for us, but that was about it. It would have been nice if they had been praying, but what we needed were real people with compassion to help us deal with the suffering. Prayer is always appreciated, but we also needed ears that would listen and hands that were willing to help, not all those avoidant looks with patronizing hot air.

"Mama eventually had a nervous breakdown, because all the folks she had been close to for years just up and turned their backs on us. The pastor and the other church staff were just not equipped to handle real problems. They lived in their holy bubble, and that was that. I still can't help but wonder whether some of it had to do with my mixed blood? The times were different back then."

"So, what happened with your mom's breakdown?"

"She snapped. Couldn't deal with the pressure of being a divorced mother of a raped child, trying to make it on her own without any support from anyone, not even her own family. She could not believe how long it had gone on, even with her there. The state child services didn't seem too interested since the law was already involved, and we were out of the house. They didn't have any counseling or support programs back then. Both sides of the family—hers and my stepfathers--pulled away to distance themselves from the shame of her bashing his head with the baseball bat and calling the police. They felt their family names had been publicly tarnished. They all said it would have been best if she had kept everything quiet and had come to them instead. The problem is they never dealt with internal family issues. They always just swept them under the rug and turned their heads.

"It didn't take long before she began blaming me for what had happened. I know in my heart that she didn't mean it, but she just couldn't cope anymore. She took to drinkin' then started cussing me. She said that if I hadn't worn those terry cloth short shorts in the summer that let my ass hang out, or if I hadn't run around the yard topless under the sprinklers and things like that, he never would have been tempted to do what he did."

Sherri-Lynn grew quiet.

"Are you okay back there?" Pae asked.

"I don't know?"

"What's wrong?"

"The day my mama snapped, she called me a little half-breed whore." Sherri-Lynn wrapped her right arm and leg around Pae then clung tightly, sobbing. "That hurt like hell, Pae! It was a thousand times worse than that man's filthy claws digging around in me! She was my mama, Pae, my own flesh and blood! Why did my mama call me that then disown me? Why?"

Pae was silent. He wanted to console Sherri-Lynn, but he knew there were no words that could ease that kind of pain.

"Damn it, Pae! Why?" Sherri-Lynn choked the words through a barrage of tears.

Pae rolled over to face Sherri-Lynn. He caressed the side of her face. "That is not you, beautiful," Pae said, as he looked into Sherri-Lynn's shimmering, tear-filled eyes. "That is not you." He rubbed her soaked cheek, and the bridge of her nose where the tears had puddled then kissed her forehead. "Your mama didn't hate you, Sherri-Lynn. The world broke her. She didn't have your strength. Please, don't take this the wrong way, but I think she might have called you that horrible name because of something in her past? Some kind of pain she never worked through."

Sherri-Lynn continued to sob. She pulled Pae as close as she could. "I know, beautiful man, I know. Why are people so ugly to each other, especially to children?"

SEPTEMBEr 1: PRESERVEd ANd UNKNOWABLe

Minutes passed like hours. Sherri-Lynn regained her composure. Pae swept his left hand through her bangs and caressed her hair. He rubbed her brow then continued to wipe her tears.

"The day mama had snapped," Sherri-Lynn said, "I came home from school and discovered she had packed her things and left. She didn't leave a note or anything. It was about a week before my teachers figured out something was wrong.

"I ended up living with my aunt and uncle until I was sixteen, but I couldn't put up with their self-righteous attitudes, with all that was happening under their roof, so I just up and walked away. I stayed in sheds and backyards, and the bedrooms and garages of friends, and I sometimes slept on the school grounds or in the woods.

"One day, the original owners of this place ran across me. They already knew I'd been on my own. Word gets around small towns quickly. They promised to give me room and board and a fake adult I.D. if I were willing to work here serving drinks and taking care of the place. They also promised to put me through junior college if I wanted. They kept all their promises. Really good people. Sad."

"What's sad?"

They were not church-going folk, but they treated me the way the preacher was always saying the Church should treat others. The Church failed us. That's what was sad."

Sherri-Lynn and Pae lay without a sound for a few minutes. Pae broke the silence. "Are you okay, beautiful?"

Sherri-Lynn rubbed Pae's cheek. "Give me another minute."

"Take all the time you need."

Sherri-Lynn moved her hand from Pae's face to his chest. She stopped where his heartbeat felt strongest through his shirt. He placed his hand over hers and pressed on it.

Sherri-Lynn was silent for another minute before she went on. "I got a two-year science degree in physics if you can believe that crazy shit? It took me three years with all the math and science that was involved, but it went quick. I love math.

"Anyway, they didn't let me go topless until I really was legal, and the full nude stuff didn't start until after they sold the place to Spanky about twenty years ago. By then, I was grown and established from saving my tip money and living rent-free. I had the degree, but I loved my life as it was, so here I am.

"I stopped entertaining full nude when I started aging and packing on the pork. These days it's in style, but not back then. Even so, I just don't do it. A few jerks tossed some boiled peanuts and *mooed* at me one night. Tiny worked 'em over pretty hard. They never came back. Another one on a different night had the balls to call me Jemima. I won't tell you what became of him. Suffice it to say he now has a lifelong reminder to seriously consider his words before opening his mouth to people, especially a lady.

"The company I keep helps make sure I never have to deal with people trying to take something from me that I ain't willing to give. They respect my personal boundaries, and I respect theirs. No, it's not a movie star life and a far cry from a moral one, but I'm still working on the moral part. At least it's more moral than forcing sex on a child."

Sherri-Lynn slid her hand from Pae's chest and placed it flat upon the side of his face. She rubbed his brow with her thumb. "How did you manage to get counseling? It's pretty expensive, isn't it?"

"Some churches are different now than in the old days. I found one that offered reduced rate counseling services by qualified Masters, Ph.D., and M.D. holders who did it for the love of helping people. They were bonafide licensed therapists, who were no strangers to real people and real problems. Best of all, they were practicing Christians who seemed to live what they preached, and as far as I could tell, they didn't put on holy shows in public while living like devils at home like so many of the people I was raised around."

"Were your parents that way?"

"No. They were nearly the exact opposite, as straight-laced as they could be in public and in private but still just as ineffective. In their minds, bad things were what happened to other people. Looking back, I exhibited all kinds of indicators that something terrible had come upon me, but my folks had seemed oblivious to every single one. Either they were truly naïve or in extreme states of denial? Whatever the case, I felt I could not approach them for a number of different reasons, the greatest being shame. I waited for many years before I finally opened up to a solid, real-deal Christian counselor."

"That's important to you, huh? The Christian part?"

"Yes, very. After years of counseling, I decided I couldn't blame those boys for what they had done to me. I wasn't feeling it at all at first. I wanted them to die. But I was losing my mind over things that are long gone, things I had no power to change. As hard as it was to accept, I decided to forgive them and try to let go of the pain they had caused."

Sherri-Lynn pondered Pae's words. "That's awfully mature. Not many people have the strength to forgive."

"Yeah. As you could see, a lot of pain is still there. I don't know if it will ever go away completely? My psychiatrist was quite patient with me over the years. She took meticulous care in helping me confront myself."

"She? You had a female psychiatrist?"

"Yep. Her name was Sandrea."

"Defender of mankind! Wow!"

"Huh?"

"Sandrea is a name of English origin. It means, defender of mankind."

"Well, I'll be John Brown and his brother George! I had no idea! I'd always wondered whether it was Gaelic? I never bothered to look it up, though."

So, why a female counselor, Pae?"

"The male sex, the gender, is just awfully tough for me to relate to. I'm not mean to them, I'm just still not comfortable around them. They're all dirty in my mind. Even if they're absolutely wonderful, subconsciously, I see them as inherently filthy at worst and untrustworthy at best. Yet, here I am, also a male. Because of this emotional deficiency, I couldn't bring myself to seek a male counselor. My childhood also hindered my willingness to trust God, knowing he is referred to in the masculine sense."

"Well, maybe you still need a bit of a female shoulder to lean on?"

"Yeah." Pae smiled. "It's obvious I do, but you know something funny?"

"What's that?"

"I carried shame for a huge portion of my life. Can you believe that? I carried shame, guilt, and disgust toward myself over something that was far beyond my control, something someone else did. I clung to God for deliverance from that internal hell while wondering whether I was actually some kind of an abomination for having been sodomized and raped as a seven-year-old? Eventually, my intellect knew better. My spirit knew better. But my emotions? The child inside of me? I don't know which was worse: the doubts or that I have no idea who those boys were? I never saw them before, and I've never seen them since. I grew up without any hope of justice and thinking that God hated me because of what they did. That little girl triggered memories of all that past pain."

Sherri-Lynn kissed the tip of Pae's nose.

SEPTEMBEr 1: AfTERNOOn

He enjoyed sitting in the woods. He would have lived there if he could, but there were not enough wild berries or other edible plants, and he did not appreciate being treated as food by insects. He loved watching the gray squirrels play. They were always energetic, and they appeared happy and carefree running up and down tree trunks and leaping across limbs, chasing each other in games of hide-and-seek. He thought they were funny when they stuffed their pouches with acorns. Sometimes, he giggled when they uttered weird, obscene-sounding noises. The odd calls reminded him of adult humans. He hated it when they used profanity, but for some reason, it was funny when the squirrels cussed.

Birds were amazing! They could sing, and they could speak to each other in their own unique languages that no one else understood. Yet, they all seemed to comprehend each other well enough to know when to take turns chirping. He imagined they were telling each other, *good afternoon*. Best of all, the birds could fly! He often daydreamed of that ability. He would have given anything to be able to fly away and never return. He had tried a few times but could not get off the ground. Once, he had climbed onto a low tree branch to gain leverage. He leaped off and flapped his arms vigorously but plummeted a few short feet to the ground and banged himself up. He decided that flying was best left to the birds.

He liked to potty in the woods. It was a lot better than dealing with it at home. At least here, he did not have to sit by it or in it until someone cleaned it up, cursed him, and slapped his face. Besides, he loved the light tickle of a breeze on his underside while he pooped. He seldom wiped afterward. No one had taught him how. He had acquired the behavior through necessity. When he did wipe, it was with his fingers, but that was usually too nasty for him to tolerate. He had washed in the creek a few times until he had discovered minnows living in it. He could not bring himself to do it afterward for fear of contaminating their home. Leaves were no good. They were always too crunchy, too slick, too sharp, or too rough, and they almost always caused some kind of an itch. At least he had learned to pull off his clothing before going. That made things easier, but it did nothing for the itching and chronic rash. That was the way it was. He had never known any different.

After being dropped off from a job, the boy would often stroll into the woods to his favorite spot, then sit and wrap himself in his arms. He would rock back and forth, and cry then look skyward, and mumble words he had invented.

Today, however, he did not cry. This day was special. The boy's mind was far from the squirrels and birds and other random critters, and far from his tormentors. The child heard an approaching freight train in the distance. He scurried deep into the woods and made his way to the track as swiftly as his little feet could move. The lad stripped his clothes along the way, leaving them scattered on the trail. The tyke arrived at his usual viewing spot just in time to see the lights on the engine's nose emerging from the trees as it rounded the bend several hundred feet away. The youth removed his boots in eager anticipation of its arrival. The ground vibrated beneath the boy long before the train reached him. A heavy rumble permeated his body and settled within his chest. The closer the train drew, the more intense the bone-penetrating pulses. The sensation was other-worldly. The boy's eyes widened, and his heart thumped as the tremors engulfed him. He spread his feet apart and his arms wide, then extended his fingers and wiggled them. The lad marveled at the powerful vibrations.

As usual, the engine's air horns belted two quick blasts just before it met its tiny spectator. The shrill, ear-splitting charges used to scare him, but he had learned to expect the powerful greeting. He had no idea what this enormous metal serpent was, but it fascinated him to no end. The fact that it always bellowed hello filled his heart with joy. This colossal steel beast never threatened him in any way. It was the most humongous moving entity he had ever witnessed. The engine's horns fell silent as it continued down the track, around another bend, and disappeared once more into the woods. The cars continued for a while. The boy was enthralled by the clanging, hissing, rubbing, and screeching, as he watched the towering metal serpent slither by. His nostrils filled with the odors of hot steel, grease, rubber, and an occasional spark. The springs on the wheel trucks compressed then extended again as the freight cars floated by on wavy rails. Tethered hoses, lines, and chains swung back and forth beneath the bulky metal knuckles that joined the wheeled containers. The freight carriers' shapes were basic, but the details of the objects upon those shapes captivated the boy's imagination. Tankers, gondolas, hoppers, bulkhead flats, livestock transports, and even boxcars, all paraded their metal mysteries. The small child wondered about the ladders, handles, brake wheels, and hatches. Repetitive *clack, clack, clack, clack* noises filled the boy's ears and thumped the ground beneath him as the train thundered by. He was enraptured!

The train passed. The boy heard its air horns in the distance. The blasts lingered much longer than when it had greeted him. It was the same every time. He imagined the prolonged calls were greetings to groups of other children. The child closed his eyes. This had indeed been a special day. The train had made it complete. He set his mind on the cool September breeze and upon the only friend he felt he had in the world. He slid back into his boots, then made his way along the trail to gather his clothes. Once all were collected, the youth moved to his favorite spot near a stream. He sat upon his clothes, covered in goose bumps. There were no mosquitos; it was an unusual treat, *icing on the cake*. Though in practice, the day had been no different than any other, it was special because, for the first time in his life, the tyke had experienced a sensation he had never felt and could not define: hope had stirred. The little one hummed while he twisted the fingers of one hand in his hair and drew patterns in the dirt with the other. His eyes were bright as he lifted them skyward. A faint smile spread across the tot's lips.

sEPTEMBEr 1: LATe AFTERNOOn

Pae arrived home just after 4:00 PM. Sherri-Lynn's Fabulous Feline persona had invited him to visit the club anytime he liked. Sherri-Lynn, the newfound companion, had asked that he purposely return so they may become better acquainted. In past years, women had taken advantage of Pae's genuine nature and led him *down the garden path* to get something from him, usually monetary favors. Sherri-Lynn did not seem the type. This became obvious to Pae after he walked through the front door of his house and discovered that at some point, she had returned the one hundred dollars he had tipped her. She had slipped the money into his pants pocket.

"Huh," Pae grunted. He counted the cash. "Interesting."

Pae thought about Sherri-Lynn and Charlene. He wondered whether there was one true love, a genuine companion, someone out there who would not take advantage of him in a third dead marriage, and consume his remaining years for the sake of their psychological starvation, emotional gluttony, their ego, and material gain. He wondered whether he should tough it out by living single throughout the remainder of his days.

Pae settled in and drew a hot bath. The level rose an inch or two before he slid in and patiently waited for the antique cast iron tub to fill. When the water reached the base of his chest, the man eased forward and used his toes to twist the knobs. He grinned over the sensation of his flaccid penis and testicles, pointing upward and bobbing under the water. It was the apex of relaxation! The bulky, muscular male's eyes fixed on the two brass valves, the curved spout, and the brass pipe that joined all three in a squared, U-shaped pattern before retreating into the wall. Pae's smile grew, and his eyes twinkled as he recollected his steamy encounter Sherri-Lynn, but then his light grew dim. He dwelled on the knowledge that he had sex out of wedlock, and in ways with which he had always morally struggled. The man's thoughts clouded as he descended into a downward spiral of self-condemnation. Pae tried to focus on more positive thoughts.

He drifted to the platinum blonde haired girl. He wondered about the mysterious little ghost and began to doubt whether he had interacted with her, but then he recalled the man in the pickup truck. *Nope. She's real, alright. What happened to her? Where is she?* Pae closed his eyes and prayed.

After bathing, Pae sat on his sofa with an old King James Bible that his grandfather had given him as a teen. He opened it and started reading at Luke chapter seven, verse thirty-six. It was a story he had remembered hearing many times of a prostitute who had been accepted by Jesus at the protest of religious leaders. Pae read through verse forty. The language was archaic, but he understood, as he had been raised in churches that had taught from the old English of the Authorized King James Version.

He thought about Sherri-Lynn's experience as a child and about how the religious leaders and her own family had ousted her and her mother for defending themselves from a sexual predator. Like the prostitute in the Bible story, they had been shut out for the sake of reputation. They would rather have run Sherri-Lynn and her mother out of town than to love them and help them through their pain. Jesus had shown a professional sex worker, a societal reject, a whore, that her life had legitimate value she did not yet understand. Sherri's life and her mother's had value too, whether they realized it or not, so did Pae's. It had taken him a lifetime to recognize his. He set the Bible on a sofa cushion and prayed again.

There was a knock at the door. Pae was not dressed.

"Just a minute!" he shouted. He arose and went into the bedroom and slipped into a pair of sweat pants. He withdrew a pistol from the nightstand then walked to the front door.

Pae called in an authoritative tone, "Who is it?"

The voice from the other side responded, "It's Charlene! I was wondering if you wanted to talk? Maybe hang out a little?"

Pae opened the door enough to peek through, leaving the side of his foot against it. When he saw she was alone, he moved his foot and opened the door a little wider, staying behind it. "Hi. Long time, no see."

Charlene's eyes widened. She had never seen Pae with his shirt off. "Oh, *Lort!*" she remarked. She covered the side of her face with her hair. "I'm sorry I've been so scarce." She released her hair. "I can explain."

"Please hold that thought. I need to put some clothes on. I'll be right out."

"Lord, have mercy! You do that," Charlene agreed. Pae closed the door, then opened it a few minutes later and stepped outside. Charlene stood near the road, smoking a cigarette and holding a beer. She wore a loose turtleneck sweater and a pair of bleached denim shorts.

"Yeah, I know," she commented when she noticed Pae looking at her white shorts. Don't worry, it's not Labor Day yet."

Charlene was barefoot. Her feet were a different strawberry hue than her hands and face. Several blue, spider-webbed, varicose veins were high up on the side of her left thigh. Pae had not noticed them the last time he had talked to her. He could not help but wonder whether she had circulation problems from smoking.

Charlene dropped her head and shifted her eyes left then right. "I'm sorry that I came on so hard that one night. I was buzzed from the booze and the pot. I ain't felt that great in the company of a man in a long time! It kind of freaked me out. I hope you can forgive me?" She lifted her head and met his gaze.

"No worries," he replied, "I felt great, too."

"You're too kind."

"No, I'm serious," Pae assured her, "I'm not just *blowing smoke*. I really did enjoy myself. It was refreshing."

Charlene turned up her beer and took a long drag off her cigarette.

Pae asked, "Do you know the other folks on this road?"

"Kinda." Charlene exhaled smoke. "The ones in that house up yonder," she pointed in the direction that led to the state highway, "is elderly. They're real quiet. They're friendly enough. They just don't get out much.

Every now and then, he'll go out in the backyard and smoke a big ole *stogie* and start talking to hisself, and then he'll hobble back in. His wife used to bring over a peanut butter cake once in a while, but I reckon her health got too bad to walk this far? I see 'em getting in the car about once a month for a grocery trip. A teenaged young'n' follows 'em back and takes in their bags for 'em. He shakes the boy's hand, and she hugs him. They try to slip him some extra money, but he always refuses. Good ole souls, all of 'em. I drop by and say hey to 'em from time to time."

Charlene pointed to the house opposite the elderly couple's. "That house across the way... Them folks is about my age." She looked at Pae. "I reckon I got you by about ten years or so?"

"You say that as if I'm a spring chicken?"

"We're both a little past our prime sugar, but we got more than enough miles left in us. Even so, I'm sure I'm your elder by at least a few years? That said, I'm not quite as old as I might look? The years have took a toll on me, especially since I got hooked on meth after I shot my second husband and ran off. I don't remember if I told you, but he's the one who filed for divorce on me. Tried to give me everything, but I told him just to cut me loose, and we'd be square. He signed the papers and ran off with his tail between his legs. I never seen hide nor hair of him again. He ain't important.

"Anyhow, these folks up the way in that other house, they're about my age. His wife used to come out and talk to me by the mailbox every other day or so, but it was mostly small talk. She wasn't really all that sociable, just trying to be neighborly and biding her time, I guess? Now, they're almost never home. I think they might be living somewhere else? They pop in every now and again for only a few minutes, and then they go on their way. Checkin' on the house from time to time, I reckon? They never bother to say hey when they drop by. Kinda sad, because she did seem like an okay person. I thought she was warming up to me, but I guess not? That's about it."

"What about up that way?" Pae looked in the opposite direction.

"You don't want to wander off that way. That dirt portion is private. There's a sign posted right over yonder." She pointed to a distant tree. The sign was covered by a cedar sapling, but an outer edge was visible. "They got more of 'em scattered here and there, the further up you go. Them folks that live up in there, they ain't right."

Charlene took another long drag off her cigarette. "I'm sorry. I like to try to see the best in everyone, even in people like my exes, I honestly do. I don't like people talking about me behind my back, and I don't like to talk about others. Gossip and slander just ain't me. I'll talk about someone just enough to tell you the story of how I came to be where I'm at, or where I think they stand, but I won't go around smearing folks just to do it if you get what I'm sayin'?"

Charlene up-ended the beer bottle again. "But I tell you, there's just something wrong, really, really wrong with them people."

Pae's neighbor took another drink. "I run across 'em now and then when I'm out and about at the convenient store or out grocery shopping'. I come across'd 'em once or twice while I was takin' a walk around the park near Main Street down in Palafox. I tried saying hey a few times, especially when I recognized their truck coming up this way, but they just gawked at me with crazy eyes. Out in town, they act like I don't exist, except for the one time the man's wife made a point of spitting in front of me when I was coming out of the store. She spit right in my path then stared me down like she wanted to kill me. For the life of me, I never figured out why."

The woman swallowed more beer. "After a while, I started to notice that they're rude as hell to nearly everybody except for a few, and them folks are the same way. But those eyes! Damn, those eyes! It's like looking right in the face of the devil himself, both the man and his old lady. It's like I can actually feel evil when I get anywhere near 'em. Sends a chill up my spine just talking about it."

Pae's neighbor took yet another drink and a drag off of her cigarette. "She's a fiery carrot top, real heavy set and soggy. Don't take care of herself at all! Looks like a damn swamp hag!"

Charlene dropped her head and raised the beer bottle. "Lord, forgive me! I said I don't like to talk down on people, but some you just can't help!"

There's that cute, back-woods pronunciation again, Pae thought. *It sounds like she's saying, "cain't."*

Charlene lowered her hand. "She's got to be at least forty years old and pregnant as shit? Looks like she's carrying triplets, but she's so damn heavy, to begin with, I can't really say for sure. It looks like she ain't never run a comb through her hair or even washed it. She usually keeps it pulled back in a low ponytail like a man would. Sometimes, she has it braided in cornrows. Makes my stomach turn when I see it. Once in awhile, I'll see her out in town, in dark blue lipstick and eyeshadow, and her hair pulled up into two of them Chinese bun lookin' things on top of her head. She'll be in a god-awful mini skirt, with that pale, ghost white, freckle-covered skin, with cottage cheese dimples stickin' out everywhere, lookin' like a crack whore."

The woman shook her head and placed her left hand on Pae's chest. Her cigarette was sticking up between her fingers. "I know that's mean! I should not have said that but in all fairness, I was literally a crack whore for a while, so I know that of which I speak! I finally hit rock bottom and swore off men for a while. Until then, I was suckin' every swingin' dick I could find to support my habit. I've been down that road. I can spot 'em a mile away."

Charlene removed her hand from Pae's chest. "I'm sorry. I'm probably making you uncomfortable? If you don't want to ever talk to me again, trust me, I'll understand. I been gettin' along fine here by myself. It took me a long, long time to be able to do it, but I can, and I do."

Charlene shifted back to the subject of the redheaded woman. "I ain't never actually seen her with nobody else, so I don't really know for sure if she was trying to hook? But I can pretty much guarantee you she was. On one end of the spectrum, you got them high-dollar escorts, and on the other end, you got them alley cat, two-dollar fuck pigs. She's way south of them."

Charlene shook her head, "I hope to *hell* she wasn't trying to score herself a lay! If she was, I shudder to think what kind of a person might have gone for that? I mean, *damn*! There's 'love the skin you're in' and 'don't body shame' and all that happy horse shit, but *damn*, at least try to make a real effort to look halfway decent, even if you are a heavy humper! What's sad is her face is gorgeous! She's fuckin' beautiful, Pae! She just don't take no care of herself, and when she tries, she looks like a damn whore!"

Pae was beginning to regret spending time with Charlene, but he felt the core information was important, so he bit his tongue and put up with her.

Charlene kept going. "Her husband is a skinny-assed little prick with black and gray hair halfway down his back. He looks like a heavy metal reject. They both sport a few tattoos that look homemade like they got 'em in the county lockup or the state pen or somethin'? He seems to be a little older than her, but I can't say for sure."

"Do they have any children?"

"Just one that I ever seen, but that was nearly a year ago. She used to walk up and down the road by herself. I tried to talk to her once, but she told me, 'Fuck off, you ragged old, used-up cunt,' in them exact words, so I never tried again. She must have been about twelve years old."

"Ouch! That's harsh!" Pae's face registered confusion. He turned his stare from the road to look directly at Charlene. "Twelve, you say?"

"Yessir," she ran the two words together, "twelve."

Pae chuckled. "Why did you call me 'sir?'"

"It may be way too soon, but I kinda respect you. I've been around more fakes than you can shake a stick at. Many fooled the hell out of me up-front, and a few others for a very long time, but I just sense something way different about you. I don't know? It's like I can *feel* what you're all bout just standing next to you? Do you get what I'm saying?"

"Kindred spirit?"

"Yeah! Like that! A kindred spirit!"

"I'll take that as a compliment."

"Is there any other way?"

"I reckon not?"

"As for that child, I'm near certain she was about twelve. Could have been eleven? Young little thing. Too thin and undeveloped up top to be older. She was flat-chested but beginning to bud a little. I could tell she wasn't in a training bra yet. Beautiful legs for a kid her age, not all gangly and knobby-kneed like a grasshopper. Her arms were thin as spaghetti straps, though. She was wearing cutoff shorts, and if you ask me, they weren't fit for a young'n' that age. Her little ass was split right up the middle and was hanging all out the back. She had way too much sass in her walk. Way too much sass in that ass! She picked it up from somewhere. It wasn't natural. And let me tell ya, that ass was the kind that most grown women would kill for! Pure genetics."

"I'm surprised you paid that much attention."

"Honey, it's impossible to ignore somethin' like that struttin' up and down out here, especially a girl that age! There's more and more of it everywhere you go, but it still don't make it right. And out here? In the middle of nowhere with all these dang skeeters and horseflies, and shit tryin' to chew your ass off? There's just no call for it; no call for it at all!"

Pae glanced at Charlene's bare legs.

"Yeah," Charlene said then inhaled her cigarette. Smoke was mingled in her exhaled response. "I hear what you're sayin': shut up." She stuck her tongue out.

Pae grinned. "I didn't say anything."

"No, but you thought it. I might be a dumb ole Alabama hillbilly, but I ain't that dumb. Anywhow, where that little girl is concerned, something's up with that. Makes me doubt that big redhead is her biological mama. She sure don't make that child dress right. They don't look a thing like each other, either. That woman ain't nothing but bag-ass, soggy cottage cheese, and pits, not an ounce of muscular tone anywhere. But then that child don't look nothin' like her daddy neither, so who's to say? But no, just one hundred percent wrong what she was wearing. I could see the insides of her pockets sticking out up-front. Way too tight. Disgusting. The seat of her shorts was cut too high and had holes wore through it. Never wore panties as far as I could tell. Beautiful girl, to be honest, but a foul mouth, and those same dark, sinister-looking eyes as her folks, eyes that just don't look anything like little kids' eyes, you know what I mean?"

"I'm trackin' with ya," Pae affirmed. "I get what you're saying."

"She would stroll up yonder-way until a big, expensive luxury car picked her up; same car every time. A few hours later, it would drop her off, and she would wiggle her happy little ass on home. On that same day that I tried to say hey to her, and she cussed me, I was sittin' on the front porch drinkin' when she walked by on her way back. She stared at me and damn, if looks could kill, there'd have been nothing left of me today!

"Not ten minutes after she disappeared up into them woods, their pickup truck come haulin' ass on by. The daddy was drivin'. The mama chucked a big damn open garbage sack onto my mailbox, and he hurled an empty vodka bottle over the roof in my direction. He stomped the gas and shook the ass end of that truck halfway down the road. The big red bovine flipped me off."

Charlene shook her head and raised both her hands. "Lord, forgive my language again, for callin' that woman a bovine! I swear, I swear, I *swear*, I don't mean no harm to nobody!" She lowered her hands and took another drink, emptying the bottle.

"Anyways, my mailbox was covered in opened-up, shitty baby diapers, and rotted potato peels, and eggs, and all kinds of other nasty crap. There were a few used syringes tucked away in some of that trash, and a shit load of tin can lids without the cans. They were probably hoping I'd get my ass stuck or sliced open?"

Pae was deep in thought. "You have any more problems with them since then?"

"Naw. I called the Sheriff."

Pae paid close attention.

"They asked me if the mailbox had been damaged. Can you believe that? I have baby shit and hypodermic needles scattered all over the place, and they asked about my damn mailbox?" Charlene turned up the beer bottle, but it was empty. She shook the final drops onto the road. "God, forgive me for my foul mouth. You too, sweetie pie."

Charlene stopped shaking her beer bottle and looked at Pae with a grin. "Pie! My pie in the sky! My sweetie pie!" She grabbed one of his belt loops and tugged on it then let go.

"Anyhow, they said a mailbox is federal property, so they wanted to know if it had been damaged. I told them no. They told me that since no real crime had been committed, there was nothing they could do."

Charlene *hotboxed* what was left of her cigarette, wearing it down as rapidly as she could. She burned it to about a half-inch from the filter then pointed at Pae with the smoldering butt sandwiched between two fingertips.

"Let me tell ya, I...got... *PISSED*! I said to that fuckin' sheriff, 'How in the hell is it that vandalism of private property--my yard--and illegal display of power in a motor vehicle, used hypodermic needles with who knows what kinda damn diseases on 'em, not to mention an obvious threat of physical violence against my person--that bottle being tossed at me--*hello?* are not a problem, but a mailbox falling off a stick is a high crime against humanity? What the hell?'

"The asshole told me to calm down and not call-in to an emergency number drunk again, or else he'd come out personally and arrest me on the spot for public intoxication. I politely thanked the corrupt bastard for his time and hung-up on him. Little Miss *It on a Stick* stopped walking back and forth a little more than a year or so after that. This was about six months back, give or take. Since then, it's been quiet as a mouse around here."

"I'm sorry you had to go through that," Pae told Charlene.

"Well, it wasn't all bad. After I picked up the garbage, I went inside and filled the tub with bubble bath, downed some Jack, and smoked a huge-ass joint while I listened to some shit-kickin' good ole boy music. I de-stressed the living shit out of myself with the help of a waterproof buddy! Damn near electrocuted myself, though. Thank God I kicked the *boom box* onto the floor instead of into the tub with me, else my ass would have been deep-fried! It was completely worth it, though! I went into seventh heaven: screamed like a banshee in that bathtub!"

Charlene placed her hand on Pae's chest. "Sorry! I'm gettin' all wound up thinking about that shit. You can probably tell I've had a little to drink today, can't you?"

"Say it ain't so!"

"You must think I'm the nastiest skag alive?"

Pae looked into his neighbor's eyes. "I think you're human."

Charlene giggled. "Where the hell did you come from? Did it hurt when you fell from heaven?" She laughed louder and squeezed Pae's arm. "Stupid line, I know! Not really a line, just a pathetic attempt at humor. I just feel such a weight lifting off me. No man, and I mean *no man*, has *ever* given me half the attention that you have given me in what? Only two days if you count that first day we met? Not really even that long if you add it all up. Thank you!"

Pae's discomfort with Charlene had grown. It did not help when she added, "If I weren't committed to taking care of myself and thinking straight, I could easily see myself falling for you. I'll bet you'd gladly have me, too, wouldn't ya?"

Charlene threw a hand up with her palm opened toward Pae. "No! Don't answer that! Please, don't even try to talk to me about it. I'm not trying to be a bitch. I know it seems like I'm a flirt and a tease."

That was the deal-breaker. Any sliver of a hope that they might form a solid bond had just dissolved. *I am not on a wild scooch hunt*, Pae thought. *She does not have an ounce of respect for me; she has already made that clear in several ways since July.* Pae considered that he could be over analyzing Charlene's words, but there were just too many red flags to risk ignoring. *Sad*, he thought. *She is mighty carefree and an awful lot of fun. She's not for me, though. At least Sherri-Lynn told me she's not interested in a long-term commitment despite the morning we'd had together.*

Charlene grinned. "Okay, I am a flirt and a tease, but not like that. I'm not a user. Anyway, thank you again for your company. It's been wonderful, just like last time! I better go now before I open my mouth too much. As fun as that night was in July, we can't afford a repeat."

"I'm sorry if I'm running you off, somehow?" Pae asked, trying to be cordial, though he was glad to hear Charlene's words.

"No, you're not running me off. I just got things going through my head, is all."

Charlene took a few steps toward her house when Pae asked, "Are you sure they have no other children?"

Charlene stopped and replied, "Only that one. Why?"

"Just curious. I keep to myself, but it's good to have at least some idea who's around me."

"We'll talk again soon." Charlene smiled and winked, then turned and went her way, adding a little extra wag to her walk. She did not look back.

SEPTEMBEr 30: EVENINg

C harlene had resumed a pattern of keeping her distance from Pae. He had begun to reciprocate, as the fun of her sporadic drunken flirtations throughout the month--usually in the street—followed by a sober, cold shoulder had worn thin. Whatever she may have thought she wanted out of life, Pae knew it did not include him. He was a temporary diversion and nothing more. He did not mind; he just hated the idea of being used despite Charlene having said she did not believe in using people. But then, she had contradicted herself in several ways. He still hoped to build a friendship, but doubts continued to mount. Pae was convinced his association with Charlene would remain superficial at best.

Charlene had begun leaving her house at sunrise. She often returned after midnight but occasionally would not show up until a day or two later. Her mannerisms troubled Pae, but he respected that she had her own life. He missed her, regardless.

Of little consolation was Pae's relationship with Sherri-Lynn. Though frequently together, they were not attached at the hip. Like Charlene, Sherri-Lynn was cautious and more reserved than in their initial meeting. She had not subsequently admitted any overt romantic interest in Pae, although she had dedicated a majority of her free time to him. Despite more her restrained behavior, the woman's fondness for the man's company was evident. Sherri-Lynn's countenance seemed to glow when they were together. On a few occasions, she had asked him to not visit. Though skeptical of his friend's unspoken reasons and tempted to give way to old insecurities, Pae elected instead to be content with Sherri-Lynn's requests. There were days he could have visited but had chosen not to. He had his own commitments just as Sherri-Lynn had hers.

Over the years, Pae had learned to quench his attachments to women who had no desire for him. With few exceptions, a majority of his perceived friendships--male and female--had been one-way streets.

Pae prized wisdom, emotional maturity, and consistency, but he often struggled to maintain a level head, especially when the pendulum swung in the opposite direction. Depression had been as integral a part of his life as joy: until recent years, it had dominated the man's behavior.

Pae attracted a wide range of personalities. Unfortunately, he lacked strong social skills. As a result, the awkward male had tended to over-attach himself to anyone willing to offer sympathy, comfort, or friendship. He had discovered the roots of his clingy habits during cognitive therapy, and through practice, had managed to kill most of them. With few exceptions, Pae had learned to distinguish the differences between when to engage in unfettered communications and when to participate in idle chit-chat. Even so, social interactions still seemed a rockier process of trial and error to Pae than to most people he knew, at least from his perspective.

Pae enjoyed Sherri-Lynn's friendship but was careful to respect her boundaries and even more mindful to guard his own. If she needed time alone, that was fine by him. Sherri-Lynn had proven herself reliable by returning to Pae's company at each appointed time and place. She never *flaked-out* on him by changing her mind at the last minute or by not showing up, as was Charlene's habit.

Pae continued his routines of gym and spa visits, bookstore and coffee shop loitering, and exploration of other towns. He attended the church in Palafox on Sundays and helped with volunteer activities during the week, although he still had difficulty with crowds--a mild phobia with which he had struggled since childhood. Even if a particular experience had been among the best Pae could remember, he would sometimes take a break from people. Personal hangups notwithstanding, it was good to have life settle into a predictable rhythm and more fulfilling despite the hide-and-go-seek behaviors of his female companions.

OCTOBEr 28

October drifted by as uneventfully as September. The little platinum blonde girl had not returned. Pae had entered the woods behind his house many times but had uncovered no evidence she had been there. She was gone.

The turbulent dreams and the night terrors had subsided. Pae continued to pray for the girl and her family. He had passed the longhaired man who had claimed to be her father several times in Palafox. The man had ignored him even when they had once collided after cutting a corner on the same aisle in the grocery store. He had not so much as given Pae the *stink-eye* but had instead corrected his stride and kept moving. Pae had no idea what to make of this, but it did not sit well with him.

Public contacts with the longhaired man and his associates caused Pae to consider the years since his second divorce. Though he had encountered many bumps in the road, life had been the most tranquil he had experienced. Internally, he still had a lot of rough patches, but he had grown in leaps and bounds.

Peaceful habitations were unusual. Seven years of relative serenity did not fit the irregular and disruptive patterns of previous decades. Life had never afforded Pae this much long-term serenity. His spiritual life--the practice of his faith--had diminished over the years. Tranquility had made him complacent.

Until his meeting with Reverend Smalls, Pae had ignored increasing urges to mingle with society. Relative anonymity had become comfortable, but it bothered him. The more involved he became with Reverend Smalls' ministry, the more these concerns rose to the forefront of his mind. He started making strides to break free of complacency. His faith was building once again after almost a decade of lying dormant. In the light of this upswing, Pae sensed an approaching shift. He did not know why it troubled him.

WiNTEr: ONe YEAr PRiOr

Fear-induced adrenaline raced through the boy's veins. He quivered from the biological tempest that swept his body and from winter's penetrating chill. The ground moved back and forth beneath him as he swung suspended from a tree branch by one ankle. The rope dug in like teeth. Pressure mounted in the small child's head the longer he hanged. He screamed but was silenced by duct tape. His other leg and his arms were free. He flailed about with his fingers spread, trying to grab hold of anything he could to steady himself. The boy's buttocks flexed and seized, and his legs stiffened as something struck his bum, hard. The frigid late afternoon air licked the child's new wound like acid.

"You gonna bite another customer, you worthless little shit?" a tall, slim, tattoo-covered man with long, black-and-gray hair barked with a reserved calm in his voice. He held a heated, two-foot segment of rubber garden hose. He was dressed for the cold, as were a girl and a large redheaded woman who were both spectating. The females sat upon the steps of an old refrigerator-white trailer, huddled together as they poured brandy into steaming mugs of cocoa. They watched with sadistic pleasure.

"You wanna keep those teeth, you filthy little cock sucking faggot?" The man whacked the boy a second and third time in an X-pattern across his lower buttocks and upper thighs.

"Do you like that? Huh? Did that feel good? Was it worth you sinking your teeth into that customer's balls, you little man-whore?"

The man removed one of his gloves and used his bare fingers to twist a large welt that had formed on the rear of one of the boy's thighs. The child writhed in agony. Rapid, low-pitched noises escaped the duct tape. The child's face was red. Veins stood out as his head turned purple.

"Evil little queer!" the large redheaded woman shouted. She swished some brandy in her mouth then spat it in the direction of the small, dangling boy. "You're full of Satan, you nasty little demon!"

The girl giggled, "*It* sure acts like it belongs tied up outside!" She smirked at the woman then called to the younger child, "You're not supposed to bite the balls that feed us, you dumb little hillbilly!"

The little boy gagged on his saliva. He snorted and choked as mucus filled his nose. He cried and flailed and screamed. He clawed at the tape over his mouth. His hands and arms were met with fiery pain as the cut segment of hose struck them in retaliation.

"You bite another customer, and I'll knock every damn one of those ragged little teeth out of your sorry little head. Then you can swallow cock like Grandma Moses! Hell, they might even like that better? How's that grab you, you little shit stain? You can gum for cum!"

The man striped-up the boy's backside again. The child swayed and uttered a terrified, muffled scream. The man pulled a large knife out from under his coat and cut the rope that suspended his ankle. The boy's outstretched hands broke his fall. The frozen ground felt like cement, and the leaves, twigs, and dead grass like needles.

"*It* looks like it's cold." The preteen girl observed the beaten, pale, shivering boy as he lay on the ground. "I could squat and piss on *it*!" She laughed.

The large redheaded woman chuckled and sipped her brandy-laced cocoa. "Hell, I could sit on *it*! I'm sure I could conjure a fart or two to warm the nasty little cunt!"

The man directed the girl, "Candy! Get *it* up from there and take *it* inside. Pile some blankets on *it* until *it* settles down and gets its color back. We don't want the damn thing to go defective and break or stop working altogether."

"Can't I take *it* to the van and leave *it* with that other one instead? Why does *it* have to keep stayin' inside with us?"

"Do what you're told!"

"*It's* kinda heavy," the girl complained.

"So? Drag *it*."

The girl sat her mug beside the trailer steps, then took the child by his ankles and rolled him onto his back. The large woman stood and opened the trailer door then stepped aside.

"I think *its* dirty little pee-pee is about to snap off. *Its* nasty balls already turned blue and sucked up inside."

Candy dragged the naked boy across the frozen ground and up the metal trailer steps. A trace amount of blood had dried in the child's nostrils along with a wad of green mucus. Tears dried on his cheeks. The boy's bloodshot eyes were narrow, puffy slits. The stabbing hot pain from the raised red welts was intensified by the abrasions from being dragged. He continued to vibrate from adrenaline, fear, and cold. His mind drifted.

He thought about the warm season and the playful squirrels and birds, and the frogs, crickets, and other woodland creatures, even the snakes. He thought about the trees, the wild daisies and dandelions, the honeysuckles, blueberries, and blackberries, the wild scallions, and the sour green clover. He recalled the creek with its minnows, crawdads, and tadpoles. He considered the vast blue sky, and the sun, the stars, and the moon. He reflected upon all the wonders in the great big world out there. He sobbed, masked by duct tape, and silently cried out in his secret language, just as he had for as far back as he could remember.

OCTOBEr 29: AfTERNOOn

"**Y**ou really gotta give him a bath! He's getting ripe!" Pae overheard a low voice not far above a whisper in the adjoining diner booth. He was not sure, but he thought he recognized it from the unsavory encounters in late July and mid-August. He sipped his coffee and attuned his aural sense.

"The part that needs to be clean gets cleaned," a second low voice replied.

Yep. That second voice is definitely familiar! Difficult to forget someone who talks so much while they make threats. No doubt it's that longhaired fellow and his buddy from the blue pickup truck. I don't remember seeing it in the lot, but then I wasn't looking for it.

"They're starting to complain," came the voice of the longhaired man's companion.

"Well, if they really want *it* to get cleaned up that bad, they can do it theirselves," the slender man replied.

It was difficult for Pae to hear the men's conversation past the tall wooden partition that separated the booths. He was careful to avoid making too much noise while he sipped his coffee. It was too easy to drown out their muffled words. Pae's hearing had suffered during the war. He could no longer receive some frequencies.

The longhaired man continued, "*It* gets cleaned once every two weeks, and if *it* ain't up to their liking, they can go to hell! Damn in-laws! Their whiny asses will get charged double if *it* comes back any different than *it* goes out. They can wait six months for their next visit, too. See how they like that!"

Pae thought he heard the larger man mumble something. The slender one responded, "Don't look at me like that! That's the way it is, and that's how it's gonna be! They can kiss my ass or kiss each other's asses for all I care."

"Well, damn, Mark, at least wash his clothes!"

Mark, huh? Pae thought. *At least now I know his name, not that it does me any good. I see he's still the same character as the three times he crossed me. He hasn't changed a bit.*

"What the hell did I just say? Huh? Did I stutter? Do you need a hearing aid? Shut your damn mouth and stop being a fuckin' parrot! You are not a go-between for them. You answer to me! You seem to have forgotten that? You wanna push it? Then, by all means, push it! See what I'll do! Try me!"

"I'm sorry, boss."

"I ain't your damn BOSS, bitch! Mind your fuckin' mouth if you value that tongue! 'Baws-man' is fine. I got no problem with that, but I ain't no damn BOSS!"

"I'll let 'em know, baws-man...double charge if they clean him up in any way."

"Damn right! Better not so much as even run a comb through *its* hair. *It* was born without a soul. *It* don't deserve no special treatment. Now, shut the hell up or talk about something else. We're in public, asshole!"

Pae avoided the town of Palafox when he wasn't engaged in church activities or buying groceries. It was a bastion of negative energy. The locals were an awkward mix of polite, courteous, and hospitable on one hand, and downright rude and nasty on the other. Sure, you get that in every town no matter where you go, but here it seemed as if it were a near equal hot-and-cold split right down the middle with no moderation in-between. The town hosted a peculiar chasm among personalities. Friendly or not, few of the townspeople were sociable. The majority treated Pae as an outsider. His church affiliation and increased exposure to the community had not changed that. The whole place felt on edge. It had been that way since Pae had visited in May after moving into Knollwood. What he had just overheard in the adjoining booth helped confirm why he had preferred to avoid this town and set out instead for the further reaches in neighboring Henshaw County where Sherri Lynn worked.

Pae raised his coffee cup and took a deep whiff of his dark roasted, caffeinated beverage. The heavenly aroma added a little joy to the otherwise unpleasant situation he eavesdropped upon. He had been on a near-complete fast from all foods and snacks for the past week and had increased time spent in prayer at the church office with Reverend Smalls away from the distractions of his daily routines. The café-diner was his refuel point afterward. Pae stopped there to drink a sweetened cup of black coffee, or to have a glass milk with a side of bacon, and a glass of water so that he would have the energy to make the drive home.

Pae wondered about the new child that had been introduced into this bizarre picture, a boy of whom he had never heard, in the same predicament as that little girl who had appeared and then vanished three months ago. He sipped his coffee and listened but heard no more conversation.

The two men sat and mumbled a few vague words over the next several minutes, then stood and departed. A waitress walked to the booth they had vacated.

Another, at the counter, asked, "Did they stiff you again?"

"Not completely. The dicks left two dimes."

"Yahoo! You're rich, bae!"

"One of the pigs left me his phone number again."

"Which one?"

"Which one do you think?"

The young lady's coworker laughed. "That Steven Tyler wannabe?"

"You got it! I would snitch-out his scrawny ass to his old lady, but knowing her, she'd snap that little twig in half then try to put the moves on me! Find her some waitress love!"

The other woman laughed harder. "I've seen her hang out with some *grody* looking women. I wouldn't doubt for one minute that she's into it!"

"Watch it, girl! You know I'm into it, but *ugh*! Not with that! I like mine clean and at least halfway domesticated! And did you just say, 'grody looking'?" The younger waitress cackled. "What, are you living back in the seventies or something?"

"That's from the eighties, my dear, and no. I'm not *that* old! Damn, girl! I pick up some outdated phrases when I visit my parents."

"As long as you don't pick up on anything too strange, I guess?"

"You got me beat on that one, bae. Steven Tyler wants to rock your world!"

"Girl, you're nasty! The real Steven Tyler can rock my world any day! I don't care that he's a male or how old he is! But that gross hick with his jungle beast? Hell, no!"

Pae chuckled at the exchange. *Finally,* he thought, *I can enjoy my coffee!*

SPRINg: TWo YEARs PRIOr

Long red orb descends behind an ashen shroud
Faceless giants loom; they stare and frown
Outstretched arms whisper in the breeze
Pale grey mistress is set free
Her veil spread wide
Draped to the earth
Three now sleep
One steps forth

The trailer was fogged with smoke. A strange, almost metallic odor filled the room, reminiscent of the smell of locked up tractor-trailer brakes. Slow, melodic, synthesizer-infused hard rock music drifted from the speakers of a portable sound dock. Two men sat at the kitchen table, playing cards. Two others sat in the living room, one in a chair and the other on a sofa. A preteen girl retrieved a bottle of cola from the refrigerator. She set it next to some rum and two glasses. A bag of ice was on the countertop. The girl wore a pair of sheer burgundy shorts-style panties that were laced on the left hip, and an elastic yellow-and-black wedding garter as a choker. The sound of growling dogs penetrated the thin exterior trailer walls. They barked then settled down after a male voice responded.

The girl poured two glasses of rum and cola as the trailer's front door opened. The chain on the top of the door stopped it from swinging too wide. Two men entered. They were dressed in denim trousers and boots, with lightweight suede leather jackets that were opened in the front. Their foreheads and the fronts of their T-shirts were soaked in sweat. Their clothing was dusted with soil.

"It's dark as hell out there," one of them remarked. "I thought we'd be burying those three little bastards all night. It would be nice if you weren't so damn picky, Mark."

"I'm a businessman, Wade," a man with long, graying black hair replied from the sofa. "I'm only interested in quality that brings in cash. Candy and that thing in there is the best two money makers I got. That other little blonde one is still pulling her weight, too. Piss on the rest of 'em! If we need more, we got plenty of connections. They can be snatched up damn near anywhere. All it takes is a dumbass woman burying her nose in her phone. *Swoop!* 'Where's my little Jethro?' Hell, we can make our own, if push comes to shove. It'll take a little time, but why not? You never can tell?"

"Yeah, well, those three are in the ground. We put 'em far enough out that your worthless-ass brother and his merry little band of swine won't come sniffing. We left the shovels against the propane tank. Why the hell do you let him anywhere near us, anyway?"

"Because he's the best security we have against his kind. There's nothing better than having a man on the inside running interference, especially if he's kin. He knows blood is thicker than water. So, what if he and a few of his deputies want to get their poles greased on the side? We couldn't secure this operation well enough without 'em. There's a price to be paid for everything. Now, quit bitchin' and make yourselves at home. Y'all boys showed up just in time."

Mark pointed toward the hallway with a longneck beer bottle in his hand. An obese redheaded woman escorted a nude four-year-old boy to the living room threshold. The woman wore a long, tie-dyed T-shirt that covered her hips. A pair of red panties showed from beneath. She ushered the toddler aside so she could continue into the kitchen without him.

"You got them drinks poured yet?" the woman asked the half nude preteen girl.

"I'm workin' on it."

The man on the sofa raised his voice, "Candy, get Wade and Bruno a couple o' cold ones!" He looked at the two men. "Grab them other two chairs out of the kitchen."

The men entered the kitchen then returned with chairs and bottles of beer.

"Hey, Lance! Bubba!" the longhaired man called to the two playing cards. "Y'all take a look at this!"

The sound of plastic stoppers skidding on vinyl arose as one of the men in the kitchen rotated his chair. The girl reached into an ashtray on the table and picked up the rolled joint the man and his card-playing partner had been sharing. She took a *hit* off the marijuana and offered it to the woman.

Once the men's eyes were on the toddler, the man on the sofa directed him, "Now, show 'em what I taught you. Sing!"

The boy held his head down and fidgeted with his hands. He glanced in the directions of each of the spectators, shifting his eyes back and forth between them and the floor.

The man raised his voice. "Don't get all shy on me now. Sing it, nice and loud so everybody can hear."

The toddler's nervous voice arose. "Yummy, yummy, yummy..." he hesitated, "I got..." the tiny tot paused again, trying to recall the words, "cum...in my tummy."

The small gathering chortled. Bruno nudged Wade with his elbow. Bubba and Lance made *catcalls*. Lance applauded. "Bravo!" he howled.

Candy rolled her eyes and shook her head. "Little bitch." She took another drag off the joint then swallowed some rum and cola.

The woman took a drink. "Yeah, I hear ya. His little golden child."

The longhaired man nodded and winked with a somber expression. He offered a slow, mocking clap with his beer bottle in his hand. "Good job, little shit." A cigarette bounced on his lips. "You earned a banana!"

Bobby hollered, "Uh-oh! Does that mean what I think it means? Which one of us gets to give it to him?"

"None of you broke dicks!" the dark-haired man replied. "You ain't got the cash, and there ain't no freebies except for the law."

"And him," the preteen girl turned up her nose. She took another drink of mixed alcohol. The woman had been a half step behind and eyeballing the young girl the whole time. She placed her hand on the child's butt.

"Bitch, get your skank paw off my ass! I don't belong to you!"

"Candy!" the dark-haired man called out.

"Yeah? What?"

"Give the knob gobbler a banana and take *it* back to *its* hole, then slide over here and warm me up some."

"I can warm you up," the large woman told him.

"I didn't ask you. You can warm me up later on when it's time to crash."

"I don't want to wait that long," the woman replied, coming in from the kitchen, holding her rum.

"Then warm up one of them!"

The men looked at each other.

"Any takers?" the woman asked as she looked at the other five men. She pulled her panties to her ankles with one hand--sloshing the drink and spilling some on the floor as she did--then kicked them into the middle of the living room floor. "I know you prefer lean beef, but we only serve up rump roast with a side of pork out here. I have an appetite for a mini fish taco, but I can't have that. My loss is your gain. I can use my imagination!"

One of the men stood. "It's your call, Mark. She's your old lady."

"Have at it, Bobby," the dark-haired man replied. "Hell, you can all swing your bats at her."

The woman took Bobby by the hand. "The more, the merrier," she grinned, looking at the remaining four.

"Naw, we're good," Lance replied as he scratched his beard and looked at Bubba sitting across from him. "We got a game to finish." He turned and addressed the girl. "Give me that *weed* back."

The girl inhaled once more then dangled it in front of him. "Tell me you love me."

"To the moon and back, darlin'."

"So full of shit," the girl said in a sarcastic tone. She returned what was left of the marijuana, then pulled on one leg opening of her panties and exposed herself. "Dream on, you fat fuck!" The child turned and slapped her butt then flipped off Lance as she grinned and winked. Lance chuckled and returned the wink.

"I'll stay in here and shoot the breeze with Mark," Bruno told the woman. Wade did not respond.

"Suit yourselves. I'll have plenty of room for seconds if y'all change your minds. Y'all's sweat don't bother me none. Hell, I like it wet and *gamey!* It's more like cooter that way."

Candy took another drink, then left the kitchen. She gave the toddler a banana without the peel. "I swear, I don't know what makes you so damn special?" she told the boy.

The little one took the banana with both hands and gnawed it. Candy yanked one of his arms and hurried him into the first room in the hallway. "At least that other little tramp in the van knows her place. It should have been you that got planted."

OCTOBEr 30: 3:12 Am

Pae tossed, and turned, and rolled. He was in a dead sleep. He placed the backs of his hands over his eyes then rubbed them back and forth while he moaned and uttered noises as if chewing his tongue in a mucus-filled deluge. He was trapped in a charcoal fog that pulled on his throat and face. His skin crawled. It felt rubbery, dry, and tacky. He thought he was covered in dried vomit. Pae heard breathing that was not his own.

"Master prepares," he heard a voice say. "Dine!"

Pae knew the words were not directed at him. He heard a low, drawn-out groan that made his stomach sour, followed by the sound of a little girl, humming.

Repeating shrieks rang out. Pae remembered such blood-curdling cries from when he was a boy sleeping at his grandparents' house, awakened by raccoons and foxes taking chickens during the night. He saw an adolescent white rabbit being dragged away by a hind leg. The tiny animal was in its death throes, splitting the air with shrill, heart-stopping screeches, certain of its demise. Pae could not see what was taking it. Soft weeping arose, followed by another sickening groan. It was slow and repetitive.

"Watcher!" a voice whispered. "Seer!"

A chill raced up Pae's spine.

A fortress wall appeared. Small, square holes lined the foundation, large enough for a single fist to reach through. Pae heard heavy footsteps like stomps on a hollow wooden floor. The commotion died.

"Touch," a low, gravel-like voice snarled. Pae felt downward pressure on his pillow beside his head.

Pae awoke. The green digital display on his clock changed to 3:13. He uncovered himself, then sat on the edge of his bed with his arms around his abdomen. He rocked back and forth, feeling sicker than he had in years. The man hurried toward the bathroom but vomited a little on the floor along the way. Once at the toilet, the weakened male collapsed to his knees and held his head over the bowl. He dry-heaved several times and belched repeatedly. He could still hear breathing but deduced it was his own. The smell of sulfur lingered in the man's nostrils. He wasted no time praying, though his face remained over the fouled toilet water. Pae knew the dream had been serious.

OCTOBEr 31: MORNINg, THe WEe HOURs

" Flower," a voice whispered. An ethereal aroma filled the air. It was delectable! Another voice said, "Open."

A hole was torn into a frail silver membrane that resembled a facial tissue.

Three others took turns, saying, "Trample," "Ruin," and "Seal."

A sixth voice hissed, "Murder."

The membrane turned black as it was shredded. Thunder rumbled. The flames of three candles struggled against a rising wind. Sprinkles of water fell, but they did not hit the shredded membrane.

A closed fist emerged. The knuckles faced upward. Wisps of pink and gold smoke escaped from between the fingers with a sickening moan. The rain intensified. The closed fist rolled over.

A charcoal gray tornado emerged from a sea of blackness. The rain turned to blood and was sucked into the cyclone with the pieces of the shredded membrane and the flames from two of the candles. The hand rose and began to open. The light from the third candle intensified. The two wicks that had lost their flames to the dark, twisting wind continued to smolder. They glowed orange, but they did not reignite. The colored smoke from the opened hand and the moaning voice were also pulled into the tornado. The images dissolved. Sounds of a violent struggle ensued.

Pae yelped when he awoke. Something had struck his jaw. He sat up, wondering whether he had hit himself. He used to flail about during night terrors in his younger years and had once slapped himself with an arm deadened from loss of circulation. He pressed his fingers against his face but sensed no residual pain. He had full sensation in both hands. All was well until he surveyed the room. It was chilled from the night air and lit with a pale, bluish-white light. He thought it was intense moonlight until he realized he could see the contents of the other rooms in the house as if there were no walls. He twisted to look over both shoulders. He saw everything in a dim haze.

What's happening? Am I still asleep? Pae looked at his clock. As with the morning before, it was 3:13 a.m.

Again?

Pae glanced away from the clock. The bedroom was as it had always been. He could no longer see into the other rooms. The pale, blue light was gone. It was dark except for splashes of moonlight sifting through the box fan and between the drapes. He sat in bed, listening to himself breathe. The house was dead silent. A faint wind whistled past the fan blades causing them to gently rotate. It was still unplugged, just as he had left it.

A little deeper in the woods, along a private dirt road, a small boy tossed and rolled as he slept inside an old mobile home. The child wallowed, and groaned, and shivered under an insufficient blanket as he dreamed in the chilled October air. The foul odor of unwashed, urine-stained material permeated the room. He heard voices laugh in his dream. He knew they laughed at hlm.

One of the voices said, "At next sunset, you will know the lie behind your name; God will not remember!"

The boy did not know his name. He had never heard it. The laughter increased. There were laughs from many voices.

"God hates! He abandons and forsakes!" the voice added.

The child sucked his thumb. He cried but did not wake. The dream imprisoned him. He heard a sound he did not recognize: the sound of shovels breaking soil.

"Six, six!" called a voice that resembled a child's. It transformed into an adult male's tone as it declared, "Seven shall not arrive! No completion!"

"At next sunset, the petals fall," the first voice muttered. "This day, the flower dies."

The boy heard another whisper, "They approach!"

"Scream your inane babblings into the ears of the deaf spirit!" a voice uttered then laughed. It shook the boy's soul.

An abrasive, raspy voice yelled, "Abandoned! Forgotten! Forgotten! No hope!"

"Sleep with them," another whispered.

The boy saw images of birds and squirrels falling out of the trees. He saw the fish and tadpoles and frogs float, stiff and unmoving, to the surface of the creek. Snakes rolled onto their backs and kinked-up into tight, contorted knots. Flowers wilted; their petals shriveled, lost their color, and fell. The tot saw the three children who had previously shared the room with him, lying side-by-side, face-down and motionless. He saw the blonde girl his own age who had recently occupied the van behind the trailer. He watched the dim, red sun sink below a darkening horizon.

The child smelled an odor more putrid than any that had ever entered his nostrils. It was worse than when he had soiled his clothing and more intolerable than the dead, swollen skunk he had come across along the state highway. He heard a low, humming growl. It accompanied quick, rhythmic thumps upon his chest out of sync with his heartbeat.

"It shall open beyond its reach," a voice quietly echoed. "The clock will stop. The dogs will feast!"

The boy felt downward pressure on the side of his face. "No hope for others! The days incomplete! In the grave, this hope shall sleep!"

The child awoke. He curled into a fetal position and pulled the small blanket over his head. He stared through the opening as he sucked his thumb and shivered. A shadow, darker than the enveloping night, loomed before him. Within the shadow was a pair of much blacker eyes. The little boy heard breathing from inside the room. It was not his own.

OCTOBEr 31: EARLy AFTERNOOn

"You get the milkshake maker cleaned up?" the slim man with long salt-and-pepper hair asked.

"Yeah, it's ready," his large, redheaded female partner replied.

"You wiped it down good? All over?"

"Top to bottom, just like you said. I used those wipes you told me to use. I did a bunch of extra detailing on the top end; spent hours on it; worked my damn fingers to the bone."

The man looked around impatiently. "Well, where is it?"

"I put it back in storage."

"Well, take it out. We got some new clients comin', and they're going to pay a premium. They got some kind of a celebration planned that they want to use it for. Halloween party, I guess? They already fronted part of the money."

"How much they gonna pay in all?"

"Let me put it this way: you'll have a real orgasm, not that fake shit you try to pull on me all the time."

The woman's eyes widened. She grinned with a puzzled brow. "You're shittin' me?"

The longhaired man took a drag off his cigarette and asked, "Do I look like I'm shittin' you? I'll be able to get you that *cherry* condition '77 Town Car over in Farley that you been actin' all stupid over for the past few months."

"What about you? What're you gonna get outa this?"

"Let's just say that you and me's both gonna be makin' out like bandits. Now, go get that milkshake maker and make sure it's presentable. Bobby and his boys have an eye on things. Lance will be along soon to pick it up for delivery."

OCTOBEr 31: DUSk

The time has come...

Autumn had delivered her annual promise of barren limbs woven into a tapestry of bright yellow, red, brown, and rust-colored foliage and evergreens against sullen gray and amber skies. The air was cool and crisp as the sun languished into a dull red ellipse and sank behind the trees. The wind carried a hint of burning timber from distant fires. The sounds of teenage horseplay arose. Barks and howls from dogs echoed throughout the tiny rural community of Palafox accompanied by knocks on doors followed by the phrase, *"Trick or treat!"*

Halloween had arrived.

The K-12 school's gymnasium and surrounding portable buildings had been converted into a haunted house as the school grounds played host to a traveling carnival. Two sheriff's department cruisers patrolled the main street through town and the intersecting residential streets. Two others sat in attendance at the school parking lot, accompanied by two state trooper cruisers and one police vehicle from a neighboring town. A fire engine and a paramedic's van were on standby.

Several dozen adults and costumed children covered the school grounds, throwing darts, plastic rings, and baseballs in attempts to win stuffed animals and nick-knacks. Some threw pies at faces peering through holes in a wall. Others entertained themselves at a face-painting booth. A small assortment of rides satisfied patrons who craved adrenaline rushes. Some rode in circles upon the backs of two donkeys, a mule, and a horse. A haunted rail car in a carnival trailer and a mirrored fun house welcomed all who dare not endure the cheap grotesque horrors of the haunted gymnasium. Some patrons strolled casually, having enjoyed their fill of carnival rides, taking breaks to eat cotton candy, caramel apples, and corn dogs. The air was filled with the odors of barbecue, mustard, and deep-fried treats. Everyone was enjoying the evening in their own way.

The sleepy little town of Palafox was abuzz with the celebration of All Hallow's Eve. As usual, those who governed, and those who most influenced them, ensured the perfect veneer of country family fun for the sakes of all who visited, especially those from neighboring towns and counties. The demons, spooks, witches, and goblins were contained within the confines of patrolled streets and monitored school grounds. Evil was latex, vinyl, plastic, and elastic. The town's devils were tidy and sanitized.

NOVEMBEr 1: MORNINg

Pae was awakened by bangs on the front door. The deadbolt rattled against the strike plate. "Damn it!" he barked as his heart shot into his feet. He arose with rubber knees, wanting to give whoever was on the other side a pounding of their own.

"Lunatic hayseeds giving people heart attacks at zero-dark-thirty in the morning!" the man grumbled. "No consideration at all!"

Pae approached the door in flannel pajamas with his pistol loaded and a round chambered. Using his slipper-clad foot as a barricade, he unlocked the door then eased it open. A dull ray of light splashed through. The sun had not yet peeked from behind the trees. Pae was surprised: a young girl with dyed black hair fashioned into hooped braids, and dark reddish-blonde eyebrows greeted him. Pae estimated she was twelve years old but no older than fourteen.

"Have you seen my little sister?" the young girl asked while chewing bubblegum open-mouthed. "She's about this tall." The girl held her hand several inches above her waist. She appeared to be at least six months pregnant. She wore a black leather jacket over a short maternity dress and over-the-knee striped socks with high wedge sneakers.

Poor hick child, Pae thought. *I'll bet this is the girl Charlene was telling me about?*

Most of the girl's proportions were different than Charlene had described, no doubt brought on by the pregnancy.

If this is the same girl, it's pretty easy to see why she stopped drifting around.

A chill ran up Pae's spine when he looked the girl in the eyes. They were beautiful, but every bit as sinister as Charlene had described. Their darkness far exceeded what he had observed in the little platinum girl.

This has to be the same girl she described?

"No, I can't say that I've seen her," Pae answered. "When did you see her last?"

"Can I come inside and wait for her?" The girl tried to look past Pae into the house.

"No, I'm sorry. If you are who I think you are, then your daddy and I had a talk a little while back. He told me to not associate with you girls. As much as I'd love to help, I can't get involved."

The girl's brows sank and narrowed. Her eyes registered confusion. She huffed, then looked away and chewed on a fingernail. After a few seconds, she dropped her head and glanced at Pae through beaming puppy dog portals. The ends of the girl's mouth turned upward in a devious grin.

"I can make it worth your while," the girl cocked her head to the side with a fingertip between her teeth. Her brows jumped. She turned aside and hiked her maternity dress high enough for Pae to see her hip. Chill bumps raised on her thigh and buttock. She wore no panties.

Why, of all the places on earth, Pae wondered, *did I think I would be able to get away from it all by moving out here? I've jumped right into the middle of it! This place is a nuthouse!*

"No, I think it would be easier for you to find her if you keep moving. She could be stuck in a ditch or something? You never can tell?"

The girl flashed an artificial smile. "Are you sure you don't want some, anyway?"

"Thank you for the offer, but no. I'm sure your little sister needs you more than I do?"

"Okay, well, thank you." The girl rolled her eyes, then turned and trotted off the shallow cement steps. "Stuck in a ditch, my ass!" she mumbled. She saw Charlene, who had been alerted by the pounding on Pae's door, watching through a window.

"What'r' you starin' at, you ragged, washed-up old cunt?" the girl howled at Charlene. "You see this?" she opened her jacket wide and hiked her maternity dress over her belly with one hand and pointed at it with the other. She was fully exposed without the slightest thought of modesty. "I got me one! Where's yours, you dried up, barren ole witch?" Charlene stepped away from her window.

Pae closed his front door. Though troubling, the girl's visit put to rest some of his fears. *She must still be alive, or at least she had been until last night?* Pae walked to the other end of the house to open the kitchen door. He propped it with a brick sheathed in a sewn, padded, cloth cover then turned on a portable music dock. He raised the volume so it could be heard from outside, then he waited. After several hours, Pae turned off the music, locked the house, and departed.

Pae arrived at Spanky's just shy of noon. As usual, Sherri-Lynn greeted him as he entered. "Well, hey there, stranger! How are you?"

Pae avoided the small talk. "Are you serious, I mean truly serious, about our friendship?"

Sherri-Lynn studied Pae's expression. He looked washed out, almost gray, and peaked. "I have a feeling you're gonna drop a bomb on me, but yeah, I am serious about our friendship. I would never have done what I did with you in a million years had I not felt something unique enough to convince me you were worth it. The times we've spent together since then have been nothing to sneeze at, either. So yeah, I meant it. Somehow, though, I doubt you're approaching me about your neighbor lady or about us? This is about that little girl, isn't it?"

"You're one hell of a smart lady. Yes, it is."

"Well, shug, I do have a physics degree and a lifetime of reading people. One has nothing to do with the other, but what they both say is that there really is a brain behind my eyes. I am not one of those Searcy's from down near Mobile. Now, before I second guess our relationship and refuse, how can I help you and that little girl?"

"Would you mind if we talked outside?"

A chill washed over Sherri-Lynn. She walked into the parking lot with Pae. He gazed into her eyes. "I might need to hide her out soon."

"Honey, you need to leave."

Pae took a step back, shocked by Sherri-Lynn's response.

"Do you have any idea the kind of trouble you could get into with the law? And you want to pull me into it with you?"

Pae bit his lip, trying to figure out what to say.

Sherri-Lynn continued. "Now, look, I appreciate where your heart is, I honestly do. If something terrible really is going on with that poor child, I can certainly understand, but you've got to seriously, and I mean *seriously,* think about the consequences if you try to take her! Bad situation or not, you're best off figuring out a way to get the law involved. I think you are a wonderful, wonderful man! You have the most awesome heart I have ever seen, but your thinking needs some work! You need to go and sort through this before you make a horrible mistake!"

Pae still did not know how to respond, so he listened.

"Now, I appreciate you coming to me, and I stand by what I said. We are friends, and on a level, I have never allowed anyone else to approach, much less during a first encounter. I think I already mentioned that? Maybe I've said it several times? I am not flippant with words like that, Pae! You are a truly special human being, but I've got to be forthright and brutally honest with you because I do respect you, and I most definitely respect myself. Your coming here to ask me something like that is pretty damn insulting! You took consideration for that little girl, and rightfully so. You took consideration of your feelings toward her situation, but you did *not* think of me *AT ALL,* short of wanting to take advantage! Not in the slightest! You take your ass on out of here and think about that!"

Pae had not expected to be scolded, but Sherri-Lynn's points were valid.

"Forgive me. I am deeply, deeply sorry! Please forgive me!" Pae looked away. His apology, though sincere, felt hollow. He was not able to convey what was going through his mind. "I feel ashamed," was the best he could offer. He dropped his head, then raised it and looked at the tree line across the parking lot and past the rural two-lane blacktop.

"You're right. You're absolutely right," Pae added, "I'll heed your words. I'll take them seriously. Thank you for your honesty, Sherri-Lynn." He knew his response sounded choppy and perhaps insincere. As in the old days during cognitive therapy, he was shutting down, hard.

Pae found the courage to look into Sherri-Lynn's eyes again. "One last thing…"

"Yes?" Sherri-Lynn angled her head to one side and folded her arms.

"You already know that Pae is my nickname. I've been told it means *peace*. My real name means *beloved one*. The historic Hebrew implication is *loved by God*. It also means *friend*. The name is quite common, but most people are unaware of the meaning. I'm telling you this because the meaning is deeply significant to me. The modern name is too common and easily overlooked. I don't know why I am only telling you this now? I just felt that for whatever reason, it needed to be said."

Sherri-Lynn glanced at Pae. She looked strange. He could not read her.

"I'd better go now," Pae said.

Sherri-Lynn did not say a word. She went back inside, leaving Pae in the parking lot. Troubled, he sighed and returned to his car. He prayed as he walked.

Tiny saw Sherri-Lynn as she passed the bar on her way toward the back. Her arms were still crossed. She was rubbing them with her hands.

"You okay, Sherri-Lynn?" Tiny asked.

"Yeah, I'm fine."

"No, you ain't. You're cryin'. Do you need me to have some words with that friend of yours?"

"No, Tiny." Sherri-Lynn stopped. "To be perfectly honest, for the first time in my life, I think I might be falling in love?"

"Oh… Well… Okay? I reckon I'll leave him be, then?"

"Thank you, Tiny." Sherri-Lynn smiled. A tear shot down her cheek. "I need some time to think."

"You got it. One more thing, little sister."

"Yeah?"

"In the twelve years I been bouncin' here, I ain't never once seen or heard hide nor hair of you ever havin' the hots for any man. You've dated a few, but I ain't never seen no real spark. Shit, you're probably the oldest virgin on the face of the planet?"

"Thanks a lot!" Sherri-Lynn tried to laugh while she wiped her cheeks.

"He must be one hell of a man?"

"Maybe worthy of me giving up the last of my virginity someday?"

"I don't know how the hell you've managed for goin' on forty years, but I have nothin' but mad respect for you, little sister. If you decide he is the one, I'll invite you two over for dinner with me and Julia. It would be an honor to dine with the man who finally won your heart."

"Thank you. I'm gonna go out back and sit in my car for a bit."

"Take all the time you need. I'll talk to Spanky and the girls. We got you covered."

NOVEMBEr 2: ONe HOUr AFTEr SUNSEt

Her dark eyes were different. Whatever had once lain dormant behind them, inoculating her against horrors unknown, had been jarred awake and thrust into cataclysm. The girl's eyes were electrified yet colder and more inhuman than any Pae had ever seen. He was amazed to see the little platinum-haired girl had returned, but something was wrong, much worse than during their initial encounter. This time, her disturbed gaze locked into his without the slightest hesitation. She did not resemble a fish. Her dull, lifeless luster was gone. This time, she looked as if her soul had been run through a blender. The little doll's eyes reflected something her premature mind could not process or convey. Pae stared back into the girl's jittering brown eyes. His spirit felt drenched in the black ugliness of hell.

The child had arrived unannounced through the kitchen door. As during their previous encounter, Pae was undressed. Though it was just past sunset, he had bathed and was preparing to settle in early. He had not realized he had left the kitchen door unlocked. It had become an habitual practice since their first meeting. Pae's brushes with the man claiming to be the girl's father had diminished his hope and curbed his expectation of another visit by the girl. But being a creature of habit, he had not given much thought to his new practice of leaving the door unlocked each night until bedtime.

Pae had dried himself and placed his towel in the utility room that adjoined the kitchen when the child had arrived. He thought he had imagined hearing the spring expand across the screen door. The twist of the antique diamond-cut glass knob on the main kitchen door had convinced him otherwise. An intruder had arrived. He had no time to race through the kitchen to retrieve his pistol from the bedroom. The door had already swung open as he had exited the utility room. He was relieved when he had discovered he would not be fighting for his life in the nude feverishly swinging a kitchen knife.

"Sweetheart, what has happened to you?" Pae raised the girl's bangs to examine her forehead. He pressed on it, then explored her temples and crown and the base of her skull.

"What's making your eyes do that? Why are they jitter-bugging?"

Pae pressed a hand against the girl's chest while he held the other against her upper back. The child's heartbeat sounded fine though the rate was a little higher than he had expected. The girl kept a bead on him. Her bizarre optical vibrations started to slow.

Pae realized he was still undressed. "We've gotta stop meeting like this," he told the child. "Wait here. Don't go away."

The girl did not break eye contact until Pae turned away. He walked to the bathroom to extinguish the flames in the antique space heater. The girl did not watch him go. She stood transfixed with her head angled upward, and her vision locked in place as if the man were still before her.

Pae turned off the heater in the living room. He kept the one in the bedroom lit. The box fan had been removed, and the window dropped. Gas space heaters made Pae dizzy. A two-inch opening had been left to vent the heater's spent fumes. An old, yellowing white vinyl blind had been pulled to the level of the window's opening and the curtains tied back.

Pae returned to the girl, wearing a set of flannel pajamas.

"Well, I did say you are welcome here anytime, didn't I? Let me take a closer look at you, angel." He crouched to the girl's level then looked into her eyes. They no longer jittered. He proceeded to examine the girl from head to toe.

"You're all nice and spiffed up."

The girl's hair had been braided into cornrows. They merged into two loose, long ponytails, cinched by elastic bands with beads at the base of her skull, behind each ear. As before, a long patch of straight bangs covered the girl's brows. Though her hair was dirty, and leaves and twigs were stuck to it, Pae could smell the lingering scent of shampoo. He also detected traces of perfume behind the child's ears and at the base of her neck.

The child's eye sockets were dark and sunken, and the skin beneath her bloodshot eyes was purple and bagged. Her left ear was lined with the same studs he had seen the first time they had met, but a few were missing. Dried blood peppered the holes and smeared her lobes.

The little one's pink jacket had been laundered. It smelled clean, but it was riddled with patches of fresh soil and other outdoor stains. It contained rips Pae had not seen in July.

The child's fingernails were clean underneath and trimmed and polished. Her hands and face were smeared with dirt. The little one's glittered eye shadow and dark mascara was also smeared. Her nostrils were lined with dried blood.

The girl's lips were painted in glittered, deep plum lipstick. Most of it had rubbed off. A thick, dark crust resided in the corners of her mouth. Pae wiped one corner with a fingertip. A tiny fleck clung to the edge of his fingernail. He rubbed it with his thumb. It left a faint, powdered red smudge.

Pae rubbed the girl's rosy cheeks, open-handed with his thumbs. They were hot and puffy. Their hue was a little too red, brighter than the last time he had seen her. He looked closer. It was not rouge; her cheeks were flushed. Unlike their initial meeting, the girl's jacket was zipped all the way up to her chin. Curious, Pae pulled the zipper a few inches. The child's neck was red, swollen, and bagged as if filled with fluid.

"Please, no!" Pae whispered. The pit of his stomach soured.

He felt the youngster's forehead. She was roasting. A putrid stench met his nostrils.

"No, no, no! God, no!" he whispered, "Please don't let it be!"

Pae stopped whispering. "Let me see, precious. Do not be afraid. I will not hurt you." He hoped she believed him.

The girl did not respond. Pae turned her around. He saw a small, dark, wine-colored stain a little below the seat of her layered orange dress. The center of his chest burned while reluctant anticipation mounted. He hesitated for a few seconds then lifted the rear of her dress. An overpowering odor assaulted him as he pulled the layers upward, revealing a much larger stain on the seat of her tan hosiery. It covered the girl's crotch and extended downward toward her right ankle and several inches down her left leg, not quite to her knee.

The man groaned and released the little one's dress then hugged her. He kissed her forehead and took her cheeks into his hands while tears eased down his face.

"I'm going to take off your jacket. I have a feeling you have something else I need to see?"

The girl remained fixed in the man's eyes. Her black pupils were fully dilated, defying the light in the room. Her expression was as black as pitch. She stood, motionless.

Pae unzipped the child's jacket and removed it. Her forearms were covered in broken elliptical bite marks. Light traces of dried blood covered one of the impressions. It was a recent wound. Others like it were older and scarred. The bite patterns indicated they had been self-inflicted.

Pae stood and walked to the kitchen window that faced Charlene's house. He pressed his face against the glass and cupped his hands around his temples so he could overcome the reflection from the kitchen light. Charlene's house was dark. Her porch light was off. He tapped on the window as he considered the situation.

"What to do, what to do?"

He retrieved his phone from the bedroom and dialed Reverend Smalls' number. It went straight to voicemail. He tried Sherri-Lynn's number. It also went to voice mail. Pae bit his lip, trying to figure out his next move. He looked at the child then returned to her after a moment of contemplation.

"I'm gonna have to get a closer look. I don't know what else to do. I need to lift your dress again, precious. May I? Is that okay?"

The girl nodded.

Pae raised the back of the girl's dress, then took the elastic waistband of her hose with her panties then peeled them. She jerked and winced. He stopped pulling. Her panties were stuck to her skin. Pae kissed the girl's forehead, then stood and thought a little more. He redialed Reverend Smalls. Still no answer. He tried calling Sherri-Lynn once more. No answer there, either. He looked through the window. This time he noticed

Charlene's car was missing from the driveway. He considered calling Spanky's but changed his mind. Spanky's was more than fifty miles out. Pae mumbled a quick prayer then returned to the child.

"Don't be afraid, love. I'm going to clean you up then get you out of here. It is going to hurt a little, but it won't be on purpose. Your underwear will have to come off so I can take care of you."

Pae hugged the child then went to the sink for a glass of water. She remained in place, like a statue with limp, hanging arms. Pae turned the faucet and let the water run. The pop of the igniting water heater and the hiss of running gas issued from the utility room. Pae placed his wrist under the faucet to ensure the water temperature was comfortable. He filled the glass and returned to the girl.

"I'm going to pour this over your behind. It might sting, but it will help loosen up the *yuckies* so I can take your panties off. Is that okay?"

The small child did not respond. She trembled as Pae lifted her dress from behind to get leverage for the glass.

"This isn't going to work," Pae said. "Raise your arms, precious."

The girl raised her arms. Pae unzipped the back of the child's dress then untied the bow from around her waist. He pulled the dress over her head and discarded it on the floor. The girl's back was covered in red scratches and bruises. Pae turned the little one to examine her chest. Her nipples were bruised black and purple with red blotches and surrounded with impressions from sets of human teeth.

Pae almost cussed, but he restrained himself for the child's sake. "Beasts!" he whispered.

Pae turned the child's back to him again then poured the warm tap water into the girl's panties. He waited a few seconds before he detached her undergarments. They were filled with dried blood, urine, feces, and perspiration. Pae pulled the child's underwear to her knees. Some of the reconstituted fluids dribbled onto the floor and onto his free hand. He sighed then repositioned himself to examine the girl's vagina.

"No!" Pae gasped.

Facing the man was a circumcised penis and a pair of testicles. The skin around them was blotched with brown and purple bruises. Pae sat on the floor for a moment letting the visuals sink in. His eyes clouded with more tears.

"You're a boy!" Pae whispered. He recalled what he had told his psychiatrist four years earlier, the same thing he had told Sherri-Lynn in September. The man's conscience blazed. His heart turned to icy-hot, molten wax. Tears gushed forth. He pulled the child close and hugged him.

Please forgive me, Pae thought. He whispered, "You are not filthy just for being a boy!"

Pae released the child, then bowed his head to the floor and prayed while he sobbed. He remained on his knees after he calmed down. He straightened his torso, then cradled the back of the child's head in one hand and rubbed his back with the other. The side of Pae's face was pressed against the boy's chest. Pae's abdomen heaved as he cried. He leaned back and released his embrace. His butt plopped onto the antique vinyl covered floor.

The boy leaned forward and cupped Pae's cheeks. The distress in the child's eyes spoke volumes. Pae's psychological wounds ripped through his being like a knife-filled cyclone. Faded, decades-old memories reached into their rotted, black caverns and retrieved visuals and feelings of past agony; Pae's former hell was resurrected.

Pae and the child peered into each other's souls for what seemed a lifetime. Tears washed down the child's cheeks. His mascara ran. His tiny hand wiped Pae's tears in silence.

The little platinum-haired boy with cocoa eyes caressed Pae's bangs and rubbed his eyebrows with his thumbs. He remained locked hard in the adult male's wrecked, tear-soaked gaze. Pae's emotions started to settle. Hell had not resurrected; it had only spat at him in a final ditched effort to poison his future.

The past is gone, Pae reminded himself. *You are no longer helpless.*

The man returned to his senses. He dried the rest of his tears and rested. He removed the child's buckle-up baby doll shoes. They were covered in dirt and fresh scrapes. He finished disrobing the boy and tossed the soiled panties and hosiery onto the jacket. Pae washed his hands, then wrapped his arms around the boy's back and hoisted him. The child's legs dangled as the man carried into the bedroom. Pae eased the youngster face-down onto the bed. The boy started to tremble. He whimpered and covered his mouth with his palms. Pae hurried to the other side of the bed to face him. He dropped to the floor and placed his hands on the boy's hands.

"Precious Love... Dear heart, please do not be afraid," Pae pleaded.

Pae was not accustomed to talking to children. He had not interacted with one in years aside from brief, casual encounters, and none had appeared psychologically damaged, at least not to this extent. Pae was unsure how to conduct himself. Therapy had not prepared him. Having avoided children most of his adult life, Pae took his cues from memories of the ways his aunt used to speak to his toddler cousin.

"Sweetheart, look at me. I am not going to hurt you. Look into my eyes, dear one. I brought you in here so I could wash you. I cannot put you in the bathtub. It would hurt terribly if you were to sit in the water. Please believe me. This is the easiest way for me to get you clean. Please do not be frightened. I love you, little one."

Pae coaxed the boy's hands away from his mouth, one by one, and kissed them then returned them to their original position. He rubbed the child's fingers.

The boy refused to look at him. He continued to shake, almost to the point of seizure. Pae peeled the bedspread from atop the pillows and covered the child. He leaned over the boy and rubbed his back, and whispered, "It's okay, little one, do not be afraid. I will not hurt you. You are safe now."

The boy's trembling started to subside. Pae pushed the boy's bangs aside and kissed his forehead, then sat on the floor and held the child's hands. The youngster panted while his tremors subsided. He pushed against Pae's hands so he could lower his own to the bedspread. He pressed his face against them. Pae withdrew his hands. The boy felt the mattress sink as the man sat next to him. He did not look up. Mild trembling persisted. Pae patted the top of the lad's cornrow-plated head then rubbed his upper back between the shoulder blades as he remained covered.

"It's okay, child," Pae tried to assure the little one. "Everything will be alright." He sat motionless for a few seconds.

The boy risked a peek at the man. Pae placed a finger on the tip of the tyke's nose. "Boop!" he said.

The little one's brows drew in, and his eyes glared with confusion.

Pae sat with the boy and rubbed his back until he relaxed, and the trembling faded.

"Let's get you cleaned up, beautiful. Wait here. I'm going to the kitchen. I'll be back in a few minutes."

Pae felt weird speaking to the boy in ways he would address a girl, but it seemed clear he had been taught to think and behave as one. There was no denying he had been dressed and made up as a girl. Had Pae not witnessed the child's genitals first-hand, he would never have figured it out, and he would not have been convinced had someone told him. Addressing the little one as a girl seemed the most logical approach.

The child remained in place when Pae walked out. He did not know what to think of this strange man's gentility and emotional softness. Most of the men to whom he had been peddled had treated him with utter disdain. A few had offered a bit of civility but to a much lesser degree than Pae. None had fed him, or washed his hands, or spoken kindly to him. None had looked into his eyes with anything but sexual desire, ridicule, tension, and contempt. No one, male or female, had ever cried with him or for him. They had yanked on him, and nudged, pushed, tripped, suspended, slapped, spit on, and dragged him. Some had extinguished cigarettes on him. He had been thrown once. They had not politely ushered, carried, or hugged him. All had laughed at or cussed him at one time or another. None had made any effort to urge him to communicate like a human being. They had expressed expectations, and issued commands, and had always gone straight to business. There were no rewards, no food or drink, no candy, no toys, no time with customers' pets, and no interaction with other children.

No one had respected the little one's body or his emotions. They had shared him with other men, and with women on two occasions. Those women had treated him worse than any man had, save for Mark. Before Pae, the boy had been nothing more than a commodity treated with less regard than animals and most objects.

Contrary to declarations that he had been born without a soul and that he was not human, the boy had a keen intellect and an inherent but limited sense of right and wrong. Pae's behavior had confirmed some of what the little one had sensed was right. What little else he knew had been learned by observing the animal kingdom.

The child lacked discernment in matters of trust. His life had been rigidly structured and closely monitored. Trust was not an option. Neither the word nor the concept existed in his world. Though allowed limited freedom to roam in the woods for short periods, he was thoroughly institutionalized.

Even so, the boy's initial encounter with Pae had been a curious experiment. He had not willingly disobeyed known expectations until that day. A fortunate deviation had occurred with a customer, so the youngster had seized the opportunity to slip through a tight window of exploration. Rules did not cover every circumstance. In fact, they addressed few; they were more blanket rules than anything else. The boy did not know how to handle the unexpected, so he had followed his instincts. He had paid a brutal price in the old tin washtub, but it had not been harsh enough to quench his curiosity. Pae's interactions had given the youth a taste of life he had only imagined. This enormous, menacing-looking male was the little one's first legitimate exposure to the concept of love. He knew he had to return, somehow, and, so he had.

Though a chilling endeavor, the tot had lowered his guard a second time. The child expected to be reprimanded upon returning to the trailer but was confident he would not be carried away as the other little ones had. The boy was marked and therefore protected; this much he knew, as he had heard Mark, the tall, slim man, declare it to others several times. Mark had shot one man to death in front of the boy to prove the validity of his word. The salt-and-pepper-haired man's corrective behaviors horrified the boy, but his protection comforted him, harsh and unfeeling as it was.

The boy's thoughts returned to Halloween night and the events that had preceded his escape into the woods. He then recalled the dark-haired man's threat to knock his teeth out the year prior. The child had naturally lost plenty of baby teeth since then. He was not familiar with rooted ones and was unaware he had them. Teeth were teeth. He figured the horrors of his struggle on Halloween were worth the impending loss. He would much rather lose his teeth than endure that again. The thought of the rubber hose was a different story. The recollection filled him with grief. He realized he had not thought things through. Teeth were no longer a concern.

The boy had followed what he had perceived were orders from Pae. He followed directions without a fuss as he had been conditioned over the years. Instant, unquestioning obedience to Mark and the others had always yielded more desirable results than resistance. Pae's ways were peculiar. They were different. They warranted evaluation.

Though void of the concepts of free will and trust, the child felt a magnetic urge to allow Pae past his defenses since their last meeting had worked out favorably. He had entered a stranger's house and had rummaged his refrigerator without reprisal, and then he had received a reward in turn. He hoped for a similar experience this time.

The boy mentally prepared himself for the receipt of torture at Mark's hands, though at present, he expected sexual exploitation from Pae despite his hopes. Lying prone without any clothing had never gone well. Thoughts of retribution and pending molestation started to overwhelm the child. He began to whisper in his secret language.

The child studied the bedroom as he whispered. He did not see the shadows that had been in his room at the trailer, the ones he often thought were laughing as he had drifted asleep, the ones that had tormented his dreams a few days prior. He was convinced the same had been responsible for biting his ankles and leaving strange blemishes from time to time for as far back as he could remember. The welts had been different than those caused by insects and had often drawn blood. This place did not appear to have any of those shadows that would whisper, and move around, or try to steal the air from his mouth, or press on his chest and head.

This man's bedroom light was dim and the house almost barren except for basic furniture and a few pictures and ornaments, but it did not feel gloomy and empty like all the other places the boy had entered, even the well illuminated and cluttered ones. The whole house made the little one feel warm, like the woods, before Pae had brought him into the heated bedroom. This house felt safe. Pae's presence was comforting and inviting like the woodland creatures and the train.

The youth remembered that Pae had dressed when they had originally met and then again tonight, a contrast to the actions of the others to whom he had been exposed. He considered that Pae had not touched him the way the others had and that Pae's *dirty little pee-pee*--as he had heard his own appendage called many times--had done the opposite of what he had expected. The boy wondered about the man's shaven and waxed physique, void of hair except for his head and forearms. He puzzled over the scars on the large male's groin, inner thighs, shins, buttocks, and back. Pae was not reactive like the men the child had seen shot, stabbed, and beaten, or like those to whom he was daily exposed. This man appeared to harbor no fear and no anger. He is monstrously large and muscular, but wounded, and soft, and gentle. The boy smiled. He continued to focus his thoughts on Pae, blocking out the world to which he was certain he would return. The little one's fears diminished. He continued to whisper as he eagerly waited to see if the huge adult male would indeed clean and not harm him. A hot rush of giddy anticipation coursed through the boy's veins. His heart leaped.

Pae returned with a few rags, a large bowl of water, and some liquid dish soap. He also had a small medicine bottle. He set the items on the nightstand.

"I am not going to hurt you," Pae said as he circled the bed with the pill bottle. "By the way, my friends call me Pae, and yeah, it sounds like pie." He sat beside the boy.

The child was still lying prone, but he no longer hid his face. He did not respond to Pae's humor. He could not relate to the pie reference. Pae extended his hand, palm up, toward the child. He took one of the youngster's hands and rubbed his knuckles and fingers with his thumb. The boy reciprocated. He closed his eyes and attempted to suck Pae's fingers. Pae withdrew. The child drew his shoulders toward his ears and lowered his head in a cowering manner. The man laid the pill bottle on the mattress then brushed the little one's bangs with his fingers.

"It's okay, sweet one. You're not in any trouble." He massaged the boy's blanket-covered back and hummed a tune until the little one relaxed enough to chance another look at him. Pae took a pill from the medicine bottle.

"This is ibuprofen. I don't know if it will help any, but I don't think there's anything else I can give you that won't cause any problems."

The man snapped the pill into quarters then laid one portion on the bed. The boy stared at it, then ate it as Pae stood. The child's face contorted. He squinted and shook his head then smacked a few times while he eyed the man through narrowed slits.

If looks could kill!

"You weren't supposed to chew it," Pae said, in a choppy, laugh infused manner. He stuck his tongue out, then returned to the bed and tousled the boy's bangs. "I was going to bring you a cup of water so you could wash it down. Something tells me you're not familiar with the concept of medicine? Oh well. That's that, I suppose? I guess I should wash you now?"

Pae stood again then walked around the bed to retrieve the bowl and rags from atop the nightstand. He removed the bedspread from the child and placed the items beside the pillow on the child's left side then slid upon bent knees on the boy's right. He dipped one of the rags in the bowl of water and lathered it with dish soap.

"I will be gentle. If anything hurts, understand that I am not doing it on purpose, okay?"

The boy twisted his torso and patted Pae's flannel covered thigh. Pae smiled at the boy and rubbed his bangs again.

"I hope you have figured out that I am not like whoever did this to you? I am really more like you except grown up. Older boys did terrible things to me when I was around your age. I understand, beautiful. I know."

The child stared at Pae's face. He lifted his hand from the man's thigh, then pointed behind him and waved. Pae cocked his head and raised a single brow. The boy huffed then repeated the action. Pae looked behind toward the wall. The youngster slapped the man's thigh, then pointed once more and grunted. They exchanged glances.

"Oh!" The man raised his brows. "You're pointing at my bum, huh?" Pae patted his own rear. "Because I said others hurt me like they hurt you?"

The boy sighed and rested his hand on Pae's leg again.

"Yep. That's right, little one. The same as you." He prepared the rag. "I'm going to start down here at your bottom end. That's where you need it the most."

With the soapy wet rag in one hand, Pae took hold of the boy's soiled bum. He could not help but notice the boy's legs were more filled out than most children his age.

"You're quite active outdoors, aren't you? It's pretty obvious to me. You have strong, full legs." The boy groaned. Pae detected a hint of emotional pain. The worried look on the lad's face confirmed it. "I'm sorry, precious. I didn't mean it like that."

Pae gently took the boy's right buttock and pulled it toward him. He gasped. "How on earth did you even get here, child?" He wanted to stop but he couldn't. The boy had to be treated.

Pae rocked back and whispered, "God, give me strength! They turned you inside out!" He leaned forward again. His gag reflex was triggered. The boy's backside looked like a jagged wad of caked, soiled, bloodied, and chewed gum. Pae looked away for a moment. *You saw worse overseas*, he told himself. He paused. His breathing tempo increased. His heart raced.

The man snapped out of his fog, then squeezed water and suds from the rag and dabbed between the child's cheeks.

"They did the same thing to me. I was only a little older than you are. There were six of them." Pae set down the rag and counted his fingers for the boy. "One, two, three, four, five, six." He wiggled his fingers. "This many." Pae was not sure the child understood, though he appeared to pay close attention.

The man resumed washing. Water dribbled, and suds oozed. When they made contact with the boy's damaged anatomy, he clenched his cheeks and clawed at the bedspread with one hand and at Pae's leg with the other. His grip felt like a tiny bear trap. The flannel pajamas were not much of a barrier. The boy did not make any audible sounds other than changes in breathing. Pae stopped to massage the child's back then resumed blotting after the boy relaxed.

"It's a wonder you stopped bleeding out there, wherever you were? I don't know how you made it here without passing out or dying? No rips inside of you, I reckon? Nothing deep, else you would have bled out for sure? I guess I'll know if I see any fresh blood? You've been missing for a couple of days. Someone came by looking for you. She said she was your sister."

The boy raised a balled fist with the middle finger extended.

Pae chuckled, with a bit of choked-up merriment, trying not to cry again. He shook his head. "Yeah, I kinda didn't think she was. How in this world did you make it here?"

"Friend of Pae...," a frail whisper came. "Shiny, yellow man."

Pae stopped. His eyes widened. "So, you *can* talk!" He sat back and was pensive. His brows narrowed, and his eyes shifted. One side of his mouth tightened. "Sweetheart, I have no shiny, yellow friend. Who is this shiny, yellow man?"

The child did not respond.

"Why was he shiny and yellow? Was he wearing a Halloween costume like a superhero or a robot?"

The boy shook his head.

Pae pointed toward the light in the center of the ceiling. "Was he shiny and yellow like that light?"

The child looked up at the dingy low watt bulb. He shook his head again. "Shiny, yellow feet."

"So, he wasn't all shiny? Only his feet?"

"Shiny, yellow feet. Shiny, yellow man. Friend of Pae."

Pae wracked his brain, trying to figure out this one. "Was he wearing rubber boots like a fisherman?" *This place is full of lakes and rivers. Who knows how someone might have been dressed?*

"Shiny, yellow feet," the boy repeated. "Eyes," he added, then twisted his torso and pointed at Pae's face. "Pae eyes."

Pae stared at the youth. "Pae eyes?"

"Pae eyes. Eyes like Pae."

"The same color as mine?"

The boy shook his head, then resumed his propped stance on both elbows. He raised his forearms and patted his eyes with his hands. "Pae eyes! Pae eyes! Eyes like Pae!" He twisted again and pointed at Pae's face. "Pae eyes."

Pae grunted and nodded. "Okay." He abandoned the questions. More pressing business was at hand. Whoever this shiny, yellow man might have been, it made no sense at all that he would have sent this boy out on his own without cleaning him up and seeking medical attention. Two nights would have been an excessive amount of time for an adult to continue in this condition but for a child this young? The fact that he was still alive was nothing short of miraculous.

But, who in his right mind? I wouldn't put it past ole shiny, yellow man having been threatened at some point just as I had? That would certainly explain his unwillingness to care for this boy. He might fear for his own life? Why didn't he at least come to the door with him? And why would this person claim to be a friend of mine? How would he even know who on earth I am?

"That mouthpiece, Charlene," Pae grumbled. *I wonder if she's been talking?*

Pae concentrated on clearing his mind so he could focus on the boy. The cleaning process was tedious. He had to be delicate. The child reacted to the pain by twitching, but he never broke down. He was tough. The boy's mood seemed to lighten in spite of his vulnerability and discomfort. Pae was impressed. He turned on the clock radio. The FM selector was already tuned to a classic rock station.

As soft rock played, Pae thought of the children whose angels are tasked with delivering their spirits back to God and laying their precious souls to rest. He thought of the torments of so many at the hands of vile men and women while on the road to their demise. He thought of their broken little hearts failing in agonizing despair, often too young to have any comprehension as terror and death lay hold. The man considered the destroyed marriages and other devastated relationships that the violent losses of children so often leave in their wakes. Pae wept as he pondered while he rubbed down the boy's legs and removed the dried, scaled blood and waste.

Too many are never found again. Survivors, such as this child and he, are left to carry living death in their minds and scars in their hearts throughout their remaining years. *Why? Where is the rhyme or reason? Where is the justice?* Pae had grappled for decades with the questions of life's cruelties. He used to dwell on such things until he concluded that informative, reasonable explanations do not exist, no matter how people attempt to engineer them in their quests to cope. His conclusions had not settled the questions, though they had reduced the frequency with which they had plagued his mind.

In the absence of logic and reason, there stands faith and, therefore, hope. Those of us who remain must keep moving forward; we must face, and resist, and overcome deep-rooted pain, and pursue life with fervor; we must excel for the sake of ourselves and others and be living medicine for the souls of those who remain broken.

This is the best logic Pae could fathom, the only answers he could derive from the unknowable and unanswerable.

Individuals need not change the world. How many possess the power to influence on so grand a scale? But everyone can be a light to those within their paths. It is as simple as making a daily decision then following through. Self-sacrificial love--even toward those we do not understand and might fear--without the expectation of anything in return, is the best anyone can do. The world can be changed that way, one life at a time.

Pae reflected a little longer until his heaviness lifted. He patted the boy's cool, goose-pimpled, rash covered, scraped, and bruised buns. He gently squeezed one buttock then drifted from reality. His face went blank, and his eyes settled onto the child's firm, meaty bum. He sat still for a time with a perplexed expression, then slowly rubbed the boy's back.

"Are you hanging in there, beautiful?"

The twin-ponytailed child nodded. Pae patted the top of his cornrow-braided head then rubbed his jaw, hoping it would further soothe the boy. "Keep hanging on. It won't take too much longer."

Pae resumed his previous train of thought. He revisited the idea of self-sacrificial love. *Greater love has no one than this, that they should give their life for their friends.*

"Huh," Pae mumbled. *I had always taken that as meaning a final act of heroism, not a living commitment. There's a bit more depth than I'd realized. It is certainly more attainable by anyone than heroism.*

Pae's thoughts drifted further. He responded to his own pondering by saying, "That's my prayer for you, child, that your life may someday be far better than these awful beginnings. I mean that sincerely, whether you understand or not."

That was sufficient for Pae. He had no answers to the *whys* of all the pain and destruction in the world, but he did have what he needed at this moment for the hand that had been dealt him and the boy. The reason was invalid. The answer, to use his time and resources in favor of the child's welfare, is where the intrinsic value of the moment resided. Nothing else mattered.

Pae sang in tune with the song on the radio as he lathered the little one with a second, clean, soapy rag. He imagined the boy freed from his prison, filled with joy and dancing, clothed from head to toe in love, and exploring the depths of his personality while having the time of his life. He rinsed the child by wringing a third wet rag, without soap, over the lathered area, then dried him by wiping with a fourth. The boy flinched and grunted several times but remained in place. Pae stopped singing when removal of the dried body fluids uncovered the full extent of the damage. He set the rag down and looked away when childhood memories flooded his brain. Pae also recalled children that had been dismembered during the war. The adult sighed then rubbed his eyes to keep them clear.

Pae picked up his phone and tried to call Reverend Smalls again. As before, it went straight to voicemail. The world was empty, and the night dark, but not as dark as the inner night. *Lord, you know what you're doing. I'm at a loss, but I trust you.* Pae patted the boy's bum. He prayed for the child again as he finished cleaning his backside. He rolled the child over.

"Just a little more, Pae assured him. "Not much longer."

Pae cleansed the remainder of the blood and feces from the youngster's inner thighs and ankles. The child's ankles were covered in scrapes, cuts, and scabs. A dark purple bruise resided between the little one's legs just below his genitals. It was surrounded by red impressions that resembled teeth marks. Matched series of small, rounded, tan bruises were on the tot's wrists, forearms, shins, and ankles. The patterns were similar to those on each side of the little one's hips, where they met his waist. Pae laid his fingertips against a row near the boy's feet then against a series on his hip. The man sighed, nodded, and whispered, "Yep. I figured as much."

A few stray marks were on the boy's ribs, and a series of scars were on his hip near his groin. Pae had missed them in the kitchen due to the shock of discovering male genitalia. The youth had been branded with scars resembling three chain links. The raised welts were aged. The word CRADLE was tattooed above the chain, and GRAVE was tattooed beneath it in fine-lined letters that were about one-quarter inch tall. The letters E-*KPm* flanked the left side of the brand in a smaller font, and 6SICK6 flanked the right. The entire composition covered the same area as two side-by-side Kennedy fifty-cent cent coins.

The boy did not express the slightest bit of annoyance at Pae's inspections. Pae decided to not wash the lad's inner thigh where the bruise and bite mark were located. Dried saliva might still be present. Unfortunately, the boy had been missing for a few days. Even in the mild temperature, there was a high probability that sweat had washed away any residual evidence of foreign body fluids.

More tears eased down Pae's face. It seemed they would continue all night. He trembled, wishing he could take the law into his own hands.

I would love nothing more than to exterminate every single one of the people on that dirt road! Well, not the pregnant teenager or the large woman Charlene said might also be pregnant, but certainly her husband and any other adults who might be there. But then, I would be no better than them. Vengeance belongs to God and justice to the law. Besides, I've been praying for those people. Boiling blood and a broken heart or not, I cannot afford to live with a divided mind. Best, I forget about them for now and keep tending this child.

The boy took Pae's free right hand and pulled it onto his abdomen below his navel then patted it. He had no tears to share with the man this time, only a stare from those dark cocoa eyes. Pae moved his hand above the child's navel, but the youth scowled then pushed it below again. Pae nudged the child, and the boy nudged back. The adult remained where the effeminately adorned lad had placed him. Pae mustered a compassionate twinkle through his swelling, tear-filled eyelids. The little one's pouty lips returned a thin smile. The boy's eyes looked warmer and more life-like than Pae had previously seen. The child continued to rub Pae's hand and study his expression.

Pae turned his attention to the boy's swollen neck and his red, flushed cheeks. He removed his hand from the child's abdomen and placed his fingers flat on his chest. The child's pulse was rapid. He checked the youth's temperature by laying a hand upon his forehead. Not surprisingly, it was still warm, but it did feel cooler than it had earlier. He placed a wet rag on the little one's forehead. *I need to get some water in you soon,* he thought.

"Who did this to you? You've been missing since at least Halloween. Did this happen on Halloween? What about yesterday or earlier today? Have you been at someone's house all this time? I sure wish I knew who that shiny, yellow man is and why he didn't bring you to me himself since he claims to be my friend?" He sighed. "I don't know how you lived through that, but I'm glad you did. I'll bet you're starving? Are you hungry?"

The boy nodded.

"I'll get you something to eat."

The child's eyes widened. He rolled his head in the direction of the wall that faced the dirt road outside.

"Don't be afraid, beautiful," Pae rubbed the side of the lad's face. "They will never hurt you again. You may eat all you want. You will not be punished."

The boy looked at Pae. His face almost beamed.

"It's true! I am going to take you away to someplace safe, but first I would like to feed you. Would you like that?"

The boy grinned and nodded. "Yes, please," his frail voice whispered. The tot's deep brown eyes peered from behind flowing platinum bangs like polished Kona beans. His lips still bore traces of glittered, dark plum lipstick, and his eyes and cheeks remained smeared with makeup.

Will he ever have any kind of a decent life? Pae wondered. He washed the boy's lips, eyes, cheeks, and nostrils, then rinsed and re-folded the rag and placed it back onto his forehead. Pae eased himself from the bed, then opened a drawer and pulled out a folded sweatshirt.

"Here, let me put this on you."

The boy sat up and raised his hands. The rag flopped into the child's lap. Pae slipped the shirt over him. It swallowed the child.

"Way too big, huh? Your shoulders are about to pop right through the neck hole. Well, it's the best I can do for now. I'll go make you a peanut butter and jelly sandwich, with a cookie, and a donut, and a glass of milk just like last time. I'll bring you a cup of milk and some water, too. How does that sound?"

The boy nodded again, grinning like the Mona Lisa.

d. bRENT iSBELL
SICKS

"Stay here, precious. I'll be right back in just a few minutes."

When Pae returned with a tray, the boy was on the edge of the bed, facing the door. The tot had removed the rag from his forehead and had draped it over his crown. His legs were dangling off the mattress as he shook his arms, entertaining himself with the long, loose sleeves the man had provided.

"Aminals! Aminals!" the boy repeated.

Pae stopped in the doorway and watched the child for a few seconds. He refrained from laughing at the sound of the boy interchanging his *n*'s with *m*'s. The youth stopped saying *aminals* then began whispering something unintelligible. Pae could not hear what he was saying.

"Here's your food, beautiful," Pae announced as he walked through the door. "I'm not real sure how we'll do this? Oh! I know!"

Pae moved the clock radio aside and set the tray on the nightstand. He rolled up the child's sleeves, then picked up the sandwich and wrapped a napkin beneath it. "Here you go, precious." He handed the sandwich to the child.

The little one gently accepted the snack. "Thank you," he whispered, with his gaze locked into Pae's.

Odd that he has manners. He says please and thank you. I didn't see that coming.

The boy patted his chest with one hand and said, "Devil child."

Pae's heart sank like a rock.

The boy added, "Full of Satan. Devil-child. It! It! Not him, it! Full of the devil!"

Pae was *floored*. He tried to decipher what the boy was attempting to communicate. The boy patted Pae's leg. "Pae, like Pae! Pae eyes. Eyes like Pae." He patted his chest again. "Nasty little pee-pee! It! It! Filth!"

"No, precious! No, no, no!" Pae said in a sorrowful, pleading tone. He sat next to the child. The boy huddled up as close as he could. Pae's tears gushed again. He wondered how much more he could take.

"Who on earth would tell you such things?" Pae asked, amid his sob. "You are not a devil-child! You are a beautiful, beautiful child, a precious little jewel!" *What kind of monsters are those parents of yours?* Pae squeezed the little one in a sympathetic hug and kissed the top of his head then told the child, "No, Precious Jewel, you are NOT a devil-child!" He swept the boy's bangs then rubbed his shoulder.

"God hates Precious Jewel," the boy said.

Pae's stomach churned. He thought his heart could not break any further this evening, but the surprises kept coming. His eyes bagged and burned from the relentless emotional barrage.

"God does not hate you, little love."

The boy looked at Pae, quizzically.

"God loves you, beautiful! He talked to me and asked me to take care of you tonight."

The boy's eyes widened; surprise was written all over him.

"I love you too, little one. God loves you, and I love you!"

"Love?" the boy asked. His eyes roved back and forth in a questioning manner. Pae perceived the boy's curiosity.

"Yes! Love!"

The boy's eyes stopped moving. He stared.

Pae placed his hand on the boy's shoulder and rubbed it. "Love."

The boy continued to stare.

Pae bent down and kissed the youngster's forehead. "Love."

The boy cocked his head.

Pae hugged the child again. "Love." He then placed his hand over the one with which the child held the sandwich and repeated, "Love."

The boy's curious look lingered. Finally, Pae drew a deep breath and slid his hand under the sweatshirt and rested it below the child's navel to the same spot the child had formerly guided it. "Love."

Something registered in the boy's eyes. "Pae loves you," the little one whispered in the form of a statement, as he took a bite and smacked on the sandwich. The concept of love had never been described or demonstrated to the boy. He had overheard it spoken many times in adult conversations at customers' houses but seldom at his own, and certainly never directed at him. He had not comprehended the meaning when he had heard. He understood Pae's demonstration. His actions had established context. The word *love* finally made sense.

"Yes, I do, beautiful. I most definitely love you! God loves you too, Precious Jewel."

The boy removed one hand from his sandwich, then raised it. He balled up his fist and extended his index finger toward the wall. "They don't love *It*. They don't love Pae, too." He relaxed his finger, then said, "Pae loves you. Pae loves *Nasty Little Pee-Pee*."

A laugh shot simultaneously through Pae's nostrils and mouth. He coughed, then closed his eyes tightly and squeezed his nose. He thought he had blown out his sinuses.

Poor thing has no clue who or what he is.

Pae felt bad for making light of the boy's situation, but something had to give. It was way too painful and sad a reality. A gloomy thought overtook him. *What if there are more like this boy out there? What if he's trying to tell me this is what they call others like him?*

The boy studied Pae's body language as he contemplated.

When Pae resumed eye contact, the child extended his finger again, then put it in his mouth, then slid it back and forth then withdrew it.

"They don't love Banana Bitch," the youth said.

The boy relaxed his finger one more time and pointed it toward the floor. "Pae loves Precious Jewel. God asked Pae to love you. God hates *It;* God loves Precious Jewel."

Pae did not respond.

"They don't love," the boy rattled on as he leaned over and patted his own behind. "Pae loves Precious Jewel," he patted his own behind again, then he patted Pae's. "They don't love Pae, too." The boy returned his hand to the fold-over sandwich and held it up to Pae. "Pae loves Precious Jewel," he whispered. "Pae."

The child took another bite, then placed his right hand behind Pae and worked it underneath Pae's pajama top and into the waistband of his bottoms. He rested where the elastic held his forearm in place. He patted Pae's left buttock. The child continued to eat with his left hand. He laid his head against Pae and kicked his dangling ankles back and forth and started humming.

Pae reached across the front of his own torso to rub the boy's bangs and pat his head. He rested his left arm alongside the child. He considered removing the boy's hand from his waistband but decided to let him be. The boy was at peace. Pae was at peace. The boy smacked away on his meal.

The boy finished his sandwich as the analog sounds of plucking strings came through the speaker on the clock radio. Pae recognized the old tune. A soft male voice followed a series of introductory notes.

"That's a froggy," Pae told the boy. The child did not react. "Froggy...you know? A frog?"

The little one's head snapped upward. His eyes lit up, and his mouth dropped open.

Pae laughed. "It's not a real frog, it's make-believe, pretend. Gobble up the rest of your goodies. I'm going to get you that milk and water now. Enjoy listening to the froggy. I'll be right back."

The boy finished his meal and glugged as much milk and water as Pae had offered. He was parched.

"We can't spend any more time here. I've got to get you out so I can take you to a safe place."

Pae gathered some clothes from the dresser. He looked into the mirror and saw the child watching him. It was eerie how the boy was a dead ringer for a girl, beautiful but spooky, none-the-less. The boy's dark, ominous expressions were long gone. His eyes remained bright. They continued to fill with life.

"Beautiful child," the boy said to Pae.

Pae smiled. "Yes, you are a beautiful child."

The boy shook his head and pointed at the man. "Beautiful child!" he repeated, louder.

"Oh! You mean, me?"

Contentment washed over the boy's face. He patted his chest. "Precious Jewel." The boy bobbed his head back and forth and made sounds that reminded Pae of an ape. The man watched him through the mirror for a moment.

"I need to get dressed. I can't leave the house in my pajamas. I will be right here in the living room."

Pae fished a full set of clothing from his dresser and withdrew a pistol from the nightstand. "I'll bring this with us in case we see any bad guys. Don't be afraid."

The man carried his pistol into the living room and proceeded to change his clothes. The boy walked into the doorway to watch. Pae caught a glimpse of the curious child. "I guess I didn't have to come in here, huh?"

Though Pae could have closed the bedroom door to keep the child contained, he did not want to risk causing any undue trauma. He thought that odds were higher, the child would have walked right out and headed up the road if he would have dressed in another room. Waiting for food was one thing. The boy had something tangible to gain from that. Despite the man's apprehension, the passing moments revealed the boy had likely not entertained thoughts of slipping away. He appeared too interested in Pae.

"Beautiful child. Beautiful Pae," the boy said. "Precious jewel."

After dressing, Pae retrieved the child's soiled clothing from the kitchen floor and placed it into a clear plastic trash bag. He walked into the bathroom then returned with the bag and a fresh towel. The man gathered the used rags and placed them in the plastic bag with the clothing. He tied it off, then wrapped the child in the towel. The little one still wore the adult's sweatshirt. Pae picked up the bag and the child.

"Come, Precious Jewel. It's time. Let's take you someplace safe. You never have to go back there again."

As Pae carried the boy to the front door and turned on the outside light, the child pointed to a small display against the wall. "Shiny, yellow man."

Pae stopped.

"Shiny feet," the boy added. He pointed to a polished brass bell Pae had purchased during his military service in South Korea.

"Like that?" Pae asked.

The little boy nodded, "Shiny, yellow man. Shiny feet."

NOVEMBEr 2: THREe HOURs AFTEr SUNSEt

Pae arrived at Spanky's and parked behind the building near the compact loading bay. The child was fastened in the back seat on the passenger's side. Pae dialed Sherri-Lynn's number on his mobile phone. She answered.

"Well, hey there, hon!" Sherri-Lynn's southern accent oozed with its usual honeysuckle sweetness, but never so sweet to Pae's ears as tonight. "How are you?"

"Not too great, to be honest. Do you have time to meet me out back near the loading area? I'm parked at the far corner on the right as you exit the building. I would not have sprung up on you like this, except that it's important, very important! You can bring Tiny or someone else with you if my request sounds too odd?"

"No, hon, that's fine. Kind of a strange thing to say, but fine. Give me a minute. I'll be right there."

Several seconds later, the Fabulous Feline came bouncing across the parking lot in all her curvy, plus-sized splendor. Her topside was covered in a flannel shirt. She ignored the chilled November air. As she approached, Pae rolled down the rear passenger's window then got out to meet her halfway.

"Thank you for meeting me here," Pae said.

Fabulous Feline glowed with anticipation. Her grin was sunny. Her expression defied the murky night around them.

"I have someone I'd like you to meet." Pae took the Feline's hand and led her to the car. As they arrived, the light from a parking lot telephone pole revealed a beautiful little girl with platinum blonde cornrow braids and a patch of long bangs, nestled in the shadows of the back seat. She was wrapped in a beach towel. The car was running, and the heater was on.

"Precious Jewel, this is my friend, Fabulous Feline. Her real name is Sherri-Lynn. Sherri-Lynn, this is Precious Jewel."

The Fabulous Feline smiled and waved at the child. "Hey there, pumpkin! How are you?"

The child stared at the Fabulous Feline.

"Is it okay if I talk to your friend Pae for a minute? We'll just be right over there so you can see us."

The youngster did not blink.

Fabulous Feline nodded. "Well, okay, then? We'll be just a minute, sugar. Hold tight, okay, honey bun?"

Fabulous Feline walked with Pae a few yards into the parking lot in line with the rear passenger window.

"Is that who I fuckin' think it is?" Fabulous Feline demanded as she pointed at the car. "Have you lost your damn mind? That's kidnapping! And why the hell did you bring her here of all places? And what's this 'Precious Jewel' shit? You're seriously scaring me, Pae!"

Pae gripped Sherri-Lynn's hand. "Come look at this!" He pulled her back to the car, then opened the rear passenger door. He unbuckled the child and removed the beach towel then pulled up the sweatshirt. "Look at his neck and chest! Tell me what you see."

"What do you mean *his* neck?"

Fabulous Feline's eyes widened as she viewed the child under the faint light that sifted through the back window and from the car's interior dome light. "Oh, my God!" She gasped when she saw the child's discolored groin and genitals, and the bruises on his nipples and legs, and the tattooed brand on his hip.

"That's nothing compared to how his poor little bum ring looks! He's shredded! It's a wonder the boy's not dead! He's been like this, and out wandering alone, since at least Halloween!"

The Fabulous Feline did not like the way Pae was barking at her, but based on what she was witnessing, she knew his tension was valid. Pae lowered the sweatshirt and wrapped the towel around the boy. He buckled the child then closed the door. He walked a few feet away again with the Fabulous Feline in tow.

"I'm taking him to the hospital here in this county. I don't dare take him to any emergency room in Empire, and I didn't want to risk leaving him in the hands of the rural paramedics. There's no telling who might have shown up? Even if the paramedics are on the level, they would have drawn all kinds of attention that this little one does not need. He is marked, and I can almost guarantee you they're crawling all over the place trying to find him so they can keep doing this! The boy is being prostituted, Sherri-Lynn! It does not matter if I go to prison for kidnapping. I've got to get this precious child some real help and hopefully take him to where he'll never be found by those people again! I did not come here to get you involved. I came here because I respect our friendship, and I respect you! I felt you should at least have the courtesy of knowing what had happened to me in case you never see me again."

The little boy's voice rang out from the opened car window. "Shiny, yellow man!"

Pae and Fabulous Feline looked at the youngster and then into the direction he was pointing. A man had walked out back to smoke a cigarette. Pae returned to the car. Fabulous Feline followed.

"Is that him? Is that the shiny, yellow man?" The little boy shook his head.

Fabulous Feline was confused. "Who in the world is shiny, yellow man?"

"I don't know. I'll explain later." He looked at the child. "Why did you say, 'shiny, yellow man,' if that's not him?"

The boy placed his hand atop his head. "Lamb hair." He mimicked the sound he had heard many times before from his toy, "Ma-a-a-a-a-a!"

Pae and Fabulous Feline looked at the man. His hair was short and white from age and filled with tight waves. "Did the shiny man have hair like his?"

This time the boy nodded. "Lamb hair."

"But that's not him?"

He shook his head again. "No shiny feet. Old man. Shiny, yellow man no old. Shiny man no old." The little one patted his eyelids with his fingertips. "Eyes like Pae. Friend of Pae."

"Friend of Pae?" Fabulous Feline asked.

"No friend that I can recall. I'm guessing it's someone who was dressed in some kind of a uniform or a costume on Halloween night and likely learned about me through Charlene? I don't know." Pae narrowed his eyes and pursed his lips. He looked at Fabulous Feline. "Do you know that man?"

"Yes, his name is Ben. He's in his late sixties. We allow smoking inside, but he likes the fresh air. Imagine that? Fresh air while you smoke. He's a regular. Been in every night for the past week from around eight until closing. Was here all night on the thirty-first, starting around sunset, when we had our annual Halloween bash. Why?"

Pae shook his head. "Nothing, I suppose? He just reminds this child of that *shiny man* character that he claims told him is a friend of mine. I don't have a clue who that person might be or how he thinks he knows me, and most especially why he would have referred to me as his friend? I can't figure any of it. Anyhow, that's not important at the moment. What is important is that I've got to get this boy to a hospital! I've wasted way too much time already."

Fabulous Feline stood with one hand on her forehead and the other on her hip. After a few seconds, she moved the one from her forehead onto her mouth. She began to pace.

"Well, I've gotta go. He needs medical attention."

"Wait!" Fabulous Feline urged. She stopped pacing. "Let me get dressed. You're not going alone!" She placed her hands on Pae's ears and pulled him toward her. She kissed his forehead then trotted into the private rear entrance of Spanky's. Several minutes later, Sherri-Lynn emerged in regular clothing accompanied by Tiny. He was on his mobile phone.

"The cavalry is coming!" Sherri-Lynn shouted. "I'll ride with Pae," she told Tiny.

"We'll meet you there." Tiny nodded and waved then got into his lifted classic 4x4 truck.

Sherri-Lynn got into the back seat of Pae's car. She leaned over and kissed the boy on his cheek, amazed at how he looked like a real girl. "Let's get this precious child the hell out of Dodge!" Sherri-Lynn exclaimed. Pae did not delay.

"Oh, my God!" a nurse gasped as she examined the boy on a gurney. He was disrobed and lying prone. Pae held his hand and stroked his bangs. The nurse walked to the doorway of the emergency room and yelled into the hallway toward the nurse's station, "Marlena! I'm gonna need doctor Woodlin to come take a look at this!" She directed her attention to the adults in the room. "He will have to be admitted. Meanwhile, I'll have the doctor take a look, and we'll do a rape kit. Are you his parents?"

"No," Pae answered. "We don't know who the parents are. He wandered up to my house a few hours ago. We brought him in together. We gave as much information as we could when we checked him in."

Another female voice arose from behind. "I'm here!"

They turned and saw a heavy-set, dark-skinned woman in her early fifties wearing prescription glasses and a pants suit.

"Hi, Carolyn," the nurse greeted the woman, "Is he one of your cases?"

"Not yet. He will be. The office is closed, so I can't get any paperwork started, but he is not going back to wherever it is he came from."

"Sir," the nurse asked Pae, "do you have any idea how this happened? Where he lives?"

"I have a pretty good idea where he lives, but I can't prove it. As to how that happened? No, ma'am, I do not. I hope I have not ruined any chances of getting anything with the rape kit? I couldn't leave him in the same condition he was in when he showed up at my house. I had to clean him up. He had blood and waste all over him."

The nurse shook her head. "I don't know. It sounds awful, but you should probably have left him as he was. Well-intentioned as you were, you may have cleaned up any evidence as to who might have done this to him. Some of that blood could have been someone else's."

"I didn't wash his pelvis or abdomen in the vicinity of those bruises, or his nipples, either. Those look like hickeys to me. If anyone else's fluids dried-up on him, they could still be there? To the best of my knowledge, he hasn't been home since Halloween night. A girl claiming to be his sister came by looking for him on the morning of the First."

A baritone male voice arose from behind the group. "Pae, you forgot these." The man was a giant. He presented a clear plastic trash bag that contained the boy's soiled clothes, and the rags Pae had used to clean him. "Sherri-Lynn told me she forgot to grab them when you were dropping her and the child off at the emergency entrance. I went back for them and locked your doors for you."

"And who are you, sir?" the nurse asked.

"My name is John Maddox, ma'am. Folks call me Tiny."

The nurse eyeballed the gigantic, *corn-fed* man from head to toe. "Uh-huh?" she mumbled.

Tiny interjected, "I know Ms. Sherri-Lynn and Mr. Pae, personally. I can vouch for 'em both. A law enforcement friend of mine can vouch for me. He'll be along soon."

"Did you say, Mr. Pie?" the nurse grinned.

Pae clarified, "Pa-e, nurse, with a slight halt and an upward pitch on the *e* sound, but Pie is close enough. It's a nickname that I have been told means 'peace' in the Thai language. I never bothered to look it up. Some Thai friends gave it to me many years ago when I was stationed there in the Marines. Long story."

"Good evening," another voice called out, "I'm looking for a Mr...Pie?"

"That's me, sir," Pae responded to a law enforcement officer who had entered the room. He wore a brown and tan tactical uniform with a collared T-shirt. A five-point star was embroidered on the chest, and a metal badge was clipped on the black utility belt around his waist.

The child raised his tiny arm and sank his teeth into it while he emitted muffled screams. His face flushed red, and the veins in his neck, forehead, and temples protruded.

"What's going on?" the nurse looked at Pae and the others. "What is he doing?"

Pae urged the man, "Officer, could we step into the hallway, please?"

"Deputy U.S. Marshal McCade, sir, and yes, let's."

"Deputy U.S. Marshal, indeed?" Pae was surprised. "I didn't expect I'd see a marshal here tonight." The two men stepped into the hall away from the view of the room's occupants.

"Good evening, Marshal." Pae offered his hand. The deputy marshal shook it. "Here's my I.D.," Pae said as he reached into his back pocket. "Pae is a nickname. I live near this child in Empire County. I called their sheriff's department in late July to report that I had suspected he was being abused and possibly even molested."

The deputy marshal examined Pae's driver's license, then handed it back and peeked into the hospital room.

"It's a boy. Trust me on this," Pae assured him. "I called the non-emergency number because I didn't actually witness anything first-hand, except that he was filthy and his clothes were dirty. They were girl's clothes. There are girl's clothes in the room with him tonight in a plastic bag. They're his. I thought he was a girl at that time, so I kept referring to him as such while I was on the phone with the sheriff's office. The boy had been drifting around the neighborhood bundled up like it was the middle of winter with no supervision at all. At the very least, it looked like neglect. So, I called, and the dispatcher connected me directly to Sheriff Busbee. He told me to stay out of people's lives and get this: he said what they do for *fun* around there is their business. It was the damnedest thing I'd ever heard! He used those exact words, *'for fun'*! I couldn't help but wonder if he'd realized what he had said? He told me to call if I ever witness a real crime, otherwise, mind my own business, and then he hung up on me."

"Approximately, what day was this, sir?"

"July 30th, 10:42 a.m."

"That's awfully specific."

"The date and time sticks because I'd never experienced anything like that before. It was bizarre as hell. I called from a payphone at a convenience store a couple of miles from where I live. It was the Paq-Ur-Saq off route 221, toward Palafox."

"You say Sheriff Busbee spoke with you directly?"

"Yes, sir, directly. He sounded pissed, too! My gut tells me he knows this child and has some idea what's going on? Another problem is that a man who lives a little up the way from my house on a private road claimed this child is his, but no one else out there acts like they've ever even seen the boy either as a male or female. As far as anyone knows, that man only has a teenage daughter who is between maybe twelve to fourteen years old, and she's pregnant."

"Pregnant? Where did you get that information, sir?"

"Some of it from my next-door neighbor. She's familiar with a lot of folk out there. Whether all of it is accurate, I cannot say. It's just what I've been told. I did see a pregnant girl that I strongly suspect is her. She came to my door, looking for her little sister. She doesn't match the description I was given, but that far out in the sticks, how many others could there be? I think she was looking for this boy."

"This neighbor of yours who provided the information, is she related? A friend of theirs?"

"No, sir, not at all. Just a neighbor who spends a lot of time out and about. She comes across those folks now and then."

"What is this neighbor's name?" The deputy marshal was writing notes on a small, pocket-sized pad.

"Charlene. I don't know her last name. We live next door to each other on the paved portion of Busby Place. I don't know her address, but it's the only house next to mine. I'm at Box 8. Busby is spelled with a *y* at the end, not with two *e*'s like some of the folk out there. As far as I know, the child lives on the private dirt road beyond it."

"You said your neighbor gave you some of the information? Who gave you the rest?"

"Reverend Smalls, out at the First Assembly Church in Palafox. He's the one who told me no one is aware of any children living out there, especially not one this young. He has a lot of ties in and around Palafox."

"You say you think Sheriff Busbee might be involved somehow?"

"Well," Pae pointed toward the door to the hospital room, "the boy didn't start biting himself until you walked in. He went right to it as soon as

~ 225 ~

he saw you. I'd say it's the uniform, no doubt. If Busbee isn't directly involved, I'd make a solid bet he knows who is. Gotta be a uniform of some kind? My gut tells me--based on that phone call--that he's covering for them. Only my opinion for what it's worth?"

"I see. Would you please ask that huge fellow to step out here? I have a few questions for him, too."

"Will do, deputy marshal. Thank you for hearing me out."

Pae entered the room. "Tiny, the marshal has some questions for you."

Pae turned his attention to the boy as Tiny walked out. He raised his voice enough to be heard by the two men in the hall, "Don't be afraid, Precious Jewel. I'm back. The man in the uniform didn't take me away. He is gone now."

The boy stopped biting himself. The nurse stopped trying to calm him. Blood oozed down his forearm. He reached for Pae. Pae walked to the gurney. The boy wrapped his arms around him and squeezed tightly. He pressed his face against Pae.

"Love!" The boy smiled.

"What is your name, sweetheart?" the nurse asked.

"It's okay, beautiful," Pae comforted the child and swept his bangs aside, "you can tell her. She's here to help just like me and these other nice people."

The boy's dark eyes filled with fire. He waited to respond. "Milkshake Maker!" he growled. *Yet another derogatory description of himself*, Pae thought.

The nurse almost laughed. "Did you say, Milkshake Maker?"

The boy nodded.

"Why is your name Milkshake Maker?"

The child grabbed Pae's hips and jammed his face into his crotch.

"Holy shit!" the nurse exclaimed.

The child sucked twice on the fly of Pae's jeans then tried to push him aside. He leaned and looked toward the hallway then flipped a bird in the direction the deputy marshal had walked. "Milkshake Maker! Hole! It! It!" the boy screamed.

Sherri-Lynn threw her hands up and turned in a circle then stood with her mouth hanging open as she stared at Pae. She lowered her hands but kept one bent at the elbow with the palm turned upward.

"What the hell?" Sherri-Lynn asked Pae. "What the fuck was that?"

The child crawled forward on the gurney and picked up an instrument that was lying on a tray next to it. He hurled the object toward the door and screamed.

"Precious Jewel, don't go back!" the boy yelled. "Pae loves Precious Jewel! Pae loves Little Pee-Pee! They don't love Milkshake Maker!" He pointed toward the door. "Fuck-stick law dawg! I smell bacon!" He slapped his chest. "Devil Man-Whore!"

Tiny peaked into the room.

"We're okay, sir," the nurse told him. "But please ask the marshal to stay in the hall. He shouldn't come back in here."

"Nurse," Pae interjected, "it's not the marshal, it's his uniform."

"Yeah, I got that."

The nurse walked into the hall and yelled toward the station, "Marlena, is the doctor on his way?"

"Yes, ma'am, he is."

She walked back into the room to address Pae again. "Sir, would you object to a DNA swab? I hate to ask, but honestly? The way he clamped onto you? That just ain't right. I need to take a sample."

"That's not a problem at all, nurse. Anything I can do to help."

Sherri-Lynn raised an open palm and walked toward the door. "I'm sorry," she told Pae, "I can't look at you right now. I know I was eager to tag along, but I didn't anticipate this. It's too overwhelming. I'll be in the hall."

When Sherri-Lynn entered the corridor, she saw Tiny hug the marshal. Two Henshaw County sheriff's deputies were standing with them.

"Thank you, Kevin," she heard Tiny tell him, "I'm gonna owe you and your bud's big-time for this, brother! I hope y'all can find enough to put that bastard behind bars."

"This sort of thing normally falls on the local jurisdiction. We don't usually touch this kind of stuff. Possible corruption and involvement of

Empire's county sheriff might change that. The county coroner will certainly have to get involved if the sheriff has to be taken into custody, and the state police might have to get called out, too. Beyond that, I can't say. The best I can do is relay the information to a few contacts I have and hope they're willing to do something with it."

Nurse Kelly rushed past Sherri-Lynn. Pae and Carolyn remained in the room with the child. "Deputy Marshal!"

"Yes, ma'am?" the marshal said as Nurse Kelly approached.

"It slipped my mind: a couple of days ago, a friend of mine who nurses over in Covington out in Empire County, told me about a thirteen-year-old boy who showed up in their emergency room needing stitches in his penis. She said his daddy brought him in. I can't help but wonder if this is somehow related? Same bunch of people, maybe?"

"What makes you say that?" the deputy marshal asked.

Nurse Kelly leaned in close and lowered her voice. Tiny stepped back. "That boy in there just grabbed that Pae-man's bum-side and locked onto the fly of his jeans! Y'all heard the commotion? It might be a stretch, and I know it's a sickening thought, but I wonder if this child was the cause of that other boy's injury? I've seen a lot of weird stuff in this profession, especially from hicks, addicts, and rich, narcissistic assholes."

"Shit!" the deputy marshal huffed. He glanced at the entrance to the emergency exam room then back at Nurse Kelly. "Did your friend in Covington happen to mention any names?"

"Yes sir, but I can't recall. Sorry. She said they did come from money, though; dressed real nice and had a premium health care plan, but they insisted on paying in cash! The hospital accepted, but they ran their information anyway. It's their policy, and it's also the law."

"Can you remember the exact date? Did she mention the time?"

"I'm not positive. I want to say Halloween night? I'm pretty sure she said that's when they came in? It was an awfully hectic night for them. It had to have been somewhere after eight because her shift doesn't start 'till then, and she was already at work. You know, I've heard of kids getting razor-bladed by apples on Halloween, but I ain't never heard of any getting their weenies hacked up by a bag of chocolate bars!"

"Thank you, nurse."

"One more thing, sir."

"Yes?"

"That little boy said, 'Pae loves little pee-pee!' If he's a stray who just wandered up to that guy, why is he coming up with stuff like that? That's a bit too personal, especially for a child that age! And he's glued to that man like he's the only one in the room! It makes no sense!" Nurse Kelly squinted and shrugged. "I think there's more going on than that big Pae fellow is letting on."

"I'll look into it." The deputy marshal finished writing notes. He flipped the pad shut then put it into his pocket. He stuffed two sticks of gum into his mouth. The muscles in his left jaw rippled while he chewed and watched Nurse Kelly return to the exam room.

"That's a little too coincidental if you ask me," Sherri Lynn overheard the marshal tell Tiny.

"Yeah, I hear you, brother."

"How much do you know about good ole, Pae?"

"I met him two months ago. He seems like a stand-up guy, on the level, as far as I've ever seen."

"Hm!" the deputy marshal grunted. "I have a feeling we'll need to lay low on this one; not go beating down any doors, right up front. If these two incidents are related, there's likely something serious going on out there. If Sheriff Busbee is involved, I'll do what I can to make sure they lock his ass up and throw away the key. Just between you and me? If there is some kind of a child prostitution ring behind this and I could, I'd arrange it so all the assholes involved would get spread as big around as beer cans while they await trial. Turn 'em all into bagel butts!"

One of the nearby deputies shook his head and grinned with his hands on his hips. His female partner could not resist laughing.

"Oh, my God!" the female deputy giggled. "That's so gross! Bagel butt! Beer-can ass! I'll never get the image of an asshole that big out of my head!

God! That's just... Is that even possible? Eww!" The deputy shook her head while she covered her face. She dropped her hands and turned in a circle while she exaggerated a shudder. "That's just nasty!" She giggled again.

"Get used to it. We're not even scratching the surface. You'll eventually see a lot of crazy shit even in *Podunk* places like this...especially in *Podunk* places like this. It's a shame we don't start in jails and courthouses out here like in other counties, else you'd be used to it by now."

The deputy marshal added as he remained standing with Tiny, "Personally, I'd love to see Sheriff Busbee get castrated if he is involved, and then planted beneath the federal pen along with his accomplices, but the law must prevail. We'll handle it the right way."

"I hear you on that. Thank you for taking the time to come out."

"You got it, brother. I better get back before my break ends, and they notice me missing."

The two men shook hands and hugged again then parted ways. Tiny returned to the exam room. Sherri-Lynn walked to the waiting area.

The doctor arrived a few minutes later as the nurse swabbed Pae's mouth. He was accompanied by another staff member with a clipboard.

"Good evening, I'm Doctor Woodlin," the physician introduced himself as he entered the room. The doctor was tall, slim, and dark-skinned, with closely shorn hair that had a part carved on the left side. His eyes were grayish hazel green, and his face had a warm glow.

"It looks like we have a full house?" Doctor Woodlin smiled. "I specialize in Obstetrics, but I am the duty physician for emergency intake this evening. This is one of our interns, Doctor Weiss. We have surgeons on duty in the main hospital. Hopefully, we will not have to call upon them."

"Doctor Woodlin," the nurse said, "This is Ms. Carolyn Jenkins."

"Child Services?" the doctor asked. "Yes, we've met. How are you this evening, Ms. Jenkins?" He shook the lady's hand.

"Fine, doctor," Carolyn smiled. "I'm doing well, sir. It's always a pleasure getting to see those beautiful hazel eyes and that gorgeous dark skin! And how are you this evening?"

Doctor Woodlin's skin was too dark to show a blush, but he could not hide the pleasure in his smile. "I am flattered, Ms. Carolyn. I am doing well, indeed. Thank you. And who else do we have here, Nurse Kelly?"

"This huge wall of muscle is Mr. Pae, and this dinky fellow here is Tiny." Kelly grinned as she peeled her blue glove and whacked Tiny's arm. "Mr. Pae has volunteered a DNA sample for the lab. I haven't started the rape kit yet. I figured it best to let you take a look first. He's gonna have to be admitted."

"He?" the doctor asked. His eyes fell upon the boy's penis. "Indeed! So, you are."

"None of these folks are the parents. He's a stray they brought in. A woman was with them. She stepped out. We don't have much information. The patient's forms are laying over there." She pointed to a clipboard on a rollaway tray.

"Well now, you're a cute little..." the doctor turned to Pae and Tiny. He raised his brows and shrugged.

Pae spoke up, "A beautiful child, a precious jewel." He nodded at the doctor.

"Quite breathtaking, indeed." Doctor Woodlin offered a warm smile that concealed his concerns not only for the boy's appearance but also for Pae's peculiar word choices. He and his assistant donned gloves as they made their way to the child. "I'm guessing the deputies are here on his account?"

"Yes, doctor, they are," the nurse replied. "A deputy U.S. marshal is here, too."

The doctor looked at each of the adults in the room. "Forgive me if I sound rude, but I will need you all to step out, so Dr. Weiss, Nurse Kelly, and I may examine the child. Please, if you will?" He motioned toward the door.

Pae hugged the boy and kissed his forehead. He cupped the little one's rosy, swollen cheeks, and looked him in the eyes. "Doctor Woodlin and these other people love you just like me. Do not be afraid. They are going to help you. I will be right out in the hallway in case you need me, okay, precious?"

The child grinned and nodded. He threw his hands around Pae and hugged him again. "Beautiful child," he told Pae. They hugged for several seconds, then Pae eased himself from the boy's embrace.

Doctor Woodlin motioned toward the door in an usher-like manner. "Please," he said. "Nurse Kelly, have you taken any vitals?" the intern asked as the others left the room.

"No, doctor. It's been a little crazy in here."

"Doctor Weiss," Doctor Woodlin said, "please take the child's vitals, and examine that swell in his throat. I need to speak with nurse Kelly for a moment."

As soon as Doctor Woodlin was convinced the others were out of hearing range, he leaned toward the nurse. "Something is not sitting right with me," he mumbled. "It's that Pae fellow. There's something *off* about him."

"You noticed it, too?" the nurse replied. "I thought I was imagining things until that boy clamped down on him."

"What do you mean?"

"He grabbed that Pae man's ass and sucked on his fly! He acts like that man's the only real person in the room! And the way he refers to that child? They claim he's a stray who just wandered up to him tonight, but the boy is way too attached! It's creepy!"

"Yeah." Doctor Woodlin's brows narrowed. He pursed his lips.

Nurse Kelly added, "The woman that's with him is acting a little fishy too as if she's uncomfortable around him? Neither one said they were dating or even related to each other. She *pitched a hissy* and stormed out when the boy grabbed him. It seems to me she has no real idea who that man is."

"I see." Doctor Woodlin glanced at the boy. "Be sure you swab that child carefully, nurse. Get his hands, forehead, cheeks, and lips, besides all the obvious areas. I want to know if there are any signs of inappropriate contact by that big Pae dude. Check everywhere. Be careful when you do.

Write down what you've already heard and anything else the child might say. Get the camera from the nurse's station and photograph him from head to toe. Take a hundred snapshots if you have to. Put it in his file."

"That bag of clothes was brought in with him. There's some nasty-looking wash rags in there, too. That Pae fellow said, he cleaned the boy before he brought him here."

"Well, there go the swabs." Doctor Woddlin sighed. "Get 'em anyway for the sake of procedure. Prepare them for the lab. I'll call ahead to Doctor Rosenthal. She and her technicians are putting in extra hours tonight. They'll probably be eager to dig into this one. I'll talk to the deputies."

"Yes, doctor."

Pae, Tiny, and Carolyn stood together in the hallway. Sherri-Lynn remained separated. The nurse at the station called to them, "Hey, y'all! We have some hot coffee on, and there's vending machines right over yonder In the waiting area if y'all'd like?"

The group agreed that refreshments would be a welcome diversion.

Once in the waiting area, Carolyn asked, "Now, Mr. Pae, I was told a little bit over the phone, and I caught what you said in the room, but is there anything else you can tell me about that child? A real name? Next of kin? An address? Anything at all?"

"No, ma'am. I don't know his name. All I know--based on what little I've seen of a man claiming to be his father--is that he likely lives on a private dirt road off Busby Place in Knollwood out in Empire County. The child had drifted into my yard in late July. I gave him a peanut butter sandwich. His daddy found out and came at me with a friend of his."

"What do you mean, he 'came at' you?"

"Threatened me with a pistol. Told me to stay away and not even look in the child's direction. He referred to him in the feminine sense the whole time, obviously."

"Did you say anything to the law in Empire County?"

"Yep. They told me to mind my own business. That's how that man and his friend found out. The law called him. Whatever's going on with that boy, they didn't want it getting out. It's not a far stretch to figure out what they were hiding."

"Oh, my sweet Jesus," Carolyn covered her mouth. "Empire County! Forgive me. It's late. I just remembered: those folks out there? Most of 'em's related. There are a few extended families that have intermarried and been ruling the roost since my grandmother's time. That little boy's gotta be a Busbee or a Tillman? I'll see if I can get the doctor to send me a confidential lab report on him so I can verify his identity."

Tiny assured Carolyn, "My old buddy Deputy Marshal McCade will help you with whatever you need to find out who he is. He has people in our sheriff's office. None out there in Empire, but I'm sure he can handle them, too."

"Wait a minute." Carolyn asked Tiny, "You were the one behind this little gathering?"

"You mean behind getting you and the law out here? Yes, ma'am, I was."

"The man with the connections!" Carolyn smiled and patted Tiny's arm. "That should make life a little easier on me. I'll need you to ask your people to help me with this as best they can. I reckon we all oughta sit down and wait for the doctor to let us know when we can go?"

Sherri-Lynn approached the small group. "I'll peek in and let them know we're in the waiting area." She avoided eye contact with Pae and kept walking with her arms folded across her chest and her head down.

NOVEMBEr 3: MORNINg

"So, you're the little shit that broke my milkshake maker? How old are you sport?" a thin man with long, salt-and-pepper black and gray hair asked a boy. The lad's hands were tied behind his back and secured to an oak tree in front of a ragged old trailer. His clothing was made of fine, expensive materials, and his hair well-groomed. He was overweight. His brows were drawn in, and his cheeks flushed. The boy glared at the man. His crystal blue eyes were ablaze. He did not answer.

The man thumped the lad's forehead with a loud thud, leaving a red mark. The boy jerked his head to the side. "I'm thirteen, you bottom-feeding, hillbilly ass-wipe!" He spat in the man's face.

The man chuckled while he wiped the saliva. "You got a little spunk there, junior! A little fire in them bones! Tied up in the lion's den, and you still choose to go toe to toe with the king of the jungle! Hell, I admire that! It still don't answer my question."

The man's failure to retaliate troubled the boy.

Mark shrugged with his eyes closed, "I got no problem with you breaking my milkshake maker," he opened his eyes, "except you didn't return it, broken or not."

The boy offered no apology or explanation.

Mark looked the teen up and down while he grinned. "It's hard enough getting my hands on one, much less programming those damn things. But getting one that works without spilling a single damn drop?" Mark dropped his gaze while he ran his fingertips across the teen's lips. "Hell, that's right next to impossible!" He rubbed the boy's cheeks.

The boy snapped his head aside.

Mark grabbed the boy's head with both hands and stared into his eyes. "I had to throw away a few because they just wouldn't get with the program, but this one was special! It was a premium brand!"

Mark thumped the boy's head repeatedly. The teen's eyes watered, and his face contorted. He cringed and shifted from side to side.

"So, where is it? Huh? Where did you and dear ole daddy dump my milkshake maker?" The man bobbed his head.

The boy remained silent.

Mark leaned to within a few inches from the lad's face. "I heard about your little hospital visit." The man tilted his head. "How'd you get them stitches in that tiny little pecker, champ?" He smiled. "What turned your pole purple? Did the milkshake maker malfunction? Did it forget what it was and think it was blender?" The man grinned with dark, smug eyes. He nodded, "It did, didn't it?"

"Your little bitch bit it!"

The man unfastened the teen's pants and snatched them to his knees. He slid the blade of a large survivalist's knife into a leg of the boy's underwear then yanked it, slicing the garment in half. The tip of the blade bit into the boy's thigh, leaving a bright red dot that swelled and began to ooze.

The man laughed and shook his head. "*Bit* is hardly the word I'd use, sport! It looks like that thing nearly got ripped out by the roots! Hell, it looks like it starred in a damn shark show!"

Mark's expression sank from gleeful mockery to somber disappointment. "I'll bet dear ole daddy took you to the hospital over in Covington, didn't he?" He tapped on the boy's penis with the side of his blade. "Probably got all kinds of attention? All kinds of people asking all kinds of questions, huh?" He paused. "Yes? No? Maybe?"

The young teen trembled with anger, not sure whether to respond while the reality of his predicament sank in.

Two men stood a few feet away with dog collars around their necks, connected to chains. One of the men's eyes were puffy, bagged, and darkened. He looked as if he had not slept in a month. A pistol was pointed at his head. The slim salt-and-pepper-haired man's larger bearded companion held both chains and the revolver. Four other men stood close by, keeping watch. The chained man's mouth and chin were coated in dried blood.

"So, you chose to use my little milkshake maker in a way it was not programmed for, didn't you? You know how I know? Your daddy's little boyfriend sang like a canary when I started yankin' his teeth out with a pair of pliers. Didn't take any effort at all to get that soft little doughboy to spill his guts."

"He ain't my daddy's boyfriend, you low-income trailer park reject!"

The slim man laughed and looked at the other men. He tousled the boy's hair. "Atta boy, sport! You're full of all kinds of piss and vinegar, aren't you? I like that! I really do! You might not have much of a dick left, but you got twice the balls of that weak-kneed sack of shit and his fat little guy pal over there."

The longhaired man looked at the bloodied, chained man while he addressed the teen. "He told me your little stick was just small around and stiff enough to force up the milkshake maker's ass end." He looked at the teen's anatomy and shook his head. "Plump little rich boy ain't got no natural endowment. Such a shame."

Mark returned his attention to the boy's face. "From there, you got too damn carried away and started hammering. The milkshake maker malfunctioned, then turned around and ripped the livin' shit out of your tiny little mushroom!"

A snide chuckle escaped the longhaired man's mouth. His eyes grew darker. "And then you lost it! You let it fly away, right out the back seat of dear ole daddy's car. Why? Huh? Why did you do that, Sparky? Tell me."

Mark placed the blade of his knife against the boy's throat. The anger drained from the boy's eyes when he felt the bite, followed by a thin, warm, trickle of blood. He sensed the game was over: something terrible awaited.

"Because your damn, dumbass daddy wanted you to feel all growed up. He figured you're finally old enough to become a bonafide part of his world. So, he threw a special coming of age party to let you play a little rich bitch game of domination, that's why. He wanted you to become a chip off the old block, didn't he? Show you what it's like to be in control? Your rite of passage into the secret man-club of Daddy Rich Bucks?"

The longhaired man pointed the knife at the boy's father. "Well, I got news for you, little man! Your daddy and his fat girlfriend, here?"

Mark waited to see if the boy would challenge him again. The boy held his tongue. "They're gonna find out what low-income trailer park rejects do when you destroy their property and lose it, and then run to the damn county hospital to give up shit-tons of information!"

The man shook his head and muttered, "Backseat of a car, no less." He turned his attention to the bound men and raised his voice, "Too damn stupid to take it home or at least get a room, miles from here! Hell, all that damn money...you coulda got a fuckin' private jet, but no! You kept that shit right at the back doorstep, in our own backyard, right where it could bail out and hide! All that money and power, and not a single, legitimate damn brain cell among you!"

The man looked back at the boy and grinned. "But don't worry! You won't miss out. You'll get to join the *real* secret male domination man-club!"

The teen's eyes widened. He trembled.

"Now, let's have us some fun, shall we?"

"Hold on, Mark, I wanna watch this!" a female voice rang out. It was the man's large, redheaded companion, Sasha. "Don't do anything yet! I'm gonna microwave some popcorn and bring us some beers!" She struggled to stand then stopped to catch her breath once she was up. "This is gonna be better'n a damn picture show!" She glared at the thin man, "Which your sorry ass ain't took me to see in a coon's age! This'll make up for it, though! Hold on now, while I go get us some refreshments!" She waddled inside the trailer.

Sasha returned several minutes later with a bowl of microwaved popcorn and a foam ice chest.

"Well, looky there! She's back! Y'all ready?" Mark looked at one of the watchmen, who was leaning against the residential propane tank anchored in the yard. "Wade?" he asked.

"Born ready, baws-man!"

Mark looked at the others. "Bubba? Bruno? Lance? Bobby?"

"Chompin' at the bit, brother! Give us the word!"

Mark turned back to the boy. "Hey sport, do you like trains?"

The teen's jaw dropped a little. His eyes glazed over. He looked like his brain had blown a fuse trying to comprehend the question. "I don't know? They're okay, I guess?"

"Oh, ho-ho!" Mark mused. "They're much better than okay! They're a butt-load of fun!"

The other men chuckled.

"You'll get to see that here soon, 'cause we're all gonna play choo-choo train, and that includes your fat little jelly caboose!"

The large woman roared with laughter. "It's too bad that pregnant little bitch Candy is out lookin' for the milkshake maker! She'd pop that bun two months early if she saw this! Y'all make sure y'all *rosebud* one of 'em! I ain't never seen that up close and personal!"

"*WOO! WOO!*" Wade mimicked a steam whistle.

Alvin chortled, "All aboard!"

NOVEMBEr 5: EARLy AfTERNOOn

A telephone rang in a large, crowded, cubicle-filled office, at a desk stacked with folders and papers. Photographs of children of all ages and more papers suspended by pushpins adorned the partitions behind the cubicle's occupant. Rings emanated from other cubicles. Carolyn looked down at her phone.

"Every damn line," she grumbled. "The sky must be falling today?" She picked up the handset and pushed one of the buttons. "State Child Protective Services, this is Carolyn, how may I help you?"

Carolyn sat and listened. "Mmm-hmm?" the middle-aged female mumbled. She pulled a thin manila folder from atop her desk, then opened it and scribbled notes. "What's that?" she asked. "Are you sure?" The woman continued to listen, making occasional sounds to acknowledge the speaker. She scribbled more notes. Several minutes passed. "Alright, now. You have a great day, Ms. Sarah Jean. Mm-hmm. Bye, now."

Carolyn hung up then tapped her pen on the open folder, leaving small black dots on one of the attached forms. She looked at the document that was clipped on the opposite side, ignoring the blinking lights on the telephone's other four lines. The social worker picked up the handset and pressed the button on the open line then dialed a number from an adhesive note inside the folder.

"Hello?" a pleasant male voice answered.

"Hello, Mr. Pae?"

"Speaking."

"Mr. Pae, this is Carolyn over at the state CPS. We spoke in the hospital a few days ago."

"Yes, ma'am, I remember. How may I help you?"

"Well, Mr. Pae, I just got some information back from the child's DNA, prints, and lab work."

"Yes?"

"It ain't good, sir. Are you sitting?"

The hair stood on the back of Pae's neck. He felt a weird twinge in his chest and a knot in his stomach. "I'm sitting."

"The boy don't exist."

Pae fell silent for a moment. "He doesn't exist? How does that happen?"

"Probably born in the back seat of a car or in a crack house? Could have been born in that clinic that burned down out in Patawnee a handful of years back. They weren't up with the times. Lost a dozen or so birth records along with scads of other information, including immunizations. Whatever the case, he's not in the public system that anyone can find. His DNA ain't on file."

"Something tells me there's a lot more to this?"

"Yes, sir, Mr. Pae, there is. No one's been looking for him. He doesn't match any missing persons bulletins. Nothing's coming up in the law's databases. They're still searching abducted and missing children's files as far back as eight years to be sure, but nothing's coming up. They just don't have enough to go on, and there are too many records that could be a match but cannot be proven. He might not be from this area or even this state, as far as that goes. He is being listed as a John Doe."

"How does that bode in terms of placement?"

"Not well, Mr. Pae. Not well at all. The state isn't gonna give him up to anyone's care anytime soon."

"What about those folks up the road from me? Aren't they his family? Can't the law question them? Get the boy's identity that way?"

"They're not related, and they have no children or any legal custody of anyone else's children. Are you sure that little boy lived out that way?"

"The way that man was behaving toward me, I have no doubt. I'm pretty sure there's a pregnant teenaged girl there, too."

"I see. I'll make some calls and see if I can turn up anything on her. Meanwhile, the boy's gonna end up housed in a psychiatric facility until they can figure out whether he's fit to go into the foster system. They don't usually check because there are too many of them from broken homes who do need observation or counseling at the least. They're giving him special consideration because of the uniqueness of his case. Honestly, Mr. Pae, that could take some time. The politics of gender isn't the issue. It's the question of whether the boy is stable enough to be placed into society, especially around other children? He's already exhibiting some major behavioral problems."

"How long is 'considerable' likely to be?"

"Truthfully? It could be years, Mr. Pae, assuming they ever let him out? He has some serious medical issues that have gone untreated. It's a wonder the child appears as healthy as he does. He has some developmental problems, too. For starters, he cannot read or write. Being five or six years old, he's not really behind, except that his vocabulary is limited. He can't express himself as clearly as other children his age.

"He has no concept of table manners or hygiene, outside of brushing and rinsing his teeth. Lord knows why, but he's adamant about that. He can gargle mouthwash, too. Beyond that, he's a mess. He doesn't know how to wipe himself. He drops his drawers wherever he's at. The boy doesn't comprehend modesty. They had to put some special mittens on his hands to keep him from getting out of his clothes every time they turned around. I was told they considered fitting the po' child for a straitjacket.

"He also has some serious psychological problems besides being emotionally detached. Except for occasional anger outbursts, he acts like he has no emotions. Although they hate the term and rarely use it anymore, they think the child might genuinely be psychotic. It's sad. I've seen so many troubled children disappear into the system. They get shut away where they can't be a burden to society, and that's that."

Pae was choked up. His heart broke. "Is there any way possible to have her, um, him released into my custody, or Ms. Sherri-Lynn's, or maybe into Tiny's and his wife's? Any way at all to put him with folks he's a little familiar with and trusts?"

"I'm afraid not, Mr. Pae. I understand your compassion for that child, I really do, but there is no way on earth the state is going to release him into anyone's care anytime soon, much less into the charge of any single folk, and most definitely not a single male. That's out of the question. I'm not trying to be mean, Mr. Pae, that's just how the state works. That poor child's been on my brain day and night. I've been praying and praying.

"Between you and me the four walls," Carolyn continued, "I really wish I could get away with doing something illegal so I can get that boy out of the system and into a real home with folks that can afford to give him the care and treatment that he needs, but that's just not going to happen. My hands are tied on this one, sir."

Pae sat in silence for a few seconds.

Carolyn could hear Pae sniffling. "Are you okay, baby?"

"No. I'm heart-broken and mighty disappointed, Ms. Carolyn. I love that little boy, and I feel horrible that I can't do anything for him."

"You've done more than enough, Mr. Pae. You brought that child to the hospital and got him away from some crazy-ass people that pimped him out as a girl. You saved his life, sir. That's all anyone could ask."

Pae fell silent again. His heart was too heavy to speak.

"Thank you, baby," Ms. Carolyn said. "You did all that you could. Now, it's my turn to do all that I can. I can't make any promises, but I can guarantee you that I will do everything within my power to make sure he gets the best care the state can provide. I realize that might not be saying a whole bunch? The system is overwhelmed. But the child will get to live, and he is out from under the roof that endangered him. I will keep you informed. Thank you, Mr. Pae."

"Thank you, Ms. Carolyn."

Carolyn could tell Pae was devastated. "Bye-bye, now, baby."

"Bye, Ms. Carolyn."

Carolyn hung up the phone and reclined her chair. She placed her hand over her forehead and eyes. "Lord, Lord, Lord!" she mumbled, "Please help us all, Lord Jesus!" She remained reclined for a few minutes, contemplating. "I'm getting too old for this. I need a vacation in the Bahamas."

Pae entered the backyard then crawled to the spot under the house where he remembered a little girl had circumvented the privacy fence. He sat upon the dirt and thought about the boy in the state system. At times the man wished he could shut off the side of his brain that emulated female traits, but he could not deny his compassion, empathy, or heightened emotions no matter how hard he tried. It was an ingrained part of the male's psyche and as much a part of him as the testosterone that helped build his thick, muscular frame. Pae, like everyone else in this world, was a unique culmination of biology, experience, and faith. Though he sometimes wrestled with his peculiarities, he accepted them. Pae prayed for the child as he sat in the dirt and cried. Rain started to fall.

NOVEMBEr 8: NOOn

Pae had felt drained since the phone call from Carolyn three days prior. Visits from investigators and the nature of their questions had not helped. Pae wondered whether they took him at his word and whether they had acquired a recording of his phone call to the sheriff's department. They had been evasive when he had inquired. Mark's blue pickup truck had made creeping passes in front of his house during the day. Pae had scarcely slept, expecting an intrusion during the night, but all had been quiet. Unpredictability made the nights seem colder and darker. This compounded his lethargy and triggered paranoia. It heightened his sense of self-preservation. Pae was exhausted and prepared for a fight to the finish.

Meanwhile, Pae had eaten one peanut butter sandwich, a soft oatmeal cookie, a powdered mini donut, and a cup of milk each day, after praying for the child. He had consumed little else. His midsection was growing soggy. He had drunk a lot of hard alcohol but stopped after he had seen Mark's truck crawl past his house. He needed to be as alert as he could manage, and he did not want to risk being influenced into making poor decisions.

Pae had never been as attached to another human being as to the nameless little platinum-haired boy. Whether the result of misplaced emotions from his childhood trauma or a healthy, sympathetic sense of compassion, he was convinced he loved the boy as his own. Considering how the world had treated the child, in contrast, the boy was more Pae's than anyone else's.

Paranoid and demoralized, Pae called Reverend Smalls to inform him of recent events. Their conversation was lengthy. Reverend Smalls was as genuine a person as Pae had ever met. He was glad to know someone in the clergy who cared, a man who had proven a willingness to act in support of those he barely knew. *There really are very few left in the world*, Pae thought.

Pae considered calling Sherri-Lynn but decided it would be best to see her in person. He drove to Spanky's. She was not there. Tiny met him at the bar.

"She hasn't been here since that night at the hospital," Tiny explained. "She took a few days off to clear her head. Didn't say for sure when she'd be back."

"May I call her? You do have her new number, don't you? Either her phone is cut off, or she's changed it? The number I have isn't working."

Tiny thought for a moment. "Well, she didn't say one way or the other, but considering you two go back a ways," Pae did not see the point in arguing the inaccuracy in Tiny's statement, "I reckon she wouldn't mind? She is awfully sweet on you, that's for damn sure."

Now, that bit of information caught Pae by surprise. If there were any words he had not expected to hear, those were the ones. Pae wondered as Tiny wrote Sherri-Lynn's phone number on the back of a business card. Tiny handed the card to Pae. "Good luck, brother."

Pae took the card with his left hand. "Yeah," he extended his right hand, "thank you." The men shook. Pae rendered a scout salute to Spanky and blew a kiss to the young greeter, Kayla, as he exited the building.

Pae got into his car and dialed the number. The phone rang a handful of times before the message system engaged. Sherri-Lynn's unmistakable voice was on the recorded greeting. He left her a message then waited. She did not return the call. After sitting in the car listening to the radio for about twenty minutes, he started it and drove home.

NOVEMBEr 9: NOOn

Pae had left a few other messages on Sherri-Lynn's phone during the hours that followed his departure from Spanky's the day before. She did not return his calls. He returned to Spanky's. Sherri-Lynn was there, greeting at the entrance.

"Please leave," Sherri-Lynn requested dismissively, as soon as Pae entered the building. He did not understand her distance. His heart sank. Pae stopped walking toward her, confused. He opened his mouth to speak, but Sherri-Lynn interrupted, "Go home."

"No, not until we talk about what's going on with you."

"GET...THE FUCK...OUT!" Sherri-Lynn shouted while she pointed to the door behind Pae.

"Okay!" Pae raised his hands and backed away. Spanky watched from the bar. Tiny entered from the hallway near the private rooms. "Okay, I'm going!" Pae exclaimed loudly enough for the others to know he was complying with Sherri-Lynn's demand. He lowered his tone and looked her in the eyes, "I am more than willing to talk whenever you're ready. You know how to reach me." Pae departed.

NOVEMBEr 10: LATe AFTERNOOn

Pae had finished shopping at a tiny *mom-and-pop* general store near Fowlers Crossroads in Fayette county. As he walked to his car, he was met by two men: one was taller than he, but neither had the muscular girth.

"My, my, my, if it isn't ole big guy Pae," the taller man said.

"Do I know you?"

"No, but we sure as hell know you! You are not easy to find these days, Mr. Moffat. We've been looking all over hell and back for your big ass."

"Yeah, well, I've been a little busy."

"I'm sure you have. It don't seem like you're home much anymore? Imagine our surprise when we dropped by here and happened to see you out strolling around! This must be our lucky day! It ain't yours, though."

"Oh, really? Why might that be?"

"You took *The Man's* property. *The Man* don't appreciate nobody taking what's his."

"I didn't take anyone's property."

"*The Man* thinks you did."

"Well, '*The Man*' is mistaken. I don't have anyone's property but my own."

"Whether you have it or not doesn't make a damn bit of difference. You took it. *The Man* figured it out when the law started snooping around. They're not as sneaky as they think they are. It's pretty obvious you ain't, either. After all, here we are."

The tall man's eyes turned as cold as ice. "You're not gonna take anyone else's property." He reached into his jacket toward the waist of his pants.

Pae could not hear anything but his own heartbeat. He could not see anything but the man standing before him. The rest of the world had faded out. Pae felt like he was floating as he dropped his paper grocery bag and charged the man

The taller man was not able to withdraw his hand before Pae drove his left fist upward into his nose. The man stiffened like timber and fell straight back. Pae did not see the man's limp body start twitching on the ground with eyes wide, mouth agape, and jaw moving as if gasping for air while blood gushed over his face and seeped into the dry, red-orange clay. Pae did not see the pistol that had slipped from the man's waistband onto the soil parking lot. He had already acquired his second target.

The shorter man was panic-stricken, staring in disbelief at the ease with which Pae had dispatched his partner. He spun open a butterfly knife, but Pae was already upon him. Pae caught the man's wrist with his right hand, and his upper arm with his left as the man leaned into him. The momentum of the shorter man's forward movement caused him to run himself through with his own blade when Pae immobilized his arm above the elbow and forced his hand back. The knife dug into the stranger's left lung between his ribs. Pae stepped aside. The punctured male fell upon his dagger, driving it to the hilt.

Pae stood motionless for a moment, trying to process what had happened. His world was still moving in a slow-motion blur without any sound except his heartbeat and his breathing. He stood with his arms dropped to his side, staring at the groaning, twitching man whose nose had been violently disfigured and the dying man who had fallen on his own blade. No lucid thoughts entered his mind. He kept looking back and forth, scanning the two fallen men, wondering what had just happened.

Pae snapped from his fog and looked down both ends of the rural county road. It was empty. The ruckus had drawn no attention from the elderly store attendants inside.

Pae gathered his groceries and got into his car. He watched the men with bewilderment from the open window for a few more seconds. It seemed like hours. Reality started settling in when he noticed the gurgling moans from the smaller, suffering man drowning in his own blood. Pae turned his head to observe the storefront and the road one last time. He eased onto the pavement and drove away.

Pae called for paramedics from a payphone at an abandoned gas station a little more than a mile away. He was careful to use a clean napkin from his center console to manage the handset. The trembling, adrenaline-filled male wiped the coins with his T-shirt before inserting them by their edges and dialed the squared, silver, numbered buttons with a pen. Pae remained anonymous during the call. He provided basic but essential information as rapidly as possible before hanging-up while the dispatcher continued asking questions.

Three more miles up the road, a state trooper's cruiser blasted past Pae's car heading in the opposite direction toward the general store with lights flashing and siren wailing. A county sheriff's vehicle was not far behind. Pae pulled onto a public dirt road and stopped at a wooded park. He transferred his groceries to the trunk then sat on a cement picnic table where he caught a glimpse through distant trees of yet another police interceptor rushing by. Pae smoked a cigarillo and prayed while images of the war and the preceding months ricocheted through his brain.

NOVEMBEr 13: BOOk Of SORROWs

Pae had scarce slept for several days. He was consumed with frustration and guilt. *This isn't the way it was supposed to be*, he thought. *Two divorces, no children, living on disability, trapped in the middle of nowhere with almost no real social life, kept at a distance by two dazzling and wide-open yet highly guarded women... Still, no idea whether way back in July, that little girl—that little boy--really did...*

Pae closed his eyes and shook his head.

That wild sex I'd had with a woman I'd never even dated, and the things we let each other do... And now, I've seriously injured two men, and maybe killed one of them, not to mention the completely underhanded way I handled that emergency call...zero integrity!

When I'm frustrated, I cuss, smoke, drink, masturbate, and go places to watch naked women... I open myself up and run my mouth like I've got no better sense. I get pissed, and I tell off God! It's a wonder I'm still breathing! What kind of a believer am I? What kind of a vile human being?

Pae felt horrible. As he sat in silent contemplation, impressions ran through his mind:

I remember that you are made of dust; I remember that you dwell within a frail tent of flesh. I know your disappointments and your fears. I hear every cry; I feel every heartache; I see every tear. You are honest with yourself, and you are honest with me; therefore, you are honest with others. You suffer because you have a heart for me, but you are also human and living in a fallen world; it is the way of things. You struggle because your conscience is alive; you care about the things of God, and you are keenly aware of your shortcomings. You are not abandoned. You are not rejected. You are growing. You are changing. You have a heart for those toward whom I have a heart. Reject the internal accusations. Turn away from negative, self-condemning thoughts and confusion. Remember the one who has preserved you and who knows the number of the hairs on your head. You are loved.

DECEMBEr 4: MORNINg

"Hey there, little Sis, how're you doin'? You hangin' in there?" Tiny asked Sherri-Lynn over the phone.

"I'm good, Tiny. Just a lot on my mind is all."

"I got some information from Deputy Marshal McCade if you want to hear it?"

"Yeah, sure. What is it?"

"He discussed things with his supervisor a few weeks ago then contacted a friend of his at an FBI field office. The feds didn't want to get involved. They said it was a local matter, but they did offer to help out if anything turned up. Kevin figured they threw in that last part as a professional courtesy but probably wouldn't get involved anyway."

"That's really sad. That poor little boy went through some awful shit. I can't believe they're not even going to try?"

"Hold on, there's more. An interesting name showed up on the Coosa County sheriff's docket last week. They arrested some guy for DWI that had felony warrants and get this: he has direct ties to somebody on an international most-wanted list of some kind. They don't know how they overlooked it before, but that's how it goes. Sometimes, things slip through the cracks. They've been after that guy on the list for domestic child trafficking and some gang murders overseas. Once they squeezed that DWI and found out he had all kinds of connections in Empire County, the fed's got all over it like white on rice! That's all I got. Kevin didn't really say anything else except that it's not looking good for the law out there."

FEBRUARy 28: MORNINg, BEFORe SUNRISe

His tongue shriveled from the bitter sea that gushed into his mouth and clawed his palate. His eyes shrieked amid fields of fire as he broke the surface, expelling water from tormented olfactory cavities. Through a dark, milky haze, he saw the blurred silhouettes of five sets of hands extended from the sides of a dinghy. He swam toward the hands under the black, starlit sky. As he raised a hand upward, his blurred, ocean-drenched eyes saw the distressed faces of five people staring back through a tumult of rising noise. He felt slaps against his fingers, then pushes against his shoulders and kicks against his face. It was then that he heard the occupants of the tiny craft screaming profanities. They hurled objects as they resisted his attempts to board.

He heard a ruckus emerge from behind the group. The sea churned violently as a larger vessel rapidly submerged. Its bow had already slipped into the murky black deluge. He treaded water, backing away from those in the boat so he could get a clear view. Those who remained on the sinking ship had hoisted a morbidly obese woman over their heads and tossed her into the sea without a lifejacket. It was then that he realized he had no life jacket, neither did anyone aboard the ship. Only the five occupants in the dinghy wore them.

"There's a choice we're making!" he heard a random voice cry out.

He watched in horror as a boy in a wheelchair was hoisted up and tossed overboard after the woman. The man's heart sank like a rock. He swam as rapidly as he could to where he had seen the woman and the boy plunge. They were nowhere to be found. He dipped his face but could see nothing. He dove into the liquid abyss, blind and reaching in hopes of taking hold of the two. He turned back when overwhelming pressure stabbed his inner ears, and his lungs constricted. He struggled to maintain consciousness as he hurried upward toward the few, faint shimmers of muted starlight dancing upon the surface.

Water sprayed as he breached and gasped for air. Profane shouts filled his ears as a naked man chained at the waist was thrown from the sinking ship. The chained man screamed at the top of his lungs. A train of other naked men, all bound at the waist and tethered to each other, slipped over the railing into the depths.

"No..." the man whispered in ghastly terror as he treaded the surface. Hopelessness settled in.

The crew members on the sinking vessel took up a feeble old man. He was also naked and chained at the ankles and wrists. The old man laughed hysterically as he was raised above the heads of those who prepared to dispose of him. A group of crying women rushed toward the elderly man. They beat upon his stomach and ribs and spit in his face while it was turned toward them. He continued to laugh. As the crowd carried the man to the side of the ship, a little girl gazed into his eyes. His laughter faded into silent bewilderment. The child reached upward and placed a cookie in one hand and a small, white bird in the other. A glimmer arose in the child's eyes as she smiled at the old man. Tears rolled down his face. He gripped the cookie tightly, then blew a kiss at the bird and released it. The bird flew away. The ship's crew hurled the chained, elderly man into the sea.

The man treading the water swam briskly toward the elderly man and cradled him in his arms. "It's okay," the old man said with a smile. "It's okay!" The old man eased beneath the surface, still smiling as the water closed in upon his face. He disappeared amid the quiet sloshes of calm ocean ripples.

The yacht was gone with all who had remained aboard her, including the child. The lifeboat had set sail under the power of wooden oars. A female voice rang through the pungent, humid ocean air, "We have saved our own lives! And I have saved this corkscrew and wine!"

The man was alone on the surface of the water beneath a night absent the moon. He stared at the shimmering white twinkles affixed to the black expanse overhead. The word *trust* ran through his mind.

MARCh 15: EARLy AFTERNOOn

"The FBI, in conjunction with the Alabama Department of Public Safety and the Empire County Coroner's Office, raided the property of Mark Busbee in Knollwood at sunrise yesterday morning," a news reporter broadcasted from a local television station. "Busbee had been under investigation for suspected ties with international gangsters and domestic child traffickers since early November."

Pae stopped walking across the living room of his apartment. The breaking story captured his attention. He stood as if rooted to the floor.

The reporter continued. "Busbee, a forty-three-year-old Empire native, was a convicted felon who had served a reduced sentence of two years in Henshaw County for outstanding warrants. Allegations of kidnapping had been brought against him, but there was insufficient evidence to support the claim, and his accuser refused to cooperate with the police. He was released three years ago. Busbee was fatally shot when he and his accomplices fired upon agents during the raid. His partner, Ms. Sasha Marquette, thirty-nine, was wounded when she attempted to surrender. She has no prior convictions or arrests and is being held for questioning.

"Busbee's brother, Sheriff Clayle Busbee, who had served the Empire County Sheriff's Department for more than thirty years, was apprehended by a U.S. marshal and taken into custody by the county coroner. Sheriff Busbee was anally sodomizing a thirteen-year-old boy several hundred yards from the site of the primary raid. He had failed to notice agents as they approached. The child had been handcuffed to a tree, wearing a dress, a wig, and women's makeup, and jewelry. Busbee was on duty and in uniform at the time of his arrest. His vehicle has been seized and impounded for evidence. The boy, who was reported missing in November, was treated at Providence Regional Medical Center and is currently undergoing a psychiatric evaluation.

"Two other men, Mr. Lance Coleman, thirty-four, and Mr. Wade Baker, forty-five, surrendered after exchanging shots with law enforcement. A fourteen-year-old girl who claims to be the daughter of Mark Busbee--but whose identity has not been confirmed—gave up after receiving a superficial gunshot wound from behind, caused by Mr. Coleman who was intoxicated. The girl had willingly fired upon agents prior to Coleman's accidental interference. She was also treated at Providence Regional Medical Center and has been transferred into the custody of the Wayland Juvenile Detention Center. She is being held without bail, pending identification, and trial.

"Meanwhile, four infants--one boy and three girls, each approximately three months in age--were caught in the crossfire, unknown to agents. They were not injured. Marquette and the teen denied any relationship with the infants, but sources have confirmed the triplets are indeed Marquette's, and the teen is the mother of the fourth. Mark Busbee is the confirmed father of the teen's child.

"Investigators say the vehicle of a man reported missing along with his son—the boy whom Sheriff Busbee had sodomized--was discovered in a densely wooded area on the property. The man's personal belongings and those of a long-time acquaintance were found inside Busbee's residence. All three have been missing since November.

"Agents also recovered the personal effects of at least four other persons who had disappeared during the years following Busbee's release from Henshaw County. The identities of the missing persons to whom the objects belong are being withheld. Their whereabouts remain under investigation.

"Three pit bulls that were chained on the property have been handed over to the Empire County Humane Society. Though kennels were found inside Busbee's residence and in a panel van on the property, investigators say there is strong evidence suggesting they had been used to house children, not animals.

"Meanwhile, the county coroner's office and state police have unearthed at least a dozen shallow graves during a comprehensive search of Busbee's five-hundred-acre property. Law enforcement agencies from neighboring counties are assisting in on-going investigations following the raid. The Empire County Sheriff's Office has been barred from participating while three of its deputies have been taken into custody. Two others have been administratively suspended without pay. Other local, county, and state officials are still being questioned. No further arrests or suspensions have been made. Neighbors and known associates are being interviewed while raids occur elsewhere throughout Empire County.

"In related news, Mr. Robert 'Bobby' Tillman, forty-nine—pictured here--also a native of Empire County is being sought as a person of interest. If anyone has any information concerning his whereabouts, you may report it anonymously to the number at the bottom of your screen.

"Some of our viewers might recall two men who were assaulted in the parking lot of a Fayette County mercantile back in November. We have since learned that those men were associates of Mark Busbee. Thirty-eight-year-old Bruno Cavallo had died from complications at Drew Memorial Hospital on the day of the assault. Mr. Arthur Weddle, thirty-five, was found dead at the scene from a knife wound to his chest. Both men were convicted felons who had served short sentences in the Alabama Department of Corrections. To date, no suspects have been identified in their slayings. We will provide more details as they are received."

Pae shook his head. "That Sheriff Busbee is a dead man." *They publicly dimed him, hung that ole boy out to dry.*

Though glad to see justice in motion, Pae was disappointed. He had prayed for those people as often as he had prayed for the little boy. He had accumulated countless hours over the months, yet the people had not changed. Instead, they continued in their ways and brought swift judgment upon themselves.

Pae recalled the two men in Fayette County.

What was it all worth? His mind filled with questions. The more he wondered, the worse he felt.

As Pae considered his mounting grief, words from the Old Testament book of Ezekiel came to mind. He recalled them as best he could: *As surely as I live, says the LORD, I take no pleasure in the death of the wicked; but I desire instead that they turn away from their evil and live.*

That doesn't help, Pae thought. His heart grew heavier. He struggled to reconcile the words with the events of the past eight months and with the television's news. He considered Second Peter chapter 3, verse 9: *God is not lazy concerning His promise, as some consider laziness, but is exceedingly patient toward us, not willing that anyone would perish, but that all might turn from the errors of their ways.*

Pae cupped his face in his hands and huffed. *Why are these thoughts running through my head? They don't fit. They're making me feel worse!*

He slipped deeper into thought. *Why did that man, Mark, have to die? Why did any of them have to? Why, even with all the prayer over nearly three quarters of a year, did those people not change? Why could I not have learned of them years ago and started praying then? Would more time have made any difference? Has anyone else been praying for them? Family? Friends? Anyone?* Pae was not sure what to make of the situation beyond the obvious.

Pae's thoughts returned to his sexual rendezvous with Sherri-Lynn. His conscience had troubled him enough afterward, but now that she was out of the picture, he felt much worse.

I blow it every time I turn around. Every major decision I make seems to kick me in the face. I suppose that's just how life is? Has any worthwhile good come from any of this?

An impression arose within Pae's mind while he sat in contemplative silence:

Sometimes, it is about you. Sometimes, it has as much to do with you as with everyone else, and sometimes even more. You learned to overcome barriers that had hindered you throughout your life and kept you trapped in a predictable but ineffective existence. You pushed aside the lies you once believed of yourself and found genuine compassion for those the world deems unlovable and useless. You prayed for those that others would rather forget, and you took life-endangering action to ensure the welfare of another outside the realm of occupational duty. You learned to stand up for yourself and to love your life enough to preserve it for the sake of others. Conversely, you acquired deeper levels of trust through your willingness to surrender your dependence upon material weapons in exchange for spiritual assurances. Your faith has increased. You have what you need to continue on the road ahead.

Pae's heaviness lifted. He received no more impressions. His grief dissipated.

Pae reflected upon the child. The little boy remained a ward of the state. Ms. Carolyn kept him updated on the boy's progress. It pained him to hear that the little one had been living in a juvenile psychiatric facility with no word on a pending release. Being the youngest in the ward and effeminate, he had been a target of the older residents since day one. The staff had cut his hair short, but neither that nor his hospital-issued uniform had helped him blend or stave off any bullies.

Pae was told the boy's incarceration had been extended for several reasons, including the performance of oral sex on older boys. He had repeated the words *outside* and *woods* each time he had been caught. One custodial staff member had been detained by security then arrested after police arrived, for having been discovered in the act of coaxing the child into oral sex in exchange for a walk around the grounds. The custodian had no idea the video and audio surveillance systems had been repaired. Aside from an extended stay, the boy's behaviors had earned him intermittent placement in isolation, accompanied by more frequent therapy sessions and increased medications.

The child had broken the fingers and busted the nose of an eleven-year-old girl who had grabbed his butt and called him a little sissy. He had also sunk his teeth into the testicles of a twelve-year-old who had picked on him since the day he had been admitted. The youngster had lured the older boy to execute his revenge. The resulting nicknames the older children had assigned the pint-sized blonde were Honey Hole, Violent Femme, and Pae-Eyed-Piper: a play on words because the boy frequently wandered the ward calling for Pae; it held a dual meaning because of the lad's reputation for "smoking the skin pipes."

The boy had been difficult to manage in the presence of other children, though alone, he was every custodian's dream. He was fully institutionalized: he followed the rules to a tee when not exposed to other youngsters.

Integration into a shared social construct was the primary aim of the child's rehabilitation, but he failed miserably at that, preferring isolation while craving the very inclusion he avoided. The other children, even the teens, were beginning to fear him as his behaviors grew more peculiar and his defensive tactics increasingly clever and brutal. He needed to learn to socialize with his peers. He was not integrating.

The doctors had hope for the child, though, as he had exhibited unexpected tenderness toward animals that had been introduced during a specialized therapy session. The boy had treated them with more compassion and more exceptional care than had any of the other children, and the animals had responded more positively toward him than toward the other residents. The doctors had changed their opinions of the psychotic and sociopathic tendencies they had observed and had decided to modify the child's treatment.

Despite the glimmer of hope, these things distressed Pae to no end. He was a powerless, shut-out, third-party spectator. All he could do was pray for the child, and send cards and letters. *That's plenty*, he told himself, though most times he questioned whether he believed it. He made a concentrated effort to pray for the boy no less than once per day and muttered a few quick prayers each time the child crossed his mind. He referred to him as "my Precious Jewel." Pae felt a moral obligation to adopt the boy in spirit. *Who else will? How many can relate to what he's been through?* Though Pae and the boy had shared limited contact during two brief visits, they had thoroughly connected. Pae's empathic traits were too strong to deny this as fact. He *knew*.

Pae had dropped by Spanky's a few times before Sherri-Lynn's final disconnect the week before Thanksgiving. He had hoped to work out what was eating her. She had avoided him each time. Pae had no interest in hanging around to interact with the other ladies. He was polite to them, but as Sherri-Lynn had observed in September, he did not care to linger and gawk at bodies.

Pae had made subsequent visits to have a few drinks and to chat with Spanky and Tiny. He ensured he arrived when Sherri-Lynn was not on shift. Since she had decisively broken contact, he felt it wise to avoid confrontation.

Spanky had a hard, guarded personality and rarely spoke a word that was not business-related. His mere presence had intimidated Pae upon their introduction. When he and Sherri-Lynn had parted ways, Spanky had dropped his menacing veneer and revealed a depth of sympathy Pae would never have imagined. Otherwise, Spanky remained hard around the edges--that was his way--but brief, private interactions had proven this man of few words had a heart of gold toward him and Sherri-Lynn. Spanky and Tiny had expressed sincere disappointment that she had kicked him to the curb.

Pae was lonely. His sexual rendezvous with Sherri-Lynn had broken his contented single existence and intensified his sense of isolation. He craved a committed relationship. In the absence of such, he chose to fill the void by getting more involved with his church and the community of Palafox, and with developing his friendship with Charlene. The gym and other hobbies remained, but Pae needed more direct human interaction. At least he had learned to give a woman her space when she wanted it. Though the man missed Sherri-Lynn, he was able to live without her. He had shaken off the desperate, empty, emotionally starved, and clingy nature that had hounded his younger years.

Charlene had initiated many small but positive changes that had strengthened Pae's resolve to let Sherri-Lynn be. Most notable was enrollment in an adult high school education program. Charlene's thinking was clearer than ever. She was becoming more responsible and nailed down, but also a lot more light-hearted and cheerful. It was almost as if a second childhood were bubbling up within a developing, level-headed woman. She was finding her balance.

Charlene loved the impact of Pae's presence and her new growth. Pae was thrilled with her changes. Though he'd had no direct influence upon her decisions--as far as she had ever stated--he was proud of her. She had at least thanked him for not having taken unfair advantage of her drunken stupor back in July. It was the number one thing that had caused her to continue associating with Pae. Charlene had indeed learned to respect him. They were bonding quite well. Even so, Pae never stopped thinking of Sherri-Lynn.

MARCh 17: SUNSEt

Sherri-Lynn sat in her car before her shift, pondering the events of early November, as she had several times over the past four months. Her latest thoughts had been triggered by recent news reports and a phone call she had received from Tiny. Her window was rolled down, and the radio was dialed to a news station. The engine and heater were running. She watched the steam from her breath as it hit the chilled dusk air. She observed the texture of her green fleece gloves while she held a Saint Patrick's Day café latte with both hands. Sherri-Lynn sniffed the minty liquid through the opening in the lid and smiled.

Sherri-Lynn reflected upon Tiny's phone call in December. Tiny's information was history. The Empire County Sheriff's Department was in shambles in the aftermath of the swift, four-month investigation. As secretive as the small-time traffickers thought they had been, too many *breadcrumb* trails had been left, and too many amateur errors made, most were drug and alcohol-related. Federal and state agents had made quick work of the situation.

Sherri-Lynn drifted back to that night in the emergency room. She kicked herself for having been on such an emotional high, only to be let down by the troubling adult-to-child interactions she had witnessed. The abrupt display of that underage child had been met quite passively by the receiver. She wondered whether Pae had secretly, in some psychologically twisted way, enjoyed what had happened? Perhaps he had lacked full comprehension of the boy's action, or worse, he did not care? Maybe a small part of Pae's mind had never fully developed past the age he was raped? She could not draw a solid conclusion.

Sherri-Lynn's doubts had grown when investigators had arrived before her departure for work this evening to question her a second time regarding Pae's role in November's events. She had also been troubled by questions about the deaths of the two men in Fayette County. Most distressing was the suggestion that dangerous men still sought Pae. Her soul was vexed.

Sherri-Lynn had been convinced she had fallen for Pae until he had arrived with the boy on that November night. The child's snap at Pae's jeans in the emergency room had dissolved her doubt. It had sealed the deal. She shuddered at the recollection.

Does the man have any boundaries at all? Sherri-Lynn wondered. *Is he actually a little self-destructive? Dangerous, but not in a fun, attractive, bad-boy way?* Pae's wide-open heart looked more like weakness than strength.

Sherri-Lynn's thoughts drifted further back. She and Pae had spent time away from her place of employment on walks and at café's, and on strolls along a nearby creek. They had also spent an evening at the Henshaw County fair in mid-October. She had invited Pae on a shopping trip to a Birmingham mall to help her select lingerie and daily underwear. He had gladly accepted and had appeared to have thoroughly enjoyed the trip. She had even selected a pair of panties for him. Pae's emotional openness and his absence of embarrassment and shame had been unsurpassed, and his zeal for life admirable.

Perhaps his openness is a strength, after all? I suppose he is fun and attractive in his own edgy way, even if he's not what anyone might consider a bad-boy? You're a strange man, Mr. Pae.

Sherri-Lynn recalled Pae's description of his first meeting with Charlene, their immodest physical exchange, and what had seemed to have been as intimate a discussion as she'd had with him. Sherri-Lynn was jealous of Charlene. Though she had willingly exposed herself and had uncoerced sex with Pae, she had not expected him to charge into her heart in full force. No other man had accomplished such a feat, much less without trying. Pae was the first.

You are indeed unique, Mr. Pae, aka peace, beloved one, friend, or whatever your real name is?

Though intriguing, the concealment of Pae's legal name was a bit of a turn-off. *Mysterious men can be exciting, but there is a fine line between mysterious and shady.* Sherri-Lynn did not think it worth the effort to sort through the hints.

Pae had expressed several times the importance and relevance of his Christian faith. During their discussions away from the club, he had seemed thoroughly convicted of what he had claimed to believe. But then, Sherri-Lynn had thought it odd that he had so loosely fit the behavioral patterns of what she had learned to expect from believers, first by strolling into her place of employment—a strip club--and then by appearing a little too relaxed there, and a tad flirty.

He let me perform oral sex on him, and then he did the same for me and anal sex on top of it! I mean, really? What honest, devout Christian does that?

Sherri-Lynn wracked her brain. Pae appeared more Christian at heart than in his behavior, but even that was not awful, just difficult to comprehend. She could not fully understand the apparent contradiction. It seemed he would have been much more conservative.

The man was a pro. He apparently knew exactly what he was doing! That only comes from experience. What decent Christian makes a habit of that? God, how could I have fallen so easily?

The confused female stared at herself in the car's rearview mirror.

Don't lay the blame squarely on Pae's shoulders. You quite willingly played your part in contributing to his compromise.

That thought jarred Sherri-Lynn.

Perhaps I was a bit too hasty to judge him? After all, he is a man, and he hadn't had sex in ten years! Whether he was completely honest was beside the fact that he started blasting off just by me touching him. And...I threw myself at him like a horny piece of meat.

Sherri-Lynn chuckled and shook her head. *I reckon that makes me a dumb bitch? What on earth have I gotten myself into?*

The early middle-aged woman continued to mull over the two months she had enjoyed Pae's company. She missed him, but still, he seemed out of balance, and more than a little weird.

"Women's panties," the green-eyed lady mumbled. She smiled.

Sherri-Lynn had not been inside a church in years, but she remembered the notion that the heart is what God examines. She also remembered that God has standards of conduct. He is, after all, holy and moral. Of that, she was certain. Pae had exemplified so many real Christian attributes, more than most people she had known, especially men. *Some of his mannerisms, though?* Sherri-Lynn pondered these things then recalled what he had been through as a child.

Tears formed. Sherri-Lynn ran her free hand through her hair and swallowed with her dry throat then took a drink of her shamrock latte. Her throat felt no less dry. She recalled that Pae had never come across as an angry man. He had seemed docile and even-tempered. That generated a little cynicism. Sherri-Lynn wondered whether he had lied about his childhood calamity, but then she was experienced in recognizing pain, and his descriptions had rung true with her own experiences. She could tell that Pae's horror had indeed been real. She recalled that he had mentioned several years of psychotherapy.

That must surely have been where he had managed to break through any anger barriers he might have had? He might still have some, further below the surface, but has learned to manage it? I know I've been down that road.

Sherri-Lynn raised her head and looked out of her driver's side car window then hung her arm out of it, still gripping the latte over the center console with her right hand. She continued to weigh the pro's and con's of a relationship with Pae as a friend, and as a possible lifetime companion and mate. The deal was not quite sealed, as she had tried to convince herself. As much as she had avoided thinking of Pae, the doubts remained. Her heart was still drawn to him.

Sherri-Lynn rolled up her window and turned off the car then called Tiny to let him know she was in the parking lot. She explained that she had a lot on her mind and might be late for shift despite being on the premises. She had never been late for work a day in her life. Tiny relayed a message that Spanky was fine with whatever time she needed, and that he had offered her the day off. She declined and remained in the parking lot, drifting away with the radio and her thoughts.

Twenty minutes passed.

Sherri-Lynn adjusted the rearview mirror so she could check her makeup. She looked at her crystal, emerald green eyes and rugged features, then examined her medium-toned, milk chocolate skin and her straight, dark auburn hair.

He doesn't see you as a peculiar, Australian-Irish southern trophy, you know? He's not after bragging rights, girl. He doesn't see you as the racists do, either. You know damn well that he would not have made a move on you had you not opened the door. Weak moment or not, he respects himself, and he respects you. He's not picky about your features, your skin color, or your build. He's as open and as real as they come, maybe because he is fully self-aware and is all he claims to be even if it doesn't all make sense? He cannot hide that he loves you for you, beautiful! That much is absolutely guaranteed! You know you love him, too...

Sherri-Lynn stared intently into the rearview mirror. She broke her gaze then turned the ignition to ensure the radio had not drained her car's battery. The car started. She ran it for a few seconds and glanced at the clock on the instrument panel.

I will call Mister 'Pae' Moffat--whatever his real first name is-- tomorrow, but now, I need to get my ass to work.

MARCh 18: DAWn

Pae's heart was heavy. He sensed he was having another *empath moment*, as he had often referred to them. His spirit was overcome with a peculiar intensity he could not quench. Exercise, music, television, casual reading, and attempts to study his Bible had not settled his unease since waking before sunrise. Nothing held his attention for more than a handful of minutes. Unlike other empath moments, however, he did not feel emotional, just indescribably disturbed. His dreams had awakened him over the past several weeks, though they had been more peaceful and more abstract than in the months leading to the child's rescue.

The dream that troubled Pae most had crossed into an old memory of a game of *Lifeboat* during a college course. Only five people could enter the lifeboat while their ship sank. Three of the eight eligible contenders had to be voted out and left to die. Pae remembered that among the three voted out, the first choice was a Christian minister. Of the reasons given by the group of thirty classmates, two had stuck with Pae over the years. The first was that the minister had no practical life-preserving skills like the doctor and the professional survivalist. The second was that no one needed a "self-righteous windbag" who would surely try to control the behaviors of the others or at least criticize and judge them to no end. Pae recalled the heated debates. Only five of the class' thirty participants, including he, had defended the fictitious character's seat in the boat. The majority had felt that a man whose moral character was based on the ages-old and disputed "Word of God" had no intrinsic human or societal value. They had reasoned that humanity was good by nature, so a "preacher" had no place. The game's participants had voted out the minister, and also the mentally impaired woman who had no arms or legs and could not speak. An elderly man had been the last one voted out. After all, he had already lived his life. Pae had considered this dream-memory combination for days. The indecipherable message troubled him.

Pae started praying. He continued intermittently for the better part of two hours while he moved about the apartment. The man focused on the child's safety but found no peace in that. He figured something else must be at the root of his trouble, and it must surely relate to the *Lifeboat* memory. He decided to abandon his spoken prayers in favor of allowing his spirit to groan while his mind wandered.

Pae removed himself from potential distractions by settling onto the floor in his bedroom closet. He leaned against the wall. The man closed his eyes and cleared his mind as best he could then muttered several unintelligible words. An intense electric chill filled his brain. The sensation affected the large male's exterior, causing the hair on his head and the back of his neck to rise. He increased the frequency of obscure words in mumbled prayers. Scriptures came to mind. Pae meditated on them as he continued.

The man's pulse slowed. He involuntarily kicked the base of the wall, and his torso jolted as he relaxed. The static charge grew. It spread to Pae's shoulders and the remainder of his body, leaving raised skin and standing hair in its wake. Pae felt detached. The sensation bordered on ecstasy. He was swept away into a vortex of intense, focused prayer that he had no desire to disrupt. Though conscious and aware of his surroundings, Pae slipped into a dream state...

A little girl's blue eyes shimmered like sunlight dancing off the ripples of a sunbathed lake. Her hair reflected a resplendent cinnamon hue. A pair of faerie wings constructed of plastic rods, vinyl, and crepe pulsed with life from behind her shoulders. She took Pae by the hand. Her skin was warm and soft, and her tiny grip firm. The heat from her palm permeated his arm and filled his heart.

The girl's blue eyes turned purple. The teeth fell from her sunny grin, and her gums withdrew. Her eyes faded away, leaving black sockets. She squeezed Pae's hand as he was pulled toward a hole.

"One score and five," the child whispered. "Pray, pray, pray!"

The girl squeezed Pae's hand tighter. Her hair turned blonde then fell from her head. Flickers of light danced in her cavernous, black eye sockets, and the crown of her head illuminated.

"From this day, enumerate five times minus a sunrise," the girl whispered. "The life shall ebb forth. Pray, pray, pray!"

Shadows danced across Pae's face, and a flapping noise arose as the girl dissolved from his sight, singing:

"To death, I reach,
to death, I reach:
Beautiful orchid,
kiss me fair.
To thee I cast the life I surrender;
fragrant lilac, fill the air."

Pae was inside a consuming black abyss. He heard moans, groans, weeping, and wailing. A tormented male scream pierced his mind, followed by a loud call:

"Not hell, yet, hell! Hear the stories we shall tell!"

The back of Pae's head struck the closet wall when his relaxing muscles contracted then released. He remained in his semi-conscious dream state with eyes closed, simultaneously aware of his visions and of the material world. He fell deeper into his electrical trance. A sensation like ants crawling from every pore enveloped his skin from head to toe. Pae imagined he was being sprinkled upon by grains of salt.

More screams arose accompanied by the cries of children. Pae heard the screech of sliding metal followed by echoing clicks and clacks.

"Here," Pae heard a voice he could not recognize as masculine or feminine. "Speak."

Pae was confused. "What shall I say?"

The voice replied, "Tell."

Pae did not know what he should tell. He smelled olives. The peculiar aroma compelled him to open his mouth. The intense, tingling sensation in his head converged with the one in his chest. A refreshing, bizarre, cold heat rushed off his tongue like peppermint chased by ice water. Pae's stomach was in knots. He smelled the same delightful odor of incense he'd had in a dream, months earlier.

The shapes of two heads appeared like fogged blotches against the pitch-black backdrop. The heads contained no details. Each exhaled their own flavor of incense and color of smoke, one gold and the other dark brown mixed with turquoise. A third head appeared. Bars covered it. Male and female voices took turns emanating from the bars. Two distinct patches of pastel vapors arose. One smelled of incense and the other of cloves. They converged.

A small hole formed in the black canvass of the abyss. Light filtered through. Pae heard a child's laugh. He saw a gray mist without form shoot through the hole, leaving the blackness he inhabited. Other children's voices continued to cry, scream, moan, and wail.

"More," Pae heard the strange but pleasant voice tell him. He opened his mouth, and again, a refreshing, icy-hot flow blasted forth. This time, it was like horseradish. Once more, the man's stomach knotted, but the discomfort was not as severe as before. The void remained unchanged.

"Speak once more," the pleasant, neutral voice said.

A harsher, more bitter flow proceeded from Pae's mouth.

Still, the abyss remained unchanged.

"Show," the voice told Pae.

"Show what? I do not understand."

"Show: demonstrate! The gates shall not prevail against thee; the violent take by force. Open; remove; take from within. Show. One score and five," the strange voice said.

Pae saw himself removing his shoes. He gave them to one of the indescribable white mists. His feet started to bleed. He saw himself remove his jacket and give it to another fog-like image. He felt the chill of winter's cold. The same he did with his shirt and with his pants. His heart sank when he held his hands upward, and his underwear started to slip from his waist.

"Stop!" a booming male voice shouted. Pae's heart skipped a beat. His knees struck each other. He dropped his head with his eyes closed tightly, drawing his arms against his torso as he crouched in terror at the sound. He did not know to whom it spoke.

"You shall not!" the overpowering voice sharply commanded, before issuing the demand, "Preserve!"

Something scraped Pae's hips from front to rear on either side, followed by an irritated scream that faded into the distance. Pae's underwear had been returned to his waistline.

Pae felt hands holding him up and another hand on his shoulder.

"Speak again," the pleasant, neutral voice encouraged him. "Speak, demonstrate. One score and five."

Pae turned toward the darkness and opened his mouth while his feet continued to bleed. The scent of olives lingered heavily in the air. More holes opened in the blackness. More laughter, like the sounds of children playing, arose amid the misery. Other faint, gray mists shot through the illuminated rips.

Pae's energy drained to the point of exhaustion. He no longer felt the hands supporting him. He recalled one particularly grueling forty-hour cycle of no sleep during the war under a seemingly endless barrage of enemy fire in 124-degree heat. He had only one packet of rations per day and two canteens of water to sustain him. His other two plastic flasks had been consumed. Pae felt knife-like stabs in his stomach. The skin on his face and around his eyes grew leathery. It drew in and clung to his bones. His mouth was stuffed with cotton. His feet still bled. The skin fell from his shins and from his bruised, bleeding waist like flakes of powder. He noticed his underwear was soiled and torn. It barely covered his dignity.

"Do not faint. Continue," the strange voice encouraged Pae. Naked, he dropped to his knees in a cold stream. A torrential rainstorm swept over. Lightning flashed and thunder peeled. Pae flopped, face-down into the water with his arms by his sides, and his head turned. Large, bloody tears issued from his eyes, swept away by the rushing water.

Pae opened his mouth in one last depleted breath while water rushed down his throat. The scent of olives intensified. The refreshing, minty sensation issued forth from his mouth once again, more dazzling than before, pushing out the intruding deluge. Pae's stomach filled with warmth. The blackness around him carried sounds of joy. Visions of white, shining holes increased in number and size until the abyss ripped open. Pae was blinded by the intensity of the light as the darkness parted like a theater curtain. He heard the laughter of a little girl accompanied by the pressure of a warm embrace around his torso.

Another, more pleasant voice Pae could not discern as masculine or feminine said, "In the shoes, I ran; with the wings, I soared; Through the words, I lived: here am I."

Pae's ears clapped, and his chest vibrated from deep, thumping pulses that thundered throughout his body.

"Well done, dear friend," the previous, nondescript voice said. "One span of times plus one time, then two times more."

Pae's torso arched, and his limbs hung like a rag doll as he was lifted and carried into a black fog mingled with orange, rotating swirls amid the thumping, bone-rattling rumble.

Thundering blades of a low flying helicopter shook Pae's apartment. It rapidly faded as the aircraft descended toward a nearby airstrip. The man's eyes flickered open. The heaviness in his spirit broke. He stood and waited a few seconds before exiting the closet. His entire body, even his eyelids, nose, ears, and other extremities, still tingled like a limb without circulation. The sensation dissipated within seconds. Pae pressed two fingertips against his neck. His pulse had speeded up from having been surprised by the helicopter.

Pae sauntered into the living room and glanced at the wall clock. He rubbed his eyes, then listened for the clock's tick. It was still running. Pae returned to the bedroom to confirm the time via the digital clock radio. He had been praying in the closet for thirty minutes; he thought it had been less than five.

Drained from the morning's experience, Pae lay on the sofa, prepared to nap. A knock arose on the apartment door. Pae eased himself up then looked through the peephole on the apartment door. He saw two men in dark suits. One was holding an open wallet displaying a badge and credentials within view of the sight glass. Two sheriff's deputies stood behind the men. Pae recognized the deputies from the hospital in November and one of the detectives from a visit to his former residence in Empire.

"More questions," Pae Moffat mumbled. He opened the door and greeted the authorities.

d. bRENT iSBELL
SICKS

d. BRENT iSBELL
SICKS

DISJOINTED TIMe; THiS FACe Of MINe

A face looks across an empty room; a face looks back.
The room is silent; no words are spoken.

What are you?
That I am.

And what is that which you are?
That which resides in-between.

What is in-between?
This point in time.

And what is this time?
The time is now.

But it is only us in this time now.
Yes.

We are in this room.
That we are.

What shall we do?
That which we can.

And what is that which we can?
Observe, listen, and wait.

Who are you?
Not yet me.

Then, we shall observe, listen, and wait.

The room remained silent; no words were spoken.
A face looked into a dull, steel mirror; a face reflected back...

d. BRENT iSBELL
SICKS

aPRIL 3: A nEW dAWN

Dawn had arrived two hours prior, hosted by a lazy sun shrouded in a dark blanket of nimbus clouds. A chilly mist fell while a thick bank of white fog hovered over a murky, violet-gray lake and concealed the horizon. Though several weeks in, spring had not sprung. Winter languished.

A woman stood on a park sidewalk that paralleled the lake's shore, dressed in fine apparel. There was no hiding the fact that she possessed wealth. She was in her early middle-aged years and weathered. Amid impressive grooming and a tidy appearance was fair skin that looked a little rubbery and creased as if she had spent her life in the sun without the benefit of a deep tan.

Another female approached with a man on the sidewalk. The middle-aged woman watched the younger one dance like a puppy around her companion. She had dishwater blonde hair. Her upper torso was bundled in winter attire, mismatched by high-cut denim shorts and cowgirl boots. The giddy lass moved with fluid ease as if in a pair of *sneakers*. Small tattoos decorated her thighs. She reminded the older woman of a playful nymph without a care in the world.

The man was reserved. He walked in a straight line up the path with his hands in his jacket pockets while his female companion skipped and danced around him. He glowed with a content, rosy-cheeked smile. The older woman considered the warm colors in the approaching man's face might be the result of the cold weather snapping at him but thought it more likely an emotionally triggered blush. The man's eyes twinkled.

You're trying to hide it, but you clearly look entertained by your little friend's silly antics, the older woman thought as she observed the man. *Good job keeping your cool.*

Though behaviorally contrasted, the younger couple appeared to be two peas in a pod. The man had dark hair and an appealing, not quite rugged, facial structure. The older woman had seen what she had considered better-looking men over the years, but at least this one was easy on the eyes. A far cry from a supermodel or daytime soap opera material, she ranked him as acceptably cute, and quite a hunk. The younger man was bundled for the cold, but the woman could tell that a massive, muscular physique with a lean waist resided beneath the layers. The bulk of the man's chest, shoulders, and back, and the circumference of his thighs were clear indicators he was in top physical condition for someone likely in his early to mid-forties.

The older, middle-aged woman stepped back to the edge of the sidewalk to allow the couple to pass. The younger female scurried behind on the grass, paying her no mind. She smelled peculiar.

Ah! I recognize that smell, the older woman thought. *She's high on the wacky weed. That explains at least part of her child-like giddiness.*

The man's eyes twinkled at the older woman as he strolled past. His smile was warm and pleasant. She winked at him. His smile grew. He turned his attention back to his giddy friend, who skipped in a zig-zag pattern on the sidewalk.

The woman continued to watch the couple after they passed. She lingered a bit too long. The man glanced over his right shoulder and caught her eyeballing them. He was too distant to see the touch of sadness in her eyes. She flashed a guilty grin then turned her attention toward the frigid lake. The woman watched the fog as it loomed several feet above the surface. A light, frosty breeze kissed her face with a soft whisper. Though dressed for the dreary weather, she kept her arms folded across her chest.

Several times, the middle-aged woman turned and glimpsed at an elderly man who sat upon a nearby bench. He did not appear to pay her any notice. His gaze was set on the waterfront. The woman paced a few steps back and forth as she looked toward the lake's far shore. She repeatedly glanced at the man, unable to resist the nagging draw of his presence. Ignoring the possibility of stains on her elegant, weather-treated boots, she ambled toward him through the soft soil and damp grass.

As the woman approached, the old man estimated her height near six feet until he noticed the thick soles and tall heels of her boots had elevated her several inches. She had a medium build: it was evident by her form-fitted pants. The old man could not help but notice the shapes of her thighs and calves. *Impressive*, he thought. Her full, high hips were enhanced by her long coat's belt, smartly cinched at the waist. He observed that her feet were wide. He did not know women's sizes but guessed hers near a man's 9E, or perhaps a slightly smaller eight. *Why is she walking toward an old relic like me?* the elderly man wondered.

"May I?" the woman asked when she reached the man. She slid her right earmuff behind her ear, leaving the left in place.

The old man stood and smiled, taking note of the woman's warm, dark eyes. He bowed and motioned his hand toward the bench. "Please, do!" His face beamed. He cautioned the woman as she prepared to sit. "Here, let me take care of that for you!" He wiped some of the dew off the painted green boards with his black leather-gloved hands.

"That is quite alright. Please do not trouble yourself, sir." The woman's voice dripped with the sweetness of a ripe, violet muscadine ready to be plucked. Her southern accent was apparent, and her words proper and distinct, with a bit of chain smoker husk. "It is only clothing. The material might melt, but I will not," the woman joked then grinned.

The old man waited for the middle-aged woman to sit before he settled back down. He took note of her features. She had straight, bright, strawberry blonde hair. It was cut in a shoulder-length bob with long bangs that had been tousled by the chilled breeze, giving the appearance of a natural cowlick. Tiny drops of moisture clung to the strands of the woman's bangs like miniature, crystal Mardi Gras beads.

The bridge of the woman's nose was significant compared to most, and it had a slight lean to the left from the old man's perspective. *It's a handsome nose*, the elderly man thought. Though he had always admired more delicate features, somehow, it fit. *On second thought, it's quite beautiful*, he concluded.

A light patch of freckles was sprinkled upon the woman's strawberry cheeks, lending a youthful glow. Her makeup had been modestly applied with enough contrast to cause her natural features to stand out. The brilliant whites of her eyes were most notable. The man appreciated what he saw.

"My name is Victoria Richmond." The woman offered a gloved hand. It was narrow, and her fingers slim and short. The old man removed the glove from his right hand. It was tanned and meaty and appeared to have seen a lot of hard physical labor in its day.

The woman added, "I do hope you will forgive my breach of etiquette? The air has a dreadful chill. I would not have been offended in the least had you chosen to retain the wear of your glove."

The two strangers shook.

"It's my pleasure, ma'am. Nothing to forgive." The old man's dark, cocoa brown eyes shimmered in the pale morning fog. "Victoria Richmond, you say? You're the lady who owns that big magazine and those web sites, and several other businesses, and who gives to all those charities?"

Victoria closed her eyes and nodded. "I am she." When she opened her eyes, the man could not help but notice a peculiar spark.

The man added, "You give proportionally more than anyone I have ever seen. If you don't mind my asking, ma'am--I hope I am not being too personal--what brings a woman of your standing out here, on a day like this?"

The woman grinned with her hands upon her lap. She sat up straight and pulled her shoulders back, then turned her face toward the water, closed her eyes, and drew a deep, cold breath into her nostrils. She opened her eyes as she exhaled a cloud of steam. "Some days, I just need to get away and *air out*. I love the life with which God has blessed me, but it requires an intense commitment. When I feel overwhelmed, I come to sparsely populated locations such as this, to think and to pray, and to recover. Do not get me wrong: I adore people, but sometimes I just need some *me* time."

The middle-aged woman looked at the old man and smiled. "And you, sir? Why are you here alone on such a day as this?"

The old man's dark eyes shimmered as he returned the woman's smile. "You don't have to call me sir, though I do appreciate the courtesy. I might be ancient, but I'm not really worthy of such a title. Honestly, it surprises me that a woman of your wealth and influence would even take the time to sit with an average Joe, much less an old codger like me? Thank you. I'm here because I need to 'air out,' too. Since my beloved wife passed, I've kept busy finding reasons to continue. I do fine most days, but there are times like these when it catches up with me. It happens more frequently the older I get, and the more my body breaks down. I suppose I'm not quite ready to give up the ghost yet, but I am tired. I'm pretty worn out."

The woman placed a hand upon one of the old man's. "I am sorry, sir." Her dark eyes reflected a look of genuine sympathy. "How long ago did your wife pass?"

"It's been two years now. I was convinced I would have joined her within the first few months. I ended up in the hospital, and I nearly went tits-up. Oops! Forgive me. My filter doesn't work as well as it used to. Anyhow, I thought I was a goner, but no. I've always been stubborn." The man grinned. "I get along, though. You see a lonely old man sitting here in the gloomy wet cold, but I am not as lonely as you might think? I spend most of my time staying as fit as I can for my age and volunteering at the local men's *halfway house*. That's where I first heard of you. You're quite the celebrity among the downtrodden, even those who are too proud to admit it. The guys are particularly impressed with your work in the children's ward at the psychiatric hospital."

The woman's weathered, freckled glow intensified. She withdrew her hand from the old man's. "Forgive me. I am a touchy-feely type by nature."

"No worries, ma'am. I appreciate the personal touch. Thank you."

"And I appreciated your fine compliment, sir, especially concerning the children's psychiatric ward. I generally keep that under wraps. The poor dears do not need the media following me in there."

"Your work there might not get much media coverage, but it sure gets the attention of the guys. You are quite a celebrity to them. They respect you tremendously. A few have children there."

"I owe my success to God. I cannot take credit."

The man tilted his head. "It's refreshing to see true humility from the elite. Please don't take that as an insult, ma'am. It's just that I'm so used to people with your wealth and influence looking down on folks, with their noses in the air. And to give credit to God when not in front of a camera or a large audience? That's mighty unusual these days!"

"Well, I truly cannot accept credit. I have had to put forth the lion's share of effort over the years, and I still work myself ragged, but none of it would have paid off had God not given the ideas, led the way, and provided the opportunities. It was all his doing. It was slow going at first. Like those poor children in the state hospital, I thought I was doomed to an aimless, meager existence for the first handful of years of my adult life. I did not come from money, no sir, far from. I will not go into any details, but suffice it to say humble beginnings were the catalyst that helped push me to where I am now, once I recovered from prostitution and alcoholism."

The old man snapped his glance from the lake to Ms. Richmond. His surprise was undeniable.

The woman's eyes remained warm but took on a solemn, piercing quality. "Though often in the public eye, it is no secret I am a staunchly private woman. There are a few personal secrets of which I never speak openly; five, to be precise. I do not mind telling you three of those secrets." Victoria felt it wise to refrain from declaring she is a carrier of HIV and Hepatitis C. "I have never divulged these secrets to the public. I do not know what compels me to do so now, but I am willing, as long as you promise to not sell to the tabloids and gossip columns, or plaster it all over social media?"

The old man grinned and turned his face toward the lake. He extended his right arm across the back of the bench behind the woman. He wagged his left hand. "Bah!" He turned his head to face her again. "You have my word. I'm too old to chase that kind of foolishness."

The woman echoed the man's sentiment. "Me, too! It does get old, believe you me." She shifted to get more comfortable. "Okay, so here it goes... Are you ready for my first secret?"

aPRiL 3: sECRETS

The old man wondered what crazy skeletons the famed female philanthropist could possibly have in her closet, and why she was willing to tell him? Surely, she was exaggerating their importance? He was thrilled to have her company, so he gladly humored her.

"Fire away," the elderly man said.

"My first big secret is that I am a nudist at heart." Victoria giggled after disclosing the information.

The old man blushed and turned his head. "I didn't see that comin'!" he said after he turned to her again. His eyebrows jumped, and his lips drew in as if he were going to whistle.

"I am not an exhibitionist, mind you, but a nudist. I especially love prancing naked in the woods, but do not worry: I do it alone on my private estate, not on public land, and not in the company of others. The woods are where I feel most connected with myself and with God." Victoria patted the man's left shoulder and chuckled. "Please forgive my indiscretion. I hope I have not embarrassed you?"

"No, no, not at all, miss. My bones are old and creaky, but I was young once, like you."

Victoria chuckled and waved a hand in front of herself. "You call *this* young? You, sir, stop tickling my fancy!" she quipped in a sarcastic tease. "Seriously, though, thank you! Some things I just have to get off my mind now and then. It is rare I have a discreet audience. It is not always freeing to tell a paid professional."

"I'm not so sure how wise it is to tell a stranger like me, but with all due respect, ma'am, that is your business, not mine. I am honored, and I agree: professionals do have their place, though sometimes it is more therapeutic to tell a regular person."

The unlikely companions exchanged nods and simultaneously remarked, "Indeed!"

The woman giggled again. "It is like we are cut from the same cloth?"

"I wouldn't exactly say that, ma'am. You're quite the classy woman: cultured and accomplished, and maybe half my age? I'm just an old fart!"

Ms. Richmond smiled. "Do not sell yourself short. No, there is something else about you." The woman scanned the old man's face. "I felt drawn from the moment I saw you sitting here. It is almost as if in some weird way, you and I are connected? Soul mates?"

"Well," the man laughed, "Flattery will get you everywhere, missy, but honestly, soul mates might be a bit of a stretch?"

"The concept is more prevalent among the young; that is certain. They often apply it to deep, romantic love interests and shallow crushes. This feels a bit more substantive than that. I feel at ease conversing with you. It is as if I can sense the quality of your soul?"

"True flattery," the elderly man nodded. "Now, you're tickling *my* fancy!"

The two shared another laugh as they gazed upon the lake.

"No swans or geese out," the old man said.

"They have better sense than us," Victoria joked.

"I reckon so."

The couple sat quietly for a moment.

Ms. Richmond's eyes rotated upward. "Now, where was I? Ah, yes!" She dropped her skyward glance and turned to the man. "Another secret is that I am covered in tattoos."

The man rotated his body toward Victoria. "Now, that's a bit more of a shocker! I never would have guessed! I suppose they're in areas that are easily covered? I don't recall ever seeing them in any photos or the few times I've seen you on TV. I have a handful of tattoos myself."

"It is true! One of them is a crude *tramp stamp*, as they were once referred, on my lower back at the hip. It is a large butterfly with some tribal designs and is my pride and joy." Victoria rolled her eyes with a gleam of sarcasm.

"An older teenaged acquaintance applied it when I was thirteen years old. The pain was nearly unbearable, but my will was iron. I took hell from my foster parents for that! I thought I was a goner! No, sir, they did not appreciate that one bit! It did not help that embedded in the design is an arrow pointing south flanked by gothic letters that read, 'NO ENTRANCE! KEEP OUT! I thought they would flat die!"

Victoria laughed after describing her tattoo. "My foster mother had walked in on me after a shower one day. I had forgotten to lock the door. I was drying off with my back to it when she caught me. She had a royal cow!"

A hearty laugh escaped the old man. He blushed and looked at the ground then back at the woman. "Now, *that is* a little embarrassing! I can only imagine!"

"As long as you do not imagine *too* much!" Victoria teased and patted the man's shoulder again. "Some of my other tattoos are quite sinister. One could argue that a few are even demonic, though I do not recall what was going through my mind when I got them. There is one that I honestly cannot remember receiving. My drunken youth was a blur. It would not be fair to say they represent demons, not fair to me, that is. It might be different if I could remember what I'd had in mind, but no. I was bombed half out of my gourd in those days. Benefit of a doubt."

"Please forgive my prying, miss, but why *do* you keep them? Why not have them removed or covered with different patterns? Surely, you have the resources?"

"I have wrestled with that a great deal, believe me. I had prayed over it for years on end. Eventually, I found peace in the idea that keeping them would serve as a reminder of the demons God has vanquished on my behalf."

"Speaking of demons, ma'am, I wanted to volunteer at that children's ward, but they wouldn't allow it. It's a long story. No sense in me getting into it."

An inquisitive look entered the woman's eyes, but she did not press the man. "We all have secrets we never tell, sir. That is our prerogative. This brings me to the third, and one of my most closely guarded secrets."

Victoria looked at the lake and drew another deep breath, then exhaled a plume of vapor and sat for a moment, with a classic *thousand-yard* stare. She returned her attention to the man and swept a hand through her bright, strawberry blonde hair. The woman twisted the ends for a moment then rested her hand on her neck. Her eyes shifted as she studied the old man's facial features. Victoria dropped her glance, then raised it again and met his eyes.

"What is your name, sir?"

"Cagle. My last name is Cagle."

"Unusual. It has a strangely calming feel. Interesting... Mr. Cagle, I asked your name because what I am about to tell you is of an extremely personal nature. I have never uttered this secret outside the confines of a psychiatrist's office; therefore, I prefer to be at least on a bit of a personal level--a slightly even keel--with the one to whom I have chosen to reveal this information. I have held this secret for too many years, even from the psychiatrists, once I left the foster system. My juvenile records are sealed. Quite frankly, I am tired of holding it so close."

The woman's words piqued the old man's interest. She had his full attention.

"I have yearned to divulge this secret, but I have never found the right time, place, or person. Though it has weighed heavily upon me for years, I do not feel those hindrances today. My soul is at peace. *This* is the day, sir. *Now* is the time."

The elderly man was all ears. He raised his left brow in curiosity but remained silent.

"All kidding of tabloids aside, sir, are you prepared to hold this in the strictest confidence? My life might literally depend upon it."

The old man's face filled with grave concern. His brow furled. "I have no idea why you're opening up to me with these things? Me, of all people, and in a place like this? But if you feel you must, I'm sure you have your reasons?" He patted Victoria's knee and offered a reassuring smile. "You're safe, my dear. Say what you will."

"Mr. Cagle, I was not born female. I am transgender."

The woman paused for the man's reaction. He held his peace.

"Does this disturb you?"

"At my age, about the only thing that disturbs me is shitting the bed in my sleep."

The woman's eyes widened like saucers. Her mouth dropped open. She covered it then burst into raucous laughter. The old man's face flushed with glee as he watched the pent-up tension explode from the woman's heavy heart.

"Of all the responses I could possibly have imagined, kind sir," Victoria struggled to spit out the words while she laughed herself silly, "that was certainly not among them!" She coughed a few times, then caught her breath. "That *is* quite disturbing!"

Mr. Cagle joined Victoria's amusement with a hearty chuckle. His face grew redder with embarrassment, but his smile brighter.

Victoria leaned against the bench, tossed her head back, and looked into the battleship gray sky. "Oh, dear!" she huffed. The woman's chest rose and fell with relief as she caught her breath while the hilarity subsided. The transformed female dropped her head and shifted her eyes while nibbling the outer seam of one of her gloved thumbs. Victoria paused to re-engage her company.

"It is a long story, Mr. Cagle. I cannot speak for any other transgender women, only for me. I despise men in general. I always have. Even so, I have had intense homosexual urges for as far back as I can remember." Victoria nibbled her thumb and shifted her eyes again. Mr. Cagle observed. Victoria paused once more and added, "It is an awful *catch-twenty-two*, rooted in cognitive dissonance, the professionals say." She nibbled again.

"I am familiar with the term and its meaning," Mr. Cagle assured the woman.

Victoria stopped chewing her thumb. She rested her hand on her lap. A sober look entered her eyes. "I will not make any excuses, Mr. Cagle. I do not believe I was born this way. I have carefully considered reasons that support that belief, but they are much too involved to discuss here, and frankly, not worth it. I am what I am, no matter what anyone else believes or how society and politicians would like me to think.

"My journey toward a female identity began long before my relationship with God. That was not easy. I had grown up believing he hated my very existence, but something inside would not accept that. After all, if he is real and he created me--formed me in my mother's womb--and ensured my safe delivery into this world and my subsequent preservation, why then, would he hate me for having been born? That would be ludicrous! I do not believe God is schizophrenic, Mr. Cagle. I believe that he is entirely stable and single in purpose. He is not divided. I am convinced God loves me. That is my 'it in a nutshell' observation. I am certain I need not tell you it is far more complex a subject."

Mr. Cagle nodded.

"My life before God was a wreck, and it was growing worse with each passing year. The intense beatings I had received at the hands of the fearful and two stabbings..." Victoria shook her head.

"Believe it or not, ma'am, I understand where you're coming from. I've been there."

Victoria paused and looked toward the lake. "Did you notice that couple that passed through here?"

"Yes, ma'am, I did. The young lady was having a time, wasn't she?"

"That she was. Did you perchance notice the man that was with her?"

"Yep. They were a bit of a mismatch. Do you know them?"

"No, sir, I do not, but he did look awfully familiar, not so much in the face or skin tone, but in his overall build and the way he carried himself."

"I cannot say I have ever seen those two before, but then I don't spend a whole lot of time here. I try to stay as busy as I can. Why?"

"No reason, really. I would be lying if I said I did not think he was cute besides looking vaguely familiar. His eyes were gorgeous!"

"Sorry, Miss Victoria, I wouldn't know anything about that."

"I do not mean to embarrass you, kind sir. I just had to say it. I spend so much time keeping myself in check, it is good to state how I feel to another living soul outside of a psychiatrist's office and during my quiet time with God."

"This old man does not judge you. It is an honor to see a compartment of your heart that nearly no one else gets to see."

Victoria sighed. "I am stalling, sir. Forgive the candor in what I am about to tell you. It is quite vulgar, actually, but it is also a fact of my past. Given what I have already revealed, I feel it must be stated."

"Trust me, Miss Victoria, you truly cannot shock these old ears. Do not hold back on my account, ma'am."

"Okeydokey. Here it goes..."

d. bRENT iSBELL
SICKS

aPRiL 3: tHAT i aM, aM i

Victoria paused to give Mr. Cagle an opportunity to reconsider the information she was preparing to share. She wondered how much he might accept before asking her to desist. He remained steadfast.

Ms. Richmond proceeded. "I was anally sodomized against my will four times as a preteen then twice as an adult." Victoria pursed her lips and dropped her head.

Mr. Cagle nodded, but Victoria did not see. He waited for her to reengage.

"Please forgive my lack of boundaries, sir," the middle-aged woman whimpered. "I do not know what got into me?"

"No worries, pretty lady." The old man rubbed the woman's back just below her neck. "Life knocks the piss out of all of us. We have to release the pressure once in a while, even if our venting is unsavory. God preserves us through the ugliness. He weathers the storm beside us and pulls us up when we sink. Our pain does not shock him. Your pain does not shock me. Do not fret your words, wonderful lady."

A tear streaked down Victoria's cheek. She bowed her head again and sniffled twice then returned her attention to Mr. Cagle. She swept her long, damp, strawberry blonde bangs aside with one hand. The pearly whites of her eyes had turned faint pink from the steady flow of restrained emotion.

Ms. Richmond flashed a thin, downcast grin. "I knew there was something kindred about your spirit from the moment I laid eyes on you. I knew there was a reason I felt comfortable with divulging these secrets. You are a believer, are you not?"

"I make no personal claims that people cannot first recognize, ma'am."

"Yep," the woman affirmed, "You are. I can see it as plain as day."

Two more tears shot down Victoria's cheeks. "I slit my wrists in a hot bathtub when I was eleven. I clearly remember doing that. It was mid-March, the eighteenth, to be exact. That date is burned into my brain. I had not learned an effective method for opening my veins, else I would not be here today. I will not list the gruesome events that shaped my youth. Suffice it to say that when it all came to a *head*, I was prepared to meet God, whether I thought he hated me or not."

Ms. Richmond twisted the fingers of her left hand in the ends of her bob cut and pulled it beneath her chin while she stroked the same plug of hair with the right. "This might sound strange, Mr. Cagle, but I am convinced Jesus appeared to me."

Victoria pressed against the inside of her upper lip with her tongue while she nervously played with her hair. "You probably think I am a *kook*, now?"

Mr. Cagle squinted in a broad smile that accentuated the *crow's feet* wrinkles beside his twinkling brown eyes. "Not in the slightest. I am quite intrigued, Miss Victoria. I have never met a wealthy, highly educated, accomplished, and level-headed person such as you, much less one who is a kook. Besides, wouldn't you be more of a kook if you didn't actually believe he was real and capable of showing himself yet tried to follow him anyway?"

Victoria snickered. The old man's quick-witted logic was refreshing. "Thank you, sir, and thank you for still calling me miss instead of mister. You have no idea how that touches me."

"I respect you, ma'am, and I understand. I also believe you are everything you say, and that includes being a woman. I believe that you saw what you say you did. I have no reason to doubt you."

Victoria wiped her tears. She was silent for a moment then continued, "Your average person meets God through pure, simple faith, and nothing more. Do not misunderstand: faith is precisely what it takes, simple, willing trust, like that of a small child toward a loving adult."

Mr. Cagle thought it peculiar that Victoria had chosen the word *adult* instead of *parent*, peculiar, but not beyond reason. He wondered whether he was over-analyzing. Still, the detachment within her statement, whether intended or subconscious, made sense.

Victoria continued. "It takes faith to accept the idea that there is a way to a working, personal relationship with our creator." She paused. "I might be sounding a bit preachy? Forgive me?"

"No, ma'am, you're fine. Say what's on your mind, Miss Richmond."

"I am most certainly not discounting the indispensable act of faith. What I *am* saying is that I am convinced I saw *him*: I believe I saw Jesus face to face, though at the time, it had not occurred to me."

Victoria stopped to read her companion's body language. He was still at ease. "I cannot, for the life of me, recall any physical details, just a vague recollection that he looked nothing like any artwork I had ever seen. He did not resemble a blue-eyed Renaissance-hippie mix with hair halfway down his back. That much I remember. Somehow, I recognized him, regardless. I also believe I conversed with him the way you and I are speaking now."

Victoria tilted her head. "You do not appear skeptical? Kidding of kooks aside, I thought for sure you would be reacting as if I have lost my mind?"

"Miss Victoria, you would not believe the things I have experienced throughout my life, but then perhaps you might? Trust me on this: I have heard stranger things and from folks every bit as competent as you."

"Thank you for the support, Mr. Cagle." Victoria gazed at the lake again. "Had I been hallucinating? Possibly? It had occurred while the paramedics were fishing me out of the bathtub. I had lost a lot of blood. I could easily have been conversing with one of them and not realized it? I could have imagined the conversation. Was my encounter real?" She looked into Mr. Cagle's eyes. "In my mind, yes, sir, it was, very much so. It was as real and as vivid as you and me sitting here now. It was quite visceral."

Victoria stopped speaking for a moment then tilted her head again. Her brows narrowed, and her mouth opened a little. She rested the tip of her tongue between her lips then pursed them.

"That's an odd expression. You look, perplexed?"

"I never thought about it, but I think I might have seen him once before when I was quite young? I cannot remember for certain. Chunks of my childhood have been pushed from my memory."

"Don't feel bad, Miss Victoria. Most of my earlier life is a blur like yours. Honestly? I think it's part of God's way of helping us let go of this place in preparation for what lies beyond? He helps us forget some of the pain so we can keep moving forward. He also intensifies the good memories of what we've lost to the point that they transform into pain. I believe that is so we may look forward to leaving this world and entering our eternal home. That's what I'm holding onto, anyway."

"That is indeed an excellent way to look at it," Victoria nodded and smiled, then added, "an excellent way. Interesting perspective, for certain."

Ms. Richmond sat quietly for a few seconds. Her mouth dropped open, and her eyes narrowed. "Revelation... Revelation...what? What, what?"

"I beg your pardon, ma'am?"

"Nothing. I drifted again. I tried to connect some dots that weren't quite adding up. I remember a vague biblical reference, but for the life of me, I cannot recall exactly what it says or where it's located."

The younger couple passed again on the sidewalk between the park bench and the lake. The dishwater blonde in cutoff shorts and cowgirl boots laughed while she ran with the man's coat in her hand. Being at least twice her size, he lacked his speed. She slowed to let him catch up. The man scooped the petite woman into his arms and tossed her over his shoulder.

The early middle-aged woman reached in the direction of Victoria, and Mr. Cagle then yelled, "Lord have mercy, I've been abducted by a great big horn dawg! Don't save me! Don't save me! Mama's cooter is hungry!" She laughed hysterically.

The man slapped his captive's butt with his left hand.

The woman yelled, "It looks like this big ole horn-dog wants the boo-tay!"

Victoria laughed and waved back. "Bon appetite!" she called.

"Thank you!" the younger woman waved again. She giggled and started patting the man's behind with her free hand while she remained flopped over his shoulder, clinching his coat.

Victoria and Mr. Cagle looked at each other and chuckled. They shook their heads.

"Young love," the elderly man said.

Victoria's smile was bright. "Young love, indeed."

They watched until the couple passed from hearing range.

Let me see," Victoria said, "where was I? Ah, yes! I cannot lie and say everything turned rainbows and butterflies after I opened my heart to God. Life had become much worse from several perspectives, especially the outside pressures. But inwardly, something had shifted in a way I had neither anticipated nor dreamed. I had begun to discover strengths I could never have imagined before my personal relationship with the lover of my soul."

"The lover of your soul, you say? You know, I have not heard anyone say that in eons, it seems. That's gotta come from an exceptional place? Such words do not naturally spill from the lips of most people, not even Christians."

"Have you ever had anyone love your soul so deeply that you knew it without words?"

"Yes, ma'am: my beautiful wife. Outside of her and the Lord? No. Some came close over the years, but no."

"Only one human being has ever come that close to me, sir, but now God holds that title exclusively."

"That other person, Ms. Victoria, did they love you because of your transgender body, or maybe leave you because of it or your faith?"

"No, sir, nothing like that. Life was just moving way too fast. Time and circumstances split us apart. I moved past it, though. He never stopped living in my heart. Eventually, I recognized God's presence. He had been there since day one though I could not see him. Faith opened my eyes. For the first time in my life, I was able to face all of the ugliness that had come upon me and not run from it, even when I thought I might implode. By then, I was so deep into this female transformation that it had become dangerous for me to back out. Honestly, I did not want to. I had begun to love myself on the inside. What was outside did not matter quite so much. Why heap more distress upon myself by putting my life at risk? It was easier to keep pressing as a female."

Victoria stopped playing with her hair. "I bet you are wondering how someone like me reconciles her life with the Church and with the world at large?"

"Well, yes, that could be quite a problem. How *do* you reconcile?"

"The short answer is I do not. What I am cannot be reconciled to the Church or to society, not even among those who claim to love, support, and accept those such as I, at least not from what I had experienced years ago as a youth when I was open about it. I had received large doses of negative treatment in those days. Each side of the morality and political acceptance coin talked a big game, but when it came to making the actual plays, each wanted me wholly in their court. They expected me to be either all in or all out, with no gray areas. Those who do not fit into a tidy, predictable box, those who function within the gray areas, scare people. But people like me *are* walking gray areas. The Church calls it confusion, and rightfully so.

"For many years, I was perplexed and excessively distressed living in that confusion. I was destroying myself, trying to escape the pain of my youth, and that lingered for a good long while after God began changing me on the inside. Despite having a new perspective on life, I had no peace, none whatsoever. I almost attempted suicide again as a reborn believer."

Victoria paused.

"I hope you're okay, Ms. Victoria? Please continue, ma'am, if it is not too painful?"

"Not too painful at all, sir. Self-reflection steals my attention. I apologize for my intermittent drifting."

Victoria paused, then continued. "At some point along the way, I found the answer that eventually brought peace. I chose to give up seeking acceptance from society and from the Church, but that was not my answer. My answer was contained within a decision to abandon my transgender identity so that I may dedicate the rest of my life to living as a celibate woman, to think of and conduct myself as an authentic female and disconnect from unnecessary emotional distractions. At first, I argued with myself and with God, thinking I was letting my imagination run away with me. After all, I had been born male. It seemed to fly right in the face of all that I knew of basic morality and of the biological sciences. That wreaked havoc on me, sir. Abandoning a transgender identity felt like an unfair conclusion, as celibacy was a vital part of that decision. Why could I not have my cake and eat it, too? Live as a woman and marry a man? Do you know what God said to me?"

Mr. Cagle raised a curious brow.

"He said, 'You *can* have your cake and eat it, too, but my blessing is not there; it is on the difficult path. Few there are who are willing to walk that path. The joy of the life I offer is inherited by those who overcome.'

"He did not say that audibly or necessarily in those specific words. I have never met anyone in their right mind who has audibly heard from God. That does not mean they are not out there, but that I have never met one. His voice comes to me as thoughts, impressions, and feelings that I cannot shake, and most often, when my mind is settled and at peace. I then search the scriptures to validate those impressions. When they line up, I accept them as being God's voice."

"No need to explain, Miss Victoria. I can relate."

"That got my attention, Mr. Cagle. God did not tell me I could not continue in a way that seemed to make more sense, to appease my craving for shallow male sexual relations under the cloak of living as a female. He made no passive-aggressive threats or wag his finger or shake his head in disapproval like the dozens of well-meaning people I had run across in my earlier years. He did not blatantly threaten me or throw any sugar-coated, sarcastic insults my way, not like so many of his followers I had reached out to.

"The sense of peace I had during those talks was far too valuable to relinquish. Though not easy, I chose the better way. I found my true identity in him. The opinions of the Church, and of society, and of politicians no longer mattered. My exterior did not matter, and in time, my urges subsided: they no longer ruled me."

Victoria's thousand-yard stare returned. Mr. Cagle patiently watched until she spoke again.

"The choice was completely mine, and I was absolutely free to make it." More silence followed. Victoria resumed eye contact. "That's powerful, Mr. Cagle."

Victoria paused for a few seconds more and then continued. "Once I had settled upon my decision, I thought I would hate celibacy, but honestly? That was exactly what I needed to get my head clear. It was a rough ride for a while. Life-changing decisions are always easy to plot, but the self-discipline to follow through is a force to be reckoned with. Temptation crawls out of the woodwork almost immediately, and it seems to almost never ease up. But it does get easier to resist, and so I did. Since then, I have been living one hundred percent as a celibate female. The dicey beginnings were worth it. Now, it is second nature, well, first nature, actually. I will not lie: I still crave indulgence with a man every now and then, but I do not follow through, and I have not since that day many years ago. I find my strength through my relationship with God."

Victoria paused once more. "I hope I am not melting your brain, Mr. Cagle? I have been told I could talk the ears off a brass monkey."

The old man chuckled. "No, my dear, not in the least. I certainly have no other place to be today. You may talk the ears off of this old monkey for as long as you'd like." He smiled reassuringly and patted Ms. Richmond's knee.

"Truth be told, everything has been a blessing in disguise. I have never had a *first true love* outside of my relationship with my creator. My true love can never be a human being, sir. The capacity for such was stolen during my youth. Perhaps the saddest part was that it had occurred at such an early age that I had no idea it was missing. I lacked awareness of such things. I cannot even lament my virginity because the concept had never held any value. I had been robbed of it long before I comprehended it. But God gave me in its place the ability to love in different dimensions, to empathize with the pain of others in ways that many might never experience. It has turned out to be a worthwhile trade. As horrid as my beginnings were, I would not change my life for anything."

Victoria was interrupted by a squirrel as a few more tears eased down her face. The bushy-tailed gray rodent jumped onto the bench beside her. It sat curiously, twitching its tail.

Mr. Cagle remarked, "Well, would you looky there?"

Victoria spoke to the squirrel, "I am sorry, little friend, I do not have any food for you today."

The squirrel lingered. It placed its forward paws upon the woman's thigh and begged for a few seconds. Victoria gently rubbed the fur on the tiny creature's head. "Next time," she told the animal in a loving tone. The squirrel flailed its curved tail a few times then scurried away.

Victoria watched the tiny rodent depart. "I did not expect to see him today. I thought he would be huddled up in a nice, warm nest. I feed him and his little friends from time to time." She slid the fingers of both hands through the ends of the hair that lay over her left shoulder.

"Getting back to the tattoos," the middle-aged woman continued, "I often examine them in the mirror, then I consider my imitation female physique: the wide, high hips, thick thighs, and flat stomach, and the small but firm, non-augmented breasts. It was a complete fluke that I had grown some respectable little goose eggs. I had no desire to augment. The female hormones had worked favorably in that regard, and I thought they might also have stunted the sizes of my hands and feet until I learned I had been born with Klinefelter Syndrome."

"I am not familiar with that term."

"I was born with an additional X chromosome."

"Ah! That I am vaguely familiar with. I remember a lot of public talk about X and Y chromosomes years ago. I've never known the clinical name."

"It contributed to a number of natural feminine features. My hips, feet, and hands are among those. I had also lactated a time or two before I started hormones. The double-whammy of estrogen treatments and Klinefelter worked well in diminishing most of the common transgender earmarks I might otherwise possess. My *Adam's apple* is even small."

Mr. Cagle narrowed his eyes as he tried to focus on Victoria's throat. "I can't see it, even knowing it's there."

Victoria smiled. The old man's simple compliment warmed her heart. "You are too kind, sir."

"No, no, I mean it. You are one cute patootie!"

Ms. Richmond blushed and smiled, then lowered her head and closed her eyes. "You are a charmer."

"I used to be."

"You still are. Thank you again."

Victoria lifted her chin and opened her eyes. Her face was aglow. "I consider all these things when I look in the mirror, and then I view my shrunken male genitals. I never got *the operation*. I still have my *little six,* except it is in centimeters instead of inches."

Victoria chuckled at her own statement while she looked away. "Ole millimeter peter," she joked." She turned back to the elderly man. "Sorry."

Mr. Cagle had an open-mouthed grin and was shaking his head. "You embarrassed me that time!" He stuck his tongue out.

Victoria giggled. "Truth be told, it was never as large as six inches. I have never had a real *whacker.* My entire *package* had always been small compared to other boys my age. At one point, I had been nicknamed Peanut Patch."

Mr. Cagle's blush intensified.

"Forgive me." Ms. Richmond smiled and looked into the old man's eyes as she placed the fingertips of her left hand beneath his chin.

Mr. Cagle returned her smile. "Nothing to forgive."

Victoria smiled and withdrew her hand. "These things cause me to reflect upon my life's choices. It is quite sobering. Sometimes, I beat myself up so badly that I cannot even look in the mirror or leave the house for days. The self-condemnation can be quite miserable. But then God reminds me that we are all broken in some way, even the most squeaky-clean and perfect in appearance. Even knowing all our flaws, all our secrets, God loves us unconditionally. The way in which he reminds me is as gentle as this breeze."

Victoria closed her eyes once more and inhaled the crisp, moist air. A faint, icy breeze drifted across the lake and licked her face.

The old man waited for the woman to finish savoring the moment then asked, "How does God remind you, if I may ask?"

"With the lyrics from an old Anne Murray song, *You Needed Me*. I learned those lyrics forward and backward, inside and out. They resonate deep inside my soul, Mr. Cagle. Those words come to me every time I am feeling desperately low. Regardless of how the artist might have intended the lyrics, I imagine the words being whispered directly to me from *the Comforter*, the Spirit of God, every time I listen to or recall them. They are a part of me, sir."

Victoria's eyelids fluttered as she fought back tears. Her nose was red. "Excuse me for a moment, please." She withdrew a handkerchief from her coat pocket then turned away. She wiped her eyes and blew her nose then stowed the cloth.

Mr. Cagle marveled at this beautiful creature. That she had been born male did not bother him in the least. Her heart was what mattered. *God can truly work miracles*, Mr. Cagle thought. *No one is terminally lost while they still have breath in their lungs. Jesus can save and give purpose to anyone.*

Victoria turned back around. "I apologize that you had to witness that. There is nothing feminine or dignified in snarfing a wad of honker juice."

A sharp laugh escaped Mr. Cagle. He shook his head again. "Honker juice, indeed! Oh, Lord, that reminds me of a childhood friend who used to refer to wads of *snobber* as, 'holy honker juice!' Good googly-moogly!"

Victoria shared Mr. Cagle's laughter, then calmed and continued. "We are all but works of clay in the master's hands. He adds his unique 'living water' to soften us, then reshapes the warps and molds us into something beautiful and fit for noble service toward those who suffer. When this realization comes, I shake off my self-pity, and I remember that I am not garbage. I am not all of the awful things that people have said that I am. I am not an artificial person. I do not have a deceptive heart. Some could argue quite logically, that I am the epitome of deceit, but I am not, Mr. Cagle. I am a reborn soul, living in a corrupted body."

The man and woman exchanged looks. Mr. Cagle patted Victoria's knee and squeezed it. She placed her hand upon his and looked toward the lake. A single tear rolled down her right cheek.

"I look at myself—my female physique, male genitals, and dozens of tattoos--and I see children who are tormented, as I had been. I see those who have no one standing in their corner, those whose families refuse to offer support for fear of being exposed in some way. I see those who are too terrified and hidden away to have any voice at all. My heart melts for children forced into prostitution, especially boys. I can imagine nothing more emasculating than that. I lived through it." Ms. Richmond wiped a second stray tear. "It did things to me."

"Is that why you volunteer at the psychiatric hospital?"

"Yes, sir, it most definitely is, and it is also why I donate and spend time with children in the regular medical wards."

Mr. Cagle nodded. He faded into his own thousand-yard stare.

Victoria went on, "It is not terribly difficult for society to feel compassion and want to come to the aid of a girl living in that hell, but for a boy? I do not understand it, sir. I have never understood why boys get swept under the rug? It does not help that boys are not naturally wired to express deep emotions. Girls will often bottle up their pain for long periods, but it almost always comes to the surface. They deal with it. Boys generally do not. They end up getting left behind by society and by their families, even by each other, especially when they attempt to open up about it. The world collectively backs away. Males do not build social safety nets like females. They are quite different in that regard, even the ones like me, who take hormones and grow boobs. Looking female does not necessarily produce female; it takes effort. Without a support structure, we are walking time bombs. Few overcome it in a healthy way. It has been like this for as long as I have been alive. Some things seem to never change.

"Those who succeed, are they who learn to open up and make themselves vulnerable by exposing their abuse, but they create a void by doing so. They must fill that void with goals that help them find a sense of purpose. Those whose goals include compassion toward humanity find a wonderful thing, sir. I do what I can to help ruined, hopeless male victims find their value, and if possible, to find it in our creator. It is my life's work. I have a unique advantage in that I am a woman in their eyes. They see a nurturing mother, a sister, an aunt, and a friend. The younger ones see a loving grandmother. They see an approachable human being who—by virtue of being female--is not a threat and who identifies with their pain. They are amazed by the depth of my understanding of the inner-workings of their minds. They do not know I am one of them. God has turned my weakness into strength. He has turned my lie into truth. The so-called 'filth' of what the self-righteous had said that I am, is now become beauty.

"God changed me through the message of the cross: the final demonstration of the love Jesus gave his generation and the first demonstration of his love for me. The receipt of his love through precious few people before I ever understood is what eventually won my heart. My hopes, dreams, desires, efforts, and broken heart were not nearly enough, not even that encounter when I slit my wrists. The receipt of genuine love is what pointed me to the cross, and that is what ultimately saved my life and taught me how to renew my mind. This is what I share with these devastated boys and men, and sometimes girls, and women who think they are unwanted and unlovable."

The old man's glow diminished. His eyes watered. He removed a glove and wiped his tears while he lowered his head. "Forgive me, Miss Victoria. You've touched a soft spot. I sure wish I had known someone like you years ago. A person like you could have tremendously helped someone I had met."

aPRiL 3: oLD mAN wiNTERS

Mr. Cagle lifted his head then turned to Victoria. "I probably shouldn't say anything else? If you knew my past, you would likely not be here telling me these things? I should have warned you up front."

"Why should I not offer you the same grace you have afforded me? You are not beneath me, dear sir."

More tears ran down the old man's face. "I was locked up in the federal prison system for twenty-five years. They bounced me all over creation. It's just as well, I suppose?"

Self-condemning thoughts flooded the old man's brain. "So many decisions throughout my life had seemed to make sense at the time I had made them, but they always seemed to turn sour. As a result, I had often questioned the purpose of my existence. At times, it had seemed clear, and at others, it was a complete mystery.

"I doubt you will believe this, but I was not entirely guilty of the charges that were brought against me, at least not in the way they were presented. I'll just say that I was the defendant in what they used to call back in the old days, a *kangaroo court*. The judge had politics to contend with, and the jury had an axe to grind. The facts were of no real consequence. The case was in court for only three months, and it took the jury less than two hours to convict me. It all happened in a flash."

Mr. Cagle offered a melancholy grin. "Yeah, I know," he turned his head away from Victoria, "none of us old jailbirds did it." He dropped his head. "We're all innocent." He glanced at Victoria.

Victoria's fogged, wet eyes were filled with compassion. "I am not here to judge you, sir. You have served your time. Your debt to society is paid. The reasons are no longer relevant."

"Thank you, Miss Richmond." The old man paused, then sighed. "My beautiful wife, God bless her soul, waited for me all the years I was locked up. She owned a business but sold it to meet me here after I was released. This is as far as they would send me on the bus. I didn't have a penny to my name. I learned early on to not accept any funds from the outside to avoid being extorted by other inmates.

"When I arrived here, I had to check into a halfway house. I still wonder to this day why God seemed to have dumped me here of all places? My wife's town was okay, and she would gladly have taken me back there, but she was ready for a change. It goes without saying that I needed a new start. I really did not want to return there, so here is where she drove to meet me, and here is where we settled."

The old man shook his head. "If I could possibly count all the endless days, I had prayed to be released someplace where my weary old carcass could find joy for the remainder of my years, not fleeting emotional happiness, but lasting contentment down in my bones? I had that until my sweetheart was taken, but now?"

Mr. Cagle's expression broke up. His breaths were quick and shallow. He sighed and looked upon the fog-shrouded horizon. Though the sun was still rising, the temperature had dropped.

Victoria became aware of the droplets of mist tapping her chapped face. She sensed Mr. Cagle's isolation. The old man's chest heaved for a few seconds. He swallowed as he gained his composure and returned his attention.

"I never understood exactly what she saw in me? We discussed it frequently, so I do have the answers; they're just hard to fathom. Tough for it all to sink in. She was so forgiving and understanding, so inhumanly patient. She was unique. We never had any children.

"I sometimes feel like I was put on this earth to serve as an example of what not to be? So many times, from way back in my youth, I was essentially disposed of, and it continued throughout my life in some way or another.

"I felt God had thrown me away when I went to prison. I thought he had finally buried me for good. But you know what? He didn't. He said, "You have not been buried; you have been planted." It was during that one session of calm, focused prayer that I finally understood. God helped me grow In the darkness into what I was always meant to be: his nourishment for those emotionally wrecked and spiritually starved men. He needed someone on the inside who wasn't a cop, a counselor, or a chaplain. God transformed me into something they had never seen before. Through me, he revealed himself to many."

"Revealed..." Victoria piped up. "Revealed... Revelation, Revelation, The Revelation... I am sorry to slip that in at such an awkward moment. That biblical reference is stuck in my brain. It is bugging me. I am listening. You keep triggering something vague, and now that brief passage of scripture will not let me go." Victoria squeezed Mr. Cagle's hand. "Do not mind me. I am sorry I interrupted. Please continue."

"That's quite alright, Miss Victoria. I suppose it goes back to that sentiment of us being soul mates? After all, it is widely accepted that soul mates bring out all kinds of things in each other, do they not? If I happen to somehow draw that mystery out of you, you're more than welcome to cut in at any time.

"As far as the federal pen goes, God took excellent care of me. I did not suffer the same fate as many convicted of the same kinds of crimes. I am here, after all. Incarceration initially terrified me, but it gave my life validation, *real* validation. I met so many that no one else could or would help. Society keeps men like me locked away in their minds even if we never get thrown in the *pokey*. What real difference does it make whether we are outside or inside prison walls if they shut us out when we try to speak up?"

Ms. Richmond's brows drew in, and her eyes narrowed. She appeared confused. She could not quite piece together to what Mr. Cagle was alluding.

"I can identify with boys who are sold into prostitution," Mr. Cagle added. "I had been in the middle of some horrible things in my day."

A chill rushed down Victoria's spine.

"I have a secret too, Miss Victoria. Cagle is not my legal last name."

Victoria maintained her intense expression. She looked pale as the blood drained from her cheeks. Confusion was replaced with concern.

"My wife fought like hell to help me legally change my last name after prison, but the law wouldn't let us, so I started using the name Cagle in social settings. I still use my legal name on official paperwork. If it's all the same, ma'am, I'm not comfortable sharing it. No disrespect intended, especially in light of all you've shared. I just don't honestly see the point. I can see how withholding it can make me seem shifty?"

Victoria squeezed the elderly man's hand again. "Well, sir," she said, "not any shiftier than I might seem to you knowing I am a man in a make-believe woman's body?"

The man rubbed the top of Victoria's thigh near her knee. He bobbed his head and twitched his lips back and forth while he looked upon the lake.

"Sir," Victoria added, "I am convinced of your sincerity and of your heart even if you are not as comfortable with sharing as I."

The old man nodded, then resumed his story. "Many survivors were there, but I never got to speak to them. They were housed in the protective custody units. Believe it or not, I stayed in the general population at most of the facilities except the ones that gave me no choice. I could have PC'd-up into special housing units from the open yards, but in the beginning, I was at such a low point emotionally that I figured I'd help God finish me off by not requesting protective custody and letting the other inmates do me in. I felt like living human waste. But God had other plans. I had no clue I could relate to anyone there, but I was able to connect with many...so many! It was there that I gained the realization that God truly is hope in hopelessness. It was through the injustice of my trial and the following prison sentence that he showed me his love by delaying justice."

"Begging your pardon, sir? I do not follow?"

"Prison was full of people—men--whom society had disposed of in the name of justice, me included. Most belonged there. Some deserved much worse. Others should not have been there at all. Some received letters from their victims, letting them know that there was no way they would ever receive enough justice in their eyes; there wasn't enough in the world for them to be able to atone for what they had done. I saw hard men cry like babies, and soft men wreak horrible destruction. Most of those men were young, but a few were aged.

"I remember one old convict in particular. He was on his fifty-third year into a triple life sentence without parole. That man died in his cell the day before his seventy-fifth birthday. I overheard the *White Shirts*--corrections officers--say that he had gone out with a smile on his face clutching a letter from one of his victim's granddaughters. It said that she had forgiven him and that God loved him in spite of his crimes. The *Shirts* scoffed about it and made jokes. One laughed and mocked the deceased by pretending to be him suffering in hell. He went to caterwauling and flailing his arms. It broke my heart to see that.

"Old man Winters—the con's last name was Winters—had told me that on the day he was sentenced, he laughed at the victim's family in the courtroom and made some vulgar remarks toward them. He said he had spat at the ones who were crying as the bailiffs walked him out, and had even sung a vile limerick. He said that at the time, he was proud of what he'd done, but the years started to work on him. His victims' family sent him hateful, threatening letters for years, wishing him extreme suffering, dismemberment, and death. He deserved the very worst of God's judgment as far as they were concerned, but God delayed his justice for that man's sake.

"The light came on for me, Miss Victoria. I recognized a sour attitude I'd had toward people who had done things to me. I saw the shoe on the other foot. God is indeed just, but he is also merciful. The way I see it, there is no greater justice than mercy, to be pardoned for our crimes against each other and against God despite what we all deserve. Regardless of how many might or might not agree, I have found great comfort in that. It increased my capacity to forgive and to exercise self-restraint."

d. BRENT iSBELL
SICKS

aPRIL 3: wHAT's iN A nAME

"People have said that religion is a tool used to control the masses," the old man who calls himself Cagle told the middle-aged, transgender woman who calls herself Victoria Richmond. "That may well be? But a relationship with God? That's different. He teaches me to control myself. I need not control anyone else. The way I see it, real religion is a relationship with God, like the relationship I had with my wife. It is not a pile of rules used to scare and guilt people into staying in line. That kind of relationship is doomed to fail like a fake marriage. I need not control anyone or anything but me. I need only to love and respect others the same way I love and respect myself, if not better."

Victoria's eyes watered again. "Profound words, Mr. Cagle. I do not know if you realize it, but you have been living that philosophy the whole time I have been conversing with you." Victoria sniffled. Tears shot down her cheeks. She wiped them with a gloved fingertip. "If it is not too intrusive a request, may I hug you, sir?"

The elderly man smiled. His warm yet somber brown eyes twinkled amid rosy cheeks. "It would be my pleasure, ma'am. And thank you for still calling me Cagle."

Victoria erupted into a light sob while she slid closer to the aged man. The two embraced. "My pleasure, sir," she said.

The old man clung tightly with one hand and rubbed the woman's hair behind her earmuffs. He continued to speak as they held each other and gently rocked. "There were so many men I prayed for in prison," Mr. Cagle said. "I prayed for them for years and years. Some died, some were released, and some were still there when I left. God gave me a lot of time to pray, unhindered and uninterrupted, for one very special person."

The companions mutually released each other. Victoria slid back to her original position on the bench. She wiped her eyes again.

The elderly man went on, "I prayed endlessly, it seemed. Finally, about fifteen or twenty years into my incarceration, give or take—my memory is slipping--my prayers kind of dried up. It was not that I had lost hope or interest, but that I had felt a release. It's like something inside me had said everything was okay: I could ease up. Still, my heart breaks, knowing I will never get to see him again."

The old man cleared his throat. "I will never know what became of him. I am convinced I will know in heaven…" the old man had difficulty finishing his thought, "but it's not the same, Miss Victoria. It's just not the same to this weary old soul that's been tossed about for more than eighty years."

Tears washed down the man's face.

"And now, my wife is gone. We had twelve glorious years together after my release. We had married when I got out."

The old man inhaled deeply then released a quick burst of steam into the cold April air. The skin beneath his eyes was bagged and dark.

"But now," he shook his head, "what further joy have I to look forward to, aside from passing from this world? I prayed, and I believed God heard and answered, and for a while, it was obvious to me that he had. Now, I don't know what to think, Miss Richmond? Why would he answer my prayers by restoring my joy but for a brief period? I knew the day might eventually come that my wife would pass before me, but I didn't foresee this emptiness."

Tiny capillary veins reddened in the old man's chapped cheeks in the cold, heavy mist.

Victoria leaned toward her elder companion and caressed the thinned white hair sticking out from the earflaps of his cap. "It's okay, hon," she relaxed her speech, "God will restore your joy. Don't let go of your faith."

The old man sniffled and grinned amid clouded, downcast eyes. "No one has called me *hon* since my wife passed--my beautiful Sherri-Lynn, my Fabulous Feline--God rest her soul. She was the second *precious jewel* I had lost."

"Revelation 1:14-15, Authorized King James Version!"

"Ma'am?"

Ms. Richmond stopped caressing the old man's hair. She fixated on a snowy white lock she had twisted around her finger.

"His head and his hairs were white like wool, as white as snow; and his eyes were as a flame of fire; And his feet like unto fine brass, as if they burned in a furnace!"

The middle-aged woman peeled her gloves. She took the elderly man's face into her trembling hands and leaned closer. Her dark eyes peered deep into his soul. Two heavy tears raced past her quivering chin and thumped the lapel of her coat. The woman's aged voice cracked, as she said in a tone reminiscent of a six-year-old girl's, "Mr. Pae? The friend of the shiny, yellow man with lamb hair?

The tiny white rabbit's wounds had healed; the nondescript bird's shackle was gone. God remembered little Zechariah; God loved David. The bird spread bright, multi-colored wings and ascended into heaven.

www.ingramcontent.com/pod-product-compliance
Lightning Source LLC
Chambersburg PA
CBHW071242170626
46809CB00001B/51